Praise for Sara E. Johnson

Molten Mud Murder
The First Alexa Glock
"Johnson provides a fascinating vie
into the Māori culture… Armchai

T0044425

"The novel is a page-turner par excellence, with vivid characters and an enthralling plot, all wrapped up in a most charming evocation of New Zealand's landscapes, people, and local politics. I highly recommend this debut novel!"

—Douglas Preston, #1 bestselling co-author of the Pendergast series

"Johnson gives us a compelling picture of modern New Zealand overlaid by Māori culture with its strict taboos and amazing artifacts. Alexa hopes to stay in New Zealand, and if this leads to a full series, my fingers are crossed that she gets her wish."

—Margaret Maron, *New York Times* bestselling author

The Bones Remember
The Second Alexa Glock Forensics Mystery
"At the exciting climax, Alexa uses her wits, not a gun or martial arts skills, to take out the bad guy. Hopefully, this refreshingly normal heroine will be back soon."

—*Publishers Weekly*

"Ready for some armchair travel with a hint of *Jaws*? Sara Johnson provides the ride in her second New Zealand–set Alexa Glock Forensics Mystery, *The Bones Remember*. Once you discover, with this dauntless forensic investigator, the wilds of

Stewart Island, you'll want more pages. And the shark attacks and treachery along the way will keep the pages turning."

—Kingdom Books Mystery Blog

The Bone Track
The Third Alexa Glock Forensics Mystery

"Johnson's wonderful descriptions of New Zealand's natural beauty immerse the reader in her action-packed tale, and the relationship between Alexa and Charlie adds a layer of emotion and regret to the well-plotted adventure. Fans of internationally set mysteries will enjoy this dangerous ride."

—Sarah Stewart Taylor, author of the
Maggie D'arcy Mystery series

The Bone Riddle
The Fourth Alexa Glock Forensics Mystery

"There's much to enjoy. Bonus: those New Zealand landscapes the victim seemed determined to destroy."

—Kirkus Reviews

"Forensic technology, a rising body count, and romance abound in Sara E. Johnson's new thriller The Bone Riddle.

—Criminal Element

"Johnson expertly balances her lead's personal and professional lives and maintains nerve-shredding suspense throughout. This gives every indication that Alexa can sustain a long-running series."

—Publishers Weekly

Also by Sara E. Johnson

The Alexa Glock Forensics Mysteries
Molten Mud Murder
The Bones Remember
The Bone Track
The Bone Riddle

THE HUNGRY BONES

AN
ALEXA GLOCK
FORENSICS
MYSTERY

SARA E. JOHNSON

Poisoned Pen
PRESS

Published by Poisoned Pen Press, an imprint of Sourcebooks
P.O. Box 4410, Naperville, Illinois 60567- 4410
(630) 961-3900
sourcebooks.com

Cataloging-in-Publication Data is on file with the Library of Congress.

Printed and bound in the United States of America.
VP 10 9 8 7 6 5 4 3 2 1

In memory of the Chinese gold miners in New Zealand.

"Gold, Gold, Gold
bright and yellow, hard and cold,
Heavy to get and light to hold
Stolen, borrowed, squandered, doled
Price of many a crime untold."

—CHARLES THATCHER, GOLDFIELD BALLADEER

Chapter One

"The mouth and hands of anyone at the scene are the biggest source of contamination," Alexa Glock replied to the question. "Wearing masks, barrier clothing, and gloves is crucial."

Professor Campbell, one of three on the interview committee, frowned from the upper-left Zoom box. "Anything to add?"

Alexa glanced at her image: behold the winner of the Bed-Head Hair prize. She refrained from taming it. "Protect the scene. Use disposable equipment when possible and sterilized equipment when it's not." This was Forensics 101 stuff.

Professor Campbell, whose specialty was DNA, leaned so close to her computer that Alexa could see her nose hairs. "Are you familiar with the Phantom of Heilbronn?"

Even though it was two a.m. in New Zealand, Alexa perked up. "She was Germany's most wanted woman. She left DNA at forty crime scenes, but in the end, it was found she didn't exist, and the DNA came from contaminated swabs."

"Aye." Professor Campbell relaxed into her seat and studied Alexa's curriculum vitae. "No PhD?"

"I have two master's degrees."

"No DMD?"

Most odontologists—Alexa's specialty—were Doctors of Medicine in Dentistry, so the professor was right to inquire. "My university created a special master's program because of a shortage." *Two years of nothing but teeth.* Should she share her motto with the professors? She tongued her top incisors and went for it. "Lips may lie, but teeth never do."

Lower-left box—Assistant Professor Abby Akintola, specialty bloodstain patterns—bared her teeth in a congenial smile, but Professor Campbell frowned. "If you joined the faculty at Abertay University in Scotland, we would expect you to complete a PhD."

Alexa liked a challenge.

Dr. Ben Odden, chair of the forensics department, upper-right box, seemed to be speaking.

"You're on mute," Dr. Campbell shouted.

A whimper came from the kitchen. Alexa's roommate's canine partner, Kaos, was stirring. His doggy dreams were interrupted. The apartment was open-concept, and there was no door to close.

Dr. Odden unmuted. "I see you submitted an article to *Forensic Science Today.* "Bacterium in Great White Shark Bite Lacerations."

"They've expressed some interest." If Alexa took a university position, she'd have more time for research and writing.

"What are you working on now?" Dr. Odden asked.

Alexa had a professional crush on Ben Odden. She'd devoured many of his published articles over the years and had used some of his cutting-edge techniques. It was a thrill to "meet" him. "The pink tooth phenomenon. I was recently involved in a case where the deceased presented a pink molar."

Alexa was chuffed by the interview committees' rapt attention, but she wasn't sure she wanted to leave her traveling forensic investigator job. Especially after her boss had called earlier.

"Your friend Dr. Luckenbaugh requested you. She received approval to exhume a Chinese gold miner, buried around 1900. She needs an odontologist. Can you get to Arrowtown tomorrow?" Ana Luckenbaugh was a forensic archaeologist who worked for a firm called Preserving Heritage. Alexa had already booked a flight. But first she wanted to ace this interview.

Kaos howled.

"What's that?" Professor Campbell shouted.

Alexa popped out of her Zoom box. She ran to the kitchen and opened the crate. Kaos jumped on her. "Down. Hush."

She ran back, the gangling dog at her heels. She pushed Kaos's butt down, whispered for him to sit, and slipped back into her chair. "It's my roommate's dog." She hated the sound of that. On the verge of thirty-eight and living with a roommate. "I'm looking into the relationship of pink tooth phenomenon and head position." She flashed back to her last away case. The deceased had been found head-down. The positioning had accelerated decomposition in his facial area. And possibly the PTP. The image of maggots in the corpse's orifices crawled into her head. She shook it away.

The interview went on for twenty more minutes. Kaos pushed his head into her Zoom box once and charmed the scientists, even Dr. Campbell.

"We'll be in touch," Dr. Odden said. "Maybe get you over to Dundee to check *oot* our facilities."

His Scottish brogue was sexy. Alexa clicked Leave Meeting. She took off the blouse covering her sleep shirt and realized her abrupt Zoom departure to fetch Kaos probably revealed her shortie pajama bottoms. *Did that constitute a flash?* She snorted, turned off the light, and laid on the couch, fingers buried in the remnants of Kaos's puppy fur. Did she want to leave New Zealand for a job in Scotland? In the darkness, skeletal remains of gold rush miners staked a claim on her thoughts. She pictured the teeth protruding from their jaws.

夏季

SUMMER

1880

Precious MaMa,

Our ship from Hong Kong almost sank in a storm, but we made it to Sun Gum Saan. Uncle Cheong Tam translated: New Gold Mountain. He told me to buy boots, woolen pants, a coat, and a hat. Five of us walked eighteen days, over bare mountains, rivers, tussock, rock to New Gold Mountain. White men think the gold is already gone. A little boy grabbed my queue and made pig sounds.

Shining rivers flow between this village and the many mountains. Uncle Cheong Tam and I built a mud hut along the creek where other Chinese stay. The birds, MaMa. They sing strange songs and keep me company. My rice bowl made the journey. You filled that rice bowl, MaMa; now it rests in my hands, the painted crane's wings spread.

Crane: the prince of all feathered creatures. Wings: your gift to me.

On my third day I found a nugget in Arrow River. My first Gold Letter for you: a seven pound cheque I earned from the nugget. More will follow and then I will come home, a rich man.

Faithful First Son, Spreading Wings,
Wing Lun

Chapter Two

Natalie, in full uniform, hovered over her. "Kaos needs to sleep in his crate. He needs boundaries."

Alexa winced at the crick in her neck and tried to straighten her legs. The dog took up half the couch. "What time is it?"

"Five-thirty." Natalie held the dog's leash. "Come, Kaos."

He hopped off, tail wagging.

"I've got an away case in Arrowtown." Alexa stretched her legs. "I'll be gone for a couple days."

"Pack your puffer and beanie. What's the case?"

First she translated. *Puffer: warm coat. Beanie: hat.* Would she need them in May? "Something about exhuming a Chinese miner for repatriation. A benefactor wants to bring him home."

Natalie's young forehead creased. "There's a Chinese belief that a soul can only find peace if tended by family members."

Natalie was only twenty-seven yet possessed an elder's collected knowledge that often surprised Alexa. She also possessed a teenager's ability to sleep through dog howls in the middle of the night.

"That doesn't sound like a crime," Natalie said. "Why are you going?"

"Teeth are why." She thought back to the details Dan had sent in an email. "I'll measure the strontium isotope in the enamel to find out where it's from."

"Strontium isotope," Natalie repeated slowly. "What's that?"

Alexa stumbled to the kitchen to make coffee. "It's a trace

element found in rocks. It works its way into water, soil, plants, on up the food chain, so that animals and people consume it. The amounts of different strontium isotopes in your enamel vary depending on where you grew up."

"So my teeth can tell you where I grew up?"

Alexa added ground coffee to the French press. "You are *what* and *where* you ate."

"Sweet as."

Alexa beamed. "Then we'll extract DNA from the pulp chamber. See if it links either of the skeletons to the benefactor."

Natalie leashed Kaos and left. After a blissful cup of coffee, Alexa lugged the couch against the wall and did a twenty-minute kickboxing routine to her throwback playlist. She was psyched about the day ahead, but U2's "I Still Haven't Found What I'm Looking For" bothered her. *Shuffle, jab, cross, hook.* What if she *had* found what she was looking for? She loved her job. And maybe Bruce as well, the detective inspector she'd been dating. Her brother, Charlie, always accused her of running away from commitment. Said it was a pattern.

Jab, cross, undercut.

She showered, dressed, packed, and drove to work where she spent a couple hours in her cubicle at Auckland Forensic Service Center finishing reports. At noon she checked in with her boss, Dan Goddard.

"Ready to fly?" he asked.

Alexa tried to stem her excitement. "I just finished that robbery report."

"If a crime case comes up, I'll need to pull you away," he warned.

Even though it was a Wednesday, she felt like a kid on a Friday afternoon.

It was a two-hour flight from Auckland on the North Island to Queenstown on the South Island. Her crime kit barely fit in the overhead compartment. She never left home without it. Alexa was glad the woman next to her was absorbed in her *NZ Herald* crossword. She opened her laptop and reread the email from Ana Luckenbaugh.

Kia ora Alexa,

The dig I've requested your assistance with is being funded by an elderly woman, Corrie Wong, in Guangzhou, China. Ms. Wong wants to spare no expense in repatriating her great-great-grandfather. He has been calling for her to bring him home. That's why I need your teeth expertise to see what we've got. We don't want to return the wrong remains.

My graduate assistant and I don't know why this skeleton was left behind (I will explain "left behind" when you get here). We've determined it's the remains of an adult male. I'm waiting for you to arrive before I examine the skull.

Shelby and I will pick you up at the airport. You can stay at our cottage.

—Ana

Chapter Three

Mountains perched in every direction, and the trees crowding the roadside, tinged with yellow and orange, reminded Alexa of fall in Raleigh, North Carolina—her home prior to moving to New Zealand. She shook her head: autumn in the month of May was topsy-turvy. "The leaves are pretty," she said.

Ana, at the wheel of the Toyota Highlander, gestured with her hand. "It's not natural, this color. Comes from non-native trees. European settlers planted them to look like home."

Alexa was glad Ana returned her hand to the wheel. The road curved, dipped, climbed, and now spanned a foaming emerald-colored river by a narrow bridge. Alexa squinted down—way down. Three red jet boats lined the bank and another took off in a blur. Her new glasses were stowed in the case. She had moderate nearsightedness, which the ophthalmologist said was common with age. *Yikes.*

She focused on a jagged mountain looming straight ahead. Past tree-height it turned stark and bare. She wondered how the gold miners traversed such a harsh landscape. The thought reminded her of why she was headed to Arrowtown, which Ana had said was only twenty minutes from Queenstown. She opened her mouth to ask Ana how they'd located the skeleton if the grave was unmarked, but the four-year-old singing loudly in the back seat drowned her attempt. Shelby was not the graduate student.

"Daddy shark, daddy shark, doo, doo, doo."

On repeat. Alexa had forgotten Ana had a daughter.

"Do you like my song?" she screamed from her giant car seat.

Ana, whose thick braid draped over her left shoulder, shot Alexa a look. "I've been on travel a lot lately, so I didn't want to leave Shelby behind." She had to raise her voice. "I asked Mum if she'd come with and do the child-minding. She's a freelance reporter and can work anywhere. God bless her. She's at the rental house. It's called Prospector's Cottage."

Shelby kicked the back of Alexa's seat. "Nana shark, Nana shark, doo, doo, doo."

Alexa was more interested in exhuming skeletons than being serenaded by a preschooler, but she was looking forward to working with Ana. They'd met when Alexa had been called in to examine the teeth of nine skeletons unearthed during a road construction project. Well…it turned out to be ten. An infant—whose teeth never had the chance to erupt—had been cradled in one skeleton's arms. Ana worked for an Auckland archaeology firm that specialized in cultural heritage remains. Alexa had thought at the time, and still did, that Ana could be her sister. They were the same height, five-seven, both had hazel eyes and pale complexions with a dust of freckles. Ana tamed her unruly hair with a braid. Alexa, whose hair was shoulder-length, preferred a ponytail.

And a childless existence.

"I'll show you downtown before we drop Shelby off. It's busy with tourists because of the autumn color."

The road curved past a lake, a golf course, and then a school. A Go for Gold sign adorned the front entrance. The tiny town came into sight. They passed a storybook church and modest homes. Ana stopped at a crossing. "This is Buckingham Street."

"Sounds British," Alexa said.

"Sure, most immigrants during the gold rush were English, Irish, and Scottish," Ana said. "Arrowtown was settled on their backs. The Chinese were recruited once the settlers thought they'd squeezed all the gold out of the river. Turned out the dregs were plentiful."

The little library on the corner had a sign out front. Alexa squinted to read it: STORY TIME FOR DOGS WED. @ 10:00.

"Stop at the sweet shop!" Shelby shouted.

Alexa decided she liked the kid. "How big is the town?"

"Around three thousand residents. During the gold rush, fifteen thousand people lived around here."

Buckingham Street was canopied with elms and oaks, their leaves just past peak. Alexa lowered her window and smelled rich decay and a hint of winter. A row of closely spaced bungalows— two-windows-and-a-door-wide—charmed her. She imagined hitching posts out front and horses tethered to them.

Ana waited for two women to cross the street before turning. "Those are original miners' cottages from the 1870s. European miners, mind you. The Chinese settlement was down at Bush Creek. No cozy cottages for them."

The business district had one- and two-story buildings with false fronts like a Western movie set, the mountains behind them looming like a fake backdrop. There was a pharmacy, a bakery, and a store called The Wool Press. She blinked. An actual hitching post was out front. The Fork and Tap, across from the library, had a yard filled with picnic tables. People in sweaters sipped beer and laughed. The red-roofed Post and Telegraph had benches on its porch.

Ana parked in front of a gift store. They crossed to the sweet shop. A bell jangled when they entered, and the ceiling was festooned with fairy lights. Alexa inhaled the chocolaty aroma and went straight for fudge. Shelby and Ana created a mix 'n' match bag from jars of candy. "Pick something special for Nana," Ana said.

Alexa, who treated, bit into her chocolate sea-salt fudge before they were back in the car.

In three minutes, Ana turned onto a small road lined with purple-leaved trees. "The Chinese planted plum trees," she said. "They missed trees from home too."

The miners were gone, but their trees—or the descendants of their trees—lived on. Alexa liked the living connection to the past.

Ana pulled into the driveway of a modest blue house. "It's a perfect location. Close to the cemetery and town."

A woman with spiky gray hair came out onto the front porch. Shelby unbuckled herself, opened the door, and ran. The woman scooped her up and kissed her all over her face.

The scene tugged at Alexa's heart. Her mom had died when she was six; her grandmother when she was sixteen. She gathered her crime kit and suitcase and trudged to the porch.

"Mum, this is Alexa," Ana said.

"Nice to meet you," Alexa said.

"*Kia ora.* Call me Pam." She was trimmer and shorter than Ana and casual in jeans and a red turtleneck. "You get the room at the top of the stairs. There's a view of Bush Creek from up there. I've left a spare cottage key on the dresser." She released her granddaughter. "You'll have to come downstairs to use the loo."

"No problem. Thank you for making room for me."

Shelby ran to the door. "*I'll* show you."

The wooden floor was painted light gray, and the ceiling rose to a peak above twin beds. Shelby climbed on one bed and pointed to the other. "Sleep there." Her golden-brown pigtails went up and down as she bounced on the duvet. The knees of her jeans were dirty. Alexa set her suitcase at the foot of the bed and pulled back the gauzy curtain of the single window. Water glistened through the trees. The segment of creek she could see was maybe ten feet across and strewn with boulders.

Shelby stopped bouncing. "That's where Nana and I hunt for gold."

Alexa turned. The child's brown eyes glittered. "Have you struck it rich?"

Quick as a rabbit, Shelby hopped off, calling, "I need my pan." Alexa guessed it was a panning-for-gold pan. She might like to try that so she could tell her brother, Charlie. He was a geoengineer and loved all things rock. She grabbed her jacket and followed the kid downstairs. When Ana said she and Alexa had to go to work, Shelby's face screwed up. Alexa braced herself.

"Your candy is in the kitchen," Ana said. "You can have one more before tea."

Shelby skipped off. "Dodged that one," Ana said. "Come on, let's walk. Exercise will be good. We've a bit of daylight left."

Alexa zipped her "puffer," eager to view the bones. "Should I bring my kit?"

"Wait until morning. We'll just see what my graduate assistant has been up to." She glanced after Shelby. "And stop at the pub. Bye, Mum," she called.

The chilly walk felt good after the confines of the flight, much of which had been bumpy. "Is your grad student staying in the cottage too?"

"Olivia is staying with friends in Queenstown."

Alexa thought of the skeleton. "You mentioned the grave was unmarked. How did you find the bones?"

Ana bent down and tightened a bootlace. "We knew the general area where the Chinese were once buried. We used ground-penetrating radar."

Once buried? "I got to try GPR at a body farm when I was in graduate school."

"Never been to a body farm," Ana said.

"There's one in the North Carolina mountains. But we used GPR to locate buried pigs, not people. The more decomposed the carcass was, the harder it was to detect."

"Historic remains, especially when there's no coffin, provide weak responses," Ana said. "We looked for evidence of a grave shaft. The GPR readout indicated the soil had been disturbed."

After few minutes Alexa spotted a tall obelisk atop a steep hill. "Is that the graveyard?"

"That's the war memorial. The cemetery is behind it."

A beautiful rock wall separated the cemetery from the street. Alexa looked left and right. There was no tent in sight; she wondered where the dig was. A mixture of old and new graves sprawled in both directions. The rear border was separated from a mountain flank by a strip of tall grasses dancing in a breeze. The surroundings made Alexa think of Mom again. Ellen Rose Glock's remains rested in a cemetery along the banks of the French Broad River near Asheville. Alexa had a blurry memory of her father and grandmother throwing handfuls of dirt on top of her coffin.

Mom's tombstone said BELOVED WIFE AND MOTHER and had her birth date and death date. *Oh, God. When was Mom's birthday?*

Dammit.

Alexa shook her head. *It was April 7th.* Solace replaced her momentary panic.

A red van was parked behind a Honda in the lot. *Preserving Heritage* was scripted on the side. Ana pointed to it. "Olivia drove from Auckland so we'd have our equipment. I never minded a road trip when I was her age."

'Driving from Auckland' meant taking a car ferry across Cook Strait. The waters separating the North and South Islands could be wicked.

"Olivia is excited about your expertise in teeth."

Alexa liked a groupie. "Where is she?"

Ana pointed right. A hill dipped to a copse of trees and a grassy expanse. Beyond the trees and another rock wall, she spotted the top of a large tent.

"So you found actual bones? They hadn't disintegrated?" Bones could last thousands of years—under certain conditions—but the average life span of buried bone was one hundred years.

Overripe fruit littered the grass below a nearby apple tree, and Ana kicked one off the path. "The soil, drainage, and temperatures worked in our favor," she said. "From what I can tell in situ, the skeletal remains are intact."

Alexa was used to how Kiwis pronounced "skeletal" now. *Skel- lee-tal.* They watched a large rabbit hop across a grave.

"That's another thing the settlers brought from home: Rabbits," Ana said. "Now they're a huge pest."

"Did you find artifacts with the bones?" Alexa asked.

"A thin chain, I think gold. I've dropped it off at The Gold Shoppe to learn more about it. We also found some buttons and a pair of boots. The boots were beside the remains instead of on its feet." Ana stopped. "Would you want to be buried in your shoes?"

Alexa looked down at her blue Keds fondly and nodded. She followed Ana, weaving through headstones, some so eroded that the names and dates were obscured, and others toppled or split in two. This appeared to be the older section of the cemetery. One faded inscription caught Alexa's eye. She dug out her glasses and made out the words.

In Memory of
Robert Brodie
b. at Stronsay, Orkney, Scotland 14 Dec 1847
d. 22 Oct 1885

He died the same age she was now, far from home. She shivered at the thought. Next to Robert's grave, she read the words etched on a stone below a white cross:

Sacred to the memory
of William Danforth,
native of Arbroath, Scotland,
drowned in Bush Creek 11 Feb 1865
agd 34 years

The same creek as the one she saw from the cottage window. She imagined it morphing into a torrent, like the river on the hiking vacation she had taken with Charlie a couple months ago. It had pulled him in and twirled him like a rag doll.

He's okay, she reminded herself. She stepped forward, felt the ground dip, and froze. She was atop a grave. Her grandmother had always said that when a person shivered, someone was walking across their grave.

Alexa stepped delicately to the side and apologized to the deceased.

Daylight was fading. She caught up with Ana, who had climbed to the other side of the rock wall and walked past a small grove of four trees toward the tent. Alexa scrambled over, the rocks cold and rough against her hands. There were no grave markers on this side of the wall—just uneven ground and stubby grass.

Alexa, suddenly spooked, hurried to catch up. A white-haired man of Chinese descent sat in a camp chair outside the tent, cap clutched in his hands, a satchel at his feet. A scent, like funeral lilies, wafted in the air. He stood stiffly as they approached.

At the same time, a young woman slipped between the tent flaps. She wore a knit beanie. Messy blond bangs covered her eyebrows. "Dr. Luckenbaugh, this is Mr. Sun."

He bowed. "Sun Shing. I am here to watch over the bones, even though Ms. Forester wouldn't let me pay my respects in person." He spoke with a Kiwi accent and gestured to a glowing joss cone. "It is customary to burn incense to honor the deceased. If his soul is wandering, the smell will lure him back."

Alexa studied his lined face. He was serious.

Ana introduced Alexa and then asked, "How did you hear about our project?"

"I'm a representative from the NZ Chinese Association. Your benefactor Mrs. Corrie Wong contacted us." He handed her a business card. "She wants the bones looked after."

Ana studied the card.

His face was grave in the dying light. "Please work in haste. Our ancestor has been hungry too long."

Chapter Four

WEDNESDAY EVENING

As soon as they stepped into the tent, Ana made introductions. "This is Olivia Forester."

Olivia's flannel shirt flapped at the sleeves and her jeans were ripped—authentically, from what Alexa could tell. She wore no makeup and had a smudge of dirt on her nose. "You're the tooth expert," she said.

Alexa nodded modestly.

In a low voice, Olivia explained that Mr. Sun would be joined by others later that night and each night the bones were exposed. "A vigil," she said solemnly. Then her voice brightened. "I recovered another button."

"Let's show Alexa what we have, and then we'll wrap it up," Ana instructed. "We call it S1, for Skeleton One."

Olivia looked toward a neatly excavated rectangle in the center of the tented area. Alexa stepped over a whisk broom and skirted a mound of dirt to peer in.

The pounamu pendant against her sternum pulsed at the odd sight. The greenstone spiral had been carved by a Māori whose bones she had discovered by a river. It stirred to life to warn her or guide her or—Alexa really didn't know what.

It looked like S1 was sleeping. It was three or so feet deep and lay on its side, tawny skull in profile, one leg bent, the other straight, much like Alexa herself slept. One arm extended. The bony phalanges of a finger appeared to point at something.

Very creepy, Alexa thought.

She studied the teeth jutting from the jawbone, noting a slight overlap and yellowish color. Alexa licked her lips. Wear pattern, crowding, color, decay, the history hidden in the enamel and DNA. *Tomorrow*, she told herself. "It's a male?" she asked.

"Femur length suggests male," Olivia said.

Alexa knew the skeletal frame provided clues to sex, age, and height but that the question of ancestry rested in the skull. She tried to remember what subtle differences might distinguish it from a European skull: something about rounder eye orbits and heart-shaped nasal holes. Luckily this wasn't her job. Ana was the expert on cranial features. "Have you determined if the skull is of Asian descent?"

Olivia's face scrunched up. "Using cranial traits to determine ethnicity is biased. The practice should be abolished and replaced with population affinity."

Alexa knew Negroid, Mongoloid, and Caucasoid were negatively loaded terms, but she thought the terms African, Asian, and European were okay. "I was just wondering…"

Olivia cut her off. "Ancestry determination leads to racial inequities. Ever heard of the white-woman syndrome?"

"Yes."

"The skeletal remains of a female of European descent?" Olivia said. "Who let the dogs out? The media and police are all over it. Skeletal remains of People of Color or Indigenous? The dogs are sleeping on the couch."

Ana put a hand on Olivia's shoulder. "Recognizing differences isn't racist, and ethnicity factors into this investigation. Skull features in Asian and Asian-derived groups vary, but in this case we know the Chinese miners mostly came from Southern China. The eye orbit suggests a geographic region consistent with that area. Alexa's tooth analysis will tell us whether this is correct."

Olivia nodded. "We have to be careful."

Alexa had done a lot of spouting off herself in grad school, and Olivia had made valid points about sexism and racism in archaeology and policing. She smiled at the young woman and leaned back over to examine the yellowish-brown teeth protruding from the jaw. She wanted a closer look but could wait until the morning.

The teeth had tales to tell.

秋季

AUTUMN

1884

Precious MaMa

My claim has been good to me.

The Reserve Bank is crowded on the sixth day each week. Diggers arrive with handkerchiefs of gold, and buyers inspect them before purchasing. If the gold is pure, the digger is rewarded handsomely.

The gold goes by horse over the mountain to a big dark lake with a beating heart. A steamship takes it to the other side of the lake. Finally, a train takes it to the port city, Dunedin.

I wait for a while before I enter. The buyer looks at me with disdain but takes my flakes and peers at them with his jeweler loupe. The flakes have no skin color. When he is satisfied, he pours them onto scale and adds a counterbalance. He gives me a paper with the amount, and I take it to the bank teller. Here, MaMa, is my month's wage. Build well for our family.

New friends that come here face a poll tax. Celestials, as they call us, must now pay a great sum. I am lucky that I came before the poll tax. I am also lucky for my schooling, for which you sacrificed on my behalf.

Here the rich celebrate, and the poor bury their sorrow with grog and opium. I planted two plum trees like at home. Their blossoms will one day banish the bitterness and cold.

Faithful First Son,
Wing Lun

Chapter Five

WEDNESDAY NIGHT

After declining Ana's invitation to join them for a beer, Olivia climbed into the van. Before driving away, she said to Alexa, "Wait until Dr. Luckenbaugh tells you about the corpse ship."

Alexa had obviously misheard. "The courtship?"

Olivia drove off without answering.

"Let's get out of here," Ana said.

Darkness had settled in during the twenty minutes they'd been inspecting the bones. Alexa looked back toward the tent, guarded by Mr. Sun in his lonely outpost. The thought of sitting all night long next to a graveyard gave her the willies.

She and Ana trekked down the hill toward town, a ten-minute walk. The lights of Buckingham Street twinkled in welcome. The Four Square grocery store was still open. Across the street from the candy shop, Ana cut through a narrow alley and stopped at a low, blue wooden door. "This is my new favorite bar," she said. "It's better I tell you about the corpse ship away from Shelby. It might give her bad dreams."

"Corpse ship?"

Ana opened the blue door.

Might give me bad dreams, Alexa thought. She ducked her head and stepped down into the square room.

The stone walls, low-beamed ceiling, and flickering flames in the fireplace cast the smallish room in a golden hue. Alexa counted six rough-hewn tables—three occupied—and a couple of tall oaken barrels with bar stools around them. Two twenty-something men leaned against the bar. They glanced at Alexa and Ana and then resumed their conversation.

"This was a cold storage room back in the day," Ana said over her shoulder. "Sometimes for bodies before burial."

A morgue-cum-pub? This was a first for Alexa.

Ana pointed to the slate floor. "They had to excavate it to turn it into a bar. Otherwise we'd have to crouch. That's why I like it."

Alexa took note of the easy smile Ana gave the lanky bartender. Easy smiles weren't Alexa's forte. She was too uptight, too suspicious. Being in a relationship with Bruce, and disappointing her brother by calling a time-out in that relationship ("Running away as soon as things get serious, right Lexi?"), had ignited a dormant self-awareness, as if she were an omniscient narrator watching her own life. *Smile more, judge less,* the narrator said.

"It was an opium den at one time too," the bartender said.

"Is that right?" Ana laughed and ordered two Boomtown Blacks.

Alexa cracked a smile and took the proffered bottle of beer to a table near the fireplace. She read the inscription on the label:

It's 1862. Māori Jack with a pan of black sand from the Arrow River, a crescent of gold sparkling in the sunshine and the rush to this Boomtown is on. An uplifting brew for those empty-pan days.

She pointed to the label. "Who is Māori Jack?"

Ana eased onto a stool. "He was a sheep shearer. He found the first gold, though *Pākehā* took credit."

Alexa knew *Pākehā* referred to white New Zealanders,

Ana flipped her braid to her left shoulder. "I'll show you the spot in the river. There's a plaque for Māori Jack. Word spread, and by the end of the year, this place was crawling with European gold diggers."

Boomtown Black had a hint of chocolate that Alexa didn't like. She thought it best to keep chocolate and hops in separate corners. "What about the Chinese? When did they come?"

"After the European miners moved to other goldfields, the Otago government 'invited them.'" She used air quotes. "'Coolies were docile, cheap, and hardworking.'"

"That's an ugly sentiment."

Ana shrugged. "What can I say?"

Alexa sipped her Boomtown Black. With a start she realized she still wore her new glasses. She slipped them into the pocket of her coat. She wasn't *that* nearsighted.

"The government wanted to keep people here finding gold, even if it was just the dregs." Ana's eyes skimmed the cozy room and then settled on Alexa. "By the 1880s, there were five thousand Chinese in the region, maybe more, and almost all men. The miners came to escape war and famine. To help their families back home."

"You know a lot about this."

"That's my job, to understand the history and culture surrounding each of my digs." She dug dirt from under one of her short fingernails. "The Chinese never wanted to settle here like the Europeans. They considered themselves visitors. But way leads on to way, right?" Her eyes stayed downcast. "Many of them died here anyway."

Alexa moved her chair a little closer to Ana, whose voice had softened.

"The winters are freezing. There are floods from snowmelt. And sickness? Flu or typhoid? A broken leg? Forget it. There were no medical services for the Chinese. Maybe herbs or ointments, if you had the means." She clinked her beer bottle against Alexa's. "Like the label suggests—there were more empty-pan days than not. Lots of them died with empty pockets."

Alexa's neck prickled. She turned quickly. No one was standing behind her.

"There's a Chinese proverb." Ana's voice went husky. "Falling leaves return to their roots."

The door swung open, startling Alexa. Like leaves, two colorfully dressed women blew in. They joined the men at the bar in a swirl of laughter. "A white wine," said one. The other ordered an old-fashioned. Something fruity—maybe the drink or maybe perfume—wafted in the air. When one couple kissed, Alexa thought of Bruce. *Will I ever kiss him again?*

When the foursome settled at a table, Ana cleared her throat. "The Chinese believe that after death, the soul hovers over the grave until he is home. Those buried far from home are hungry ghosts."

The fire snapped and crackled. Alexa thought of Sun Shing's words: *He has been hungry too long.* She reminded herself that she believed in science, not ghosts.

Ana raised and lowered her shoulders. "The miners returned home in one of two ways. Save enough money to go home a hero. Buy a bowler hat and a ticket to Hong Kong. Sail on a steamer." She paused. "That's the first way."

Alexa tensed.

"The other way was to go home in a bag of calico." Ana's eyes teared up. The firelight turned them into liquid emeralds. She used a bar napkin to wipe them. "Sorry. I usually disassociate myself from my digs, but this one has gotten to me. All those lonely men, aging and dying far from home."

A lump formed in Alexa's throat. She gulped her beer.

"That's where the corpse ships factor in," Ana said quietly.

Alexa scooted even closer.

"Chinese benevolent societies arranged the ships," Ana said. "If you paid in advance—most miners or their families did to avoid the calamity of being abandoned—you were guaranteed a trip home if you died. The first corpse ship, the steamer *SS Hoihow,* was successful. Members of the Cheong Sing Tong society exhumed almost three hundred miners from graveyards all over Otago, including Arrowtown Cemetery. They cleaned every bone and bagged them together in calico bags. Then they enclosed the bags in zinc boxes covered with wood. Small coffins."

Alexa tried to imagine the scale of such a mass disinterment. The idea repelled her—*What happened if the bones still had flesh on them?*—but she kept her expression neutral. "What did the locals think?"

"They thought it was barbaric. They worried about disease. The smell. But permission was granted and, in 1883, the Hoihow took the remains of 286 miners to their families."

Alexa wondered if Charlie or her father would ship her "home" if she died in New Zealand? *Where was home?* She was coming up on her one-year anniversary of living Down Under.

"That was the first voyage." Ana paused. "The next tomb ship was nine years later. Exhuming enough graves to fill it took three years."

Three years?

"The *SS Ventnor* sailed from Wellington on 26 October, 1902, with 499 skeletons aboard."

That funny feeling prickled her neck again. Alexa restrained from turning around. Instead she turned up the collar of her blouse.

"Seven elderly Chinese men were given free passage home in exchange for attending the coffins."

With the pulsing of her greenstone pendant, Alexa sensed their presence: privileged to be alive amid so much death. The weight of their responsibility. The hope of reuniting with loved ones. When the pub's blue door opened with a bang, Alexa jumped. An older woman stuck her head through and gazed around the room, maybe searching for someone. She left as quickly as she'd entered. Alexa turned back to Ana.

"At midnight the ship hit rocks." Ana shook her head. "The captain backed off them, but instead of heading to port, he made the decision to keep going, to try to reach Auckland."

"Oh, no," Alexa said.

"Somewhere off Hokianga—the far north of the North Island—the *Ventnor* went down, taking all those hungry ghosts to the bottom of the sea. Five of the attendants, too."

The bar had quieted, as if others had listened to the sad tale.

Ana swiped at her eyes. "The miners died twice."

Chapter Six

THURSDAY MORNING

Light from the hallway jerked Alexa out of her steamy dream. She opened her eyes to see Shelby standing in the doorway. "I wanted to see if you was asleep."

Alexa blushed as if the child could see Bruce's naked body evaporating in her head. She sat up and checked the time: six twenty. "Was I?"

"I *tink* so. But now you're not." Shelby stepped into the room and appraised Alexa's red NC State T-shirt. "Is that your pajamas?"

Alexa turned on the lamp. She wasn't experienced talking to small people in narwhal nighties. "I like your pajamas. Do you go, um, to school or anything?"

Shelby nodded.

Alexa shivered as the cool air hit her bare arms. "Okay. Um, do you want to go downstairs while I get dressed?"

"No."

Shelby helped her pick out khakis and the new green knit top she'd bought in an attempt to update her Lands' End no-iron wardrobe. ("Makes your eyes pop," the saleswoman had said.) Then she showed the kid her crime kit and took her fingerprints the old-fashioned way. At the bottom stair Shelby waved the blurry fingerprint card and called, "Mum! The lady did my fingers. I'm a twirl."

"A whorl." Alexa had gotten most of the ink off Shelby's fingertips with a wet wipe.

Pam had coffee and oatmeal waiting in the tiny kitchen. "Sleep well?"

"I did." It was partially true. A pressing question woke her at two a.m. *Why hadn't the benefactor's ancestor's bones been on the corpse ship?* She'd been so wrapped up in Ana's telling of the *Ventnor* last night that it hadn't occurred to her to ask.

She liked her coffee strong and was relieved at first sip. "Ana said you're a freelance reporter. Are you working on anything now?"

Animated voices—Ana's low and Shelby's high—drifted from a bedroom. Pam flipped a dish towel over her shoulder and leaned against the counter. She wore the same red turtleneck and jeans she'd had on yesterday. "I'm writing about New Zealand sentencing laws."

The lines etched around her mouth deepened. "A sixteen-year-old boy was given a life sentence for murder. He was fifteen when he stabbed another boy. I don't believe in life sentences period, but at fifteen?"

"Are you booking my daughter for breaking and entering?" Ana said from the doorway. Her hair was down, wavy and wild, and she held a brush in her hand.

Alexa laughed. "Sorry about the ink on the nightie."

Ana walked over and hugged her mom.

"You need a haircut, luv," Pam said. "Something professional instead of the Heidi look? Don't you think?"

Ana caught Alexa's eye and rolled hers. She handed her mom the brush. "Will you do me? Like old times?"

The closeness between the mother and daughter gave Alexa a pang. She looked away as Pam brushed and braided Ana's hair. *You'd think I'd be over missing my mother by now.*

Ana ate oatmeal as she checked her phone. "Olivia will be late. She's picking up extra transport boxes and stopping by the cemetery office to let them know about the remains. They might shed some light. We've got a big day ahead. Let's skedaddle."

Alexa put her dishes in the sink, thanked Pam, and took the stairs two at a time to get the crime kit and her jacket. She met Ana in her car.

The defroster ran full blast. While they waited for clarity, Alexa asked, "Was it hard to get permission for the dig?" She recalled an exhumation that took place a couple of years ago in Raleigh. A body was exhumed after three months because the man everyone thought had been buried turned up alive. A mix-up like that was sufficient cause.

"It's a laborious process, but I'm used to it." When the windshield was clear, Ana pulled onto the street for the short drive to the cemetery. "The Ministry of Health issued us a disinterment license for cultural reasons. We've got to figure out if it's Ms. Wong's ancestor and, if not, what to do about it."

Teeth would hold answers. Alexa ran her tongue across her top teeth, considering their wonders. Each tooth wore a suit of armor. Instead of bronze or iron, the armor was made of dentin and enamel. Other body parts—the flesh and blood parts—degrade, but teeth stand the test of time. In the lab she'd crack the armor. She remembered her pressing question and asked, "Why weren't Mrs. Wong's ancestor's bones dug up for the grave ship?"

"Mrs. Wong thought they were." Ana stopped for a woman and dog to cross the road. "Until recently everyone believed the names of the exhumed miners sunk to the bottom of the sea with the bodies. That's what authorities said for over a hundred years. That's further injury to the families, don't you think?" Her voice deepened with anger as she turned onto Durham Street. "I don't think it would have happened if the remains had been *Pākehā*. About a year ago, Archives New Zealand conducted a major re-cataloging, and guess what?"

The cemetery parking lot was just ahead. "They found them?"

"Bob's your uncle. For over a hundred years the Ventnor-related records had been misfiled. Mrs. Wong thought seeing her great-great-grandfather's name on the list would bring her peace."

Alexa held her breath.

"Mr. Lun's name wasn't listed."

She let the air go in a whoosh.

"Mrs. Wong didn't know what to think until she found a stash of letters in her grandmother's trunk. That's when she contacted Preserving Heritage, my archaeology firm. She made a copy of one of the letters and sent it to me. I'll show you the translation." Ana parked behind Mr. Sun's Honda and turned off the car. She retrieved her phone, found the letter, and put it in Alexa's hand.

夏季

SUMMER

1904

MaMa,

It is my twenty-fourth season in Arrowtown. The plum tree blossoms fade as do I. No longer am I a young man. I own a cradle made from a spirit box and start each thaw to see what the winter uncovered. I stand in cold water, shake the box back and forth, coaxing the gold to the base.

It is more ritual and tribute. Bush Creek and Arrow River have nothing left to give. The birds, MaMa. They still bring joy. The funny one with the white puff throat makes a sound like the gong calling me to temple.

Use this money for a feast for our family from First Son.

I have a garden and Cheong Tam's store. Three years ago the town men beat Tam and cut off his queue. They forced it in his mouth. He died of shame and left his store to me. He is not a blood uncle, but we became family for each other.

I am a proper shopkeeper. Townspeople buy my cabbage, swedes, lotus root, and silverbeet. My English gets better but their Chinese does not.

I thought in death Tam made it home, but this did not happen. I cannot leave. I wish I could tell you why, but only time will reveal my heart.

Faithful First Son,
Wing Lun

Alexa was quiet for a second and then asked, "What's a queue?"

"His pigtail," Ana said.

Her stomach hurt. Her eyes flickered to the top of the letter: SUMMER, 1904. The *SS Ventnor*, with a belly full of calico bags, had sailed in 1903. Wing Lun had missed that fateful journey.

Chapter Seven

The pink sun crested a mountain as they crossed the gravel lot and entered the cemetery. Alexa saw mountains in every direction, crowding and shoving for attention.

"First we'll examine the skull in situ," Ana said. "Then you can extract the teeth you need and head to the lab. You can drive my car."

"I only need one tooth."

"All good," Ana said.

Mist coiled and crawled around them as they traipsed between the graves. Alexa stubbed her boot on a footstone and stopped to read it.

MARIE O'BRIEN MARSH
WIDOW OF JOHN MARSH
B 22 MARCH, 1845
D 13 FEBRUARY, 1871

Right next to Marie Marsh's marker was another:

JOHN MARSH KILLED IN A MINING ACCIDENT
B 01 JAN 1841 ORKNEY
D 12 DEC 1870 ARROWTOWN

Had a broken heart killed Marie three months after her

husband died? Was that even possible? That was a reason not to hitch your cart to a man. That, and infidelity. Alexa shook her head. She needed to sever things with Bruce or accept the fact that he cheated on his then-wife and let their relationship unspool.

"He didn't cheat on you," Charlie had said.

If he cheated on his wife, he could cheat on me. Was she a Victorian prude?

She spent a moment with a police officer: Chief Kevin Emanuel Haywood, born Arrowtown 1870, died 1951. PUT TO DEATH WHAT IS EARTHLY IN YOU was his epitaph.

Put to death? Alexa caught up with Ana at the tent. Sun Shing and a man in his fifties set aside thick blankets and rose from their camp chairs. Mr. Sun placed a steaming thermos cup— Alexa smelled tea—on the grass and took off his woolen cap. "Good morning," he said.

In the light Alexa saw that Mr. Sun was in his mid-seventies. She wondered how he'd weathered the overnight temperatures. It had dropped below fifty last night.

"This is Mr. Richard Lumb, the Otago representative of the New Zealand Chinese Association," Mr. Sun said.

Ana introduced herself and Alexa. "How was your night?"

"His soul was soothed by our presence," Mr. Sun said. "And we were soothed by blankets and hot tea."

Mr. Lumb, also of Asian descent, was thin and angular. He studied first Ana and then Alexa. "We value what you are doing here. The souls of the departed desire to be returned to their beginning."

"We understand," Ana said.

He folded the blankets and stuffed them in a backpack. "We don't want the bones to languish in some university basement for forty years like Mystery Miner."

"Are you referring to the skeleton found at Cromwell Gorge?" Ana asked.

Mr. Lumb nodded. "Dug up during the construction of the dam. The bones would have been flooded if the archaeologists hadn't moved them, but they shouldn't have been neglected so long."

"He wasn't in a basement. Two professors rescued him off a shelf in the anatomy department," Ana said. "They eventually did the teeth test and found out he was of western European descent."

"He finally got a proper burial at Cromwell Cemetery," Mr. Lumb said. "That's what we want for Mrs. Wong's great-great-grandfather, a proper burial, and in his homeland."

"That's assuming the remains are related to her," Ana said. "Ms. Glock will be extracting a tooth today."

Alexa let the crime kit slide off her shoulder to the ground. She nudged it with her hiking boot. "I'll extract a second molar and take it to a specialized lab. The enamel from the second molars represent the childhood location."

"Just the one tooth?" Mr. Lumb asked.

Alexa nodded.

The men looked at each other. Mr. Sun, the elder, nodded slightly. "Teeth chatter, but a single tooth cannot."

Alexa silently disagreed. *A single tooth has a lot to chatter about.* "I'll use the same tooth for a DNA sample to compare with Ms. Wong's."

Mr. Sun picked up his mug, but instead of sipping, he poured the tea into the earth. "To appease his thirst."

Mr. Lumb collapsed the two chairs and leaned them against the tent. He looked toward the grass and raised his arms. "There may be more."

"More skeletons?" Ana asked.

He nodded.

"We plan to check."

He nodded, seemingly satisfied. "We'll be back tonight."

Mr. Sun started stiffly across the dewy grass. Rabbits hopped out of his way. The sun, less pink now, was half obscured by low bruised clouds. Mr. Lumb watched Mr. Sun's progress as he spoke quietly. "*Shān yǔ yù lái fēng mǎn lóu.* Coming events cast their shadows before them."

Alexa checked the sky: *Yep. Shadows.* It made her shiver. She and Ana watched Mr. Lumb catch up with Mr. Sun and offer his arm. They walked along the rock wall until they came to a gap and passed through.

"Our skeleton hasn't cast a shadow for over a century," Ana said. "Now it gets a second chance to tell its story." The sun broke through the clouds, painting the cropped grass gold. "I try to separate the bones from the people, but this case is hard," Ana said.

Alexa cared about this left-behind miner too. She identified with it. At the heart of Mrs. Wong's quest for the repatriation of her ancestor was love and home, two things she struggled with. She followed Ana into the tent.

She sniffed the air: freshly turned soil mixed with a hint of polyester tent and lingering incense. She set the crime kit by a folding table she hadn't noticed the night before. When Ana switched the light on, she saw the table was covered with boxes, skeletal charts, plastic trays, a hand broom, paintbrushes, trowels, and picks. Tricks of Ana's trade. "Look at S1's boots," Ana said, opening a box.

Alexa stared down at the darkened blotchy leather boots. The toes had rotted away and the insides were caked with soil and grime. They smelled musty, rotten.

"Classic late-Victorian," Ana said.

Some of the eyelets were missing. Unbelievably, one stiff leather lace, doubled around the ankle, was in a bow. What had the man's thoughts been when he tied that lace? Was he excited about his prospects that day? Did he have a bad feeling? Alexa backed up; fearful her breath might make the fragile loop disintegrate.

Ana closed the box. "Ready?"

Alexa's eyes flickered to her crime kit. It contained her own tricks. She masked up and double-gloved before approaching the hole. "I'll take photographs first." She readied her camera and circled the remains, taken aback again by the odd sideways position.

Ana's hand rested on her hips. "S1 is telling us something. Bones never lie."

"Teeth don't either," Alexa said. "And they last longer than bone." She would gladly debate the virtues of teeth versus bone. For instance, teeth don't remodel themselves after they are formed like bones do. Maybe over a beer she and Ana could gnash it out.

She zoomed in on the teeth. They were stained, maybe from tobacco use. She took several photos and then put the camera aside. "Can I turn the skull face up?"

Ana nodded.

The dirt around the skull had been removed. Alexa gently maneuvered the skull so that the large eye sockets now stared up at her. Soil clogged the left one.

She recalled why eye sockets were large. The sockets housed things besides eyeballs: tissue, muscle, nerves, and fat. She'd read that there was empty space in the orbital fissure to cushion the head from jolts. The workings of the body filled her with awe. When she redirected her focus to the teeth, she made a discovery. The upper and lower right lateral incisors had half-moon notches. "Look," she called.

Ana knelt near the head.

Alexa manipulated the maxilla and mandible so that when the upper and lower incisors met, despite a minor overbite, the notches formed an O. "S1 was a pipe smoker," she said proudly.

Ana laughed. "You should go into archaeology. It's probably from an opium pipe. Europeans miners tended to hold their tobacco pipes with their canines."

"Amazing that you know that," Alexa said.

Ana smiled modestly. "There was a dig at the Chinese settlement a couple years ago. They unearthed lots of opium-smoking paraphernalia."

Alexa's image of opium dens was of dingy rooms and passed-out people. "I bet opium smoking didn't go over with the locals either."

Ana frowned. "Either?"

"The digging up of the bodies."

"I've read that the Chinese miners smoked opium because it decreased libido. All their wives and girlfriends were back in China."

Loneliness in a foreign land. Alexa could relate. But here she was with a fellow geek. She wasn't lonely at the moment. "I'm going to shift the skull again, to part the maxilla and mandible." She wormed her hands under it. Her left index fingertip snagged on a jagged opening. She jerked it out as if a snake had bitten her. "I felt something."

Ana scrambled for a trowel and knelt again. "Hold your palms out." She slid the trowel under the skull, lifted it slowly, and eased it onto Alexa's waiting hands. "Lift it up."

Alexa raised the cranium as if making an offering. A small waterfall of dirt leaked between her fingers. "There's a hole in his head," she said.

Chapter Eight

The lyrics of an old banjo song exploded in Alexa's auditory cortex: *"Phineas Gage had a hole in his head, and ev'ryone knew he oughta be dead."*

Gage had been a Vermont railroad worker in the 1840s. He was tamping down explosives with an iron bar. An errant spark shot the rod in through his eye and out through his frontal lobe, landing twelve feet away. Gage supposedly lived with the hole in his skull for twelve more years.

Alexa doubted the man had lived twelve more years. *Twelve seconds was more likely.*

Ana leaned close. "A couple fractures too." She retrieved her camera. "Be super careful. It's fragile."

No pressure, figuratively and literally. Alexa, heart pounding, held the cranium so Ana could photograph the hole. When Ana finished, Alexa took it to the table where Ana had a padded box ready. Separated from the body, the skull looked forlorn.

Then they studied the photos on Ana's phone. The hole was quarter-sized and jagged. Two fractures, like tributaries, radiated from it.

"What do you think caused it?" Alexa asked.

Ana enlarged it. "A mining accident. A cave-in, maybe."

"Could it be a bullet hole?"

Ana chewed her bottom lip before speaking. "That's possible. The goldfields attracted criminals. It was rich pickings, you know. The Burgess gang, circa 1860s, were notorious. Bad dudes all the way around."

The mention of gangs in New Zealand didn't surprise Alexa. She had encountered gangs in her last case.

"Over a two-day spree, the Burgess gang shot and stabbed five men for gold dust and cash. They were eventually caught and sent to the gallows. So a bullet is a possibility." Ana put her phone away and gently rotated the skull so that the hole was visible. "There's no exit wound."

The large size of the hole and absence of an exit gave Alexa another idea. "Do you think he was attacked?"

Ana gave her a bemused smile. "I'm betting on a mining accident or maybe even a horse kick."

It did not look like a horse kick to Alexa. "Should we report it?"

"To whom? Mrs. Wong just wants to know if S1 is her ancestor. Preserving Heritage isn't being paid to do death investigations."

Maybe she'd run her suspicions by Bruce. That would give her an excuse to call him. She shook her head to clear it of morbid theories. "Is it okay if I get the tooth now?"

"All good," Ana said.

Alexa leaned over and said a silent "open wide." She noted yellow-brown plaque, two cavities that made her wince—they would have been painful—a missing premolar, and erupted wisdom teeth. There was erosion, or attrition, of molar surfaces, maybe from diet or grinding. How had the miners cared for their teeth? Toothbrushes—in one form or another—had been around since ancient Babylon, but this miner hadn't brushed twice a day.

Alexa retrieved her tools: a molar elevator—a tool with a metal-cupped wedge—and forceps. She wedged the elevator between a second molar and wisdom tooth of the upper jaw and wiggled it back and forth. After all these years of being rooted, the molar gave up the fight. She removed it with the forceps and held it to the light. Three roots, like solid tentacles of an octopus, hung from it. She dropped it into a clear bag and labeled it. Her job in the tent was finished.

"I'll walk with you," Ana said.

The air had warmed, edging toward sixty degrees. Alexa rolled her shoulders as they crossed the graveyard. The scars down her back, caused by a childhood scalding, had tightened during the extraction.

"Rush the results," Ana said. "Mrs. Wong is anxious to know."

"It will take a few days," Alexa said.

"Do what you can. I'll be checking with the authorities about what to do if the remains aren't related to Mrs. Wong. They might be given a spot in the proper cemetery." She pointed. "There's Olivia."

They watched her park the van next to Ana's car. "Hiya," she said when they reached her. She dangled a white bakery bag. "The queue was long, but I snagged the last three Nutella donuts."

This was music to Alexa's ears.

"The coroner and the cemetery director will be out here at three o'clock. They're adamant that we check the rest of the grounds. To see if there are more remains."

"That's the plan." Ana then filled Olivia in on the hole in the skull. "It looks like a mining accident."

"Or some kind of attack," Alexa threw in.

"That's dodgy. Maybe he died in a fight with townies. The 'Yellow Peril' stuff. There might be newspaper articles about it," Olivia said. "The Arrowtown Museum has them archived. That would be the place to look."

"Let's focus on the mission," Ana said.

Olivia opened the bag and extracted a puffy yeast donut

leaking goo. Alexa kept her eyes on the bag until Olivia offered it to her.

"Thank you." Alexa took a donut and napkin and then passed the bag to Ana.

Ana traded keys for the bag. "Dr. Sally Weiner is expecting you. She's the director of the chemical analysis section of the lab."

On the twenty-minute drive to Queenstown, Alexa took the curves like a pro—she liked the high vantage point the Toyota Highlander gave her—and thought about the true-crime podcasts she loved listening to, except when they botched the forensic science. The miner would make a good story. She imagined being interviewed as an expert.

> **Producer**: How did you determine where the skeleton was from?
> **Alexa**: The enamel from its teeth contained the answers.
> **Producer**: How does that work?
> **Alexa**: Teeth, while they are forming, lock in a chemical signal from a geological area...

How should she put it so laymen could understand? She munched her donut contemplatively as she turned right onto State Highway 6.

> ...like a "You Are Here" flag.
> **Producer**: How is the enamel extracted?
> **Alexa:** First the tooth will be cleaned. Then we'll use a diamond bur—that's a dental tool with a...

A glop of Nutella slid onto her jacket, terminating the interview.

Chapter Nine

"I'm Alexa Glock," she told the male receptionist at the Queenstown Medical Center. "Dr. Weiner is expecting me."

"I'll let her know you're here. Have a seat." He gestured toward a waiting area. A couple sat on a couch clutching hands.

Alexa pushed her glasses higher on her nose and browsed a rack of pamphlets: PATERNITY TESTING, TWIN TESTING, PEACE OF MIND TESTING—*whatever that was*. They were all DNA-related. She'd taken a DNA analysis class in graduate school and recalled deoxyribonucleic acid was discovered by a Swiss researcher in 1869—ha! a coincidence to the same-era tooth in her tote. It wasn't until the late 1980s that DNA evidence was used in court to convict criminals. And now genealogy testing was all the rage and might indicate Mrs. Wong was related to the miner.

A tall blond woman in a lab coat called her name.

"Dr. Weiner?"

"Call me Sally." Her voice was loud, authoritative, and she looked to be in her forties. She checked her clipboard. "Dr. Luckenbaugh said you'll be conducting a strontium isotope analysis and DNA profiling from historic teeth."

The couple holding hands looked up in surprise.

"If you'll hand me the sample, I'll have the tooth decontaminated. It will take a couple hours." She looked at her watch. "If you'd like to meet me back here at one o'clock, so you can complete the procedure?"

Alexa didn't realize the cleaning would take so long. The interview with the Abertay professors popped into her head: *The mouth and hands of anyone at the scene are the biggest source of contamination.* Not to mention contaminants from the soil. Any of these could cause erroneous results. She dug out the package and handed it over.

Back in the parking lot, she checked her phone. It was only ten a.m. Should she stay in Queenstown or head back to Arrowtown? She'd been to glitzy Queenstown once with Charlie. They had defied death by bungee-jumping off a crazy-high bridge not far from Arrowtown. Her stomach lurched at the memory; she defied death in a case she'd been on and had felt invincible.

Right.

She wasn't a tourist or invincible. She decided to spend a couple hours at the Arrowtown museum that Olivia had mentioned. She wanted to see if any old newspapers contained articles about the violent death of a Chinese miner. Mrs. Wong's ancestor—Wing Lun was his name—had been alive in 1904. She'd start there.

The Lakes District Museum was on a corner just past the European miners' cottages. Driving helped Alexa visualize how Prospector's Cottage was one point of a triangle. The other two points were the cemetery and Buckingham Street. She had recently learned about the Polynesian Triangle: an eight-hundred-thousand-square-mile area of the Pacific Ocean with Hawaii, Easter Island, and New Zealand at its corners. Seafaring explorers had spread to the three points. Alexa's triangle could be explored on foot.

She parked behind the museum. Across from the lot she spotted the Arrow River rimmed with trees and scree. She remembered the beer bottle label from last night: Māori Jack discovered gold in the Arrow River in 1862. She wanted to see that very river. She crossed the road and scrambled past a skateboard park—empty—and down to the bank. The river ran swiftly and shallowly, as if it had urgent errands around the bend. The water—green and gold—sparkled with promise. An unpaved track followed beside it. Her feet itched to run it. Maybe tomorrow morning. She breathed in deeply, glad to be outdoors and on an interesting case.

Glad to be in New Zealand too, she realized.

A group of wiggly school kids blocked the information desk inside the museum. A woman behind the counter was doling out wide flat pans. "Plenty of gold left," she told the kids. "Remember me if you strike it rich." Alexa was tempted to accept a pan too. When the mini miners left, the woman smiled pleasantly.

"Is there gold left in the river?" Alexa asked.

"I wouldn't lie to the chooks, now would I? Ten years ago, a young lass I handed a pan to found a nugget worth two thousand dollars. People find gold flakes every day."

Alexa scanned the sign. Admission to the museum was ten dollars and "Gold Pan Hire" was five. "I'd like to use the archives."

"Do you have an appointment?"

"No. I'd like to see old newspapers."

The woman—her name tag said Stephanie Pincock—checked a computer screen. "It's appointment only. Would you like to make one?"

"How about for right now?"

Her eyes twinkled. "Ms. O'Brien is booked. A few reporters, you know, because of the release. Want to dig it all up again. She has some time in the morning."

Alexa had no idea what the woman was referring to. She reserved the nine a.m. slot.

"The museum contains heaps of old things. You can learn about the moa, the Māori greenstone gatherers, the gold rush, the Chinese settlement."

Alexa forked over ten dollars. The collections were housed in a warren of dimly lit rooms. She walked past a glass case with a huge leg and foot bone of a moa. She read that some moas were ten feet tall. Animated talk filtered from an old-fashioned schoolroom with wooden desks. Girls and boys shuffled in. A woman in colonial dress with frilly bonnet stood at the door. "I'm Schoolmarm. Quickly take a seat."

Alexa squeezed in beside a woman who was dressed normally. She smiled at her. "Mary Ross. Third grade. Queenstown Primary."

"Alexa Glock. Forensics."

Mary's eyes got big.

"You've been to the creek and the Chinese settlement, eh?" Schoolmarm said to her classroom of wiggling third graders. "I can tell because your gummies are muddy."

Gummies? Alexa was flummoxed until she noticed the kids all wore gum boots. She'd add "gummies" to her New Zealand slang collection.

"What were your impressions of the Chinese miners' huts?"

"They were like rabbit hutches," a girl said. "I wouldn't want to live there."

"The bad man was hiding in one," a red-haired boy said. "My brother said he's here," he added. "The Hammer."

The children started clamoring.

Alexa figured The Hammer was some TV show or video game villain. She edged toward the door.

"Settle down," Mary Ross said. "There's no bad man here, Alexander."

The racket faded. A girl asked, "Did whole families live in the huts?"

"The migrants left their families behind." The schoolmarm adjusted her bonnet which had slipped forward. "They often lived two to six men per hut."

Alexa stayed to hear more about the Chinese miners.

A boy shot up his hand. "Couldn't they bring their kids with them?"

"They didn't have the money to bring their families," Schoolmarm said. "They came from extreme poverty. And then there was the poll tax established in 1881."

"What's that?"

"Every immigrant from China had to pay a ten-pound tax," she explained.

"That's not very much," a girl said.

"Duh. Ten pounds was like maybe a hundred back then," the girl sitting next to her said.

Schoolmarm's bonnet bobbed up and down. "It was a lot of money, especially when you barely had any. The tax was increased to one hundred pounds in 1896 and was imposed on Chinese migrants only."

"That's not fair," two kids chimed.

"The European settlers weren't always kind. They thought the Chinese had unsanitary habits; they didn't like it that the Chinese worked on Sundays or that they looked different. Do you know what xenophobia is?"

Alexa skipped out on the vocab lesson. She had the museum mostly to herself. She skipped the fake forgery, perused a gun cabinet, and found the gold rush room. She wasn't sure how mining worked. A diagram explained the miners used wooden cradles and terraced boxes that trapped the heavier gold and let lighter rock and soil wash away.

She learned that when a miner first arrived, they used their gold pans to prospect. If they found gold in a section of a creek or river where no one else was working, they had to visit the gold warden in town and pay £1 for a Miner's Right. Then they could go back and stake a roughly thirty-square-foot claim.

Steam powered dredging and underground tunneling came later in the gold rush.

Alexa was drawn to the opium display. She stared through the glass at an assortment of vials, pipes with bamboo shafts and ceramic bowls, tin cans, trays, and an opium heating lamp. She read that the sale of opium was legal until 1901. By then, she figured, a lot of the miners were addicted.

There were many photographs from the era. Alexa studied several of the Chinese miners. They were older than she expected and posed in dignified stances: straight backs, no smiles on their thin clean-shaven faces. Some had bare heads; she suspected that thin braids hung down their backs. Others wore broad-brimmed felt hats like their European counterparts. Alexa liked the hats. Maybe she could find one in the gift store—a replacement for her dad's fishing hat that she had "borrowed" when she left for college.

Charlie said she looked dorky in it. *What does he know?*

A Reverend Don appeared in several photos with Chinese miners. One was labeled: *Quest of the salvation of the Chinese souls.*

Alexa chafed at the word "salvation" and its implied message of sin and redemption.

Some photos listed names. Alexa read excitedly, scanning for Wing Lun. She found an Ah Lum. Then an Ah Saab, Gee Wong, Sooe Loo, and a Koy Hop. No Wing Lun. She left the gold rush room without finding him and left the gift shop without finding a hat.

She checked texts and email at a picnic table as she ate a ham-and-gouda panini from the Fork and Tap. There was nothing from Abertay University. Nothing from Bruce either. She was the one who had called a hiatus and said she would contact him when she was ready.

But still...

What did she want? That was the elusive nugget she mined on the drive back to Queenstown. Her heart said to give herself over to Bruce, teenage daughters and all. Her brain said she would forever distrust him. Four weeks ago, in her apartment, he had not denied that he had cheated on his wife.

He'd said he loved her. Came right out with it. Alexa had admired his vulnerability in declaring this. She'd been speechless, and that had been thirty-one days ago. *Was there a statute of limitations on a hiatus? On love?*

冬天

WINTER

1886

MaMa,

The ice on the Arrow River is broken into shards of glass to pierce my heart. The gold I was to send for second brother's schooling was stolen from my hiding place. Respectfully, I am sorry.

I share a room with Cheong Tam on the edge of town only when the creeks are frozen. Ice glazes inside of the single window, and the light is pale like the eyes of the townspeople. As soon as it darkens, others gather here to smoke Tam's black beads and gamble at fan tan and pakapoo. They miss their wives and children and mothers. We are alone together. I earn shillings by reading letters they bring me: families needing money, deaths, births, longings. I write letters back for them. Tam wants to learn to make characters, but I fail at teaching him.

I thaw my fingers at hearth to finish my news. No birds sing in winter.

As soon as the creeks sing again I will find more gold, enough for second brother to attend school and for you to build a fine house as well. It is hard work, not like digging for peanuts. In three years I will return with honor.

Faithful First Son,
Wing Lun

Chapter Ten

THURSDAY AFTERNOON

Sally was waiting in the lobby. "The sample is ready."

Alexa smiled. Two tooth tests on the way. *Say that three times quickly. Two tooth tests. Two toot tests. Two toot tots.*

"What are you smiling about?" Sally asked.

"I'm excited. It's been a while since I've done an isotopic measurement."

Sally nodded as if she understood.

The strontium test would come first because enamel was the top layer of a tooth, like the earth's crust, and DNA was at the core.

They went up one flight of stairs and past several labs brimming with automated equipment, technicians buzzing around them. Sally stopped in front of a door and scanned a keycard. It opened into an anteroom of lockers and dressing stalls. Shelves held plastic-wrapped protective gear. "You'll have to change out of your street clothes," she said. "You can have a locker for your things." Sally handed her a package of sterile gear, took another, and disappeared into a stall.

Alexa undressed in her own stall and stepped into green scrubs and a Tyvek jumpsuit. She pulled booties over her shoes, stuck a hairnet over her ponytail, followed by safety glasses, double gloves, and a mask. Sally was waiting. When Alexa pulled the hood over her head she thought she and Sally looked like gangster snowmen.

The door to the next room opened with a pneumatic whoosh. It led to a passage with another door at the end. A large vent whirred and air brushed her cheeks. "That's the ventilation system for the clean room," Sally said.

They entered a brightly lit lab, Alexa tingling with excitement and a little nervousness. Sally pointed to a workstation. "The sample is there. I've never seen this process before."

Alexa was jazzed as she assessed the equipment: magnification glasses, wrapped diamond burs, handpiece, a Sharpie, ethanol spray and special paper towels, and a rack of microtubes. She donned the magnification glasses and covered a tray with the foil. Conscious that Sally was watching, she inserted the tiny diamond bur into the motorized handpiece, tested it, and picked up the tooth. She pictured it as a map that would show where S1 lived when his second molars erupted. She held the molar with her left hand, turned on the rotor with her right, and ran the diamond bur up and down, up and down, wearing a groove in the enamel's surface. Dust snowed onto the foil. When a minuscule pile accumulated, she turned off the motor and set the handpiece aside. Then she tilted the foil into the tube Sally held for her.

"You've a steady hand," Sally said.

Like riding a bike. She cleaned the work area.

Sally described the chemical process that followed. "After it's digested in nitric acid, we'll isolate the strontium..."

Alexa wasn't a chemist, and even though she nodded, she didn't understand the rest of it. "How long will it take?"

"Five days."

"Can you rush it?"

Sally frowned. "It will cost more. Two, three days work?"

Alexa hoped the extra money was in Mrs. Wong's budget. At the DNA extraction workstation, she looked for an analytical mill, which resembled a coffee grinder, to pulverize the molar. There wasn't one. "Um, I don't see a mill."

"We don't pulverize anymore," Sally said. "We use a drill and go straight to the pulp chamber."

Had she let her subscription to *International Journal of Forensic Odontology* lapse? Or had she been too busy Brucing to keep up? "I'm not familiar with that method."

Sally's eyes lit up. "It's a new technique. There are fewer handling steps, and you don't have to destroy the sample. Best of all, you get results in a few hours. Shall I demonstrate?"

Alexa hated to relinquish control but was excited to learn the new technique, "Thank you, yes."

Sally placed the tooth on a piece of gauze and then took a tiny drill out of a sterile bag. "I'll cut a one-millimeter furrow. Then I'll open it with the chisel to expose the pulp chamber."

The drill hummed to life. Sally made the furrow halfway between the root and crown, her hands steady as stone. Then she switched to a dental chisel and deftly split the furrow open. The tooth was now in two pieces. She used a probe to carve out the hardened pulp which she deposited into a microtube. "You'll have your DNA results tomorrow."

Chapter Eleven

It looked like Olivia was mowing the grass near the cemetery tent, although there was no sound of an engine. She pushed her wheeled machine in a straight line, biting her bottom lip, intent on the screen attached to the handle of the ground-penetrating radar. Hair stuck out of her wool beanie like straw from a scarecrow. A tui squawked from the top of a cross. Alexa tore her eyes away from Olivia's progress and watched the bird puff its iridescent plumage, extend its neck, and emit a series of clicks, tweets, and a chiding for good measure.

Two men—one tall and one short—stood by the tent with Ana. "All done at the lab?" she asked when Alexa reached them.

Alexa let the crime kit slide off her shoulder to the ground so that she could unzip her jacket. "We'll have DNA results tomorrow and the strontium in a few days."

"Brill," Ana said. She turned to the men. "Ms. Glock has conducted dental tests so we can uncover more information about our remains."

The taller of the two stuck out a fist. "Alan McKenzie, Queenstown forensic pathologist."

Alexa bumped his fist and glanced at Ana. *Why was the forensic pathologist here?*

"I pulled some strings to get Dr. McKenzie to have look at our bones. He's an overachiever and has a PhD in archaeology in addition to a medical degree."

"No strings needed." He had bushy eyebrows and hair starting to gray.

The second man, dapper in a dark suit, said, "I'm Quentin
Howard, Lakes District Cemetery director." He brushed a
spec from his lapel and then checked the other side. "I handle
Queenstown, Frankton, Wanaka, Cardona, and Arrowtown.
Busy, busy. People dying to get in."

"Mr. Howard heard about our skeletal remains," Ana
explained.

"There's no record of the burial. No information at all." Mr.
Howard swayed a bit as he talked. "Discovered outside the plan,
outside the boundary. In all probability, you know, it was left
behind. Those dreadful coffin ships? Highly irregular. We need
to know if any other plots are occupied."

"That's what Ms. Forester is trying to determine," Ana said.

Mr. Howard wasn't finished. "In Drybread Cemetery—
that's near the Dunstan Mountains—they discovered twenty
unmarked graves along the fence line. All gold rush era. Took all
the remains to somewhere."

"Otago University," Ana said. "There's an ongoing study."

"Your girl there should stay closer to the wall."

Alexa bristled at "your girl." She noted that Olivia had spray-
painted red grid markers on the brown grass. They ended ten
feet from the tent.

"Thinking ahead. Thinking ahead. I expect we'll extend the
cemetery this way, eh? We're chock-a-block on that side." Mr.
Howard indicated with his thumb. "We can't bury someone
in a plot that already contains remains, pfft." He shielded his
eyes from the weak sun. "Does she see the body right on that
screen?"

"No," Ana said. "The machine measures the speed at which
radio waves travel through the ground and back to the antenna.

When the waves go from one type of soil to another, or hit a rock or void…"

"Or bones?" Mr. Howard asked.

"…the readout will indicate the disturbance," Ana finished.

Olivia made a careful U-turn, one strip closer to them.

Mr. Interruptus was wearing thin on Alexa. "I'll check in with Olivia," she said. She hustled across the grass. Olivia stopped walking. "Hiya."

"How's it going?" Alexa asked.

She pointed to the screen. Alexa saw a black-and-white graph. Parts of the graph were shaded. "The survey tracks my progress."

No buried treasure or outline of a dinosaur—that was *Jurassic Park* stuff—but the bare-bones graph was a letdown. When she'd used ground-penetrating radar at the body farm, the buried pigs had at least shown up as shadowy gray ridges.

"When I finish going this way," Olivia said, "I'll turn ninety degrees and repeat the scan. Then we'll have a look-see at the results." She tucked a clump of hair in place.

"Need help?" Alexa asked.

"All good here." She pushed onward.

Ana and the men had disappeared into the tent. Alexa walked in as the forensic pathologist pulled on gloves. She set the crime kit in an out-of-the-way spot. S1's skull had been reunited with its body. Mr. Howard, hands behind his back, frowned down at it. "Never seen one of these, even though I've coordinated hundreds of end-of-life services, eh?"

The profile position hid the hole in the skull.

"If you'll please move, Quentin," the forensic pathologist said.

"No problem. No problem at all." Mr. Howard shifted to the base of the grave, shaking his head. "This burial position is highly unusual. Highly unusual. On its side? No undertaker would arrange the deceased like that. It's pointing a finger. Don't like that. Don't like that at all."

"We agree it's unusual," Ana said.

"I'll take a wee stroll. See if the girl has found anything." Mr. Howard pivoted. Alexa moved aside so he could slip out the flaps.

"Quite the ear bash from that one," the forensic pathologist commented. He knelt to study the skull. Ana watched intently, reminding Alexa of a mother hen. He cleared his throat. "The cranium is characteristically male." He gently turned the skull to the side without the hole and then to the damaged side. Alexa saw his brow furrow. "A single penetrating trauma with no exit hole. Left parietal bone. Two fractures radiate from it." He probed the wound with a single finger and spoke matter-of-factly. "The hole is irregular and has an inward bevel. It's possible it was an accident, but no other area is damaged. My guess is the sharp end of a pickax."

A chill skittered up Alexa's spine.

"If the remains weren't historic and abutting a cemetery," he said, "I'd request an inquiry."

That didn't sit right with Alexa. There was no statute of limitations on murder by pickax. "Can't you still?"

"There's no one left alive who knew the man," he said.

"There might descendants." She wondered how old cold cases were before they were permanently shelved. She might text Bruce and ask.

"Perhaps there *was* an inquiry," Ana said.

"I have an appointment with the archivist at the museum tomorrow morning," Alexa said. "Maybe I can find out."

Olivia popped her head through the flap. "I've found something!"

Ana and Alexa followed her across the grass. The GPR was

parked ten feet from the tent. "See how the ground right here dips a little?"

Alexa saw a slight depression.

"Now look at the screen," Olivia said.

Alexa knocked into Ana's head in her haste to see. In the place of the graph was the fuzzy gray background of an ultrasound image. The surface of the ground was delineated by a bold black line. In one patch below the line, wavy lines contrasted with the areas on either side of it. Olivia put her finger on it. "That's a disturbance. It's different compared to the area around it."

"It could indicate reworked soil," Ana said.

"As in someone might be buried there?" Alexa asked.

The women nodded.

How could a job at Abertay University compete with this?

The cemetery director hurried over and peered at the screen. "What's this?"

"We aren't sure," Ana said. "We'll need to excavate."

Another hungry ghost was Alexa's bet.

Chapter Twelve

THURSDAY EVENING

Mr. Howard wrung his hands. "Bodies everywhere. Not what I wanted. Not what I wanted at all." He whipped out his phone and smashed some numbers. "Eh, Harry? Quentin Howard here. Need you to run the digger back out to Arrowtown Cemetery."

Alexa scanned the graveyard as Mr. Howard finished his call. Shadows stretched like fingers from the tombstones, greedy for the night. The mountain was a shaded beast. A solitary bird sang frantically.

"Harry is on his way," Mr. Howard said. "He'll take the top-soil right off."

"All good," Ana said. "It will be dark soon. I'll get the portable lights ready."

Mr. Howard watched Ana walk off and then turned to Alexa. He was an inch or two shorter than she was. "Can't stay. Can't stay. The missus has pickleball. Just me and the boys tonight. Do you have children, Miss Clock?"

"Glock." Alexa hated the "children" question. "I have two nephews."

"Never too early to think of the future, eh? Especially when you don't have children. Never too early to plan your service, pick out a casket, prepay. Are you interested in a DIY coffin kit? Fine, affordable underground furniture, we call it."

"No thanks." Alexa crossed the grass to Olivia who still stared at the GPR screen.

"I did another sweep to guesstimate the dimension of the disturbance," she said. "It corresponds with the shape of a grave. Let's measure the outline before the digger gets here. You can hold the pigs."

Kiwis had a way with short *e* vowels. "Pigs" was "pegs," "six" was
"sex." Both had stumped Alexa a few times. She stuck a peg in the
ground each time Olivia indicated until they had a four-by-eight foot
rectangle. Then Olivia handed her a bottle of spray paint. "Outline it
while I put the GPR in the van. Then you can pull the pigs."

Alexa shook the can. The dark red paint that dribbled on her
hand looked like blood.

———

Harry removed eight inches of topsoil and dumped it six feet to
the side. The freshly turned soil smelled of minerals and tannin
and decay. *Secrets, too*, Alexa thought. After Harry drove off,
they erected a new tent around the hole.

Olivia made another trip to the van and returned with a folding
table. Ana positioned the lights and fastened the tent flaps open.

Alexa fetched her crime kit from the other tent and cast a
quick look at S1. *We haven't forgotten you.* On her way to the new
tent, she stopped and surveyed the graveyard. She had a feeling
that she was being watched. Why not? Tents, diggers, skeletons.
Townspeople were probably curious.

Olivia and Ana arranged tools in a certain order. Ana opened
a new case file on her tablet. Alexa felt in the way and knocked
over a bucket.

"I need to call Mum," Ana said. "Tell her we'll be late for
dinner." She stepped out, but immediately returned. "Mr. Sun
and another man are on their way. I'll give them an update."

"It's good someone is here to watch over the bones," Olivia
said. She unrolled a tarp. "This is for fill dirt. Everything will

need to be sieved. We're going to dig a thirty-centimeter-deep perimeter." She gave Alexa a shovel and grabbed another.

Olivia bore down with her boot, wedged the shovel head back and forth, scooped dirt, and emptied it onto the tarp. Alexa copied her from the opposite side; the exertion felt good. Bruce popped into her head. She yearned to call him and describe the situation, the mystery of it, her role with the digging and the teeth. Ana walked in as they finished.

"There's no sign of a coffin," Olivia said.

Ana was quiet for a moment. "Just like S1. Very odd. Mr. Sun and another man have set up their vigil in front of the other tent. I told them we might have another skeleton. Mr. Sun said he wasn't surprised. That there's a disturbance in the air. He'll calm the spirits with incense."

Olivia nodded. "I feel it too."

Alexa looked into the four corners of the tent as if spirits lurked. *Science, not superstition*, she reminded herself.

Olivia took a bamboo pole and moved to the top left corner of the possible grave. She poked it down into the soil, plucked it out like a toothpick from cake, looked up when Ana took a photo, and repeated the probe every three inches. When she completed one path, she moved three inches down and repeated, leaving a trail of holes. On her third go, near the center, her face broke into awe. "Resistance. Half a meter down."

The three of them dug from the sides, deepening the hole and closing in on the object. They switched to trowels and then spoons. Abertay University, Bruce, even her empty stomach receded as Alexa scooped and dumped. She thought of S1 and its pointing finger. She mapped its direction in her head; it seemed to point right at this tent. Her greenstone pendant pulsed against her sternum. She unearthed a tawny bulge. "Here's something!"

Olivia stopped digging and grabbed a whisk broom.

"Move," Ana said.

Alexa scuttled back, happy to relinquish her spot. She didn't want to damage bone—if that's what it was. She watched, engrossed, as a rounded object—roughly three feet deep—was exposed. Between each of Ana's spoonfuls, Olivia whisked aside dirt.

"It's a cranium," Ana said.

Alexa, knees numb, hobbled to the other side and peered down, expecting a sloping forehead and dirt-filled eye orbits. Where were the jaw and the teeth? The term *blank-face* popped into her head—as if someone erased the eyes, nose, and mouth. Confusion muddied her brain. When she figured out what she was looking at, her heart pounded.

The skull was facedown.

She leaned closer and made out the faint Y-shaped sutures that connected the posterior bones of the skull.

Ana reached for her camera. "I've seen a few sets of remains on their sides like S1, but I've never seen a face down."

"Someone must have hated him," Alexa blurted. She fought the urge to lift the skull and flip it.

"I took a mortuary customs class." Olivia took off her beanie and swiped the hair out of her eyes. "There's a Bronze Age burial ground on a Swedish island where fifty prone burials were discovered. They were mixed in with regular graves."

Did Bronze Age or Iron Age come first? Alexa wondered.

Olivia's eyes gleamed. "They thought prone burials prevented the dead from coming back to haunt the living."

"Prone burials are sometimes referred to as deviant burials." Ana turned off her camera and set it aside. "You might find evidence of torture or even decapitations."

Alexa scanned the cranium to see if it was attached to a neck. Dirt hid the answer.

"But not always." Ana picked up her trowel. "In medieval times the prone position was believed to be a gesture of humility toward God. Right now? Let's focus. I want to move slowly and document S2 carefully. Facedown and a shallow grave might mean it was clandestine."

The word *clandestine* made Alexa uneasy.

Olivia pulled her beanie back on and tucked her bangs away. "Sometimes prone burials occur in a double grave."

Alexa looked at her feet. Was she standing on another set of bones? "Side-by-side?"

"Stacked. One body is supine, and the other is placed prone on top of it."

Nose to nose for eternity.

"I don't see evidence of that," Ana said. "Olivia, take the upper leg area. I'll dig for the ribs. Alexa, take the neck area."

As they dug, Olivia hummed something catchy that Alexa couldn't identify. Alexa was careful not to dig too deep or fast; neck bones were tiny and fragile. She looked up when Olivia stopped humming. "I see femur."

The strongest bone in the body, Alexa thought, and critical to standing and moving.

Ana took photos as Olivia exposed the upper left and right leg bones. She set the camera aside and grabbed a tape measure. "What's the formula to predict how tall the deceased was?"

Olivia closed her eyes: "For a male, femur times 2.23 plus 69.08." She took the tape and measured. She used her phone to multiply. "One hundred and fifty-five centimeters. A tad over five feet tall. He's short, possibly because of poor nutrition."

"Maybe," Ana said.

The way Ana said "maybe" made Alexa wonder if S2 was female. But that didn't make sense. The Chinese miners had been male.

Alexa tunneled closer, visualizing the seven stacked bones of the neck. She alternated between gently scooping with a spoon and brushing aside soil with a whisk. And there it was: the topmost vertebra, the atlas. "No beheading," she said. "The skull is connected to the neck."

"All good," Ana said. "I didn't want a decapitation situation."

"Like Marie Antoinette," Olivia said.

"Or Mary, Queen of Scots," Ana said. "It took two blows to behead poor Mary."

Olivia stopped troweling and hoisted an imaginary head. "When the executioner lifted her head, it rolled away because her wig came off."

Alexa listened to the morbid banter. She liked working with these women. She scraped away more soil, exposing the second cervical vertebra. She marveled at how neatly it stacked against C1. She twisted her own head, left, right, surprised her neck was stiff. Then her stomach growled so loudly that Ana laughed. "Mum has made beef stew. You'll come over, right Olivia?"

"Ta, but I need to get back to Queenstown."

Alexa salivated at the thought of stew. Chuck roast, onion, carrots maybe, potatoes, herbs. All a guess because she'd never made a stew. The next two vertebra looked out of alignment. She brushed away a dust of dirt. Instead of stacked snugly like it should be, C3 was a half inch to the right of C4. "Maligned" popped into her head. Wasn't that another word for evil? A spinal injury like this was severe. Maybe fatal. "Look at this." Her voice was hoarse.

Olivia scrabbled over and leaned in. "The neck is broken. Ow."

After a minute of silence, Ana said, "We're done for now. I'll ask the forensic pathologist back out to take a look, and I'll need you to do the tooth tests, Alexa. S2 might be Mrs. Wong's ancestor. The whole area will need to be scanned. Who knows how many more graves there are."

Chapter Thirteen

FRIDAY MORNING

Alexa was pulling on her running tights when Shelby barged in like she owned the place.

Her hair was flyaway, and her narwhal nightie was inside-out. "Where is you going?"

"Running." She parted the sheer curtain; it was still dark.

Shelby made a beeline for the crime kit at the foot of the spare bed and slipped her tiny hand into the outer pocket. "Why?"

Alexa lifted the kit away. "This is, um, off-limits." She set it on a high shelf in the closet and closed the door. She pulled on her fleece. It was cold in the bedroom. "I run out of habit."

"What's habit?"

The kid asked intelligent questions. "Something you do over and over."

"Like kiss Mummy?"

Alexa nodded. "That's a good habit."

Shelby twirled and ran downstairs. "Mum," she screamed, "the lady is doing habit."

Smiling, Alexa emailed her boss Dan with updates. Then she checked for messages: nothing from Bruce. He was giving her the space she'd requested. *But still.*

Pam was in the kitchen, reading on her laptop. "Coffee?" she asked.

"No thanks. I'm off for a run. I'll be back in forty-five minutes or so." She patted her pocket to make sure she had the cottage key.

"Still dark out," Pam said.

Alexa pictured the track along the Arrow River she spotted yesterday; it had looked perfect for running. "I have a headlamp."

"Like a miner," Pam said without looking up.

Her breath came in misty puffs as she stretched on the driveway. Tomorrow was her birthday. Should she mention it to Ana or Pam? That seemed presumptuous—as if fishing for a party or cake. She did a set of uppercuts, hooks, and jabs and then set off. Thirty-eight would happen with or without cake.

But she loved cake.

Like a cyclops she glided through the sleepy town, catching glimpses of early morning kitchens and upsetting a free-range dog. "He won't bite," a disembodied voice trailed.

By the time she cut past the museum and followed signs for the Arrow River Trail, a fine mist coated her face. The riparian path—at first shoulder-to-shoulder with the twisty river and then climbing ten, twenty feet above it—was slippery with leaves. Any light of day was blotted by the dying leaves still clinging to overhead branches. River sounds intensified and receded, intensified, receded, mesmerizing her as she found her stride. She stayed left, like a proper Kiwi, away from the tumbling edge, and picked up her pace.

As the path climbed higher over the river, her thoughts darted from Bruce—she missed sharing case details and a bed with him—to meeting the archivist at the museum. What would she find out about accidents or attacks on Chinese miners? A shy dawn broke in time for her to see a waterfall and, past it, a swinging footbridge spanning the river.

Swing bridges terrified her. Her mind bounced to the one that had flipped her brother almost to his death. But she wanted an aerial view of the river where Māori Jack discovered gold. She turned off her headlamp, grabbed the slippery cables, and stepped up three steps and onto the slats.

Movement on the far side caught her eye. A person in a black raincoat—hood cinched—stood on the other side of the river. A soft, fat raindrop blurred her vision. For a crazy second she was sure it was a gold miner off to his claim. The person raised his or her head, caught sight of her, and slowly evaporated into the trees.

Any thoughts Alexa had of crossing the bridge likewise evaporated.

———

The archivist at the Lakes District Museum was the opposite of the mousy bespectacled one Alexa had envisioned. "I've lived here all my life," Maggie O'Brien bellowed. Behind big square lenses, her eyes were rimmed with blue eyeliner. "I know everyone and their cuzzy." Despite her girth and age—early sixties— she was quick-footed. Her bright gold T-shirt said BE NICE TO THE ARCHIVIST.

Alexa followed her up a flight of stairs to a slightly off-kilter hallway. The back of her T-shirt said I CAN ERASE YOU FROM HISTORY.

Ms. O'Brien opened a door and turned on the light. "This is it!"

Alexa forced a smile. She had expected enormous file cabinets, narrow aisles between stacks, ladders on wheels. The reality was two long wooden tables, bare but for a stack of photos, and two computer cubicles facing the back wall. The single window looked out on Buckingham Street. Ms. O'Brien pointed to the closest table. "Put your things there."

Alexa obeyed quickly; she was a little afraid of the woman. She'd left the crime kit and laptop in the bedroom at Prospector's Cottage, so all she had were her tote and a notebook.

Ms. O'Brien poked the stack of photos. "Gayle must have

left these out." She picked up the top one: a black-and-white image of a young girl in a white pinafore. She was squeezing a cat. Ms. O'Brien turned it over. "Lucinda Parnell, aged eight, 1909. Always label your photographs. It makes my job easier." She guffawed. "What photos, am I right? No one prints photos anymore. All Insta this, tic-tac-toe that. We're digitizing our collection. Gayle is our chief digitizer. Knows everything about Arrowtown history."

Alexa tucked that tidbit away. She might want to talk to this Gayle.

"Her family go way back. They donated the funds for our expansion. Did you see the gallery next to the lobby?"

"No," Alexa said.

"That's thanks to the Frost Family Foundation."

The next photo was of a Chinese man holding an umbrella for a European woman. The street behind them was unpaved. Alexa's heart drummed. Maybe she found Cheong Tam or Wing Lun. "Can I see that photo?"

Ms. O'Brien leaned in. "That's Buckingham Street."

Alexa turned it over, aware her greenstone pendant throbbed against her sternum. Faded scrawl read *Pearl Haywood About Town, 1903.*

The archivist looked at her watch. "If you had sent a request earlier, I could have pulled whatever you needed in advance. Is it about Cindy Mulligan?"

Alexa looked at the next photo in the pile. Same era: A family group dressed in heavy wool finery stared at the camera with stern expressions. A dog in the photo was blurred. "Who's Cindy Mulligan?"

Ms. O'Brien's brows knit together. "Haven't you been keeping up with the news?"

"I guess not."

"American, are you?"

Alexa set the photo down and nodded.

"I could tell by your accent. Cindy Mulligan volunteered in this museum, before my days. A docent. Played the schoolmarm. Helped establish our archives. She was murdered in 1998. Not far from here." She shook her head so that her chin jiggled. "Out for a jog. Her body was found by a gold prospector. Imagine that." She paused to catch her breath. "Took a couple weeks to catch the man. He spent twenty-five years in prison. The parole board just released him. Cindy Mulligan is gone forever, and Earl Hammer is free as a bird."

His debt has been paid, Alexa thought. But had it? What was owed when someone maliciously took a person's life? Her expertise in forensic science was her way to seek justice for the dead. She preferred not to think about what happened to the guilty after her role was finished. She knew crime left a spiraling vortex in its wake.

"What *can* I gather for you?" the archivist asked.

"I'd like to see newspapers from the gold rush era in regard to the Chinese miners, especially anything to do with crime or murder."

Ms. O'Brien's eyes widened. "Like your Wild West our goldfields were."

Alexa thought of the letter Ana had shown her. "I have two names." She spelled out Wing Lun and Cheong Tam.

"In Chinese culture, the surname comes first. My name would be O'Brien Maggie."

"I didn't know that. I guess check the names both ways. Wing Lun and..."

"Lun Wing," Ms. O'Brien finished. She plopped down at one of the computers. "Our papers have been digitized. I'll start with the newspapers that covered this area." She typed in the parameters. "Only one match for the names. Here it is. I'll print it for you."

It was an *Otago Witness* article dated April 1901. Alexa read over Ms. O'Brien's shoulder.

> *A Chinese grocer named Cheong Tam, who occupies a store at Bush Creek, was discovered yesterday afternoon on Buckingham Street with abrasions and somewhat suspicious circumstances. Chinese gold seekers use Tam's store to purchase teas, rice, pickled lemons, ginger, spices, opium, gambling pieces, and smoking accessories. The store also serves as an informal bank, a meeting place, and gambling den. Tam was removed to the hospital, but he refused treatment.*

Alexa wondered if this assault was the same one Wing Lun had written about to his mother. Maybe the suspicious circumstances included his pigtail cut off and shoved in his mouth.

"That store still stands," Ms. O'Brien said. "It's part of the restored Chinese settlement down at the creek." She stood and patted the chair. "You've got plenty here to read."

"I'd also like to see the records of Chinese burials in the Arrowtown Cemetery. Since its opening to around 1910." Alexa frowned. "Would there be records of unmarked graves?"

Ms. O'Brien looked like a bird dog on scent. "I'll find out. The cemetery records are housed downstairs."

Alexa thought of something else. "When was the police force established in Arrowtown?"

"The first jail was a log. Prisoners were chained to it."

"A log?"

Ms. O'Brien smiled triumphantly. "I'll see what else I can find. You can print to the copier in my office."

When she left, Alexa snooped through the pile of photos,

worried she was committing an archival misdemeanor. They were gold rush era photos: muddy streets, men in tall hats and vests standing in front of a hotel, a horse and buggy, St. Paul's Church, 1905. She set two aside: the one of the Chinese man holding the umbrella for the white woman and one of three older and unsmiling Chinese men. They stood shoulder to shoulder, arms at their sides. Each had a little chain arcing from their pockets to the buttons of their vests. Alexa wondered if the chains were gold. The back of the photo was inscribed *Celestials, Arrowtown, 1901.* Could one of them be Wing Lun or Cheong Tam? She would ask Ms. O'Brien for copies. She took pictures of them with her phone in case the answer was no.

Reading time. Alongside the first article, an ad caught her attention:

F. ARMSTRONG, Surgeon Dentist of Baker Street, Queenstown, Intends making a TOUR OF THE PROVINCE OF OTAGO. A Complete Outfit is carried. Continuous Gum Work, which is so like the natural gum. Bridge Work. Gold Stopings. Porcelain Jacket Crowns. The strongest system of Vulcanite work. Gas, Cocaine, or Chloroform administered.

Vulcanite was a rubbery substance used to make dentures, and cocaine was popular as an anesthesia until it resulted in too many overdoses and deaths. Alexa took a photograph of the ad because it amused her. She was glad she wasn't Dr. Armstrong's patient.

Another ad caught her attention.

A LADY, well accomplished, medium height and dark, with £100 income, wishes to communicate with Gentleman, with a view to matrimony. Letters to be addressed (accompanied with photo) to "Lonely," Box 16, P. O. Arrowtown

If she broke up with Bruce, she could try online dating. Bumbler or Tender or something like that. She wouldn't call herself something lame like "Lonely." She'd try "Odontologist" or "Rare Arch." Scientific nomenclature would garner more swipes. Her smile faded as she read CHINESE MURDER, the article next to the ads. A man named Ah Chin died from gunshot wounds. He lived in a cave along the Arrow River and was shot where he slept.

He lived in a cave? Alexa might have run above it this morning. The wounds were in the chest area—not head—so she moved to another article.

ATROCIOUS CRIME was published in 1901. A woman and her infant daughter had been butchered in a cemetery. Alexa stiffened until she learned the murders hadn't taken place at the Arrowtown Cemetery. She scrolled onward, past lots of weather reports: the weather has been boisterous, the weather is wretched, the weather expected to cause floods, the weather is desolate and cold.

She shivered.

"The Chinese Question," *Evening Star*, 1895, seemed to be in response to another letter.

Dear Sir,

"Justice" knows little in regard to the Chinese. He remarks that Chinamen are law-abiding, honest, and hardworking. I cannot possibly believe that "Justice" has ever visited Bush Creek of a Sunday evening. Gambling is not allowed by law, yet Chinamen defy the law in every possible way. They act honest, he says. That shows "Justice" knows little about the Chinese and their vile ways. Who is it that robs our girls by dosing them with opium? None other than the honest Chinaman.

Vile ways? Doping girls? The ugly head of racism. CHINESE CORPSES AND COFFINS, *Otago Gazette*, came up next.

> *With regard to the Chinese, it is well known that they observe the doctrine of the resurrectionist. They make the rounds of the colony and raise the dead, scrape the bones of those Chinese who have died a certain time before his visit—seven years, I believe—pack the skeleton with its respective pigtail in a box, which is properly labeled and sent to China by a vessel specially chartered for the purpose.*

Alexa bit her lip. This was an article about the exhumations Ana had told her about.

> *It is computed that it takes £25 per skeleton, so that it appears the dead Chinamen were worth more than the live ones.*

That haunting question: Would she have treated newcomers—ones whose skin color or eyelid shape was different than her own—with respect and kindness? Alexa prayed she would have, but history and psychology said otherwise. She tackled the next article instead of wallowing in her pale-skinned privilege.

> *Yesterday evening a Chinaman named Ah Bung fell over a precipice while carrying wood on the Arrow River foot track. He was terribly hurt, and died last night. The track at this part is too narrow, and very dangerous, and this is the second death that has taken place there since the Council cut the track.*

She needed a different running route. After printing it, she read an article about a local spinster who was missing and feared drowned in the Arrow River. Poor spinster. Had she been found? Then she read about another accident.

> *A Chinaman was killed by a fall of earth in his claim Saturday last. Deceased was working in his claim alone when the accident occurred, and life was extinct when he was dug out by some Chinamen in the vicinity. "Many bones broken," said Sew Hoy.*

Buried alive. How long could you survive? S1 didn't have broken bones, but S2 had a broken neck. Maybe more broken bones too. Ana would find out today. Alexa skipped several bankruptcy notices. With a sick feeling, she read

ASSAULTING A CHINAMAN.

> *Charles Holland (13 years of age) was charged with having assaulted Yung Tie. Accused, when asked to plead, stated that he accidentally hit the Chinaman on the head with a piece of rocksalt. When he threw it, he did not see the complainant. After evidence, the bench could not believe that the missile accidentally came in the way of the complainant. Accused had rendered himself liable to a fine of £10.*

Yung Tie received some justice. Time passed in a blur. Alexa couldn't stop digging into the past. Maybe she should have been a historian.

Someone plucked the stack of photos from the table. Alexa tore her eyes from the computer and caught sight of the snatcher's gray helmet hair and straight back leaving the room. She felt guilty having two of the photos, but they'd be reunited with the stack after she made copies. An 1878 letter to the editor caught her attention:

Dear Sir,

Everyone knows that the Chinese miners are of no benefit to the Colony; they hinder settlement wherever they go, and then leave with all their money for China. Consider that every community ought to call a public meeting and invite their Parliamentary representative to ascertain his views on the subject, and by this and other means secure men that will do all they possibly can to purge the land of this pestilence, and thus make it what it was intended to be—a British settlement.

She read a similar report from a town hall meeting. The Europeans complained of the influx of Chinamen. One man said further importation from China would be fatal to the prosperity of the European settler.

Alexa shook her head. First the New Zealanders invited the Chinese, and then they wanted them banished. SUICIDE was dated April 1902:

An unfortunate Chinaman was found quite dead, suspended by the neck, in his hut at the Chinese Camp, Arrowtown. The deceased had shown signs of mental anguish, and paid visits to the cemetery nearly every day.

Could S2, with a broken neck, have hung himself? Her eyes landed on: CHINESE SCOURGE , *Otago Times,* 1875.

There is a rush of Coolies ten miles below the Arrow at Sandy Creek. They seem to be getting gold. We have seen the sample; it is very fine indeed. The European miners are taking a stand. A notice was posted on a certain tree, saying: "Any Chinaman found higher up the creek will be instantly seized and hanged until he is dead." This seems to have the desired effect.

Maybe S2 hadn't committed suicide. Maybe he'd been hung.

Ms. O'Brien's loud voice penetrated her musings. "Found anything?"

Alexa looked up. "There was a lot of racism," she told Ms. O'Brien.

The archivist leaned over her shoulder to read CHINESE SCOURGE. "No excuse for it. I venture it was worse with your American gold rush. There's the 1885 Rock Springs episode. Wyoming, I think. Your white miners massacred twenty-eight Chinese miners."

Alexa shook her head, sad and appalled.

"I've made some copies for you." She handed Alexa a pile of papers. "The top is the history of policing in the area."

Alexa skimmed it. A Constabulary Act—whatever that was—passed in 1846 and the Armed Constabulary Act was enacted in 1867. The first national police force was established in 1886. New Zealand police history in a nutshell.

Ms. O'Brien tapped the stack. "Those next are cemetery records."

Alexa glanced at the title: *Chinese Miners Buried in Arrowtown Cemetery*. It listed names, year buried, and age buried. She scanned for Cheong Tam or Wing Lun. Ah Sing Cheong, who died in 1873, was the closest match. There were maybe thirty names on the list. "You've been a huge help. Will their graves be marked?"

"I don't know. I've also printed you an old cemetery map."

Alexa wondered about S1 and S2, banished to the cemetery outskirts. She lifted the two photos. "Can I have copies of these?"

Ms. O'Brien frowned. "Gayle might be looking for these. She's very particular. Meet me in my office."

Gayle must be the woman who had taken the stack of photos. Alexa printed one last article: DEAD CHINAMEN: EXTENSIVE EXHUMATION. It would be her bedtime reading since she could no longer stomach romance novels with their happy-ever-afters.

She stood and stretched. Her search had given her a better understanding of the gold rush era. She hitched her tote to her shoulder and found Ms. O'Brien's office. Her articles and pictures were waiting. "Thank you for your help," Alexa said.

"I also gave you a packet of Earl Hammer articles. I'm handing them out to all the reporters swarming like bees. Plus I found a letter. From a mother in China to her two sons working the goldfields. Most Chinese peasants were illiterate, so this is a little gold nugget."

Alexa thanked the archivist again.

"Just doing my job."

Chapter Fourteen

Alexa walked through the bustling town toward the cemetery. A rustling made her whip around. A cat emerged from the bushes and slunk across the street.

Had she wasted two hours? The article on Cheong Tam confirmed his and the store's existence, and she might have a lead on what caused S2's neck to break. Hanging. Lynching. Cave-in. Fall. *Pick a card, any card, your future is doomed.*

The parking area brimmed with vans and cars. Ana's reinforcements must be searching for more remains. Or maybe there was a graveside service. As Alexa cut through the lot, the cemetery director locked his car and started toward her. "Miss Clock, Miss Clock!"

He probably wanted to sell her a plot-for-one to go with her DIY coffin kit. She pretended not to hear and dashed into the graveyard. A spooky mist hovered over the ground. In case Mr. Howard was in hot pursuit, she ducked behind a tall stone angel marking fourteen-year-old Johnny Butler's passing in 1877.

ROCK OF AGES CLEFT FOR ME
LET ME HIDE MYSELF IN THEE

Let me hide myself behind thee, Alexa thought, and then mentally apologized to Johnny. She peeked above the stone angel's broken wing tip. No Mr. Howard. Between a long row of graves, she spotted a cameraman filming a woman wearing a bright yellow sweater. Alexa walked over to hear what she was saying.

"…as we know, the New Zealand Parole Board refused to listen to Cindy Mulligan's family. Now their beloved sister and daughter's killer is free. The question the residents of this quaint former mining town are asking is: Will Mr. Hammer re-offend and cause another *whānau* similar anguish? Time will tell. This is Kelly Tyerman, News Six, Arrowtown Cemetery."

The gravestone the reporter gestured to was adorned by a dewy bouquet. A sunbeam etched in the upper right corner of the stone cast its rays through the epitaph.

> CYNTHIA JUSTINA MULLIGAN
> BELOVED DAUGHTER AND SISTER
> BORN 7 APRIL 1965, ARROWTOWN
> DIED 22 FEBRUARY 1998, AGED 32
> HER LIGHT IS GOLD

Alexa had a packet of information about the guy who killed her tucked in her tote, and now she was standing at the foot of her grave. It was too weird.

The reporter handed the microphone to the cameraman and patted at her big hair. "This mist is brutal." She tossed a smile at Alexa. "Are you here to pay your respects?"

"No." Alexa's hair had increased in volume tenfold to reflect the dampness. She wished she had pulled it back. "Well, sort of."

The reporter raised a perfectly tweezed eyebrow.

Alexa clarified. "I'm working the dig. I heard about Cindy Mulligan from someone who knew her."

The reporter's eyes bugged. "May I have your source's contact info?"

"No."

The reporter looked toward the tents. "What's going on in there?"

Alexa backed up. "You'll need to talk to the cemetery director about that." He was striding toward them. Alexa walked away, hoping the reporter wouldn't follow. She wanted to find the Chinese graves. She took the "Olde Cemetery" map out of her tote and consulted it. The original burial grounds were divided into Presbyterian, Catholic, and Anglican sections. A tiny back corner was reserved for Anglican Chinese. She thought of that missionary in several of the museum photos: perhaps he'd had some success.

She turned right and stopped to read a marker: MAVIS "PEG" ALEXANDER, ARROWTOWN NATIVE, DIED 17 APRIL, 1969, AGED 98.

What was life like, Peg? Growing up during the gold rush? What did you think about the influx of immigrants? Was your father a miner? Did you ever meet Cindy Mulligan, you an old woman and Cindy a tot?

Quit talking to the dead, she told herself.

She entered an area where the graves had crumbled and epitaphs were faded. She read what dates she could: 1922, 1918, 1901. Beyond HENRY CHESTER SMITH, DIED FIVE MILE CREEK, SEPT 1897, she spotted a neglected area that corresponded with the map. She walked back and forth. There were no headstones. She toed the ground, alert for markers. None. Had the Chinese on her list been dug up? Had they made it home or were they at the bottom of the sea?

She gave up and started toward the tents. Two men pushed ground-penetrating radar machines as Olivia watched. Would they detect more disturbances? As Alexa clambered over the rock wall, a woman in a dark raincoat and green gum boots—where had she come from?—marched over. "Are you part of the dig?"

Alexa nodded cautiously.

The woman's gray hair was protected by a clear plastic bonnet tied at the chin. "You shouldn't be here. These are sacred grounds. It's not for you to disturb the past."

"Permission for the dig was granted," Alexa stuttered.

The woman's stony eyes narrowed. "A person's body and soul belong to God, and God doesn't grant permission."

"Speak with the cemetery director." Alexa straightened her shoulders, walked to the tent, and pulled the flaps open.

"Close them," Ana said. "There are too many people around."

Alexa stepped inside and pulled the flaps closed. She felt as if she'd run a gauntlet to arrive. "Some lady just complained about the dig."

"She stuck her head in here," Ana said. "Scared me to death. Quoted the bible. And there's all this activity because of Earl Hammer getting out of jail."

The forensic pathologist, Dr. McKenzie, grunted and took a magnifying glass out of his case. He knelt by the skull.

The skeleton, still facedown, was fully exhumed. One tawny shoulder knob was higher than the other in a perpetual shrug. The ribs splayed in delicate symmetry. The hips were narrow, and the bony arms were tucked under the pelvis, hiding the hands. Alexa thought of someone stripped naked, trying to cover up from hostile eyes. She had an urge to cover the bones for modesty's sake.

Dr. McKenzie examined the neck with the magnifier. "The C4 contains nerves that connect to the diaphragm. With a break like this, she'd have a hard time breathing."

"She?" Alexa asked.

He looked up. "Speculation. I can't measure the pelvis in a prone position."

"We found a few buttons," Ana said. She pointed at the table. "Mother-of-pearl. A bit feminine for a miner."

Despite his large size, Dr. McKenzie crawled alongside the

skeleton. He leaned inward, focused on the spinal column, and inched down the back to the lumbar area and halted. He grunted and leaned closer. "The L3 and L4 are broken."

Jeez, Alexa thought. A broken neck and a broken lower back.

He raised his head. "I'll clear it with my colleagues and take a closer look at the remains in the morgue. Could be a mining accident, but if it's female—that doesn't make sense."

"Should we report it to the police?" Alexa asked.

Dr. McKenzie clambered to his feet. His bushy eyebrows knit together. "We've got a mystery here, with the body, probably female, probably European, outside the cemetery boundary. The police won't be interested, but inform them that I'm conducting an inquest. Not much we can do after all these years, but it deserves a look."

Olivia's lecture on white-woman syndrome triggered an alarm in Alexa. "What about the other skeleton? Should I mention it?"

He took off his gloves and nodded. "Go ahead."

Alexa had planned to mention S1 either way.

"Did you find anything about violence on the Chinese miners?" Ana asked.

"Nothing much. No DNA results back either. I did get a list of Chinese miners supposedly buried inside the cemetery, but I couldn't locate any markers."

Ana wiped her hands on her pants. "Historic cemetery records don't always match with what's actually there. Would you head to the police station to make the report? It will take Olivia and me hours to package the bones."

Alexa agreed. She was wearing a path to town. Good thing it was close. She kept her head down as she scurried through the cemetery and back to the road. What was going on with all these damaged skeletons? Halfway to Buckingham Street her phone rang. Her heart revved as she checked the screen. Maybe it was Bruce.

Caller Unknown.

Maybe it was Dr. Weiner with the DNA results. "Hello?"

A faraway voice said, "I'm Mrs. Eugenia Petchey from Abertay University Forensic Department. I'm calling on behalf of Dr. Ben Odden and the search committee."

The phone slipped in her cold fingers.

"Are you there?" The two a.m. Zoom interview with the Scottish professors felt like three months ago instead of three nights ago. Alexa found a better grip. "Yes. Hello. I'm here."

"Dr. Odden extends an invitation to our campus. He wants to proceed with the second roond of interviews. Noo when can I get you scheduled?"

Chapter Fifteen

The mountains seemed to creep forward to listen to her reply. The way they surrounded the road in every direction, silent sentinels breathing down on her, made Alexa claustrophobic. "I'm working an away case, and I don't know how long it will last."

A pickup truck came up from behind. She hopped onto the muddy shoulder and watched it brake at Buckingham Street.

"Expenses paid, certainly," Mrs. Petchey said, "Dr. Odden wanted me to mention that."

A free trip to Scotland? "I'll call as soon as I know my schedule."

Her professional crush wanted to meet her. Ben Odden had published articles on taking fingerprints from bird feathers and on methods for recovering fingerprints from fruit, both of which she'd utilized. His latest article introduced a novel way of determining gender using lip prints. She puckered up. *Imagine working with him.* He had looked ruggedly handsome in his Zoom box too.

She slid the phone back in her tote and zipped her coat. Did she want to leave New Zealand? Start over again? Not have to worry about whether to trust Bruce? The prospect of becoming Dr. Alexa Glock, PhD—unencumbered and dedicated to forensic science—was alluring as gold.

Fool's gold, Charlie would say.

She didn't have to decide today. She retrieved the phone again and found the address of the police station on Buckingham

Street. It was open ten a.m. to four p.m., Monday through Friday. Crime in Arrowtown had weekends off.

Two blocks from the museum she found it down a little alleyway. The white stucco building had a "Community Policing Centre" sign. A notice board on the porch was pinned with announcements: *Plunket Playgroup: Support New Zealand Babies,* Te Reo Māori for Beginners, *Save Our Birds: Bell Your Cat.* She opened the door.

A teenager stood in front of a Plexiglas window. A man stood behind her.

"It fell out of my rucksack. It's brand new," the girl whined.

A middle-aged woman stood behind the Plexiglas. Her blue vest had a *Volunteer* pin on it. "So you last saw your mobile on the Lake Hayes Loop, eh?"

Alexa got behind the man and wondered what exactly a community policing center was. She didn't see any signs that this was a real police station. No wanted posters, metal detectors, or uniformed officers milling around.

The teen left. The man stepped forward. "Stephen Corrigan, *Queenstown News.* We're covering the release of Earl Hammer. Seeking local opinion. What do you think of the release?"

Alexa stepped closer. Earl Hammer name's kept popping up.

"We have to trust the parole board," the woman said. Her badge said Carrie Spindle. "Mr. Hammer is banned from coming anywhere near Arrowtown. I agree with that. And he's wearing electronic monitoring."

"Did you live here at the time of the murder?"

"No."

"I did," a voice from a back room called. "Lived here all me life." A woman in her early fifties, also in a blue vest, came out front. "I'm Lucy Laband. You can quote me. I saw him on telly. His soulless eyes, they stare right through you."

"I'll just record you then." The reporter twiddled with his phone. When he was ready, he repeated her name and asked, "What was it like after Cindy Mulligan's brutal murder?"

"I remember it like yesterday. I was working at the bank. We were scared. See? My bestie and I were flatting, and we vowed never to walk anywhere alone. Thought he was still lurking in the bush." Lucy looked off for a moment. "But sometimes you had to. I mean, no one caught him for weeks."

"Did you know Cindy Mulligan?" the reporter asked.

"Never had the privilege," Lucy said. "She was a wee bit older."

The reporter put his phone away. "How do I get to where her body was found?"

"Follow the Arrow River Trail signs," Lucy said. "You'll come to the swing bridge. That's where he bludgeoned her with a rock. I will tell you that I have *never* jogged in my life because of what happened to Cindy."

No more running in Arrowtown, Alexa vowed.

The reporter left.

Carrie and Lucy turned their attention to Alexa. "How can we help you?" Carrie asked.

Alexa focused on her mission: Report the skeletons. "Are you police officers?"

"We've been through a support training program," Carrie said.

So, no. "I'd like to speak with a police officer."

Lucy shook her head. "Our Constable Blume, he's young but I reckon competent. He comes in two hours a week."

"On Wednesdays," Carrie added.

The door banged open and a red-faced man ran in. "My wife is missing," he shouted.

Alexa jumped out of the way.

Lucy, the older volunteer, grabbed Carrie's wrist.

The man was out of breath. "I mean my ex-wife. She didn't show up at school. They called me." He leaned toward the Plexiglas. "I went by her house. She doesn't answer the door, and her car is in the driveway."

"Oh dear Jesus," Lucy said. "Earl Hammer is back."

"Don't be a nutter." Carrie shook her wrist loose. "Did you try the door?"

"It's locked." He raked his sandy brown hair. "Eileen never misses work."

Carrie lifted her phone. "I'll call the Queenstown Police Station."

Someone on the other end answered right away. "Carrie Spindle here, Arrowtown Community Policing Center." She listened. "How are you, Constable Blume? I have a man here; he's upset." She repeated what the man had said. "Yes. A missing woman." She looked at the ex-husband. "Constable Blume wants to know where you live."

The man raked his hair again. "Where *I* live? Let me talk to him."

She handed him the phone. "Paul Bowen here. My ex-wife is principal at Arrowtown Primary. She didn't show up for work this morning."

Carrie's hand went up to her mouth. "My daughter goes to Arrowtown Primary," she said.

The ex-husband paused. "Eileen Bowen." Another pause. "She doesn't answer," he roared. "I drove here because I thought it would be quicker." He glanced out the window. "I can be back at her house in three minutes."

Alexa followed his gaze. A white Subaru blocked the alleyway.

"Ten Plum Tree Terrace," he said.

Alexa's heart skipped a beat. Prospector's Cottage was on Plum Tree Terrace. Pam and Shelby were home alone. Were they in danger?

Paul Bowen shoved the phone through the Plexiglas opening and left without a word.

"The Hammer is back," Lucy said. "He's kidnapped another woman."

Carrie shook her head. "Earl Hammer is banned from Arrowtown."

Alexa backed up. The proximity between some missing woman's house and Prospector's Cottage spooked her. Throw in a paroled Arrowtown murderer.

On the sidewalk she dialed Ana's number. It went to voicemail. She swung her tote over her shoulder and started toward the cottage, telling herself everything was okay.

WINTER

1888

Dear MaMa,

As young ravens return part of their food to their parents, enclosed is a cheque for you.

Winter brings death and peril in New Gold Mountains. The postman's two horses slipped off the track into the river, and many letters and supplies were lost. Tins of black spice were saved. It arrived at Cheong Tam's store. Much excitement. Thoughts of sending money to mothers and wives vanished. Loo Lee received five pounds for a week's wages and spent all to light his pipe. A heavy smell filled the room. He fell back, and reclined on the floor. A rat ran over his legs. He did not notice. He forgot his loneliness. Now he must fast until his next payday. This vice is a precipitous leap I will not take.

Some white men smoke the pipe too. When they come, I go to the river. I wash my eyes in cold clear water. I seek my cave. By the light of my lantern, I carve a bellbird for the lady who buys my carrots and turnips. Come October the yellow bird will sound like tinkling bells.

Reverend Jesus Don stopped by again. He once visited Canton and speaks in a halting tongue of sin and judgment. He calls me Noble Son. He is kind, but I do not trust his heaven and hell.

Faithful First Son,
Wing Lun

Chapter Sixteen

FRIDAY AFTERNOON

The front door of Prospector's Cottage was unlocked. Alexa entered. "Pam? Shelby?"

The only sound was her labored breathing. She tossed her tote on the stairs and hurried to the kitchen.

The overhead light buzzed. Breakfast dishes were piled in the sink and a coloring book and crayons were spread on the table. Razzle Dazzle pink was on the floor. Alexa set it with the other crayons. She glanced through the back door window. The yard was empty, the creek hidden behind the plum trees. She checked the den and downstairs bedrooms. Empty. She called up the stairs to where her room was. "Pam?"

Silence drifted down on dust motes.

Calm down, she told herself. Pam and Shelby have nothing to do with some missing principal. They had probably walked somewhere. The gum boots and raincoats that hung by the front door were gone. Alexa stepped onto the front porch. A police car—no siren—drove by, braked, backed up, and turned into a shrub-lined driveway two houses down. Her heart, which had calmed, revved again. That's when she heard a child scream.

Her knees threatened to buckle.

The scream came from the back garden. Alexa hurtled down the steps and raced around the side of the house. She slid to a stop in a patch of grass. Between the plum trees, Pam watched Shelby in Bush Creek. Shelby was knee-deep. She dipped her gold mining pan into the water, lifted it free, and flung the contents into the air. She let go another scream as droplets, mud, and pebbles rained down, pitting the creek water. *A wild, happy kid scream.*

Alexa wondered if the police would hear and come running too. "Hey," she called.

Pam watched her cross the grass. "Is everything all right?"

"I was at the police station and, well, this man came in and reported his ex-wife was missing. He said she lives on Plum Tree Terrace. I wanted to make sure you were okay."

Pam turned back to her granddaughter. "We're fine." Shelby traded her pan for a stick and jabbed at floating leaves. "I'm a bit stir crazy. She's full on, doesn't nap." She paused, as if to let Alexa's words register. "What's this about a missing woman?"

"I don't know much." Alexa inhaled. The delicate odors of creek water mixed with dank decay and the threat of winter. *Or the threat of something.* "She didn't show up for work. She's the principal at the Arrowtown school. I just saw a police car pull into the driveway. It's two houses from here."

Pam peered into the adjoining yard. Trees and a netted trampoline blocked the view. "Why were you at the police station?"

Alexa remembered that Pam was a reporter. "Did Ana tell you we found a second skeleton?"

"In the facedown position. That's harsh."

"Ana asked me to report it to the police. I was there when the man ran in."

Pam's eyes flickered. "Ran in?"

Alexa nodded.

"I don't like the sound of that. Do you know about Cindy Mulligan's murder?"

"I learned about Earl Hammer this morning." Alexa stepped closer to the creek. Her Keds sunk in scree. She looked in both directions, half-expecting a gold miner to appear.

Shelby jabbed the pebbly bottom with her stick, intent on her mission. She hadn't noticed Alexa.

"He's out of prison and another woman is missing?" Pam said. "Hard to believe."

Alexa didn't like coincidences any more than Bruce did. "This other woman will probably turn up."

Pam lowered her voice. "Cindy Mulligan was out jogging, listening to her Discman so she didn't hear him behind her. He cracked her skull with a rock."

The clear water of Bush Creek fed into the Arrow River, where the woman's body had been found.

Shelby poked something dark and fuzzy. Alexa was afraid it was a dead bird or rat. She was about to call out her name when Shelby lifted her prize out of the water's grasp. "I caught a fish!"

The grayish object unfurled into a dripping wool hat. An image of a body tumbling with the current, hat sucked off, flashed in Alexa's head.

"Time to go inside," Pam called.

Shelby twirled around, the hat at the end of the stick trailing droplets. "Don't want to."

Then she noticed Alexa, dropped the stick, and ran at her like a big wet dog. Alexa scooped her up. It was the first time in her life she scooped a child into her arms. Over the top of Shelby's citrus-scented hair, she watched Pam wade into the water and nab the hat. She held it with two fingers. A red fabric flower—a poppy—was attached to its side. She met Alexa's eyes: a woman's hat. Anxiousness arced between them.

Shelby squirmed to get down. "My woolie!"

"No, pet," Pam said. "The woolie belongs to someone else."

Shelby grabbed Alexa's hand and pulled her to the back door of the cottage. Once inside, she pawed at her raincoat. "I can do the zip." She dropped the raincoat on the floor and then plopped down to pull off her gum boots.

Alexa saw down the hall that she had left the front door wide open. *Idiot.* Anyone could have walked in. She closed it and returned to the kitchen.

Pam walked in; the hat ditched. She pulled the back door closed with effort. "Old houses. Can you stay for lunch?"

Alexa perked up. She took the folder of articles out of her tote and set them on the table, excited to share them.

"I'm making Marmite sammies," Pam said.

Alexa changed her mind. Even though Marmite was invented by a scientist, the dark paste looked and tasted like a chemistry kit failure. "I need to get back to the dig. But thanks." She ran upstairs and grabbed her crime kit. She caught Pam's eyes on her way out.

"Lock the doors," Alexa said.

Chapter Seventeen

Alexa stood in the middle of Plum Tree Terrace to call Ana. No answer. No chance to explain what had happened at the quasi-police station. She texted: Left po. station. Checked on your mom & Shelby. All good. Back soon.

The temperature had dropped into the fifties, pulling with it a flint-colored sky that pressed down like a room with a low ceiling. *A foreboding sky*, Alexa thought.

The urge to offer assistance lured Alexa toward the missing woman's house. A second police car was now nosed behind the first on the road's shoulder. Bushy evergreens crowded the gravel driveway, which curved to hide the house. *Privacy is a good thing*, Alexa thought as she walked down the drive, *until it isn't*.

A cheery red Smart car was beside the house. An electric cord extending from an outlet on the house was plugged into the car. Paul Bowen's Subaru Forester was parked next to the Smart car.

The missing woman's two-story house was light green with large modern windows. Wilted brown plants in pots lined the ground in front of a wide porch. Alexa identified with such good intentions. When she'd lived in Raleigh, she'd bought three dozen daffodil bulbs. Were they still withering in the garden shed?

A single rocking chair was on the porch. The front door was ajar. Alexa wanted to warn whoever was inside not to touch anything. As she approached, a uniformed policeman in a bright yellow vest rounded the corner.

He breathed heavily. "Who are you?"

She hefted her shoulder up so the crime kit was visible. "Alexa Glock. Auckland Forensic Service Center."

In four giant steps he closed the distance between them. Grass and mud marred his black boots. He wore a checkered police cap and was young—mid-twenties.

Alexa read his thoughts: *Who called you? How did you get here so soon?*

When she didn't speak, he threaded his thumbs through his belt loops and widened his stance. "Constable Will Blume. Queenstown Police."

The name rang a bell. She thought one of the volunteers at the station had mentioned him. She let him think she'd been called to the scene. She hadn't said anything that wasn't true. "So this is the missing woman's house?"

He nodded.

"She hasn't been found?"

"There's no sign of her. Senior and the ex-husband are inside."

High-ranked officers in New Zealand were referred to as Senior. Alexa was used to the term now. "How did they get in?"

"Back door was unlocked."

She waited for more, but Constable Blume's light blue eyes narrowed. "Did Detective Inspector Katakana call you?"

She was saved from answering by the ex-husband and a sturdy woman in a navy pantsuit exiting the front door. The woman's black hair was knotted at the nape of her neck, and she held a picture frame. Alexa guessed she was the DI.

"Eileen wouldn't ditch work without phoning in," Mr. Bowen said.

"I've sent an officer to the school to talk with the staff," the woman said. "Hopefully, they'll shed some light."

"She never missed a day of work in the eleven years we were married. Once she went to work with a fever. Something has happened to her."

Constable Blume stepped forward. "Nothing suspicious in the back garden, Senior."

"Everything looks good inside. No sign of struggle. No sign of a purse or mobile either. That suggests Ms. Bowen left on her own volition."

"I'm telling you, something has happened to her," Mr. Bowen insisted.

"To be missing is not a crime," the DI said calmly. She turned to Alexa. "Are you Mrs. Bowen's sister?"

Mr. Bowen scowled. "That's not Misty."

"She's forensics," Constable Blume said.

Mr. Bowen's mouth dropped. "Like bloodstain and fingerprints?"

Alexa's presence was probably mystifying, but the DI didn't miss a beat. She put her free hand on Mr. Bowen's arm. "We'll wait until her sister arrives, shall we? Misty, right? She might know where Mrs. Bowen is. Meanwhile, I'll circulate this photo."

Paul Bowen jerked his arm away. "Have you tracked down Earl Hammer?"

"I have calls in to Christchurch Police," the DI said. "I'll hear back shortly."

"While you wait and circulate, that monster might have Eileen." He marched toward his car, tripping on the electric cord. Scowling, he caught himself.

Alexa hopped to the side as he backed up his car. Part of her wished she could back up too. She had let the constable think she was here in an official capacity. She lifted her chin and stood her ground.

Constable Blume's hand went to the radio clipped to his lapel. "Should I follow him, Senior?"

The DI chortled. "This isn't *The First 48*. Go talk to the neighbors. When did they last see Mrs. Bowen? Or is it Ms. Bowen now?"

"Yes, sir. Ma'am." He jogged off. Alexa wondered what Pam would think when he knocked on her door. She hoped the constable wouldn't scare Shelby.

The DI set the frame on the porch railing and photographed its content with her phone. She glanced at Alexa. "What do you call these? Glam shots? The ex didn't like it but agreed it was recent."

Alexa, mindful of the potted plants, stepped up to the railing. The fortyish blond woman in the photo wore a black dress and leaned toward the camera, one bare shoulder suggestively raised. Her coquettish smile was outlined in pink lipstick. *Desperation* flashed in Alexa's mind.

The DI texted with velocity. Without looking up, she asked, "Who are you?"

Alexa dug a card from the crime kit and held it out. "I'm a forensic investigator from Auckland. I handle travel cases."

The DI finished texting and took the card.

A surge of electricity contracted Alexa's muscles. This happened at the beginning of a case. It was the fact that the woman hadn't called in to her place of employment; Alexa couldn't conceive of not calling into work if she was detained or ill. "I'm working at the Arrowtown cemetery. There's a dig going on." She regretted putting the facedown skeleton with a broken neck on the back burner. "I was at the station when Mr. Bowen ran in."

"Right place. Wrong time." The detective inspector undid her blazer buttons as she studied Alexa's card. Her lilac-colored blouse reflected in her dark eyes, turning them into garnets. "Or is it wrong place, right time? What if I need your assistance?"

"I'll check with my boss, but I'm sure he'll okay it. So, nothing is amiss in the house?"

The DI set her hands—no rings, clear nail polish—on the porch railing, leaned forward, and did a couple arm push-ups. "We just took a quick walk-through. It was all good." The sound of an engine locked her elbows. A gray work van crept up the driveway and pulled beside the Smart car. TANDY HOME INSPECTIONS was written on the side. "Who's this then?"

A fiftyish woman in jeans and dark T-shirt climbed out. Her wide face was bunched with worry.

"Are you Misty Tandy?" the DI called.

She lifted her chin. "How do you know who I am?"

"I'm Detective Inspector Pattie Katakana, Queenstown Police." She walked down the steps and held out her badge. "Mr. Paul Bowen is concerned about your sister. He said he'd called you."

Ms. Tandy's eyes flickered to the open front door instead of the badge. "Eileen's not in there?"

"We had a look around," the DI said. "She's not home. The school called Mr. Bowen when your sister didn't show up. He's her emergency contact."

"Eileen should change that. I'm her next of kin now they're divorced. Does Paul have anything to do with this?"

"With what?"

"With Eileen gone missing." She tucked thin strands of brown hair behind her ears. "He wanted to know if Eileen was with me. I left straightaway. Thought he'd be here acting all gutted."

The word *acting* caught Alexa's attention.

"Mr. Bowen just left," the DI said. "When is the last time you spoke with your sister?"

Ms. Tandy climbed the steps of the porch. DI Katakana followed closely. Alexa wondered if the sister was going to enter the house. Instead, she plopped on the rocking chair. "The weekend. We're still sorting boxes." She rocked in choppy jerks. "Father passed a year ago. Mum died a couple years before."

"*Ka aroha hoki,*" DI Katakana said.

"Thank you," Misty said.

Alexa figured the DI had expressed sympathy.

"Do you have other siblings?" the DI asked.

"Just us."

"Does Ms. Bowen have children?"

"No." Misty stared at her Crocs. "She dotes on my Susie. Spoils her. Eileen didn't answer when I called. Never does when she's at work, eh?" She stopped rocking. "But she's not at work?"

"No. And she didn't call in sick. How long has your sister been divorced?"

"A year?" She glanced at Alexa. "Came through right after Father died. Eileen bought this house with her inheritance, then poof, filed for divorce. Paul? I never liked him."

Hurried footsteps silenced the sister. Constable Blume loped up the driveway, his eyes on the boss. "Did you hear?"

The DI frowned. "What?"

"He hacked off his tracker. Earl Hammer is loose."

春天
SPRING
1892

Precious MaMa,

With gladdened hearts our brothers Ah Mee and Fon Yim start their journey home. General consent and £2 is paid to the cemetery employees to re-open their graves. The diggers wear somber faces and leave in haste, not wanting to witness the opening of the caskets.

A woman shouts from the gate, "No bone scraping" and "You will burn in hell."

Hell is an earth prison far from home, MaMa.

We used a pick to pry the lids. Ah Mee waited longest for his journey home. His bones are clean. We bleached them one by one. His queue was beautiful even in death and we placed it with the bones. It took seven hours.

Fon Yin died in the last blizzard. It took from sunrise to sunset to scrape and boil the flesh from his bones. Brandy and carbolic proved useless against the smell of the hungry ghost.

It took three days for the bones to dry. Chong Tam provided boiled fowl, cooked rice, and a paper of lollies. Too Fong brought drinks of grog and tea. Jin Lee burned joss paper so our brothers have spirit money for their journey. I worry that my fate is that of my brother and save for my passage if I die here. The gold is gone, and only Chong Tam brightens my day.

I bow in hope my brothers reach the soil of their birth, and prosperity rains upon their wives and daughters.

Faithful First Son,
Wing Lun

Chapter Eighteen

An image of an animal escaping a cage and dashing through the woods flashed in Alexa's head. Earl Hammer, free from bondage.

The DI's face, when Alexa refocused, was fierce. "On the chance he's come this way, I'm convening a search for Ms. Bowen."

Misty Tandy jumped up. "Oh, my God, oh my God, poor Eileen."

The DI held her hands up. "This is a precaution. I'm sure Hammer will be picked up in the Christchurch area. I'd like you to go in your sister's house." The DI glanced at Alexa. "To see if any of her things are missing. If she packed a bag."

"But her car is here," Misty said.

"There's Uber, eh? Or a friend picking her up. Does she have a boyfriend?"

Misty's thin brown hair escaped her ears, obscuring her eyes, but she made a scoffing sound. "A jet boat driver. Lang somebody. He works at Kimiākau Jet."

Alexa had seen the high-speed boats, full of tourists, careening down shallow rivers. *No thanks.*

"She might be with this new bloke. Playing hooky," the DI said. "When you're finished here, call her friends and acquaintances. Maybe she's with one of them, eh?"

Alexa thought of Paul Bowen. *Had he done something to prevent his ex from moving on to a hot dog adventure guide? But then why report her missing?*

Constable Blume kicked the ground like a horse in the starting block. The DI motioned him over. "Take Ms. Tandy's information. I'm headed to the Policing Centre."

He opened his mouth, closed it, then whipped out a notepad. "Eh, Miss, let's get started."

DI Katakana motioned for Alexa to follow her down the driveway toward her patrol car. She pointed to the crime kit. "Are you a storm chaser?"

Alexa liked the image: chasing criminals instead of tornadoes. "I never leave home without it."

DI Katakana opened the car door and slid onto the seat. "Based on Earl Hammer's connection with Arrowtown, I'm reclassifying this as a missing-critical. Better safe than sorry. Take the sister into the house. Look for anything that might help us reconstruct events or anything out of place. Ms. Tandy can judge." She paused. "And get a scent article."

"A what?"

"Something for the tracker dogs."

Alexa's thoughts flew to Kaos, with his highly sensitive olfactory system. One of his brethren was on the way.

The DI looked rapped a knuckle on the dash. "Who's your boss?"

"Dan Goddard."

"Give him a ring and make this official." She gave Alexa her card. "Call direct if you find anything suspicious." Without waiting for a response, she shut the door and drove away.

The shrill siren kick-started Alexa's heart. She glanced toward Prospector's Cottage. Pam and Shelby were probably eating their Marmite sandwiches. There was no time to check on them. She took a deep breath and prioritized:

Call Dan.

Call Ana.

Kit up.

Enter house.

But first she checked the news on her phone. Two articles popped up: "Murderer Ditches Anklet," and "The Hammer at Large." They both contained the same photograph: a close-shaven man with deep-set black eyes and jutting ears. She skimmed an article.

> Police are searching for 49-year-old convicted murderer Earl Hammer, who was released from Christchurch Men's Prison four days ago. Hammer served 25 years for the brutal murder of Cynthia Mulligan in 1998. His GPS tracking device was found in his reentry apartment Thursday morning. Hammer's parole liaison went to check on him when the tracker didn't detect movement for eleven hours.
>
> "The liaison thought he was sleeping. Fewer than 1 percent of released offenders go on the run," Corrections spokesperson Richard Wilmer said.
>
> Hammer is 176 centimeters tall and weighs 86 kilograms. He was last seen wearing gray sweat-pants, a black T-shirt, and a gray jacket. Do not approach if sighted.

Got that right.

Alexa kicked at a clump of moss as she explained the situation to her boss. "The Arrowtown school principal didn't show up for work this morning. DI Pattie Katakana of the Queenstown Police has requested my assistance."

"Pattie Katakana is the first female Māori detective inspector," he said. "I haven't met her, but I hear she's good. I won't ask how she knew you were around."

Alexa ignored that comment. "Have you heard of Earl Hammer?"

"He was released from prison a few days ago. You're in Arrowtown, and that's where he killed that woman all those years ago. It was all over the news when I was a kid. Then it died away. They caught Hammer within a month. He was arrested for something else and when they fingerprinted him, they matched one left at the scene."

"Chalk one up for friction ridges," Alexa said.

"And the victim? Blond. Pretty. Single. Her photos were plastered all over the news. The whole nation held their breath between the time she went missing and when they found her in the river."

Alexa thought of Eileen's glam photo. She was blond, pretty, and single. "Did you hear he ditched his tracker?"

"Hammer?"

"Check your news feed. How long is the drive between here and Christchurch?"

"Four or five hours."

Enough time for Hammer to be here and hunt down a new victim. Had he been planning this the whole time he was incarcerated? Alexa checked the street in both directions. It dead-ended three houses past Eileen's.

"Where do things stand with the exhumed miner?" Dan asked.

Gnats of guilt swarmed about her head. "The teeth tests are pending."

"So you're finished?"

"Not yet. We found a second skeleton. There might be more."

"A hot case takes precedence. Open a new case for the missing woman."

Alexa took a deep breath. Permission was what she wanted,

but it was hard to switch gears. She promised to keep Dan apprised. Then she walked toward Prospector's Cottage and called Ana.

The archaeologist answered on ring four. Her voice was excited. "I just heard the news."

Alexa was glad she didn't have to explain. "I've been hired to help find her. There's going to be a search."

There was a pause. "For who?"

Alexa was confused. "What news did you just hear?"

"The lab director called with the DNA results. Skeleton 1 is related to the benefactor, Connie Wong. Our hungry ghost can go home."

Tears welled in Alexa's eyes. A revered son could return to China. Make that a revered great-great-grandpa. Mr. Sun would be happy. She blinked to clear her vision. "I can't wait to see the report."

"Did you let the police know about S2?"

"I didn't have time." She was in front of Prospector's Cottage now. She didn't like it that Pam was stranded without a car. "I've just been assigned to a new case. A woman who lives two doors from our rental house is missing."

"Two doors away? Is that why you stopped by to see Mum and Shelby?"

"I wanted to make sure they were okay." She studied the cottage like a stalker. There was no movement through the window. She should have told Pam to close the drapes. "It gets worse."

"You're scaring me."

A siren pierced the quiet. Alexa heard it through the phone and through the air: a warped stereo. "That man who got out on parole?"

"Hammer?"

"He hacked off his GPS tracker. No one knows where he

is." The siren repeated, and she had to hold the phone closer to her ear.

"Oh, my God. Do you think...?"

"I doubt he's come back, but it's weird, right? There's going to be a search for the woman. I'll call as soon as I know the details."

The siren tapered.

She stuffed the phone in her pocket and dug out a pineapple lump. She popped the chewy candy into her mouth. It in no way or form resembled pineapple, but it would stanch her hunger. She trudged back to Eileen Bowen's house, contemplating the task ahead. She was usually called to a scene because a crime had taken place. Maybe even a murder. This was different. Her job was to collect any evidence that might help the police locate Eileen Bowen—maybe she'd acted out of character and taken a spa-cation—or identify her if she turned up dead. Alexa had a bad feeling. She joined the constable and Ms. Tandy on the porch.

Constable Blume flipped his notebook shut. "Mrs. Bowen doesn't have a history of disappearances, and she wasn't depressed or suicidal."

Ms. Tandy gestured to the yard. "Why would she be? She has all this, a good job, a new bloke."

"It's a standard question," Alexa said. "I'd like to take your fingerprints before we go into the house."

Ms. Tandy's mouth dropped.

"It's for process of elimination. Ms. Bowen's prints will be on file because she's a school employee, but you've touched things inside the house as well, right?"

"Anything to help us find her," Constable Blume threw in.

Ms. Tandy's face relaxed. "I've never been printed before."

Alexa opened her kit. Below the ink pad and tenprint stack she'd used with Shelby, the portable scanner seemed to puff out its little black chest: *Use me. I'm the latest and greatest.* She'd been a Luddite, preferring the old method. There was something about rolling a flesh and blood finger that thrilled her. The pulse. The heat. What would the outcome be? An arch? A whorl? A murderer?

Dan had insisted. "It's a fantastic piece of kit. You'll know immediately whether the prints are in the National Fingerprint Section or AFIS."

"Yeah, yeah," Alexa said. She'd miss returning to the lab and submitting the prints herself. The tense delicious moments of waiting passed while holding a tree pose or, if she was alone, jabbing the air or executing a few side kicks.

She turned the handheld device on and pointed to the small square touch pad. "Start with your right thumb, Ms. Tandy."

"You can call me Misty." Her nails were bitten short. She wore a small solitaire diamond on her ring finger and had a patch of scaly red skin near her wrist. After she pressed the left pinkie on the box, Alexa, more to convince herself, said, "Isn't that cool? You don't need to clean off any ink."

Misty shrugged. "Do you work at the Queenstown station?"

"I work at Auckland Forensic Service Center. I was working a dig at the Arrowtown Cemetery."

"A dig? What kind?"

Establishing rapport with the missing woman's sister was important. "We exhumed a Victorian era goldminer. Then last night we found a second skeleton." Facedown, but she didn't share that. She stepped aside to view the results. In less than a minute the little screen flashed an alert. Misty had lied. Her fingerprints were in the automated fingerprint data bank, and she had a record.

The constable cleared his throat. "All good then, eh?"

She met his light-blue eyes and then looked away, weighing whether to confront Misty and risk alienation, or continue as if she didn't have a police record.

Eileen Bowen was the crux of why Alexa was here. She could wait to find out what Misty had been arrested for. "DI Kanakata has asked—"

"DI Katakana," Constable Blume corrected.

"DI *Katakana* has asked that we enter your sister's house to look around. See if she's packed a bag or if you notice anything unusual." She pulled out protective booties and gloves and asked Misty to put them on. She did the same.

Constable Blume opened the door for them. "I'll wait out here."

"Thanks," Alexa said.

A faint charred odor in the entryway reminded Alexa of her attempt to make baked chicken topped with cream of mushroom soup for Bruce. *No fail*, the recipe on the can claimed. *Ha!* Alexa pointed to a raincoat, a fleece, a purple puffer, and what looked like a man's coat hanging by the door. "Are any of her coats missing?"

Misty wrapped her arms around herself. "She has a dress coat. It's long and black. It might be in her closet."

In the den, an L-shaped beige couch and two easy chairs looked comfy, inviting. The decorative couch pillows had migrated to one end, mail and magazines stacked on the coffee table. *The Waikato Journal of Education* was on top. Alexa liked that the principal cared about research and data. She noted it was a current copy. An *Otago Daily Times* was on the floor. It was dated three days ago, and Earl Hammer's face was plastered across the front page. "Arrowtown Murderer Gets Parole" was the headline.

Misty stood next to an open box pushed against the wall. A blue bowl peeked out. "That's our Mum's fruit bowl. Mum would be frantic if she was alive. She doted on Leeny." Her phone rang. She turned her back and answered. "Marty?" Her voice caught. "Did you hear about Earl Hammer? He might have Eileen." Pause. "I'm helping at the house. *Eileen's* house. I'm with a policewoman." She paused again, frowning. "I had to take the van. How else would I have gotten here?"

Whoever Marty was, he sounded angry. Alexa peered through French doors into the backyard. Beyond a pergola-covered patio, the grass was scraggly, and the clothesline was empty. Shrubs and trees hid the creek.

Misty terminated the call, her eyes manic-looking. "That was my husband."

Alexa smiled sympathetically. "When was the last time you were here?"

She shook her head. Frowned. "It's hard to think straight. Maybe three weeks ago? I picked up Susie. My daughter. Auntie is way cooler than Mum. Do fingerprints last that long?"

Alexa suppressed a laugh. "It depends on the surface and environment. In a house they can last forty years or more."

Misty's eyes darted around the room. "I don't like this, poking through Eileen's house without her."

It *was* weird. The principal might walk through the door, demanding to know what was going on. But that would be a happy ending.

The geometric tile backsplash in the galley kitchen hurt Alexa's eyes.

"She redid it, all posh," Misty said. "New counters, appliances, everything."

An unzipped briefcase—soft leather—leaned against the tile. A laptop and some manila files were visible. The electronic guys could get buckets of information from the laptop. Alexa wondered where the missing woman's phone was. What if it was in the briefcase? "Can you call your sister?"

"I've called her already." Her eyes looked alarmed. "She doesn't answer."

"Do it again."

Misty complied. Alexa held her breath, but no ringer or buzz sounded from the briefcase. There was no sign of a woman's purse either. And no brochures for a luxury spa.

Three stacked dishes and two short, clear glasses were in the sink. A faint lipstick print was visible on one glass. Alexa picked up the lipstick-stained glass and sniffed; she detected a faint fruity smell. She smelled the other glass but didn't detect an odor. *Water, maybe.* Mindy watched as she wrapped the glasses separately. She'd dust them for fingerprints in the lab.

What lab? She had a moment's disorientation. She shook it off as she labeled the evidence bags and wondered what Misty had been arrested for. Should she fear the woman?

The trash contained food scrapings and a used coffee filter.

An Arrowtown Primary School calendar was taped to the refrigerator. Term two had started May 2nd and would end July 8th. The school was closed for parent conferences yesterday and a board meeting supposedly took place at eleven a.m. Alexa's pulse sped up; yesterday had not been a regular school day. *This might be significant.*

Next to the calendar was a photo of a teen girl in a school uniform.

"That's my Susie," Misty said.

Alexa saw the resemblance. "Does she go to Arrowtown Primary?"

"She's too old. She's Year Ten. She goes to Wakatipu High School." Her voice cracked. "What if The Hammer has Eileen?"

"You're doing everything you can to help find her. Let's finish up, so you can get home."

Upstairs were two tidy bedrooms and a full bathroom. "Susie stays the night sometimes," Misty said, looking around. "I don't see anything missing or messed up."

Alexa saved Eileen's first-floor bedroom and bath for last.

The floral duvet was pulled up, but rumpled, as if Eileen had sat on it to pull her socks and shoes on. Or off. High-heeled dress boots leaned against the duvet. Maybe the principal had changed from work shoes to a more comfortable pair.

A photo of a bearded man in sunglasses, white teeth flashing, sat on the nightstand. Alexa pointed. "Who's that?"

"That's the boyfriend. She's head over for him." Misty shrugged and looked in the walk-in closet. "I can't tell if anything is missing or not."

Alexa left the frame and looked around. Pantsuits and dresses hung on one side, casual clothes on the other. The hamper had a few days' worth of undergarments and a blue blouse. Alexa counted twelve pair of shoes—lots of pumps—nestled on a shoe rack. Ugg slippers waited under a waffle-fabric robe. So she hadn't taken off the boots and switched to slippers. Sneakers, maybe. Eileen Bowen was a neat person. Samsonite luggage— one carry-on and one medium—were tucked in the corner. There was no way to tell if any luggage was missing. "Do you know how many suitcases your sister has?" she asked.

Misty shrugged.

She moved to the bathroom while Misty checked the dresser drawers. A glass shelf held an array of Smashbox and Nu Skin cosmetics. She opened the medicine cabinet: ointments, lotion, over-the-counter painkillers. She closed the cabinet door.

A single toothbrush leaned in a cup. No one leaves without their toothbrush. Alexa was being overcautious, but went ahead and asked. Dental X-rays were one way to identify victims when facial recognition wasn't possible. "Who is your sister's dentist?"

Misty's eyes widened. "I don't know. Why?"

"It's a standard question to ask when someone goes missing."

She avoided Misty's eyes as she grabbed a floral nightgown hanging from a hook.

Chapter Nineteen

Alexa longed for a car; ten-toeing it was getting old. Especially with the heavy crime kit. "Can I get a ride to the Community Policing Centre?" she asked Misty. They stood on the porch again.

Constable Blume's radio made them jump. He stepped aside, but Alexa and Misty could hear the broadcast: "Ten-nine. All units. Missing woman. White. Forty-two. Point last seen Arrowtown School, two p.m. Thursday."

"All units" chilled Alexa. The police were taking the disappearance seriously. She needed to get the scent article to DI Katakana STAT.

Misty's eyes darted to the van. "See, it's Marty's. He needs it, needs me to get home. He's got a job." She pointed to the TANDY HOME INSPECTION logo.

Was she kidding? Her sister's life was at stake. Alexa's face must have registered disbelief because Misty shuffled and said, "I reckon it's okay."

"Thanks. I'll be right with you. I need to speak with Constable Blume."

Misty trudged to the van. As soon as she got in, Alexa motioned Constable Blume over and whispered, "Misty has fingerprints on file."

He glanced at the van. Misty was checking her phone. "Dodgy. What for?"

She fished the fingerprint scanner out and rechecked the results. "All it says is that her prints are on file for an arrest. Can you find out?"

"Let me see that," he said.

She gave him the scanner.

"If you press here, it shows the specifics." He pressed a link Alexa hadn't noticed.

Constable Blume chewed a thumbnail while they waited.

"Here it is," he said. "Larceny. A Schwinn Paramount bicycle." He paused, reading the minuscule print. "She was fifteen. Her surname was Emerson. The record should have been expunged. Lots of kids' records are expunged if they meet their parole obligations. Not automatic, though. You've got to apply."

He gave her the scanner. She begrudgingly admired the information it had provided. "Teenagers do dumb things." Maybe if she had had a merry band of friends in high school, she might have too. Instead, she'd been licking her wounds. Her back muscles constricted at the thought of the three years of skin grafts and surgeries she'd endured after the accident. She'd need to stretch tonight. "Misty might not know her prints are still on file or even remember she'd been fingerprinted. She's giving me a ride to the Policing Centre."

The constable pouted. "While I'm stuck here."

"Any news on that escaped guy?"

Constable Blume shook his head solemnly.

She paused on the bottom step and looked up at him. The Community Policing Centre in Arrowtown didn't have a forensics lab. Queenstown was twenty minutes away. "Does the Queenstown Police Station have a lab?"

He brightened. "It's got all your fingerprint gadgets. Leigh Walker is the new lab tech."

Alexa's life as a traveling forensic was a rotation of lab techs and police officers. They had to get to know her, and she had to get to know them. A job at Abertay University would bring the merry-go-round to a halt. But she liked riding the pony up and down to various crime scenes throughout New Zealand, and she was learning that she didn't need to always ride solo. "Can you call Ms. Walker to come pick up the evidence I gathered in the house?"

"Ay. Ms. Walker will want to be involved." He dug in his pocket. "Here's her business card."

Alexa accepted the card and then carefully filled out time, date, location, and description on each sealed bag, signed her name, and watched Constable Blume do the same. Chain of custody transfers had to be meticulously recorded or evidence might end up inadmissible. She thought of the two glasses. Had Eileen Bowen invited anyone in for a drink?

"What's the word on canvassing the neighborhood?" she asked.

The constable frowned. "Everyone's been diverted. The search is priority."

She hoisted the crime kit, thanked the constable, and climbed into the van. Misty backed out as Alexa buckled up. The van smelled earthy, which Alexa supposed went with inspecting homes. A perforated panel separated the front seats and the cargo area.

Prospector's Cottage flashed by. "I keep thinking what he might do to her," Misty said.

Alexa didn't know if "he" was Earl Hammer or the ex-husband. "Who?"

"The Hammer." She sped up, then slowed down, casting glances in the rearview mirror as if Hammer might be following them. Alexa almost turned to see. The Lonely Prisoner Seeks

Pen Pal scenario popped into her head. "Has your sister ever contacted Earl Hammer or met him?"

Misty's mouth dropped. Her bottom teeth were crooked. "Are you bonkers?"

Probably. Everyone was leaning toward Hammer as a suspect. What if he wasn't anywhere around Arrowtown? Misty had mentioned she'd never liked Eileen's ex-husband. "Is there a chance Mr. Bowen might have something to do with your sister's disappearance?"

Misty braked at the stop sign. "Paul fought for a part of the house they sold, but Eileen fended him off. It was in her name."

Alexa had no idea what divorce laws were like in New Zealand, but she knew in the States women were often left with a decline in income. But Eileen had a good job, and it sounded like she'd inherited some money from her parents. Misty probably had too.

When they arrived at the Community Policing Centre, Misty jerked to a halt. "What should I do?"

"Go home. Be with your daughter. Call Eileen's friends. Ask if they've heard from her." She dug into the side pocket of the crime kit. "Here's my card if you find out anything."

"Find her," Misty said.

"We're doing everything we can." Alexa hoped it was true. She didn't know boo about her new team.

One of the two blue-vested volunteers tried to block her entry into the center. "We're closed for an emergency."

"I'm working the case," Alexa said. "Forensics."

It was the younger one, Carrie. She looked tense. "I remember you from earlier. I'm only here until more officers arrive. There's been an All Points Bulletin issued."

Alexa counted four additional people inside the center: two men in police uniforms—one tall, one short—a man with a silver-gray ponytail and beard, and DI Katakana. A table and chairs had been set up in the middle of the room. DI Katakana smoothed a map out on its surface. Then she uncapped a Sharpie and handed it to the shorter of the two officers. "Do some grids. School has let out early, and volunteers are gathering there to start a search. The community wants to be involved. Ms. Bowen is one of theirs." She noticed Alexa. "Ms. Glock. Have you got the scent article?"

Alexa lifted the bag out of the kit.

The taller officer took it from her. His thick dark hair was gelled to a side swell and the bronze flesh of his left arm was a swirl of tattoos. "Did you touch it?"

"I wore gloves," Alexa answered stiffly.

Police Dog Service was stitched on the pocket of his shirt. "You better come with me to the school. Just in case."

"In case what?"

"Any of your scent transferred. I need to introduce you to my partner so he can eliminate you."

A police dog lunging for her jugular flashed in her mind. Her roommate's dog Kaos had wormed his furry way into her heart, but other dogs made her nervous. She'd never had a dog.

"This is Alexa Glock, everyone," DI Katakana said. "I have her on retainer from Auckland Forensics Service Center. Did you find anything at Ms. Bowen's house?"

Retainer? "Everything is neat. There are two suitcases in her closet, plus a toothbrush still in the cup."

"I located the boyfriend the sister mentioned," the DI said. "Langston Johnston, shocked she's missing. Said they were close, serious even."

"Maybe he wanted things to be serious and she didn't," the shorter cop said.

"Johnston last saw her Saturday, the eleventh," DI Katakana

said. "He said they were planning to get together this Saturday evening."

"That needs verifying," the older guy said.

"Maybe she owed money, did a runner," the DI said. "I'm waiting to hear from her bank."

"A principal makes good money," Carrie said.

"Account details, contact information, and even financial information can be handed over without a search warrant," the older guy said. He had a narrow face and hollow cheeks. "You never know if she was up to something. Embezzlement, maybe."

Carrie spoke up again. "That's treating her like a criminal. She's missing, needs help."

"We've got to cover all angles," the older guy said.

Alexa cleared her throat. "Two glasses were in the kitchen sink. I bagged them." She hoped the lab tech would get the drinking glasses into the fuming chamber right away. "Yesterday was parent conference day and a board meeting at eleven."

"I heard a year-eight parent gave Ms. Bowen an ear bash about not suspending the boy who's been bullying her kid," Carrie said. "The bully is in my girl's class, and he's a tyrant through and through."

"What's the parent's name?" DI Katakana asked.

"Janet Lakosil."

"I'll look into it," the gray-haired man said.

Alexa kept waiting for introductions. Bruce always made sure everyone working a case was introduced to each other.

"Ta, Mike." DI Katakana removed her blazer and hung it on a chair. "The school CCTV showed Ms. Bowen leaving yesterday, on foot, at 1:40 p.m. Secretary said she walked to and from school most days. Eco-conscious, she is. She hasn't been seen or heard from since and hasn't called 111."

A chill danced up Alexa's spine. Eileen had walked to and fro through Arrowtown like she'd been doing, and had vanished.

"We're starting the search from the school," the DI added.

"Has her phone been pinging?" the Mike guy asked.

"You know that takes time to get the records. We've only just been called in," DI Katakana said. She reached for a cup of coffee on the table, sipped, and grimaced. "What about the sister? Was she a help?"

Alexa debated mentioning the larceny charge and decided against it. "She mentioned the ex-husband and Eileen disagreed about splitting property during their divorce."

"Get that ex-husband back in here."

"On it, Senior," the shorter cop said. He pirouetted and left.

When the door shut, the Mike guy said, "Our man is Hammer. Son of a bitch is back."

"We don't know that," DI Katakana said.

There was tense silence. Who was Mike? Alexa watched him pick up a fax from the table. CHRISTCHURCH POLICE DEPARTMENT ran across the top.

"Eileen Bowen has been missing for twenty-five hours," he said. He shook the paper. "Hammer's last recorded movement was Wednesday at ten p.m. The tracker was found Thursday at nine a.m. That gave him plenty of time to get here and strike again. Same modus operandi : blond, young, single."

"Eileen Bowen is forty-two, and I don't see Hammer pissing his freedom away," DI Katakana said. "But we'll consider all possibilities, eh?"

Something niggled at Alexa. "Can I watch the CCTV recording?"

"It's all over social media that Earl Hammer is in Arrrowtown," Carrie interrupted. "People are scared." She scrolled through her feed. "Listen to this. TuiTerri said a man ran through her back garden this morning."

DI Katakana stared at the post. "Follow up. Let's get the search started."

Mr. Canine rocked back and forth on the balls of his feet. "I need a head start with the dog. Don't want the scent trail contaminated."

"Go. You too," the DI told Alexa. "Join a search team. We've got to find this woman."

The niggle persisted. "Can I see that CCTV first?"

Carrie motioned Alexa into the back room. The recording was set up on a desktop computer. Carrie rewound and pressed Start. The security camera was directed at double glass doors to record people entering and exiting. The bottom screen was labeled Front Entrance, and displayed the time and date. Two women pushed open the door, chatting, and exited the school. One carried a backpack. The other had a bulging satchel. They headed toward the parking lot.

"Teachers," Carrie said. "My girl had Flora Richards last year. The other is Ms. Denny, a maths teacher for the threes and fours. DI Katakana is tracking them down. Principal Bowen will come out next."

Everyone knows everyone in small towns.

Sixty seconds later Eileen Bowen exited. She wore a dark thigh-length coat with a drawstring waist. The coat had a sheen—maybe it was made of nylon. Her blond hair was clipped at the nape of her neck with a large barrette. Her black pants tapered at the ankle and showed off black boots with two-inch heels, similar to the boots she had seen next to Eileen's bed. Her heartbeat thudded in her ears. *Don't leave,* she wanted to shout.

Eileen turned around and tugged the door handle. The door

appeared to be locked. Had she forgotten something or was she checking the security?

The briefcase hanging from her shoulder switched Alexa's niggle to an electric shock. The briefcase now leaned on the counter of Eileen's kitchen. DI Katakana was wrong.

Eileen turned toward a worn path crossing the grass. She dug into her coat pocket and pulled out a woolen hat. Gray with an appliqued red flower.

Alexa's stomach dropped ten floors. Shelby's "fish" was Eileen Bowen's hat.

Chapter Twenty

Alexa yelled for the DI.

She ran in. "What?"

Alexa took a deep breath to calm her heart. She pointed to the frozen screen, time suspended. "That briefcase Eileen is carrying? It's in her kitchen. I just saw it."

The DI absorbed the news quickly. "You're saying she made it home?"

"I'm saying a briefcase like the one she's carrying is in her kitchen."

"How could I have missed it?" She shook her head, frowning. A wavy lock escaped her knot and draped along her neck. "I walked through the house with the ex."

Alexa realized it was a big oversight.

"'Course, I was looking for signs of disturbance." DI Katakana tucked the lock back in place. "Everyone expects to start the search from the school." She turned to leave the backroom.

"Wait." *Brace yourself*, Alexa wanted to add. "I'm staying at a rental house two doors from Eileen's. Remember I told you that? My friend's little daughter Shelby was playing in the creek an hour or so ago." She pointed to the fixed image of Eileen Bowen. "See that hat?" She should have bagged it. She had no idea what Pam did with it. "Shelby fished it out of Bush Creek with a stick."

"*Tūtae!*"

Tūtae was "shit" in Māori.

The older man and Mr. Canine hurried in.

The DI looked stricken. "Eileen Bowen made it home, and her hat, that hat," she jabbed at the screen, "was found in Bush Creek."

"Bloody hell," the older guy said. "Call in the Eagles."

Alexa's mind flew to the American rock band. She wasn't a fan. "The Eagles?"

"Police helicopters." He stuck out his hand to Alexa, who shook it. *Finally*, she thought.

"Mike Unger, retired DI. Live by the river. Soon as I heard Ms. Bowen was missing I offered to help."

DI Katakana held up a hand. "We don't know Earl Hammer has anything to do with this, Mike. He's probably up in Christchurch, doing the pokies."

Charlie had played the poker machines when he visited. Alexa had thought it was a waste of money.

"Eileen Bowen never missed a day of work," he countered. "That's what the school secretary said. So where is she?"

"It does seem if she did a runner, she would have taken her own car." She beckoned for the canine officer to come closer. *Sergeant Grant Strawser* was embroidered on his vest. "Change of plans. Start tracking from her house."

"On it," he said.

"As soon as reinforcements from Queenstown get here, I'm resuming door-to-door in the neighborhood. If she made it home, someone saw her. If she was abducted, she'd fight back. Someone heard her scream, eh?"

Fear landed on Alexa's shoulders. The hat in the creek implied something sinister. Maybe this retired DI was right.

Carrie pressed Start. They watched Eileen Bowen cut across the grass. "She might be alive," Carrie said softly. "Maybe someone stopped by her house and gave her a ride, eh?"

"Then where is she?" DI Katakana said.

"Every minute that ticks by without the woman showing up is more proof something bad has happened," Mike said.

The dog guy headed to the door. "Until we have a body, we work on the assumption Eileen Bowen is alive." He spoke to Alexa. "I need to pick Dax up at the school. Given the new information, we'll start the search in Ms. Bowen's yard. We need to do that scent elimination. Want to ride with me or follow in your car?"

"I need a ride," she said.

The DI's hand went to her radio. "I'll alert the search coordinators."

"What would you like me to do after his dog, um, eliminates me?" Alexa asked her.

"Scour Eileen Bowen's yard for evidence of abduction. Have Constable Blume assist you. If something turns up, call me. If not, you're free to go. Maybe join a search team."

Alexa hefted the kit to her shoulder and followed Mr. Canine to the street. She gulped fresh cool air. Events were unfolding rapidly, and she needed a clear head.

"Call me Grant," the dog guy said. "Is your name really Alexa? Like 'Tell me the weather' Alexa?"

The algae bloom lights of Amazon Alexa were inconsequential at the moment. She nodded. "I have to make a quick call."

The Dog Unit patrol car was in front of the Fork and Tap. Grant bleeped the car open and got in. Alexa stood by a chalkboard menu and dialed Ana, who picked up on the first ring. "Are you okay?" Alexa asked.

"Why? Where are you?"

"I'm leaving the Policing Centre."

"Any word on the principal? Has she turned up?"

"No word. Have you, um, checked on your mom and Shelby?"

"You said they were fine. I'm waiting for Mr. Sun to arrive. What's going on?"

An image of the hat dangling from Shelby's stick jabbed at her. "The police suspect the principal was abducted from her house." She cleared her throat to continue. "Shelby was playing in the creek when I stopped by. She fished out a hat that looks like the one Eileen Bowen was wearing."

"From the creek? What?"

"That guy, Earl Hammer, he's still on the lam." She had always wanted to say "on the lam," but the fact of it sucked out the thrill. "Maybe Pam and Shelby should leave Arrowtown. Go home."

"I'm on my way," Ana said.

Grant had started the car and tapped the steering wheel. She was holding up the search. "Wait," she said to Ana "Your Mom took the hat." DNA could be found on clothes of drowned victims hours or days after being submerged. There was a chance the hat might yield evidence. "Can you find it and put it in a plastic bag? Wear gloves. I'll stop by to pick it up."

"Okay," Ana said.

The heaviness lifted from her shoulders. Shelby and Pam would be safe. She glanced at the cafe menu displayed on the chalkboard—her eyes landed on truffle curly fries. *Dammit.* Her stomach growled as she got into the vehicle.

Grant pulled into the street before she buckled. The car smelled like wet dog. Her appetite subsided. "How will Dax eliminate me?"

"He'll give you a whiff is all, ay?" Grant tapped the steering wheel as a cluster of middle-schoolers jaywalked. The kids didn't look concerned about an escaped parolee or a missing principal.

"Has he found people before?"

"Ay, yeah, sure. Last month he found a lone tramper in thick

West Coast bush. Our fellow was a couple kilometers off the track, eh. Amazing how easy it is to lose orientation."

Alexa thought of the Millford Track she had hiked with Charlie. She understood dense wilderness.

They turned onto Lake Hayes Road. "Time before that, he found a care home wanderer."

"Has he located dead people?" she blurted.

"Nah, yeah. He has a different bark for that."

She prayed she wouldn't hear the death bark.

Grant rubbed his chin. "Do you know who that bloke Mike is?"

"He said he's a retired detective inspector."

"DI Michael Unger. He was in charge of Cindy Mulligan's murder case. Worked it day and night. He lifted a fingerprint from the Discman found by the river. It was used to convict Hammer."

Alexa sat up straighter. She loved it when forensic science nailed a baddie.

"Everyone called him a hero."

They pulled into the school parking lot. Alexa recognized the Go For Gold sign out front. Another sign said *Years 1–8* and *Haere mai ki te Kāmuriwai.* "What does that mean?" she asked Grant.

"Come let's sit together."

Rather than sitting together, cops and adults, maybe twenty-five in all, stood together on a blacktop. A man in an orange New Zealand Search and Rescue jumpsuit seemed to be talking to the crowd; maybe he was relaying DI Katakana's message.

Grant parked next to a police car. "There he is!"

Alexa's mind jumped to Earl Hammer. She looked to where Grant pointed. An officer held the leash of a German shepherd. The dog sat tall, ears pricked and tongue lolling. He wore an orange vest.

"I'll update Constable Hicks and grab Dax."

The dog greeted his master with two sharp barks that Alexa heard through the cracked window. Grant rubbed behind the dog's ear and talked to the officer. Then the dog tugged Grant to the car. The closer the dog got, the bigger he looked. Alexa shrank in her seat as Grant opened the hatchback. "Crate," he commanded.

The dog hopped in. Alexa turned. Dax's fur was black underneath and tawny on top like he'd been highlighted. His amber-brown eyes met hers. Should she look away or hold her ground? *Jeez.* She shouldn't be afraid of a highly trained search and rescue dog, a Kaos cousin, but her nervous system hadn't gotten the memo. Grant closed the hatch and got back in the car.

As they left the school parking lot Grant gave a woman walking along the side of the road a wide berth. Alexa recognized her plastic rain bonnet. It was the woman who had complained about the dig.

They turned onto Plum Tree Terrace. No car in the driveway of Prospector's Cottage yet. *Hurry, Ana.* They parked behind Constable Blume's patrol car. Alexa grabbed the kit and got out.

Grant released the dog and held him on a short leash. "He's my boy."

The "boy" showed Alexa his teeth. She knew that a dog's forty-two teeth had many jobs: Nip. Crush. Grind. Tear. Hold. Strip. Meat from bone, that is.

"Come closer," Grant said. "Let him smell your sleeve."

"Will he bite?" flew out of her mouth.

Grant scrutinized her face. "No worries. At home Dax plays with my ankle biter. Gentle as a kitten, he is."

An ankle biter was Kiwi-speak for a toddler. She extended her arm. Dax's moist nostrils quivered independent of each other, centimeters from the fabric.

Grant jerked the leash and said, "No seek."

Alexa retracted her arm. She'd been silly to be nervous. The dog was here to help. "Won't Eileen's scent be all over the place? It's her house and yard."

"Dax can differentiate fresh scent from old. He'll follow the most recent."

That was amazing. She watched as Grant slipped on a backpack and fitted a transmitter with a little antenna to Dax's vest. "In case he has to go off lead."

Constable Blume came to meet them. Grant filled him in on the latest news. "Blimey." He stood taller. "I'm at the center of the storm."

"You're to help me search the grounds," Alexa said. "Has my evidence been picked up?"

"Ay. Ms. Walker said for you to call her."

Grant slipped on gloves and pulled the nightgown out of the bag.

Alexa stepped forward. "Let me see your boots." If there were bootprints in the yard or by the creek, she needed to know whether they belonged to Grant.

Dax's nostrils quivered as Grant lifted a foot: "Keens. Size ten."

Alexa took a photograph.

The German shepherd sniffed at the nightgown's folds the way Alexa had pictured.

"Seek," Grant said.

Dax lowered his nose to the ground. Before Grant had returned the nightgown to the bag, the dog tugged him toward the Smart car, then to the mailbox, then to the side yard. He was on the scent.

秋季
AUTUMN
1893

Precious MaMa,

Saturday New Gold Mountain bustles and swells. It smells of raw lumber and horse droppings. Rain turns the streets to mud, and carts get stuck. There are now two hotels, two bars, a grocery, and a chemist.

By Bush Creek we have China Town. Gold is slow to trickle in. There are only twenty of us left. We burrow like rabbits. Sometimes boys from town come, throw rocks, call us bad names, and steal. They broke my crane-with-spread-wings rice bowl, and with it my heart.

Autumn Loo grabbed his shovel and chased them. He is a bent man, sixty years old, and he came back sobbing.

Our friend Kong Kai, blind in one eye, has been missing for three moons. We searched Eight Mile Creek where he has a cave in the ledge above the creek. Only his skeleton, picked clean by birds and rats. He was not murdered because he had seventy pounds in his pocket.

I sent the money to his MaMa. I can only send to you my token of love and esteem.

Faithful First Son,
Wing Lun

Chapter Twenty-One

Constable Blume cordoned off the front and back yards as Alexa watched. Then he followed on her heels as she walked to the backyard. "Forensic evidence connecting a perpetrator to a crime enhances the chance of solvability," he said.

Alexa stopped and stared at him. "Um, that's true." Otherwise she wouldn't have a job.

He continued. "A more important factor is identifying a victim-perpetrator relationship. Someone the principal knows or a family member is more likely to have kidnapped her than a stranger."

He was spouting police basics. She raised her index finger. "Ex-husband Paul." She raised another finger. "New boyfriend. Langston Jet Boat." She continued counting on her fingers as she considered Eileen's position at Arrowtown Primary. What had been the focus of that board meeting yesterday? "Maybe an angry parent from school or a disgruntled employee." Her last finger—well, thumb—represented a family member. "Maybe the sister? Their parents are dead, and there aren't any other siblings."

The constable's face screwed up. "Can't see how Misty would snatch her only sister and then come over here to help. That would be ballsy. There's the fact Earl Hammer has gone AWOL. Gotta factor in Stranger Danger."

Charlie had informed her the term Stranger Danger was no longer valid: Kids sometimes *needed* to ask a stranger for help. If

Shelby was lost or hurt, a stranger such as a store clerk or… She digressed. Probably from hunger pains. Would Earl Hammer toss his spanking new freedom away by kidnapping and possibly killing another woman? That was hard to believe unless he was a sociopath. *Or was it psychopath?* She got the terms mixed up, but both conditions were dangerous.

Stranger or acquaintance, the principal was out there somewhere, dead or alive, and most likely needed help. Alexa discounted the notion that Eileen Bowen disappeared on her own accord. Walked off. The hat in the creek indicated something suspicious had happened. She wondered whether DI Katakana had brought the ex-husband or new boyfriend into the center. Grilled them. The case was digging its claws into her.

She searched the sky: cloudy, but no imminent rain. Maybe two hours until dark.

They walked a grid in the backyard: back and forth, eyes sweeping left and right. Leaves, stubby grass, empty clothesline, distant voices. Nothing else. The black coat Eileen had been wearing on the CCTV wasn't hanging by the door. It seemed as if she'd come home, dumped her briefcase in the kitchen, changed shoes, and then left on her own accord, taking her purse and phone. Her car was here, so who picked her up? The boy toy? Alexa didn't know if the jet boat driver was younger than Eileen, but it seemed like an under-thirty occupation.

Then they scoured the creek bank. She photographed the Keen boot impressions and paw prints on the soft sand. They ended at the water; there was no backtracking. "Dax and Grant must have crossed the creek." She scanned the opposite bank. Man and dog were gone.

They found no other footprints. There were no drag marks on the grass or creek bank.

"Ready for the front garden?" Constable Blume asked.

They combed the front yard and ended with the Smart car.

Constable Blume circled it twice, his eyes on the ground. "No sign of drag marks on the gravel."

The Mini was locked, but Alexa could see through the windows that the interior was neat. Constable Blume had looked at her strangely when she ripped opened a box of rolled sterile cotton, tore off a chunk, and fluffed it up like a snowball.

"You're using fluff?" he asked.

"Fluffed cotton is quicker than a brush and covers a wider swath." Plus she could throw it away afterwards, reducing the risk of contamination. She'd dipped the cotton in gray powder and lightly dusted the car around the handle, enjoying the constable's rapt attention.

"I'm going to try that," he said.

The results had revealed four fingermarks above the handle and a few singles below. She photographed them and then lifted them onto backing cards. They'd probably match Eileen's, but what if someone else drove her car?

She was cleaning up when her phone buzzed. Caller ID Unknown. "Hello?"

"This is DI Katakana. Anything to report from the yard?"

"No signs of disturbance. It looks like Eileen left willingly. Any word on Hammer?"

"Still missing. There's a major manhunt going on—a team, helicopters, an appeal to the public, his picture flashing everywhere. They're concentrating on areas where he has connections. Here, plus he has *whānau* in Ashburton and Manukau." She paused. "I've a Search and Seize for all of Eileen's electronics and mobile records. If she has her phone, we can use the pings to track her. A constable is on the way to pick up the laptop. Have it ready."

Alexa heard a siren in the distance. "I lifted some fingerprints from the car door handle that need to get to the lab." The poppy hat flashed in her head. "And the hat that Shelby—that's my friend's daughter—fished from the creek. It might yield touch DNA. I can head to the lab with them."

"No need. The constable can deliver them to our Ms. Walker. A Search and Rescue team is on the way to conduct a creek sweep from the subject's yard. You're free to join them." The DI abruptly terminated the call.

Alexa was miffed at being "set free." She expected to be a team member. In on the investigation. Wanted to be, though her boss, Dan, had warned her not to overstep her boundaries. "There have been a few complaints," he'd said at her six-month review.

Yeah, well. When she took liberties, cases got solved.

She updated Constable Blume and told him she needed to run to the rental house to collect a piece of evidence. He looked perplexed.

"I'm staying practically next door. I'll be right back. If the officer gets here to pick up the computer, tell him to wait for me."

She ducked under the caution tape and jogged up the driveway—the kit banging into her thigh—and out onto Plum Tree Terrace. Pam was loading suitcases into the Highlander. Shelby was sitting in her car seat but climbed out. She ran to Alexa. "You can come too. We going to ride a team boat."

"Steamboat," Pam corrected. "A touristy thing on Lake Wakatipu."

"That will be fun. Where's Ana?"

"Bananas," Shelby said. She tugged on the crime kit. "Can I see what's in there?"

Alexa, confused again, lifted the kit to her chest. "Not now."

Shelby shrugged her little shoulders and climbed back into her seat.

"Let me get this poppet buckled up," Pam said. She harnessed Shelby like a pro and ushered Alexa from the car. She lowered her voice. "You should come with us."

"I can't. I'm working the missing principal case."

"Your safety is more important than work." Her eyes bore into Alexa's. "I think Earl Hammer is back. He's taken that woman."

Suddenly Alexa wanted to climb into the back seat next to Shelby. To be sheltered from harm. But she had a job to do. "I don't know. I'm about to help search for her."

"I covered Hammer's trial," Pam said. "I watched him for six weeks. It's imprinted on my brain. Remorseless every single day, he was, even with Cindy Mulligan's parents sitting in the front row. He claimed he was innocent, in spite of the evidence. Fingerprints don't lie, right? That's what the expert witness said. He should never have been released."

Alexa's eyes darted to the backyard. The creek. The bushes.

Pam gave her a hug. "No jogging, right?" she whispered.

"No jogging."

Ana was in the kitchen. "I didn't think I'd see you. I'm collecting bits and bobs," she said. "We're about to leave until this mess is sorted."

"I'm glad you're going. I need to pick up the hat."

Ana retrieved a plastic bag hanging from the doorknob. "I didn't touch it. Any word on Earl Hammer or the principal?"

"No. I'll call you if there's any news."

Ana lifted a bunch of bananas from a bowl, handed one to Alexa, and stowed the rest in a grocery bag. "Dr. Weiner from the lab called. The latest round of test results came in. The Sr isotope ratios from the molar are compatible with southern China geologic regions. Isn't that exciting? I'll email the report to you."

Alexa forced her brain to switch gears. "That makes sense, since he's related to Mrs. Wong."

"Most of the Chinese gold miners came from southern China," Ana said. "I've spoken to Mrs. Wong. As soon as the bones are released, she plans to repatriate the skeleton. She'll bring S2 home too, if it's also from southern China. 'I cannot leave a hungry ghost behind,' she said. But I doubt it. Chinese women didn't come here."

Alexa had trouble assimilating all this news. Ravenous, she peeled and ate the banana. She glanced around the kitchen, hoping to spy more food on a counter—even Marmite—but the counters were clear.

"I've ordered the excavator to fill in S1's grave. We took that tent down and moved everything into the smaller tent," Ana said. "Open graves are a liability."

Falling in a grave. Add it to her list of fears, Alexa thought. "Have both skeletons been removed?"

Ana nodded. "Dr. McKenzie wants us to re-sift the grave dirt of S2. That's why I'm keeping that tent up."

"Where is Olivia?"

Ana looked uncomfortable. "She wanted to search for the principal, but I said no. She's my responsibility. My employee. What would I tell her parents if something happened? She's spending the weekend with friends. Mum has me rattled about Hammer."

Alexa felt like the last one on the lifeboat. "Did you send Dr. Weiner S2's molar?"

"She's going to work it in tomorrow. She needs you to do the isotope test; she's not qualified. She'll meet you at the clinic early tomorrow morning if you can get there."

"I'll try."

"Can you meet with me and Dr. McKenzie afterwards? He's agreed to examine S2."

The drone of a copter filled the room. It was setting down

somewhere close by. *The Eagle has landed.* "I'll try," she repeated. She lifted the bag with the hat. "I've got to go."

"*Kia tūpato,*" Ana said.

"What does that mean?"

"Be careful."

Ana's warning and Pam's concern hovered in her mind as she hurried upstairs. She switched to hiking boots and assembled another small crime kit: flashlight, camera, fingerprint kit, gloves, boot-cast material, a few evidence containers. She stuffed everything in the drawstring bag she had for this purpose. She withdrew the fingerprints she'd lifted from the car door and then stored the big kit in the closet. She grabbed the plastic bag with the wet hat and went downstairs, locked the front door, waving as Ana, Pam, and Shelby drove off. She retraced her steps to Eileen's house.

"That was quick," Constable Blume said.

"Location, location, location," she said inanely. A patrol car pulled up. A female officer got out and flashed a badge. "DI Katakana sent me for Eileen Bowen's laptop, to take it to the techies." She held up a large evidence bag.

Alexa slipped on a fresh pair of gloves and took the bag. "I'll fetch it."

Eileen Bowen's house already felt neglected. She thought of what Eileen had been wearing as she left school, and popped into the bedroom to peek in the closet. The black coat was missing and there were four pairs of black pants hanging up. She couldn't be sure if Eileen had been wearing one pair and had changed from them to something else. She took a picture of the boots leaning against the bed. That, at least, proved she had changed shoes.

In the kitchen she unfolded the jumbo bag and slid the gaping briefcase into it. She could see a slim laptop nestled between files and hoped Eileen's calendar, emails, or search history would help locate her. Maybe the physical files would yield information too. Maybe there would be notes from the board meeting. Outside, she filled out chain of custody information and signed for the transfer to the officer. She also turned over the fingerprints from the car door and the hat. "These go to the forensic lab."

As soon as the police officer backed out of the driveway, Alexa took out the lab tech's card and called. She introduced herself when Leigh Walker answered.

"*Kia ora,*" Leigh said. "The two drinking glasses are fuming."

A vision of a fuming chamber materialized in Alexa's head. When Super Glue, or cyanoacrylate, is heated, it forms vapors that adhere to nonporous surfaces. Whitish fingerprint patterns should appear on the glasses from Eileen's sink. Presto.

"I have a copy of Eileen Bowen's fingerprints ready to compare," Leigh said.

The lab tech had done exactly as Alexa would have. She explained more fingerprints were coming and about the hat. "I'm hoping for touch DNA." In the distance a dog barked. Alexa froze. Was it Dax's death bark?

"Won't the river water have eroded the DNA?" Leigh asked.

"There's a chance it survived. Let it air-dry, no fan, on a rack. Twenty-four hours should do it. I'll get to the lab tomorrow and take a look." *Meaning let me do it.*

"All good," Leigh said.

Alexa hung up, satisfied the lab tech was competent.

Voices caught her attention. A tall lanky guy in an orange Search and Rescue jumpsuit led two men and a woman up to the caution tape. She and Constable Blume went to meet them.

"G'day. I'm Julian Getz with Otago SAR." His short beard was ginger-colored, and he looked to be in his early forties. "I've been assigned a quick creek sweep from the search subject's yard." He gestured to his group. "This is my crew of volunteers. Is it okay to traipse through the garden?"

"We're done," Alexa said. "But a dog and tracker have already been up the creek."

"The dog couldn't get a scent," Julian said.

Then why cover the same ground? Alexa wondered. Of course, she didn't know which way Dax had led Grant. Maybe across the creek and into the woods. She lifted the caution tape for them. The volunteers wore yellow safety vests and held poles. "Ta," the woman said. She and the two male volunteers stared at Eileen's house as if it held answers.

"Do you have room for another searcher?" Alexa asked Julian.

He nodded. "Need all the help we can get."

Chapter Twenty-Two

FRIDAY EVENING

Alexa and the other searchers stood on the bank. Bush Creek scurried by in rivulets and channels. *Not as wide as the Arrow River, but it means business*, Alexa thought.

The female searcher looked vaguely familiar. She whispered to Alexa. "I'm Connie, and this is my husband Jack." The younger of the two male volunteers nodded at her.

Alexa wondered why Connie was whispering. She was about to introduce herself when Julian said, "Thousands of people go missing in New Zealand each year." He fiddled with a radio.

Jeez, Alexa thought.

The other male volunteer had thin silver hair. He asked, "How many get found?"

"Most get found safely within seventy-two hours," Julian said.

"How long has Ms. Bowen been missing?" the woman searcher asked.

"She was last seen over twenty-seven hours ago."

Alexa toed the damp scree with her boot tip. The Norwegian hiker she had identified by comparing the young woman's post-mortem dental X-rays with her social media selfie smiles hadn't been found safely or within seventy-two hours. Her skeletal remains were found in a ravine a year later. She prayed the same fate didn't await Eileen Bowen.

Julian scanned the sky. "We've an hour of daylight. Who besides me has a torch?"

Alexa was the only one. She felt a sense of urgency in the waning light.

Julian pointed ten yards up the creek. Boulders spanned the banks. "We'll split up. Two on that side, three on this side. Arm's distance apart. Inspect the bank and creek closely. Poke your stick into mounds, brush, crevices, ditches, wells, shelters. Look for foot tracks, broken branches, personal effects. Listen for cries of help, moans, anything out of the ordinary. We'll shoot for the Chinese settlement, 'bout two kilometers." He contacted someone by radio. "Team C starting from search subject's backyard."

"We hear you, mate," came the reply.

Alexa was elected to cross the creek. It was only ten feet across where they stood, but the banks were steep. The man with silver hair jumped boulder to boulder and billy-goated up the bank. She followed suit until the last rock. One boot slid into the creek. Frigid water seeped down her ankle.

The man extended a hand and pulled her up. "I'm Dr. Wiggins. Dr. Getz recruited me. We worked together."

So Julian was a doc. If she got a PhD at Abertay University she could reply, "I'm Dr. Glock." As it was, she said, "I'm Alexa."

"Like Amazon?"

She ignored the comment and hoped he and Julian were PhD scientists. Epidemiologists or entomologists, maybe. Something good. "What kind of doctor?"

"Geriatrician."

Oh well. "What's your first name?"

"Joe. Stick close to me. That escaped convict might be using these woods to hide."

"He isn't an escaped convict. He was paroled."

"Same difference. I wouldn't let Mrs. Wiggins search. Too risky."

Mrs. Wiggins? This man annoyed her. Plus she didn't need his protection.

"Are you visiting from the States?" he asked.

Hadn't he seen her lift the caution tape in Eileen Bowen's yard? "I'm working here. I'm a forensics investigator."

"The missus likes *My Life is Murder.* It' a TV series. That woman's name is Alexa too. "

Lucky her, Alexa thought.

There was no path. Joe walked closest to the creek, poking his pole into piles of debris. The woods at Alexa's side thickened with mānuka trees. Or was it kānuka? Both trees were common natives, but it was mānuka that the bees loved. Alexa spotted a good walking stick and wedged between small prickly leaves to reach it. The foliage blocked the view. It would be a good place to stash a body.

Why was she thinking *body*?

Eileen Bowen had been missing for more than twenty-four hours now. This was out of character for her, everyone agreed. Her hat in the creek fueled Alexa's foreboding. Goose bumps broke out on her arms. She grabbed the stick and pushed through to the creek. Julian and the other searchers' bright vests made them visible on the far bank. She heard their voices but not their words. Beyond them, she spotted the back of a house. If Eileen Bowen had been thrown into the creek as the hat suggested, it had to have been from somewhere close by. She hoped DI Katakana had followed through on her house-to-house canvass.

Cindy Mulligan's body had been found in the Arrow River. "How far are we from the Arrow?" she asked Joe.

"Bush Creek feeds into it just shy of the Chinese settlement."

She heard about the Chinese settlement when she was at the museum. The kids in the fake schoolroom had been there. She was curious to see it.

"I holidayed round here as a child." Joe stepped onto a sand-bar and poked a pile of trapped brush. It floated clear. "There's a caravan park nearby. We'd play in the creek, build forts, pan for gold."

Alexa stabbed a rotten log and watched as her stick stirred up feasting beetles. "Did you find any?"

"Some flakes in my pan—always very exciting. A Southland man found a huge nugget a couple years ago. He was snorkeling in the Arrow River."

"Really?" Snorkeling belonged in places like the Bahamas—not where the water was snowmelt-fed. And the river she'd jogged along this morning hardly seemed deep enough.

They trudged along the bank for ten minutes. The creek widened, and the voices of the other searchers faded. Alexa's left boot sloshed. Around a bend the creek narrowed, funneling water between an island and a rock cliff that cast them in shadow. A shoulder-high opening in the rock startled her. "Look."

Joe followed her gaze. "That's large enough to squeeze through. Might be a mining tunnel. Surprised it's not blocked off." They stared into the dark recesses. The opening zigzagged like an angry mouth a kid would draw. Joe leaned forward and stuck his head in. "Some tunnels go down twelve meters or more."

"Down?"

He backed up. "The miners used pickaxes and shovels to dig below the water table when the creeks had been ravaged. They went for the subterranean veins."

That sounded like an attacker going for the jugular. Alexa didn't like it.

Joe blew a whistle. Julian dashed to the opposite bank. "We've got a cave entrance," Joe yelled. "Want us to take a look?"

River burble stole Julian's reply, but he nodded. Alexa's heart sank; she didn't like caves. In a previous case she had dodged a killer by hiding in a cave. Glowworms had hung from every crevice. *Light of the enduring world.* If she survived that one, she could survive entering this one. She clicked on her torch.

Joe nodded. "Mind your head. I'll be right behind you."

Alexa snorted. No more "stick with me, I'll protect you."

She propped her stick against the entrance and scuttled through. She didn't have to worry about snakes; New Zealand didn't have any. The opening curved left, subjugating natural light. She stepped tentatively, aiming her beam at the sand and gravel beyond her boots and groping the wall with her free hand. She didn't want to fall in a hole. She searched for footprints or drag marks. Nothing looked disturbed and there was no deep tunnel. The air was dank and cold. Three more steps in, she sensed space and slowly straightened. She aimed the light at dry rock walls. Something tickled her nose. She recoiled, banging her head on rock. "Dammit."

She heard breathing. Nearby. She turned the Maglite in the direction of the sound.

Joe blinked. "Ey."

"Sorry." She rubbed her nose and shined the light around, surprised to be in a cell-sized space where she could stand erect. She'd read that the first evidence of Neanderthal Man was found in a cave in Germany. The article interested her because she learned that Neanderthals' teeth grew faster than modern man's teeth. Alexa gritted hers. This cave sheltered no Neanderthals. No bodies either.

Her beam landed on a shovel close to the wall. She walked toward it. "Wow. Look."

Joe followed and nudged it with his boot. The head was corroded with rust and the handle was broken. Who had last touched it? She'd read at the archives about a miner who lived in a cave along the Arrow River. He'd been murdered. Her breath caught. *Could this be the cave?*

No. They were walking along Bush Creek, not the Arrow River.

A tin lantern rested on a ledge above the shovel, blackened by age or soot. The nub of a pale candle waited in its confines. Had it provided the only source of light for whoever sheltered here?

She moved the light in a circle looking for more evidence of inhabitancy: a sleeping loft, a pipe, or a ceramic jar of tea. There were no more remnants, but she sensed the cave had once been a refuge. "I think a miner lived in here back in the day."

"Might have," Joe said. "Would have kept the rain and snow off, anyway, but no sign of the missing principal."

She searched for a passageway to more rooms, but the rock walls didn't part. This was a dead end. The fractured skull of S1 popped into her head, and she thought wildly of taking fingerprints from the shovel handle. She had the supplies in her mini-kit. Maybe she'd come back.

Julian Getz waited outside the entrance, scaring her as she emerged. He had what looked like a miner's helmet on with a headlamp. "Anything?" he asked.

"Empty," Joe said.

Alexa clarified. "There's an old shovel and lantern. You know, from the past."

Julian raised an eyebrow. "But no sign of recent entry?"

She shook her head.

"The Chinese settlement is maybe ten minutes. We'll meet up there." Julian hopped back over the creek. The woman searcher waved her pole, and Alexa waved back. She filled her lungs with fresh air. The sound of a helicopter made her jump. She covered her ears as it crossed above. She hated helicopters ever since her Milford Track hike with Charlie. A helicopter pilot had tried to behead her with his dangling ton of rock.

"They'll start using night-vision goggles shortly," Joe said.

The creek curved sharply for a hundred meters. Individual leaves, a twig on the path, rocks, and scree faded to gradients of gray. She and Joe walked parallel to Julian and the two other searchers across the creek, who wove in and out of trees like forest sprites. At the convergence with the Arrow River, Julian and his crew crossed to their side.

Daylight hung on by a thread when the first miner's hut—a wooden structure—came into view. It pressed its back against the hillside, and was half-hidden by draping vines. Its sharply pitched roof might have been made of straw and wood—Alexa couldn't tell in the gloaming. A wooden railing extended like bony fingers from it. There was a door-shaped entrance. The single window was barely large enough to fit a head through.

The woman searcher pointed at it with her pole. "That's the first of five reconstructed huts. It was originally built in 1883 by Loo Lee."

Alexa did a double take. Now she knew why the woman was familiar. She was the schoolmarm. "You work at the museum, don't you?" she asked.

"Part time."

Her husband checked his watch. "This isn't time for one of your tours, Connie."

"I know. But I feel a connection. The first woman he killed…"

"Who killed?" the husband interrupted.

"Earl Hammer. The first woman he killed had the same job I do. Cindy Mulligan was a docent at the Lakes District Museum."

"Whoa," Alexa said.

Julian cleared his throat. "Ms. Bowen may be alive, and we don't know Earl Hammer is involved." Connie nodded. "It's just, well, I'm devo we didn't find her."

It would have been more devastating if we'd found her body, Alexa thought.

"It's too dark to continue searching if you don't have a torch," Julian announced. "Does everyone know how to get to their cars from here?"

"I'm at the car park," Joe said. "Anyone need a lift?"

"We can walk home," Connie said.

"See you tomorrow," Joe said to Julian. His eyes landed on Alexa, and he gave a courtly bow. "Make sure you walk this little lady home."

Alexa tightened her grip on the Maglite so she didn't bonk Joe on the head with it. *Little lady.* "Do you want me to stay?" she asked Julian.

He nodded and said, "We'll just check the huts and then you can be off, eh?" He turned on the headlamp and took out a flashlight.

She could do that. She was in no hurry to face an empty cottage.

The others faded up the path. Alexa stepped closer to Julian. "I'll check this one." He shined his light at the first hut built into a sloping terrace. "Take a squiz at the next hut. We'll alternate."

She followed the winding path. The next hut was made of chinked stone. A tiny pipe chimney poked out. The structure tapered into the hillside so that there were only three walls. She aimed her light at the roof. It was reddish thatch and extended on both sides almost to the ground. The opening was off-center and shaded by the overhanging eaves. Inside was pitch-black. She squeezed the Maglite and crept up the path.

At the threshold, her legs wouldn't budge. It was then that she thought of the kid. The red-haired boy in Connie's pretend classroom had said he'd seen a bad man hiding in one of the huts.

No one had believed him.

Chapter Twenty-Three

Alexa gathered her courage and stepped into the gloom of the hut. She swept the Maglite beam across the walls, pausing in the gray and empty corners. A crude fireplace with a mantel looked like a gaping black hole with grate teeth. A rustle came from the earthen wall; she searched it with her light. A berth was carved out—maybe it had served as a bunk. She thought of rats and backed out of the hut quickly. From the rise she spotted the lights from Julian's headlamp bouncing her way.

She stubbed her boot on a root, almost tripping, as she hustled to join him. "That one was empty." Her voice was shaky. Should she tell Julian what the kid had said? She decided against it: She'd been in the schoolroom before Hammer had gone AWOL. The kid had probably been making things up. *Kids do that.*

Alexa stuck close to Julian—just in case. He swept his strong beam around the bleak interiors of the final three huts.

The last dwelling was L-shaped with a tin roof. It stood away from the other huts as if its original builder had been a loner. "All good," Julian said. He radioed the coordinators. "Team C reporting from Chinese settlement. No sign of missing person."

"No one's had luck," a voice responded. "Ground search is terminated until morning. Regroup tomorrow at seven a.m."

"I've got clinics," Julian said. "I can join a team after work if needed."

Alexa checked the time on her phone: six thirty. A sense of disconnect settled on her like the darkness that had gathered strength. DI Katakana hadn't asked her to a briefing that surely must be taking place. Ana, Pam, and Shelby were gone. She and Bruce were on the outs. Sunday was her birthday. On the cusp of thirty-eight, and she was alone in the Southern Hemisphere. She didn't know if she was okay with that. Or not.

"Where's your car?" Julian asked.

"I don't have one."

"I'll give you a lift then. To be safe."

The offer hung in the air. They climbed a grassy knoll away from Bush Creek and the creepy huts. As they crossed a car park Julian took off his headlamp and laughed. "So long as home isn't America. Anywhere between here and Queenstown is fair game."

Downtown lights twinkled. There were people on the streets. She was suddenly weak with hunger. "I've got a date with Arrow Thai." Alexa had spotted the restaurant near the museum. "Want to join me?"

"Brilliant idea. I ate something so long ago I can't remember. Always telling my patients not to skip meals, and look at me."

Alexa did. His face—the parts not covered by a neatly trimmed ginger beard—looked gaunt in an 'I'm too busy to eat, but healthy' way. His teeth were white and straight.

"I took over the reins from Joe three years ago, and it's been non-stop since," Julian said. "That and this SAR volunteering. My life!"

Married to the job. Helping people in his spare time. She liked the man. "I have a bad feeling about Eileen," she remarked.

"Me too, but we can't assume she's dead. Presumption of death robs searchers of urgency."

Hunger was Alexa's urgent need. She felt faint.

Arrow Thai's indoor tables were full, so after ordering at the counter, they settled at a sidewalk table. Despite the chill, Julian unzipped his orange SAR jumpsuit partway. He popped open his Tui beer and sipped.

Alexa felt on duty, so she stuck with water. Her tongue suddenly tied, but Julian's persistent questions untangled the knot.

"Where are you from?" he asked.

"Auckland."

He laughed. She caught him glancing at her left hand. "Well, I'm from North Carolina. I came to Auckland on a fellowship and never left."

"A fellowship? What kind?"

She ran her tongue across her teeth. "I taught Forensic Odontology 101: pattern injury recognition, analysis, and comparison. Current methodology and trends. That kind of thing."

"So what were you doing at the missing woman's house? Do you work for the police?"

She didn't mind the questions. She wished she could think of something to ask in return, about gerontology, but what was there? *We age, if we're lucky. Then we die.* "I work as a traveling forensic investigator. I support the police."

"You're here because Ms. Bowen is missing?"

"I was already in Arrowtown. I'm working with an archaeologist at the cemetery."

"I went to a service there for a patient. Elliot Meeks. Eighty-two. Complications from diabetes. Why is there a dig?"

She described the exhumed skeletons. "There's an old Chinese belief that a soul can only be at peace if buried where he was born. Otherwise, it becomes a hungry ghost. The teeth tests I conducted revealed one of the skeletons spent his childhood in southern China." She knew it was rude, but she checked her phone to see if she had any updates on S2 from Dr. Weiner. Nope. Her phone only had three percent of battery left.

Julian didn't laugh about the hungry ghosts. Another thing to like about him. "Maybe they lived in one of the huts we just searched," he said.

The past and present were knocking heads. She looked through the glass. It was hard to reconcile the diners' smiling faces with the possibility that a convicted murderer might be lurking in the shadows or had abducted Eileen. Her wet boot and sock reminded her that Eileen might have been thrown into the creek. Or the Arrow River. She wiggled her toes and grimaced. "Do you think Earl Hammer is in Arrowtown, and has Ms. Bowen?"

"It's dodgy, her missing at the same time he is." He sipped his beer and looked thoughtful. "I had a partner. We lived together, both of us in medical school. She took off. No word. No note. The pressure of school, I think. Maybe Ms. Bowen has done the same."

A police officer walked by, snug in a bulletproof vest, his eyes scanning the street and businesses. A gust of wind pushed a paper bag across his path, and he stomped on it. Alexa watched as he picked up the trash and disposed of it in a bin. "Did your partner pack her stuff?"

"Yes. And my Xbox."

Alexa considered the possibility of Eileen being safe somewhere; it didn't seem likely.

After a waiter served their food, Julian asked, "Ever felt like disappearing?"

She shifted and thought of Abertay University. Dr. Ben Odden wanted her to visit the campus. Maybe talk over a job offer. Charlie would say she was good at disappearing. She stayed mum. Julian studied her but didn't press for an answer.

They ate with gusto—Julian Getz his tofu and veggies and Alexa her beef curry. The calories jump-started her batteries. She had never informed the police that the coroner was opening an inquest in regard to the skeletons. That was an excuse to stop by the Policing Centre and see what was going on.

She and Julian paid separately. He walked her the two blocks to the center. "Thanks for your help with the search," he said. He shuffled from one foot to the other. "Ever fancy a drink in Queenstown?"

She mumbled gobbledygook about being busy and was sorry to see him walk off, shoulders drooped from his many responsibilities, she guessed. Or maybe because she hadn't said yes. She straightened her own shoulders, wished she had a mint, and opened the center door.

The retired DI, Mike Unger, was sitting at the head of a table, watching some kind of meeting on his laptop. "Ms. Glock," he said.

"Thought I'd check in," she said.

A cop Alexa didn't recognize sat catty-corner from him, studying security camera footage on another laptop. It looked like downtown Arrowtown at warp speed.

Unger paused his meeting. He gestured to the other cop. "There are fifteen cameras around downtown," he said. "So far, Eileen Bowen hasn't shown up."

"Neither has Earl Hammer," the cop said.

Voices came from the back room. The door was cracked open, but Alexa couldn't see who was in there. Unger gestured her closer. "Look at this."

Alexa brightened. The retired guy wasn't shooing her away. She looked over his shoulder. "It's video of the Arrowtown Primary board meeting yesterday," he explained. "Full of angry parents."

He pressed play and turned up the volume. One of twenty or so people sitting in an auditorium got to her feet. It was a woman, maybe forty, her face pinched. "Our son Nick has been bullied by Ian for months. I demand a group session with the parents. Let them hear what the effin' kid did to Nick."

The man next to her rose, his eyes blazing. "He's started the stuttering again, our Nick. After years of getting it under control. You paying for the speech therapy, Ms. Bowen? You gonna suspend that kid?"

Alexa thought of Charlie, fourth grade, hair still blond and curly, refusing to ride the bus. "He'll get me again," he had pleaded. *Damn bullies.*

Her knees almost gave when the camera pivoted to Eileen Bowen, looking calm between two men at the front of the room. Her blazer was unbuttoned, revealing an ivory-colored blouse. She made a motion with her hand, and Alexa saw that her nails were polished red. "Group sessions can actually backfire, giving the child who bullies more power. Our plan is to counsel Nick and Ian separately. We're taking this matter seriously."

"I'll go straight to their house, see that something gets done," the man raged, "because you don't have the balls."

The man sitting to Eileen's right broke in. "I strongly advise against that. We've got a prevention plan…"

The door to the back room opened, and Constable Blume stuck his head out. He looked surprised to see Alexa. "DI Katakana says to turn it down."

Unger stopped the tape. "The ex-husband is here," he whispered to Alexa.

Alexa pulled out a chair and sat.

The door was a quarter open. DI Katakana was out of sight. Constable Blume sat down across a table from Paul Bowen, whose back was to Alexa. She heard DI Katakana ask, "So the last time you saw Ms. Bowen was at the Arrowtown Bakery? Was she alone or with someone?"

"Alone, but other people were in the shop."

"How did she seem?" DI Katakana asked.

"Busy. Highfalutin. The usual."

The husband wasn't waxing poetic about his missing ex. Alexa watched his foot jiggle. Constable Blume was busy taking notes, his eyes on his pad.

"Have you seen your ex-wife since?" the DI asked.

"Not since the bakery."

"You might have forgotten another encounter? Maybe yesterday?"

He scratched his head vigorously. "I didn't see Eileen yesterday."

"So the last time you saw or spoke to Ms. Bowen was early May? A Tuesday, you think?" The DI came into view. She stood next to Constable Blume and placed her hands on the table, leaning forward. "And this meeting was happenstance?"

Mr. Bowen edged back. "That's right. We live in the same small town. Something has happened to her, and this is a waste of time. You should be out looking."

"It's not a waste of time if it helps us find her." She leaned closer to Constable Blume's notebook and seemed to read from it. Then she looked up. "Were you ever aggressive with your wife, Mr. Bowen?"

"Never."

"Where were you yesterday afternoon?"

The DI was treating Mr. Bowen as a suspect instead of an ally. Alexa wondered if there was evidence to support this.

"I manage Millhouse Resort." His voice sounded resigned. "I was filling in for yet another waitperson who didn't show up for his shift. That's where I was when the school called."

"You were married eleven years, right? Did the breakup set you back a few? Misty Tandy said you picked the short stick in the dissolution proceedings."

The back of Mr. Bowen's neck colored. "Misty should mind her own business. She's always been jealous of everything Eileen has. We split the assets evenly. There wasn't a lot. The house was in her name. "

"Are you talking about the house Eileen lives in now?" the DI asked.

"No. The one we shared. She moved, bought the Plum Tree Terrace house flat out with the proceeds and her inheritance. I can't afford a house here, that's for sure. I could have asked for spousal maintenance, but it's too humiliating that Eileen out-earns me."

"So she bought a house and a new life? Resentful, are you?"

Alexa didn't blame him if he was.

"You're pestering me with wanker questions." Mr. Bowen pushed back from the table. Constable Blume jumped to his feet.

DI Katakana said evenly, "Jealous of the new boyfriend, are you? Young jet boat captain?"

Alexa heard him sigh. "Eileen is making a fool of herself with that guy, and I'm trying to help. What is it you want from me?"

Silence followed. It was a good interview technique, but Mr. Bowen didn't crack, and the DI terminated the interview. Mr. Bowen opened the door and crossed the room. He wore the same frumpy jeans from the day before. He whipped open the door and left the center.

"What do you think, Constable Blume?" the DI asked.

"Think he sounds sincere, Senior. I'll check with the staff at Millhouse. See if they confirm."

The DI emerged from the back room. "Ms. Glock? What are you doing here?"

"I thought I'd check in. See if you needed anything."

She looked irritated. "Corpus delicti. No one can be charged with a crime if there is no evidence a crime has been committed. Soon as we have a crime scene, I'll need you."

"Was there anything on Ms. Bowen's computer?"

The DI frowned. "Leave the investigating to the police, eh?"

The comment poked Alexa in the gut, but she lifted her chin and squared her shoulders. "There's another reason I'm here. To report some bones."

DI Katakana's face colored as Alexa described the dig and S1 and S2's conditions. She left out the hungry ghost part. "Dr. McKenzie, the forensic pathologist, is conducting an inquest and asked that I let you know."

"We don't have time for old bones when a woman's life is at stake."

A man rapped on the center door and then stuck his head in. "New Zealand Radio 1. I have some questions?"

"Press conference tomorrow at noon," DI Katakana said. "At Arrowtown Primary. Close the door, Constable."

Before Constable Blume could react, the man stepped inside. "Are Arrowtown residents safe tonight?"

"There are extra patrols on the streets, but people should lock their doors and leave on garden lights as a caution. Now out," she snapped.

The man opened his mouth, but Constable Blume stepped toward him. The reporter left.

"Bloodsuckers," Unger said.

Alexa pushed her notes toward him and gathered her belongings. "I'll head to the lab in the morning and then over to the coroner's office." *As if anyone asked.*

The DI frowned again. "That's all for now, Ms. Glock."

Constable Blume avoided her eyes as he held the door open. "Goodnight, miss."

Chapter Twenty-Four

FRIDAY NIGHT

The billowing wind felt good on her hot cheeks; her dismissal had been mortifying. As a traveling forensic, her duties varied from case to case and police department to police department. In this case, the DI considered her "on retainer" and not a team member.

No biggie. She'd do her job, keep her nose down.

But she didn't like being swept to the fringe.

She stalked across Buckingham Street and cut through the alley, passing the Blue Door bar—the place that used to be an opium den and then a cold storage room. Sometimes for bodies. It's where Ana had told her the sad story of the corpse ship, sinking with all the exhumed miners' remains. She wished Ana was here now and that they could drink a beer together. She was tempted to go in solo, but at the same time, she was exhausted. Her early morning run felt like two years ago. The other end of the alley spilled her out onto Arrow Street. It was suddenly quiet, just the wind riffling through the trees and the crunch of leaves beneath her boots. She speed-walked the empty uneven sidewalk, squeezing the cottage key into the flesh of her hand. Houses were set back, behind hedges, no streetlights. A dog barked. She looked over her shoulder and couldn't shake the feeling she was being watched. This whole town, surrounded by mountains, skeletal remains, a missing woman. It was crowding in on her.

The mini crime kit slid off her shoulder. She jerked it back into the right position and picked up her pace.

Plum Tree Terrace huddled in darkness. She checked over her shoulder, but it was too dark to see anything. She used the flashlight on her phone to shine the way. Prospector's Cottage was the second home on the left. Why hadn't she left a porch light on?

The phone flashlight dimmed as she aimed it at the door-knob. Her hand shook as she fed the key into the lock and turned. Her phone vibrated and died as the door swung open.

Dead battery.

She scrabbled for the hall light switch, flicked it up. Nothing. Dammit. She tried the switch again—up, down, up, down. No go. Had the power gone out?

She rummaged through the mini kit for her Maglite. The steady beam didn't let her down.

A draft of air ruffled her messy hair as she walked toward the kitchen. She fumbled for the kitchen light. Flicked it up. Power. Her relief turned to fear. The door leading to the patio was wide open. Like a mouth. Papers littered the kitchen floor and dining table. A gust of air pushed another paper off the table. The sheet of paper landed at her feet.

Was someone in the house?

She clutched the Maglite—she could use it as a weapon—and then froze. Sound funneled into her ears. Her breath. The refrigerator. The radiator. The wind. She strained to hear over the amplification. No sound of footsteps. No creak of floor-board. She thought of running out of the cottage and back to the police station.

But wait. What if in their haste, Pam or Ana had left the kitchen door unlocked and the wind had pushed it open? She remembered Pam wrestling it closed when Alexa had stopped by at lunchtime. When Shelby found the hat. Pam had made a comment about old houses.

The sheet of paper at her feet was the last article she'd printed from the archives: DEAD CHINAMEN: EXTENSIVE EXHUMATION. Other articles and photos were scattered like fallen leaves. She'd left the folder on the table at lunchtime.

She crossed to the door and turned on the outdoor light. Treetops swayed. The clothesline, empty, jingled. Nothing else. She studied the lock. It was a simple thumb-turn on the inside and a keyhole on the outside. Nothing high-tech. She tugged the door closed and tried the doorknob. It opened. She turned the lock. It wouldn't open.

The lock worked.

She looked at the linoleum, scuffed with age. There were no muddy footprints.

Her heart raced as she passed through the lounge and into the two downstairs bedrooms, turning on lights. Just to take a look-see. Beds made, everything tidy. The closets were so tiny that only Shelby could fit in them. She made herself whisk open the shower curtain in the only bathroom. Coast clear.

Conclusion: the door hadn't been properly closed and the wind had pushed it open.

She walked through the dim hallway and made sure the front door was locked. Then she stood at the bottom of the stairs. Her legs didn't believe her conclusion and refused to budge. She coaxed herself up the steps. Her little bedroom was undisturbed, and the larger crime kit was still in the closet. She plugged her phone into the charger and sank onto the spare twin bed. As soon as the phone had juice, she called Ana. "It's me." In the background she heard Shelby singing that "Baby Shark" song. "I just got back to the cottage, and the back door was wide open."

Ana's voice went high. "Are you okay? Did someone break in?"

She took a deep breath, let it go. "I'm okay and nothing is disturbed. Did you or your mom lock the back door before you left?"

"I didn't. Let me ask Mum."

Muffled sounds followed. Alexa rose and crossed to the window. The porch light gouged a semicircle out of the dark. Her foot was still wet from slipping into the creek, so she took off her boots and socks, and hung a sock over the radiator to dry.

"Alexa? Mum locked it after you left at lunchtime. But, well, I opened it to get that hat she'd left on the porch. You asked me to, remember? I don't know if I locked it. I was nervous."

"That's okay. It must have been the wind; it's kicking up."

"Have you called the police?"

"I don't think I'll bother them. They've got a lot going on."

"But what about Hammer?"

"I have doubts that Earl Hammer is even in Arrowtown. Anyway, I checked the house. There's no sign anyone was in here."

Ana sighed. "I could come get you. We're only thirty minutes away."

"No. I'm okay."

"Any news on the principal?"

"She's still missing. I helped with a search along Bush Creek, but we didn't find anything." Where was she? Alexa wondered. *Was she alive?* She changed the subject. "What did you do this afternoon?"

"We took a ride on the old steamship. It's been plying Lake Wakatipu since gold rush days." She hushed Shelby. "There were hardly any roads, so gold was transported from Arrowtown to Queenstown and loaded onto the steamer. It sailed across the lake to Kingston, where there was a train station."

The past and present knock knocking heads. Again.

"Shelby was bored until we discovered the man shoveling coal into the fire."

Alexa laughed. Probably louder than she needed. Nerves.

"Can you stop by the dig in the morning?" Ana asked. "To make sure everything's okay? I called Mr. Sun and told him the bones had been removed. No need for his vigil. But we still have the one tent up and equipment in it."

Alexa promised she would, and they said goodbye. She pulled on clean warm socks, went downstairs, checked the locks again, and boiled water for tea in the kitchen. Not that she was a tea drinker, but she craved warmth.

She found a package of Cookie Bears—probably meant for Shelby—and ate three. She picked up the papers and pictures scattered on the floor and tucked them back in the file. Earl Hammer's unrepentant face looked at her from one article. The archivist had given her articles about him for some reason. She stuffed it and two others in the trash.

He didn't deserve the time of day. Well, night.

She took the tea to the lounge, closed the drapes, and chose the DEAD CHINAMEN article to read. She curled on the saggy couch, an afghan draped around her shoulders, and read about ten "aged Celestials" who traveled to different graveyards to exhume their countrymen. The article was written in 1902. They carried out their task in multiple Otago graveyards: Skippers, Macraes, Palmerston, Drybread, Lawrence, and—yes—Arrowtown. Townspeople threw rocks and screamed insults at the men about "Desecrating God's House" and "Dirty Chinks."

One exhumation was described in gory detail. The miner had been dead five years. According to the reporter, his clothes showed little deterioration. His skeleton was examined bone by bone. Any ligaments that clung to the bones were removed.

Alexa forgot to be scared. Then the bones were laid on wire mesh suspended over a fire. An elder tended it, turning the bones with a stick or his fingers.

She pulled the afghan tighter and wondered how she would have reacted to the ghoulish sight. Hopefully, she would have shown tolerance and respect, but she was a product of her culture like everyone else. She hoped she would have at least let the old men carry out their mission in peace.

The article said that once the bones were thoroughly dried, they were placed on the grass to cool. Another elder sorted the cooled bones in batches, wrapped them in calico, and boxed them up. The deceased's pigtail, like a ribbon, was placed on top.

Chapter Twenty-Five

She finished the tea and couldn't stop herself. But it was only nine o'clock, and she decided to learn more about Earl Hammer. Just in case. She pulled the articles out of the trash, rechecked the doors, and headed back to the couch.

TOWN ON EDGE

Police divers and Army metal detector specialists are searching the Arrow River and Trail for vital clues in the murder inquiry of Cindy Mulligan, who was bludgeoned as she jogged on the Arrow River Trail and dumped in the river.

"We are tracking the movements of several suspects," DI Michael Unger said. "Residents should take caution and lock their doors."

Arrowtownians have taken heed. Quaint Buckingham Street, usually abustle with locals and tourists, was empty Tuesday afternoon. Several businesses were closed, and Don Mosley of The Gold Shoppe said he had only had two customers. "Foreigners. They didn't know anything about the poor girl's murder. I told them to stay out of the bush."

"I hope they're checking her ex-boyfriends," said Jane Besoms, owner of Tranquil B&B.

"He's still out there," a maths teacher at Arrowtown Primary said. "The dogs are gone begging for walkies."

"This is not the kind of place where something like this happens," Tiny Settles, librarian at Arrowtown Community Library, said. "We've canceled Leaf Identification Tramp and Plunket Play Group as a precaution."

Anyone with information regarding Cindy Mulligan's murder is urged to contact the Queenstown Police at 111.

Alexa thought of how DI Katakana had told the reporter the same thing DI Unger had said twenty-five years earlier about residents locking up. She popped up to make sure the windows were latched. The next article was dated a month after Cindy Mulligan's murder.

FINGERPRINT NABS MURDERER

On 26 February Cynthia Justina Mulligan, 31, an accountant at Craig, Walker & Sons in Frankton, was found dead in the Arrow River by a gold prospector. She had been reported missing two days prior by Stephen Walker, head accountant at Walker & Sons. The police searched her house, but nothing was amiss.

The Queenstown's forensic pathologist concluded Mulligan died of blunt force trauma to the skull. "She was already dead when she was thrown in the river."

Under the command of Detective Inspector Michael Unger, scores of police combed the town and woods for the culprit. In the ensuing two weeks, a host of Arrowtown residents were questioned and fingerprinted. "Nothing linked. Leads fizzled, one by one," DI Unger said. "Then I had a tip about the drifter."

An itinerant field worker, Earl Hammer of Christchurch, had been staying at Strike Rich Holiday Park and working

*at Clotilde Winery. He left the area before Mulligan's body
was discovered. He had no prior convictions.*

*Sergeant Nick Hewell, Christchurch Police Department,
brought him in for questioning. His fingerprints matched a
single preserved print left on the Discman portable music
device that belonged to Ms. Mulligan and was found on the
Arrow River Trail. He was arrested.*

*DI Unger is hailed a hero by Arrowtownians. "We're safe
again," said Gayle Frost, a Lakes District Museum volunteer
and acquaintance of Cindy Mulligan.*

*Hammer admitted bunking at the Strike Rich Holiday
Park at the time of the murder but maintains his innocence.*

Alexa wondered what type of fingerprint Hammer had. She
hoped he had something plebeian like a loop. The last article
was published after Hammer was imprisoned.

MOTHER CLAIMS SON INNOCENT

*Helena Hammer, mother of Earl Hammer, the man con-
victed of killing Cynthia Mulligan by bashing her head with a
rock and disposing her body in the Arrow River, has released
a public statement:*

*"I am sorry for Cindy Mulligan's parents and sister. It's
terrible what happened to her and them.*

*"That said, the wrong man was arrested for the murder.
My Earl did not kill Cindy Mulligan. Just because he was
in Arrowtown at the time of the crime does not make him
guilty. Earl never met her. He has been made a scapegoat
so the police could close the case. My son is a victim, too,
just because he's poor and don't have much schooling. The
system has it out for us."*

Earl Hammer is currently serving a sentence of life imprisonment with a non-parole period of at least 10 years.

What mother would believe her son was evil? How could you reconcile that? Alexa shook her weary head. She couldn't take any more Earl Hammer and chose the letter from a Chinese woman to her gold mining sons so far away.

七月一日

THE FIRST OF JULY

1887

———

Sons Fang Virtue and Chang Prosper,

Your cousin Rising Sun sent home two sovereigns to his mother, safely received, and cousin Tiger's Eye sent home three, safely received.

Why have I not received any gold letters in so many moons?

These are words to let you know in the sixth moon of this year your father left this world. We buried him in his lucky spot on Mofu Mountain, the place of his esteemed birth. Your sisters and brother are in distress. I fear they may die of hunger. The drought brought no harvest. Rice is dear. Your mother feels frail and helpless. I fear if you continue to live in a foreign land, sending no word, no sovereigns, your aged mother may be like a candle in the wind and extinguish.

I pray one thousand times over that, on receipt of this letter, you will send me a letter and sovereigns. If not, I fear you will drink a bitter regret into your soul.

MaMa

Chapter Twenty-Six

SATURDAY MORNING

God is Watching You was spray-painted in red on the tent. Alexa stumbled to the other side. *Wrath of God* dripped like blood.

She'd looked over her shoulder several times during the ten-minute walk to the cemetery. The wide-open door last night, plus her news feed this morning reported Hammer hadn't been found. He was at large, and the public was urged to take caution.

Now this.

She scanned the cemetery. Whoever vandalized the tent could be hiding and watching her reaction—maybe from behind the apple tree or a tall tombstone or crouched below the stone wall. The early morning mist didn't help; it slithered across the ground, enshrouding monuments and swallowing tombstones. A hare hopped from behind the tent, so large it looked carnivorous.

Her greenstone pendant heated up against her sternum as she called the police. She turned in a slow circle, certain she was being watched.

Constable Blume arrived in a whirl of lights and siren. He jogged across the cemetery, found the gap in the rock wall, and crossed through. "Why is the tent over here?" he huffed.

"It's where the remains were discovered." Alexa looked to where the other grave had been filled in. Mist obscured the view. "There was another tent over that way, but Dr. Luckenbaugh had it removed."

His Adam's apple rose and lowered. "There were more bodies there?"

"One more skeleton."

He looked at the tent. "Is it still in there?"

It came out in a little-boy soprano. Alexa choked back a laugh. "The skeletons have been moved to the morgue."

"Who were they?"

He must not have been listening last night when she described the skeletons. She noticed he had a shaving nick on his chin and imagined how he'd cussed and stanched it. "We think one was a Chinese gold miner. The other one might be a European settler."

He scanned the grass. "I don't see wheel marks. They must have walked."

"Might have been just one person," Alexa pointed out.

"Was anything disturbed inside the tent?"

"I haven't looked. I didn't want to touch anything until someone was here. You know, as a witness." She had grabbed her crime kit as she left the cottage. What if the bones in the morgue pointed to murder? There might be evidence in the fill-dirt, and she wanted to be prepared. She had made sure both doors were secured and locked.

She took out gloves and booties.

Constable Blume photographed the graffiti with his phone. "Doesn't qualify as a hate crime. Nothing inflammatory or threatening. Maybe get charged with property destruction," he said. "Too bad there's no security cameras here."

Alexa had already taken photos and sent them to Ana.

The constable slipped on gloves and shifted the flap open. Alexa held her breath as she looked over his shoulder. The interior was a dim jumble of overturned tables, smashed light bulbs, and a disarray of tools. The dirt Ana had wanted sieved was heaped back on the grave. The tarp was strewn aside as if it had been jerked from under the fill-dirt like a tablecloth. A shovel had been driven into the middle of the grave dirt like a knife.

Anger, Alexa thought. It looked like someone had acted out of anger.

"Has anyone been hanging around here, harassing you?" the constable asked.

The cast of cemetery characters paraded across her mind: Mr. Sun and his friend from the New Zealand Chinese Association, Mr. Howard of the DIY coffin kits, the taciturn man who had excavated the graves, the reporter at Cindy Mulligan's grave and her cameraman, the older lady with the plastic rain hat. What had she said? Something like God doesn't want you digging up the dead. Chill bumps broke out on her arms. "A woman was here yesterday. She complained about the dig. Dr. Luckenbaugh said she tried to get in the tent."

"What's the woman's name?"

"I don't know. She had gray hair and wore a clear rain bonnet thingy."

"A granny tagger." The constable harrumphed. "I'll file a report, but you know we've got a lot going on."

"It's more than graffiti. Whoever did it trashed the tent and might have compromised evidence." She heard a siren in the distance and thought of the searchers gathering for another go. "Any news about Ms. Bowen?"

"No sightings of Ms. Bowen or Hammer overnight. We heard from Vodafone. Ms. Bowen's mobile was active up until Thursday at 3:10 p.m. The last coordinate was a kilometer from Plum Tree Terrace."

A little over half a mile, Alexa converted. "What does that mean?"

He narrowed his light blue eyes, possibly aware DI Katakana

didn't consider her a team member, but his excitement took over. "Maybe her battery went dead or her phone was turned off. Or it might mean the phone was destroyed. Maybe thrown in the river. Seems to me…"

Alexa waited as he formed his thoughts.

"…that she wasn't far from her house when something happened to her. Her last text was to the boyfriend. Something like 'See ya Saturday night, heart emoji.' So she wasn't planning to see him the evening she went missing. That jibes with what he said."

A wave of anger washed over Alexa again. She wanted to be at a team meeting instead of left on the outs. *Concentrate on what you can do,* she told herself. "I'll dust the tent flaps and take a sample of the paint. Can you wrap the shovel?"

He checked the time on his phone. "I gotta be at Queenstown Airport at nine. A couple bigwigs from Auckland are flying in to help with the case." He straightened his shoulders and sucked in his stomach. "It's my job to pick them up and brief them."

Bruce hijacked her mind. He headed the major crimes unit in Auckland. Was a missing woman and an escaped parolee a major crime? Bruce didn't know she was in Arrowtown. Well, unless gossip spread from Auckland Forensic Service Center across the street to Central Police Department. It was possible, since the two of them had been seen together, out and about. But mostly they'd been behind closed doors. Bedroom doors. "Do you know who you're picking up?" she asked.

"One of them is the head of Missing Persons Unit. Don't know the other."

She half-hoped it would be Bruce and half-hoped it wouldn't. Her mind segued to the test on S2's molar that she was scheduled to perform. "Can you drop me off at the Queenstown Medical Center on your way?"

"Not really on the way."

"Thanks," she said. "I appreciate it."

He blushed and jogged off to his patrol car. Had she scared him off? She was relieved when he returned with two large paper evidence bags to top and tail the shovel.

Conscious of the time, she completed her work in a rush and left, the tent innards still a mess. Constable Blume whisked her to the medical center. There was only one car in the lot. "Nah, yeah, I'm off," Constable Blume said. He left her standing on the curb with her awkwardly wrapped shovel protruding from under one arm and the crime kit at her feet.

She texted Sally, who met her at the door. "Your firm is keeping me busy," Sally said. She looked less professional this morning, in jeans, a sweater, and tennis shoes. "What's with the shovel?"

"Evidence. I need it locked up while I conduct the test."

Once the shovel was secured, Alexa followed Sally to the locker room. It was time to disrobe, suit up, get masked and disinfected.

Sally opened a locker for her. Her Saturday-self was more relaxed. "I've been reading about the process. Did you know strontium is named after a tiny town in Scotland?"

"In North Carolina we have a Barium Springs." It was hard letting go of "God is Watching You" to focus on strontium isotope analysis, but in the end her fingers holding the molar were steady and her focus keen. Sally promised to rush the results. "I'll take the DNA sample; you get going," she said.

While Alexa and the shovel waited for an Uber, she called Ana about the vandalism.

"I saw the pictures," Ana said.

"There's damage inside the tent too. Stuff scattered and the grave half full of dirt."

"Do you think it's teenagers?"

"'God is Watching You' is a weird tag. What about that woman who complained about the dig? The one who tried to get into the tent. What did she say?"

"'Leave the dead in peace,' something like that. A lot of people think it's wrong to dig up the dead, but it's hard to imagine her spraying the tent in the middle of the night, especially with Earl Hammer loose."

Alexa agreed. "A constable came, took pictures, filed a report."

"It's a criminal offense to modify or destroy an archaeological site."

"I've got a sample of the spray paint and fingerprints from the tent flap. Your shovel too. I'll dust the handle at the lab."

"That's my favorite shovel," Ana said.

"I can eliminate your prints. See what might be left."

"I'm heading to the morgue as soon as I get the monkey situated. Can you meet me there at eleven?"

Alexa assumed the monkey was Shelby. She waved at a little green electric hatchback. She was worried the shovel wouldn't fit. "My Uber is here. Gotta go. I'll see you there."

It was a ten-minute glide to the police station. The female driver looked at the shovel suspiciously and didn't initiate conversation. After she dropped her off, Alexa stepped back and studied the Queenstown Police Station. It looked like a white stone manor house with Swiss chalet shutters.

She stood a moment longer to get her bearings. She felt like seaweed, pushed and pulled by squirrelly currents: Chinese miner and missing women. Escaped parolee and vandalized tent. A life at stake was most important. She hoped the evidence she had gathered would help find Eileen Bowen.

Three cops in full uniform glanced at the wrapped shovel tucked under her arm when she entered the lobby. She grinned: shoveled and dangerous instead of armed and dangerous. She gave her card to the sergeant at the information desk. His eyes landed on the shovel. "Digging into crime, eh?"

"I'm meeting Leigh Walker in the lab."

He called to verify. "Says she's supposed to meet you, eh?" He nodded, pulled his pants up over his large belly, and pointed toward the hallway. "Through there."

The lab tech waved to her from a doorway. "*Kia ora.* I'm Leigh." Her unbuttoned lab coat revealed an orange Jungle Juice T-shirt. A wide-eyed lion was sipping something. Alexa guessed Jungle Juice was an energy drink. She also thought Leigh, whose light-blond hair was pulled into a super-tight ponytail, looked seventeen. Alexa introduced herself and stepped in.

There was always a moment of tingly anticipation when she first saw a lab. Ideally, a crime lab had separate spaces—rooms even—for different functions: toxicology, fingerprints, firearms, trace evidence. That's how Auckland Forensic Service Center was. Not so here; everything seemed crammed into one room. She lifted the crime kit and shovel. "Where can I unload?"

Leigh cleared a desk space by stacking folders. "Cheers. Here you go."

Alexa leaned the shovel against the wall and set the kit on the desk. She washed her hands, slipped on gloves, and removed the fingerprint cards and a vial of paint. It had been tricky lifting prints from the tent flap. The polyethylene material had been shiny and slippery. She'd used black powder, a feather brush, and lifting tape. The results had been a mishmash of smeary partials. She didn't think any would be of use. She had higher hopes for the shovel handle. She filled out the custody of evidence forms, and Leigh signed off, eyeing the shovel. "Does it factor in with the missing woman?" she asked.

"I don't think so. These are from a vandalism case at the

cemetery. Let's log them in and then see where you are with the evidence I sent in yesterday." The haul had been paltry: the woolen hat from the creek, fingerprints from the Smart car door handle, and the two drink glasses from Eileen's sink. Leigh had said on the phone that she'd already fumed the glasses.

Leigh signed for the transfer. "I'll check them into the property room and get what we need."

While she waited for Leigh, Alexa studied a portable fuming chamber on a counter. She located the heating tray for the super glue pack. All the tech had to do was set the glassware inside the chamber, shut the door, insert a super glue pack onto the heating element, and press PROCESS. The heat would cause a polymerization reaction which would bond to the oils left behind in the latent prints.

Alexa thought of her middle school science fair. Her "Chamber of Secrets" shoebox had consisted of an electric coffee cup warmer, cotton balls dabbed with super glue, and a plastic Hardee's cup. She had placed the cotton balls on the cup warmer. The heat vaporized the super glue, which bonded to the fingerprints she'd planted on the cup and hardened, forming a visible, white structure.

Brilliant.

She had expected applause, but her battery-operated fan hadn't been strong enough to mask the released fumes, and Ms. Clarke had evacuated the gym for thirty minutes. Eddie Fronczak won the blue ribbon for Sailboat Stabilization. How had wine corks, toothpicks, and a tub of water beaten the miracle of cyanoacrylate?

This fuming chamber had a fume evacuation button. When Leigh reappeared, Alexa asked, "Where are the glasses?"

"In the property room." Leigh handed over two envelopes. "These are the prints I lifted from them."

The first envelope, when Alexa broke the seal, held two

backing cards. The first was labeled Sample 1, A: *t* . Alexa knew *t* stood for thumbprint. Sample 1, B contained three prints labeled *i*, *m*, and *r*. Index finger, middle finger, and ring finger. Lifting tape was smoothed flat against each card, sealing the finger marks. The little fingers were missing. Maybe the holder of the glass raised his or her pinkie while drinking, or maybe used the little finger to support the glass from below.

The other envelope held the samples from the second glass, which were labeled accordingly. Alexa took out her magnifying glass and studied the spiral-like pattern of a thumbprint. "Have you scanned them into AFIS?"

Leigh had buttoned her lab coat and looked more professional without the Jungle Juice lion staring out. "I already got the results. Can you verify?"

All results had to be verified by more than one examiner. Leigh knew to walk away. Doing so minimized bias. If Leigh thought a print was a good candidate, and they were sitting shoulder to shoulder, Alexa might agree with her. Alexa recalled a study in which examiners were told a suspect confessed. This influenced their findings. With Leigh busy doing something else, Alexa opened the file.

The Automated Fingerprint Identification System reported possible candidates in descending order. There were four. Alexa homed in on the top. She studied the print, using the software to mark it. Afterwards, she pulled up the print Leigh had lifted from the glass and followed the same process. She was comfortable they were from the same source. She quickly checked the others; they didn't qualify.

Only then did she glance at the name attached to the print on file: Eileen Bowen. "Makes sense the prints are hers," Alexa said.

"It's the same with the other glass," Leigh said. "They also have her prints on them."

Alexa left dishes and glasses in her sink too. It was embarrassing when Natalie cleaned up after her. But these results didn't get them anywhere. "What about the car door handle prints?"

"I haven't scanned them yet."

"I'll do it." Alexa thought back to yesterday, remembering how Constable Blume had looked at her strangely when she'd dusted the car with a giant cotton ball. Now, she scanned the prints one at a time, oriented each, added a filter to enhance the images, pressed Send, and twirled in the chair.

She thought of her Toyota as she waited. No one but she touched her car door handle that she was aware of except the guy at Cheap Tyres. She'd replaced well-worn tires two months ago. She anticipated that the prints would be Eileen's.

She stopped mid-twirl. Expectations were dangerous. They could lead an examiner to make incorrect conclusions and impartial decisions. Maybe Earl Hammer or the ex-husband had grabbed the handle and jerked Eileen out.

AFIS responded with a candidate list on the lower door handle prints. She quickly determined the prints were Eileen's.

But prints from above the handle belonged to someone else. Alexa did a double take. Misty Tandy was number one on the candidate list. She vacated the seat and let Leigh check the list.

Leigh reached the same conclusion. "Who is Misty Tandy?"

"The missing woman's sister."

Leigh pulled her ponytail tighter. "My sister and I shared a car when we were coming up. She was cheap as chips, always leaving it empty of petrol."

Misty and Eileen weren't teenagers, but Alexa supposed there were reasons Eileen might lend her sister her car. Alexa decided to inform DI Katakana.

The DI answered her phone with, "What?"

Alexa stammered her news. "I dusted Ms. Bowen's car door for fingerprints and some of them belong to her sister. Maybe you should ask Ms. Tandy why."

The DI was quiet for a moment. Alexa heard muffled voices, the cackle of someone's laugh. Finally DI Katakana said, "I'll send someone to find her. She's on one of the search teams that just left."

Alexa felt emboldened. "Any updates?"

"Neither hide nor hair of either Hammer or Bowen." The DI hung up without saying goodbye. Heat radiated from Alexa's core. She ripped her gloves off and tossed them. That job in Abertay was looking better and better. She took a deep breath and turned to Leigh. "Let's examine that hat now. Is it dry?"

"It dried overnight." She went to fetch it.

Alexa pulled out her phone as she waited. It was ten fifteen. She still had time before she was to meet Ana at the morgue at eleven.

They slipped on fresh gloves, sterilized a workstation, and unwrapped the hat. The red poppy applique looked wilted against the gray wool. "It wasn't home knit," Leigh said. "The tag says Great Kiwi Yarns. One hundred percent merino wool. How will you take a DNA sample?"

People left skin cells behind on everything they touched with bare hands. Alexa was banking on the possibility that Eileen's abductor had contact with the hat. She closed her eyes, imagining the scene. Eileen abducted in the woods. Screaming. Thrashing. The hat coming off. The assailant throwing it in the creek. Two seconds of contact was all it took. But where was Eileen?

"Ms. Glock? What method?"

Her eyes flew open. "Tape-lifting will be quickest."

Leigh found a roll of Scotch tape. Alexa tore off a two-inch piece. "Have a vial ready," she instructed. She pressed the tape along the headband area, plucked it up, and repeated it twenty-five times, counting silently, hoping skin cells would be picked up via the adhesive. She knew the repeated pressure increased the chances of extracting more touch DNA. Then she placed the tape into the tube, capped and labeled it, and instructed Leigh to send it off.

"All good," Leigh said.

Alexa glanced at her phone again. Ten forty. If she left now, she'd be on time to meet Ana. It would mean trusting Leigh to dust the shovel for prints. It wasn't a hard job, and the cemetery vandalism wasn't a top priority. "Will you process the shovel handle for prints? I've got a date with a skeleton."

Chapter Twenty-Seven

Alexa had hoped to walk from the police station to the hospital morgue, but the Lakes District Hospital wasn't located in Queenstown.

"Yeah nah," the Uber driver said. "Hospital is in Frankton."

Queenstown, busy with tourists, road work, and REI-type shops, flashed by out the car window. Alexa patted the crime kit next to her and leaned back in the seat. The driver, a young man with multiple piercings, was annoyingly talkative. "Must be tourist, your accent and all."

"No. I work with the police."

"They've got the cadaver dogs out now in Arrowtown. Do you know why?"

"No." And if she did, she wouldn't say.

"When SAR switches from tracker dogs to cadaver dogs, you know the police know something."

Alexa wondered if it was true.

"Saw the missing woman's husband on TV begging for information. Looked desperate."

Ex-husband.

"That Hammer dude? Bad to the bone." He swerved to miss a pothole. "The parole board up there in Christchurch is responsible. They never…"

Her phone ringing silenced him. She fumbled it out and answered.

"Hi, Lexi. It's me. Happy birthday."

Her heart melted at the sound of her brother's voice. He was the only one who called her Lexi. "Charlie?"

"Who else ?"

Did he mean who else would wish her a happy birthday? *Probably no one.* "My birthday isn't until tomorrow."

"What day is it?" he asked.

"Saturday. May 27th."

"I can't keep the time difference straight. Happy early birthday."

Alexa's mind flew to Asheville in late spring. Mountain laurel and rhododendron. Leaves the color of mint. "What time is it there?"

"It's almost seven. Mel is getting supper ready. Sweet and sour tempeh and quinoa salad."

Poor Charlie. "What are Benny and Noah doing?"

"It's Ben, not Benny. That's what he wants to be called. I told you that. He came home from soccer practice in tears. Said this bigger kid, Michael Bennett, tripped him twice on the field. He's taking a shower."

Benny being bullied? "What are you going to do about it?"

"We've talked to the coach. He'll keep an eye out. What are you doing for your birthday?"

"Maybe you should talk to the kid's parents."

She heard her brother sigh from eight-five hundred miles away. "We can handle it."

"Sign the boys up for kickboxing."

"Advice from an absentee aunt. Really, Lexi?"

Ouch. The driver pulled up in front of the hospital. "Um, Charlie, can I call you later? I'm working."

"Easier said than done, with the time difference," he replied.

"But guess what?" Alexa said. "I'm in gold mining territory, and there's still gold in the river. I'll tell you about it when I call."

"Happy birthday and all," he said, and disconnected.

She missed Charlie. And Benny and Noah. She wanted to wring this Michael Bennett's skinny little neck. Not that she would ever hurt a child. She set her phone on vibrate, in case DI Katakana needed her, and thanked the Uber driver.

In the hospital lobby Ana enveloped her in a hug. "I'm glad you're safe. The back door of the cottage being open? I would have died."

Alexa stepped out of the embrace. "I'm sure it was the wind." *Ninety percent sure.*

Ana's braid was messy, and she had circles under her eyes. "Shelby kept waking up last night. Try sharing a bed with a four-year-old while listening to your mother snore."

No mother, no daughter, Alexa thought.

"Any news on the principal or Hammer?"

"No."

Ana made room for an orderly pushing a wheelchair. "It's strange to be in a hospital. I usually examine remains at a university or a warehouse. Alan got permission for us to lay out S2 in the autopsy suite."

"Alan?"

"Dr. McKenzie, the MD PhD. He said to get started."

The morgue was in the basement. They washed their hands and suited up in the anteroom: plastic aprons, masks, hair caps, and booties. Gloves last. Alexa peered through the glass. The skeleton was arranged in an anatomical position on a metal table near a sink, though there would be no need to wash away bodily fluids.

"Ready?" Ana asked.

"Ready." Alexa sniffed the air in the autopsy room; a whiff

of astringent mixed with something earthy, like the bowels of a cave.

Four boxes lined a shelf. The bulbous forehead of a skull was visible in the first box. Alexa walked closer and recognized the hole in S1's head. *Like a pickax strike.* The next box held pairs of femurs, tibias, fibulas, humeri, and ulnas.

"Those cartons hold S1's remains," Ana said. "Olivia and I worked hard to record each bone."

The earthy smell wasn't the bones themselves but the soil that had embedded in them.

Alexa left the boxes, adjusted her mask, and approached S2. The bare bones were face up instead of prone. The hollow eye sockets staring at the bright overhead light had a haunted frightened look. And feminine too. Alexa knew that was silly; she was projecting.

"I usually start with gender identification," Ana said, "but since the frame is small, I want to make sure we aren't dealing with a child or adolescent. Can you check if skeletal maturity has been reached?"

Teeth were the best way to tell if a skeleton had reached maturity before death. Alexa was glad to play a part, even though she knew Ana was capable of counting teeth. She lifted the mandible—the strongest bone of the face. She balanced it on one hand and used her dental probe to count the slightly yellowed teeth: there were fifteen. She looked up. "Did you extract the second left molar?"

Ana stood by the lower torso. "Yes. Dr. Weiner has it so she can run the tests."

A full count of adult teeth was thirty-two, including the wisdom teeth, which typically erupt between age seventeen to twenty-one. Their presence indicated skeletal maturity, though whether wisdom teeth indicated a person was wiser was debatable. Alexa replaced the mandible and counted the teeth in the upper jaw: sixteen. A complete set, minus the one in the lab. "Maturity was reached," she said.

"I thought so," Ana replied.

A slight discoloration on a tooth in the upper jaw caught Alexa's eye. She leaned closer and probed. "Wow."

"What is it?" Ana asked.

She checked again, and when sure, said, "The right second molar has a porcelain inlay."

"Does that mean the bones are modern?"

"No." Alexa straightened. "Porcelain has been around since the late 1800s. S2 had the means to seek dental treatment. The porcelain is in good condition. No cracks. I wonder if dental records exist?"

"You mean X-rays?"

"Radiographs weren't typical until the 1950s. I mean, you know, dental charts and notes. When I was in the archives, I saw an advertisement about a dentist visiting Arrowtown." She couldn't remember if the ad had included the dentist's name and place of business. "It listed porcelain as a treatment."

Ana laughed. "I like the way your mind works, Sherlock, but let's focus on what we can determine now, such as gender."

Alexa got out her camera, took photos of the mandible and jaw, and then stood back. "Okay," she said. "Sex away."

Ana laughed again. "Been so long I've forgotten what it's like." Her face sobered as she ran a finger over S2's broad fan-shaped hip bones. "Sex determination isn't binary. The options are female, probable female, intermediate, probable male, or male."

"A spectrum," Alexa said. The world of archaeology and forensics was changing with the times.

Ana maneuvered the two hip bones together. The broad fan-shaped bones looked like wings. "See how the subpubic angle is wide and long. This is for childbearing."

Alexa squirmed. Her childbearing days were numbered. It would be a relief when it was no longer an option that sometimes taunted her.

She thought of Shelby jumping into her arms, her sturdiness and trust.

Oh, brother.

Ana ran her finger along the lower ilium where the bone curved. "The sciatic notch is wide and V-shaped. That's characteristic of a female." She waited for Alexa to respond.

"Are you leaning toward 'female' versus 'probable female?'"

"Yep. Look at the concavity underneath the auricular surface." Ana ran her finger over an upper portion of the hip bone. "It isn't present in all females, but I can feel it here." Ana replaced the pelvic bones and moved to the head of the table. She stared into the empty eye sockets.

Alexa knew she was assessing the skull for gender characteristics.

"The eye orbits are slightly rounded." She ran a finger across the golden-hued brow. "Smooth. Slender. I conclude S2 is female, and we determined in situ that she was most likely of European ancestry."

Alexa eyed the pelvis again. "Can you tell if she gave birth?"

Ana followed her gaze. "Electron microscopy might provide clues. Concentrations of calcium, phosphorus, magnesium, and sodium vary whether a female has given birth or not."

She didn't understand everything Ana was saying, but Alexa loved a fellow geek.

"Hello, hello," said a male voice. "Sorry I'm late."

Alexa jumped. The forensic pathologist loomed behind her. He was taller than she recalled. Six two or three. When she'd last seen him, he'd been crawling along S2's grave.

"No worries, Alan," Ana said. "You remember Ms. Glock?

We've determined our remains are that of a female at skeletal maturity, probably European ancestry. Teeth tests are pending. We haven't gotten further than that."

"Female, eh? Like we suspected." He circled the remains, gloved hands clasped behind his back. "I love a historic mystery. Any indications of age?"

"She has her wisdom teeth, and there isn't much wear," Alexa said. "She has a porcelain inlay, and it's in good shape."

"Dental care, eh?"

"There aren't obvious signs of arthritis. The cranial sutures are still visible, but fading," Ana said. "I'd estimate thirty to forty years old."

His bushy eyebrows rose. "Female, mature, possibly European, could afford dental treatment, buried facedown, outside the cemetery grounds. Why, we wonder? Maybe as punishment or to humiliate her."

"For what?" Alexa asked.

He shrugged. "I've read a lot about the colonial days. Infidelity, pregnancy, thievery. Maybe she was a prostitute. Or maybe she stole someone's gold. There were a few female gold miners, and miners in general were a rough and tumble lot. Suicide is a possibility."

Alexa remembered reading about a Chinese miner who committed suicide.

"Lots of stigma about suicide during the colonial days," Ana said. "That might explain why she wasn't buried within the proper cemetery. And don't discount corpse concealment."

"There's a possibility her death was violent and covered up. Pardon my inadvertent pun," Dr. McKenzie said. "I want to look at the fractures before we send her for X-rays and scanning. Let's start with the cervical spine."

Ana collected a tray and arranged the seven neck bones in

proper order. She set the tray under a magnification viewer. Dr. McKenzie adjusted the light and leaned in. "As we saw in situ, the break is between C3 and C4, eh?" He frowned, hummed, probed. "Your typical hangman's fracture is usually in C1 or C2." He poked around. "Hyoid bone is missing, but that's not unusual."

Alexa rubbed her neck.

"I don't see signs of healing," Dr. McKenzie said. "It might be a perimortem injury." Perimortem meant trauma at the time of death, Alexa remembered. Not an injury that took place before or after S2 died.

"The fracture is clean, like a snap," he said. He took his time examining the other neck bones. "No additional breaks or chips. With a mine cave-in or fall, I would expect damage in other places too."

"Could it have been caused by strangulation?" Alexa asked.

He looked up. "It's more akin to a sports injury. I've seen hyperflexion fractures like this in rugby. A quick snap back and the young bloke is wheelchair-bound or dead." He shook his head. "Let's take a look at the lumbar spinal break."

He and Ana moved back to the table and studied the lower spine. Dr. McKenzie leaned down and used a magnifying glass. "No sign of healing. It took brute force to break these bones."

Alexa's phone vibrated. She lowered her mask and groped for her pocket. It was buried beneath her plastic apron. She ran into the anteroom, tore off the apron, and pulled out the phone. DI Katakana's name flashed on the screen. "Hello?"

"We've found a body," the DI barked. "Bring your bone friend to the cemetery."

Alexa's mind blanked. "Bone friend?"

"That archaeologist. She's trained in body recovery, right? I need her assistance."

Chapter Twenty-Eight

Alexa returned to the autopsy suite. "Ana. We have to go."

"What?" She tore off her mask. "Is something wrong?"

"They've found a body."

"Another skeleton?"

"No. Body recovery."

Her eyebrows hit her hairline. "Is it the principal?"

Alexa hugged the crime kit to her chest. "DI Katakana didn't say. She asked for your assistance."

"Go," Dr. McKenzie said. "I'll take care of our friend here. I expect I'll see you later."

What he meant, Alexa realized, was that if an autopsy on the body was needed, he'd be doing the cutting.

They collected their things and left the hospital in Ana's car. They turned on the radio, but there was no news. Whatever had happened was under wraps. Ana drove quickly and silently until they crossed the Shotover River Bridge. "My shovel," she said suddenly. She still wore the plastic apron from the autopsy suite.

"What?"

"My shovel from the tent. What if that DI wants me to dig? You confiscated it."

"The police will have shovels," Alexa said. *Were the tent vandalism and the body connected?* Alexa was impatient to get there.

Ana jerked to a stop on the cemetery road ten minutes later. Cop cars and pickup trucks were parked at various angles around them. When Alexa grabbed the crime kit and got out, she heard a sharp bark. She located the barker in the back of a canine-unit car. The hatch was open, and the dog stared at her through the mesh, drooling. She thought it was Dax.

She and Ana jogged across the uneven cemetery ground, dodging headstones and rusted wrought-iron enclosures, and climbed over the stone wall.

Beyond the copse of trees and the vandalized tent, a group of variously dressed people huddled in a semicircle with their backs to Alexa and Ana: one suit, two cop uniforms, two white jumpsuits, and three orange SAR jumpsuits. She wondered if one of the orange jumpsuits was her dinner-date, Julian. The group blocked their view of the refilled grave. The suit turned. It was DI Katakana, who noticed them, and marched over. Constable Blume, one of the uniforms, followed at her heels.

The DI held a hand out to Ana. "I'm Detective Inspector Pattie Katakana. Thank you for coming. We've got a situation."

Alexa, breathing hard, looked at the gap where the DI had been standing. The grave was encircled by caution tape. Dirt was strewn around it.

Ana noticed too. "Is that where..."

"That's where we found the body," DI Katakana said.

Alexa couldn't believe what she was hearing. Or seeing.

"I had that grave refilled yesterday," Ana said.

DI Katakana's eyes narrowed. "What time?"

"Four o'clock." Ana's plastic apron flapped in the breeze. She looked down, apparently surprised, and tore it off. "I wasn't here. Harry Turner, Dig It Excavation, filled it in."

"Call him," the DI ordered Constable Blume. "Verify the exact time. And find out where the hell former DI Unger is. He's not answering his phone."

"On it," he said.

DI Katakana took off her cap and pressed it against her chest. Wisps of dark hair escaped her bun and blew into her eyes. "I need to understand a few things. There's a grave there and another grave in the tent. Both were unmarked. Is that right?"

"Yes," said Ana. "We used ground-penetrating radar to find them."

"Who was buried in them?"

"We think the one in the tent is a European settler. That one was a Chinese gold miner," Ana said. "The miner's bones will be repatriated."

The DI slipped the cap back on and pressed her hands together in prayer position. "Hungry ghosts, doomed to wander the earth. I have an auntie in Ōpononi."

"Near Hokianga Harbor, where the *SS Ventnor* went down," Ana said.

The tomb ship, sinking to the bottom of the sea, Alexa thought.

The DI nodded. "Her father found some of the bones that washed up. Didn't know what to make of them. He buried them in a Māori *urupā*."

Alexa knew a *urupā* was a burial ground. She pressed the greenstone pendant through her shirt. She detected a warmth.

The DI gestured to the tent. "Ms. Glock, Constable Blume said you discovered the vandalism. He showed me the report. 'God is watching' and so forth."

The sound of a helicopter pulled their eyes skyward. It passed without circling or hovering. When the din receded, the DI continued. "What time did you get here? Did you see anyone?"

Alexa recalled the early morning graveyard, the mist curling around the tombstones, the shock of the vandalism. "I arrived around seven thirty. I didn't see anyone." She should stick with facts, but blurted it anyway. "I had this feeling someone was watching me."

"*Mana'o kino*. I trust feelings," the DI said. "What condition were the graves in?"

"The grave inside the tent had been partially filled in, and a shovel stuck in the middle."

DI Katakana's eyes widened. "Had the grave over there been disturbed?"

"I don't know. I was focused on the tent."

The DI sighed. "Okay. The current situation?" She jutted her chin toward the group of people. "A tracker dog pulled Sergeant Strawser to that grave and started digging."

Strawser was Grant's last name, Alexa remembered. It *was* Dax in the car.

"The sergeant pulled the dog off. The lads dug until she was partially exposed. They checked for breathing and a pulse."

Alexa braced herself.

"It's our lass, Eileen Bowen. Dead."

"Oh, no," Ana said.

The DI turned to Alexa. "You've got your crime scene now."

Chapter Twenty-Nine
SATURDAY AFTERNOON

No victory dance in the end zone. Alexa would rather have been ignored than facing a buried woman who two days ago assured upset parents that a bullying plan would protect their children. A woman who was looking forward to a Saturday night date with Boy Toy and teatime with her latest educational journal.

Could Eileen Bowen have been saved? Had the police failed her? Had Alexa failed her? A small gray bird swooped by. *Tweeta tweeta tweeta*, it scolded.

"Wait for the coroner to arrive before you examine the body," DI Katakana said. Her radio cackled, and she stepped aside to answer it.

"I'll collect stuff from the tent and meet you over there," Ana said.

Two people, dressed in white coveralls, waited beyond the crime tape. The others had dispersed. Alexa put on her glasses and recognized the dog handler. When she got near, she said, "Hello, Sergeant Strawser. Grant. Who taped off the scene?"

The other guy, large and bearded, stepped forward. The cleft between his thick eyebrows deepened as he looked down at her. "I did. Who's asking?"

"The perimeter is too small," she said.

He folded his thick arms across his torso and stared at her.

Dammit, Alexa. People skills. She forced a smile. "I'm Alexa Glock, the forensic investigator. My colleague Dr.

Ana Luckenbaugh will join me in a minute. She's a forensic archaeologist."

The cleft relaxed. "Senior Sergeant Fielding, Queenstown PD."

"What can you tell me?" Alexa asked. She glanced at the grave. A sheet covered the body.

"She's buried about two feet deep. We're the only ones who touched her. We wore gloves."

Alexa nodded her approval. They wore booties too, so she wouldn't need to take photographs of their boots for elimination.

"Have you established the perpetrator's route?" she asked.

Senior Sergeant Fielding lifted his arms and let them drop. "It's not like a house with a front and back door."

Mountains, rock walls, trees, the tent, the parking area: There were countless paths to ground zero. "You don't go far carrying a body," Alexa said. "Or haul it over a rock wall."

He stared at her again. Alexa stood her ground.

"We're thinking he came from over there," Grant interceded, pointing to some scraggly bushes twenty yards away. An officer was marking it off with barrier stakes. "There's an easement on the other side where a car could have parked. We're about to conduct a primary search."

Alexa pulled on gloves. "What about a path for personnel? Everyone needs to come and go the same way."

The cleft in the senior sergeant's forehead deepened.

She couldn't stop herself. "Have you taken video of the scene? And sketched it?"

"You said crime scene investigator, right? Not deputy fucking commissioner?"

Alexa reddened. "I've seen cases get thrown out of court because of messy scene handling."

"Not on my watch," he said, and stalked off toward his officers.

Grant rocked on the balls of his feet. "We're all on edge."

"My fault," Alexa said. "Works Well With Others is always my lowest evaluation score." *Jeez.* Now she was oversharing "Why were you and Dax in the graveyard?"

He raked his dark hair so that it stood up. "We did a quick sweep Friday around noon. Nothing. Since then we've been focusing on the woods and river. Because of that hat your daughter fished out."

"My friend's daughter. Dax did good," she said.

He pointed up the closest mountain. "DI Katakana said to check the water tanks. We started there, but Dax pulled me here."

Halfway up the mountain stood three concrete tanks. They blended in like granite cliffs.

"I hate it, though. Wish we'd saved her instead of dug her up." He looked hangdog. His shoulders slumped as he departed.

Alexa slumped too, and she hadn't seen the body yet. Violent death took a toll on officers. *Search and Rescue volunteers too,* Alexa imagined. She had her private collection of tolls: a suspicious outlook, nightmares, a fear of heights and helicopters, all related to homicide cases she'd investigated. Kickboxing and running helped. She'd been avoiding her yoga mat; the practice had become too meditative. Bodies and bad guys force-entered her mind during Savasana.

Ana arrived with two buckets. Inside one, trowels, spoons, and brushes knocked together. "Got them from the tent— which is a mess. Hope that was okay."

Constable Blume followed with a tarp and a backpack. "Got my own crime kit," he said. He held up the backpack. A *for effort*, Alexa thought. She turned to Ana. "Can we excavate the body ourselves?"

"We can remove the soil around her, sure, but we'll need help moving the deceased," Ana said. They all stepped into fresh coveralls and booties.

"I'll take photographs from this side of the barrier while we wait for the coroner." Alexa spotted three or four boot impressions. How much Shake-and-Cast would she need?

Constable Blume must have read her mind. He lifted his kit. "Should I start casting?"

Alexa nodded. She respected forensic podiatry, but waiting for plaster to dry tried her patience.

Constable Blume glanced at the sheet-covered hole. He ducked under the tape and homed in on a good print. Alexa watched him add the pre-measured water to the cast pack. "Not too thick," she said.

"Nah, yeah. Consistency of heavy cream."

"You've got a future in forensics," she said.

"The coroner is coming," Ana said.

New Zealand coroners were lawyers, which made no sense to Alexa. They were contacted by the police in suspicious or violent deaths. He or she would determine if a criminal investigation should be opened—a formality here, obviously. Then the ball would get tossed to the forensic pathologist.

The coroner, already in barrier garb, crossed through the gap in the rock wall instead of climbing over. Alexa couldn't tell if it was a man or woman until she saw the face above the mask: green shadow over wide eyes and purple eyeglasses.

"Gina Cannon." She set a case down. It looked like a tackle box. "I'm the duty coroner. Got here quick as I could."

Alexa and Ana introduced themselves.

"What do we have?" Gina asked.

"I haven't looked yet," Alexa said.

Ana explained about the dig and how the hole had been filled in yesterday afternoon.

"One for the books." Gina took a video camera out of the case and handed it to Constable Blume. "Record everything I do, eh? Stay right behind me."

He nodded eagerly.

She gathered evidence rulers and hung a small camera around her neck. "Would you wait here?" she asked Ana. "Ms. Glock and I will see what we have."

"All good," Ana said.

Ready or not, Alexa thought. She had her camera ready too. They ducked under the tape and stepped to the edge of the grave as Constable Blume followed.

Bird tweets, cop voices, car engines—even Constable Blume's nasal breathing—faded as Gina pulled back the sheet. Dizziness made Alexa wobble. She inhaled to fill her lungs. The victim appeared to be on her side. The senior sergeant and Grant had removed the dirt around her face and torso; her legs were still buried. The face was in profile—right side visible. Alexa noticed the hair. It was dark red and clumped with soil. It draped across the forehead like seaweed.

But Eileen's hair was blond.

Oh. The hanks of hair were bloodied. A glimmer of blond adhered to the ear, which bore a diamond stud. Alexa tore her eyes from the strands and focused on the nose, which was prominent, and the chin, which was pointy. The lips were a horrible goth gray. The visible eye was wide open, blank. Grit was embedded in the eyelashes and eye rim. Alexa imagined how the sand must have stung and caused tears to well. Her own eyesight blurred. She blinked. The split second of darkness cleared her tunnel vision so that when she opened her eyes, she could see the profile as a whole. It was Eileen Bowen, and she looked so dead.

Alexa raised her camera. Taking photos helped her distance from the horror. The viewfinder was a shield. She had never seen a freshly buried body. *This didn't happen to me. I'm alive. I'm safe.*

Eileen's right shoulder—she was wearing a pinkish fleece—
was exposed. She was wrapped in something. From under the
gritty film coating it, seahorses smiled. *What the hell?*

"A shower curtain," the coroner said. "A cheap one. No grommets." She placed a ruler next to them and took photos.

A few of the punched holes were torn as if the curtain had
been jerked loose from a rod. A shower curtain suggested that
Eileen had been killed in a house and moved from there. Alexa
was glad. She had conjured a terrifying scenario: Eileen Bowen
roped, muffled, and buried alive.

Gina squatted and set the camera aside. "Let's see where the
blood came from."

Constable Blume stood behind her, recording.

Alexa knelt near Eileen's head, careful not to slide onto her,
and readied her camera. Gina moved the clump of hair covering
Eileen's forehead.

Click.

Gina probed the right ear, cheek, and jawbone.

Click. Click. Click.

"No sign of injury," Gina said. "I'm going to manipulate the
head." She took Eileen's face in both hands and gently rotated it
skyward. The left eye was closed, the left nostril clogged with
dirt, two top teeth visible beneath the gray lips in a snarl. The
left earlobe was ripped, bloody. There was no diamond stud.

Click.

Gina slid her hands under the skull. She stared ahead, her
eyes flaring, her hands doing something invisible. When she
pulled them out, the right glove was dark and sticky with blood.

Chapter Thirty

"Blunt force trauma?" asked DI Katakana.

Alexa jiggled the camera. She hadn't known DI Katakana was watching from beyond the caution tape, a stout tree planted next to Ana.

Gina's glasses had slipped down to the tip of her nose. She nudged them up with her forearm. "The right parietal bone feels fractured."

"By what?"

Gina leaned back on her haunches, forcing Constable Blume to hop out of her way. "That's for Doc to figure out."

"And the shower curtain, eh? Probably obtained at the scene of death," DI Katakana said. "Is she fully dressed?"

"We haven't looked yet," Gina said.

Alexa couldn't bear the thought of sexual assault/homicide. She forced herself to watch Gina remove dirt and part the curtain. Dirt slithered off its sides. Eileen wore jeans.

Alexa let out air.

"How much rigor?" the DI asked.

Gina felt along the free forearm and hand. "Rigor has passed."

Rigor mortis was the postmortem stiffening of muscles, and its stages provided time-since-death clues. The process started two hours after death and ran its course in thirty-six hours. Alexa was relieved Eileen hadn't been held hostage, frantic and afraid. But where had she been? Grant had checked the grave-yard Friday afternoon, and she hadn't been here.

She and Gina photographed the body, and then Gina wrapped it back up in the shower curtain, the smiling seahorses incongruous with death.

The DI scanned the cemetery. "We've got to find the bastard."

A chill skittered up Alexa's spine. Was Hammer out there? Hiding? Or had he gotten out of Dodge like he had after he killed Cindy Mulligan? *Got your fingerprints on file now, buddy.*

Gina faced Constable Blume and the recorder. "I'm finished. There may be additional injuries, but that will be determined at the postmortem Thank you, Constable. You can stop recording."

He lowered the camera. His freckles stood out against his pale skin.

"I'll let the forensic pathologist know he's got one coming," the coroner said. "An ambulance is on the way to transport the remains." She packed her cameras. Alexa was surprised she was leaving. She felt abandoned, which was silly.

"I'll leave it to you ladies to get her out quickly," DI Katakana said. "I'm calling Mr. Bowen to identify her. He can escort the stretcher. It helps in the long run, escorting the body."

Constable Blume cleared his throat.

"You'll assist the archaeologist, Constable. The press catches whiff, it will be all over the media. Ms. Walker is on her way, to lead the lads with the scene search."

She walked away with the coroner. Ana ducked under the caution tape and grabbed Alexa's wrist "You are not sleeping alone in the cottage tonight. Come to Queenstown."

"Sold," Alexa said.

"Okay then," Ana said. "Check the edges of the hole first.

There might be tool marks. My shovel has a nick in one corner from hitting a pipe."

A spark ignited in Alexa's brain. Tool marks can be linked to the tools that created them. If Ana's shovel had been used to bury Eileen, it was already in the lab being dusted for fingerprints. She photographed and measured what she thought were shovel marks on the sidewalls of the grave.

"Any sign of a nick?" Ana asked.

"I'll be able to tell when I enhance them."

She took three temperature readings: the air, the body surface, and soil surface. The data would help the forensic pathologist estimate time of death. When she finished, she told Ana she was ready.

Constable Blume cleared his throat again.

Ana handed them each a trowel. "Start by the feet and work upwards. It will be easy to damage skin with those," she said. "Switch to spoons, brushes, or your hands as soon as you reach flesh or clothing. We're lucky she's mostly wrapped in the curtain. We'll leave it in place and move her in it."

It was a plan, and Alexa liked plans.

The soil was easy to scoop. Why wouldn't it be? Dug up by Ana and Olivia. Piled back in by Excavator Guy. Dug up by the murderer. Shoveled back in. Partly dug up by Grant and the senior sergeant. This was just the recent excavations. It didn't count whoever buried the Chinese miner a hundred twenty-five years ago.

He had a name now: Wing Lun. He'd been the first resident of the grave. Her pendant pulsed as she thought of the way his skeletal hand had pointed at something.

They removed all the dirt piled around the shower curtain. Ana excavated the head, neck, and shoulders while Alexa and the constable worked their way upwards from the feet. Eileen wore Skecher tennis shoes. Well, shoe. One was missing. At the arms, they switched to spoons. A whiff of ripeness, mixed with the soil, made Alexa scrunch her nose. She tried not to think about what was happening inside Eileen's body. Autolysis was the scientific term. It meant self-digestion.

She lifted Eileen's right hand. As Gina had said, the digits were flaccid and pliant. Docile came to mind. Two nails were jagged. She hoped this meant Eileen had fought like hell. She hoped the nails would contain traces of skin or blood of the attacker. The forensic pathologist would swab the hands and clip the nails. She bagged the hand in one of her new Hand Preservation Bags and tightened the drawstring.

Constable Blume watched. "You're not using paper bag and tape," he said. "Don't have to worry 'bout rips or holes."

She preened. "Product of the Month in my forensic supply catalog. Made of Tyvek. They can preserve gunpowder residue too."

"Sweet as," he said.

She threw him the left mitt to bag the other hand.

Leigh Walker showed up. Her orange Jungle Juice T-shirt peeked through her white coverall. "Hiya. DI Katakana ordered me to help with the primary search and to tell you that the EMTs just pulled up."

"Keep an eye out for a diamond earring," Alexa said. "And a shoe."

Leigh's eyes widened as she looked into the grave. "Is that her?"

"Who else would it be?" Constable Blume answered.

Leigh stammered. "I just meant, well—"

"Did you have time to dust that shovel for fingerprints?" Alexa asked.

Leigh's eyes brightened. "I used black powder."

"Good choice."

"I lifted several prints that look good."

Alexa's heart drummed. "Did you run them?"

"Didn't have time."

Dammit. If she'd been in the lab, she would have done it right away.

"But, well, the prints came from two separate people. I can say that."

Alexa and Ana stared at each other. "Someone used my shovel," Ana said.

The tech jogged off to where four officers canvassed the ground near the scraggly bushes. Beyond them, the mountains stood guard in every direction. They looked closer, as if a game of Simon Says had taken place while her head was down.

Simon says take one giant leap forward.

The deceased was ready to be moved. There were no keys, purse, or phone on or around the body. Below? They didn't know yet.

As they waited for the EMTs, Alexa used her new portable scanner to take Ana's prints. "You know, for comparison with the shovel prints." She had to admit, the scanner was quick and clean.

The vandalized tent caught her attention. Did the murderer take the time to spray-paint "God is Watching You?" Wouldn't that increase his risk of being caught? It didn't make sense.

The EMTs helped Constable Blume lift the deceased, with the curtain, out of the hole and onto a stretcher. Her feet hung out. The pink ankle sock on the shoeless foot made Alexa sad. They covered the body with the sheet.

A man hurtled toward them. As he neared, Alexa saw it was Paul Bowen, the ex. DI Katakana chased after him. He knocked over a cone and crossed through the gap in the stone wall. He spotted the stretcher. "My God," he cried.

The stretcher crew froze. DI Katakana caught up to him, panting. "Mr. Bowen. This is a crime scene. You can't go bushwhacking."

"Is it my wife?"

"Ex-wife," Alexa whispered.

DI Katakana set her hands on her hips and caught her breath. "We believe so." She put a hand on Mr. Bowen's shoulder. "Are you able to make the formal ID?"

One of the EMTs lowered the sheet to expose the face. Mr. Bowen stepped to the stretcher. His face caved in. He blinked and blinked. "I told you he had her. How did you let this happen?"

"Are you formally identifying her?" the DI asked calmly.

"It's her. It's—I can't believe it. Eileen. No."

"I am sorry for your loss," DI Katakana said.

Mr. Bowen pawed at his eyes and then stared slack-jawed at the lifeless face. "Is that blood on her hair?"

The DI nodded.

"How—?"

"We don't know," she cut in.

"She's wearing her mother's diamond earrings. She, she loved them." His eyes flitted to the grave. He blinked rapidly again and stumbled toward it. "Oh, God, tell me she wasn't buried."

Alexa blocked his path. If it weren't for Earl Hammer, the ex-husband would be number one on the suspect list, and this could be a ploy to contaminate the scene.

DI Katakana took his arm. "Mr. Bowen? We're taking Ms. Bowen to hospital now. Help carry her out and then one of my officers will give you a ride."

The stretcher crew, straining from their load, made room for him to assist. DI Katakana followed behind. When her radio blared, her hand went to the dial, but she didn't answer it. An officer ran up to her and spoke. A few other officers ran across the grass, toward the parking area.

Alexa turned away from the sad scene. "Something is up."

"Let's get out of here," Ana said. "This graveyard has evil vibes."

The final task was to search the soil below where the body had been. Nothing was obvious except a darkened oval where blood had seeped from the skull wounds. Ana showed Alexa how to rake the prong end of the trowel across the smoothed surfaces. "Take the bottom. I'll start up here."

Alexa knelt near where the feet had been and raked back and forth, robotically, her mind on Paul Bowen. He'd acted as if he still loved his ex-wife. *Did Bruce still love his ex? Sharla. But why would Bruce cheat if he loved her?* Alexa understood science, not emotions of the heart. Hers, though, kept beating for Bruce.

新年快乐

NEW YEAR HAPPINESS

1900

Precious MaMa,

The Year of the Rat ushers in new beginnings. I will try for optimism in my twenty-first year in Arrowtown. We no longer call it New Gold Hills. The gold is hiding.

We cooked for three days: roast duck, roast fowl, roast and boiled pork, peas in pod, cuttlefish, and vermicelli. We invited townspeople to share our feast. Gamble, play all night, share the feast, light firecrackers, spend paper money. We wrapped long poles in crackers, lit from the bottom, and watched the crackers explode and light the way for the new year.

The Sheriff of Arrowtown spit in my face, told me I am a different race, dirty, and I should go home. My friends depend on me to write letters, be their banker, and run my store.

Faithful First Son,
Wing Lun

Chapter Thirty-One

Constable Blume returned from the ambulance. He looked over his shoulder. "Here comes Senior, running again."

The DI arrived, huffing, and pointed at Alexa. "Go see Misty Tandy. The coroner stopped by, notified her about her sister, but couldn't stay. Ms. Tandy needs details, someone to answer her questions until the family liaison shows up." She paused, catching her breath.

Alexa's dander stood. "But—"

"We're shorthanded," the DI broke in. She pointed at Constable Blume. "Go with Glock. Then head to the hospital for the postmortem. I'm assigning you as OC."

"Officer in charge of body. Okay," Constable Blume said. "But what's up, Senior?"

"Recent sighting." She took her cap off, swiped her brow, and pulled it back on. "Lone man, forties, dark hair, Chinese settlement. Matches Hammer's description and acting sus."

"Don't you want me to come?" Constable Blume asked.

The DI had already jogged off.

Ana looked panicky. "The Chinese settlement is only a ten-minute hop from here."

"You're safe, ma'am," Constable Blume said. "Cops are everywhere."

But he was wrong. The cops combing the cemetery

grounds had taken flight like a startled flock of birds. Despite the jacket under her dirty coverall, Alexa shivered.

"Go," Ana told her. "Call me later."

Alexa packed the crime kit, being careful with the footwear casts. As Constable Blume fiddled on his radio, getting Misty's address, she saw Leigh Walker, on all fours, near the leggy bushes. She jogged over. "Found something?"

Leigh nodded. "I think it's a wheel track."

Alexa frowned. A car couldn't fit through the hedge.

Leigh pointed to two depressions and a single thin tire trail. "Might be someone used a wheelbarrow to transport the body."

"Good find. Do you have a cast kit?"

Leigh nodded. "Want to help?"

"I can't. DI Katakana wants me to..." *What? Hold Misty's hand?* "...stay with the dead woman's sister until the liaison arrives. Then Constable Blume and I are attending the postmortem."

Leigh stood and looked around. "Where has everyone gone?"

"They may have spotted Hammer at the Chinese settlement. I'll see you in the lab later." Alexa took a quick look at the rutted dirt road beyond the bushes and then caught up with Constable Blume. He was quiet as they wove between graves. She was surprised when he slowed and pulled out his phone. He photographed a group of people gathered at the cemetery entrance. A cop blocked their access.

"You never know," he whispered.

"Never know what?" Alexa asked.

"Criminals. Sometimes they return to the scene of the crime, watch the goings-on."

Alexa thought that was twaddle. Nonetheless, she surveyed the bystanders: two reporters with cameras, a couple with cellophane-wrapped flowers, an elderly lady, a kid on a bike, a stooped Asian man with white hair. She fished her glasses out of the kit and pulled them on. It was Mr. Sun, the guardian of the Chinese miners' bones. His blue windbreaker was zipped up to his chin as if he was cold.

"Give me a second," she told the constable. She hurried over. "Mr. Sun. I'm Alexa Glock. We met a few days ago."

His eyes brightened. "I remember. I heard the tent was vandalized. Is that why the officer is keeping us out?"

"No," Alexa said.

He studied her. "Are there racial slurs on the tent?"

She thought of all the vitriol the Chinese miners had endured. Then she thought of the increase in hate crimes against Asians during and since the pandemic. "Nothing like that. They're keeping people out because we've found the missing woman. The principal."

He tucked his chin into the windbreaker. "Dead?"

She nodded.

"Ack. Such a waste. Where?"

She couldn't bear to tell him Eileen Bowen's body had been found in the grave of the Chinese miner. "Near the rock wall."

Their eyes met. Alexa felt held by his gaze. Thoughts transferred between them that didn't need voice: a life cut short. A maw opened for those left behind. He asked softly, "And the hungry bones? Where are they?"

"Being cared for in the hospital."

"Mrs. Wong is on her way here. When will the bones be released? "

Mrs. Wong was the benefactor, and related to Wing Lun. Alexa pictured the hole in its skull. "I'm not sure."

He held her gaze. "The bones are restless. As I sense are you."

"Me?"

"You are far from home, too," he said. "When children go far, mothers worry."

"Mine isn't worried. I'm sorry, but I have to go. It's urgent."
Alexa said goodbye, and caught up with Constable Blume. She
took a deep breath to focus on the present. "I need to ride with
you," she reminded him.

"Better we take two cars," he said.

"I don't have a car." She glanced back at Mr. Sun. *Or a mother.*

The constable's floodgates spilled as they pulled onto
Durham Street. "Wishing I could, you know, be there. At the
Chinese village. Apprehend the suspect. Be part of the team." A
patrol car whizzed toward them, siren off. The constable pulled
onto the shoulder until it passed. "Senior always assigns me
one-offs."

Alexa, a recent one-off herself, understood his frustration.
She tapped the crime kit on her lap. "Officer in charge at the
autopsy is an important job."

He sat taller. "I have to trust Senior knows my strengths, eh?
Paperwork completion. Attention to detail."

"Forensics too." She meant it. "Are we headed to Misty's
work or home?"

"Home, being Saturday and all. Fourteen Willowhaven C.
It's in Frankton."

"That's where the hospital is. Good."

"Never been to an autopsy," he said. "What should I expect?"

"The forensic pathologist will have questions about the
scene. Make sure there's a chair or bench near you. In case you
get queasy." She'd fainted during her first autopsy.

"And a bucket, in case I chunder."

"You'll be fine." *One could hope.*

The driveway to Misty's address served three houses: a two-
story boxy modern on Willowhaven Road, a smaller modern
halfway down, and a one-story clapboard bungalow at the end.
The Tandy Home Inspections van hogged most of the driveway.

Constable Blume pulled behind it. The detached garage had an old roller type door, which was open. Misty walked out of its gloom holding a basket of laundry. She stared blankly at them.

Alexa had envisioned Misty sitting on a couch, wrapped in a blanket, teary-eyed, cuppa in hand. Husband and daughter flitting around solicitously.

Not doing laundry.

They got out of the car. Misty, in jeans, dark T-shirt, and purple Crocs, stood rooted and dumbfounded. "Hello," Alexa said. "Constable Blume and I are here to stay with you until the police support officer arrives. In case you have questions."

Constable Blume sprang to her side and took the basket from her hands. "Let me carry that for you."

A mixture of darks and lights, Alexa saw. Wet and smelling faintly of bleach. The washing machine must be in the garage.

"Need to be hung out," Misty said woodenly. "Then you might as well come in."

"Let me," Constable Blume said. "Clothesline in the garden?"

He took off, leaving Alexa alone with Misty. She wished she'd grabbed the laundry; comforting people wasn't in the forensic procedural manual. "We came straight from the cemetery where Eileen's body was found. Is someone here with you?" she asked hopefully.

Misty didn't answer. She trudged to the front door, opened it, and led Alexa past a kitchen into a sitting area, where she gazed out the large picture window. Constable Blume already had a clothespin in his mouth and was shaking out a T-shirt.

Alexa gestured to a well-worn sofa. "Why don't you sit down? You've had a shock."

The couched *oofed* as Misty dropped. She put her head in her hands. Her thin brown hair parted, revealing her pale neck. Alexa believed necks were the most vulnerable part of the human body. Food and water going down a single tube; breath another. Breakage causing paralysis or death. The jugular only skin-deep. The neck revealed human fragility.

"Um, I'll just find your bathroom and wash up. Then I'll make tea, if that's okay." Misty didn't answer. Alexa hated to leave her, but she needed to pee and scrub. The bathroom was down a short hallway, opposite a bedroom. Alexa glanced in: queen bed, shades down, knickknacks, closed packing boxes.

The bathroom had a single oval sink, a toilet, and a bathtub/shower combo with a shiny blue-gray curtain. The image of Eileen wrapped in vinyl popped in Alexa's head. She pressed her nose to the satiny material and inhaled. No new smell. She pulled the curtain back and checked the liner: mold rimmed the area where it adhered to the tub.

Satisfied, Sherlock?

Out of curiosity she scanned the shampoos and body washes. They rested on all ledges: lemon and sage, royal vanilla, lavender. Someone wanted to smell good—the teen daughter, probably.

She used the toilet, and then, ignoring the scum of spit toothpaste in the sink, scrubbed her hands with wild rose hand soap. In the mirror she saw dirt on her chin and cheek. She cupped her hands and splashed water on her face, twice, three times.

The towel smelled of mildew.

She popped back into the living area. *The lounge, Kiwis called it.* Beyond it was the dining area, though the table was covered with a desktop computer and a jumble of papers and books. A home office, maybe.

"Tea?" Alexa asked. She was happy Misty nodded.

The tiny kitchen was messy. Cups, cereal bowls, and crumbs on the counter, cupboard ajar, cartons of instant noodles. *Busy parents*, Alexa concluded. *Working, raising a teenager.* She added water to an electric kettle and found some Bell tea bags and two clean mugs. Alexa wasn't a tea drinker, but it was black, and she could use a jolt of caffeine. Lunch, too, but that would have to wait. She plopped a tea bag into a third mug, for Constable Blume, and poured in the steaming water. While the tea steeped, she checked on Misty. "Is your husband on his way home?"

Misty stared at her with wide-set eyes. "Is it true what the coroner lady said?"

Alexa didn't know what Gina had said. She looked out the window. Constable Blume was hanging jeans. The daughter's maybe. They would take forever to dry on this cloudy cool day. "Let me fetch the tea, and then I'll answer your questions."

She added sugar to the mugs because that's how she liked it. Plus, it might help Misty with the shock. She put one mug in Misty's hands—they were ice-cold—and took hers to a wooden rocker across the room and sat. She burned her tongue on the first sip and looked out the window. Constable Blume was hanging underwear now. Women's. She bit her tongue to keep from laughing. Totally inappropriate. "Um, I'm sorry about Eileen. It's terrible."

Misty raised the mug but didn't sip. "She was buried?"

Gina must have told her. "Yes. We—" She almost blurted "dug her up." "She's been taken to the hospital." To be clear, Alexa added, "To the morgue. Mr. Bowen is with her."

Misty sloshed the tea on her jeans. There was no coffee table. She set the mug on the carpet, next to her feet. "Paul is still following her around? He shouldn't be there. He's not next-of-kin anymore."

Misty didn't ask to be driven to the hospital, though, Alexa noted. "Where are your husband and daughter? Do they know?"

Her face crumpled. "Martin is picking Susie up from a friend's. She'll be devastated."

"We can help you tell her," Alexa said softly.

"Martin is telling her."

The poor dad, Alexa thought. *The poor kid.* Her tea had cooled enough to sip, and she did, grateful for the warmth and calories. She thought of the van in the driveway. "Are you and Mr. Tandy business owners?"

"Marty inspects homes. I help out." She glanced toward the messy tabletop.

"Do you have any questions about Eileen?"

Misty stood, knocking over the tea.

"Crap," Alexa said. "I'll get it." She ran into the kitchen and grabbed the paper towel roll. They were almost gone, so she grabbed a tea towel too. She got on her hands and knees to mop up the spill. The carpet was beige at least. From above her, Misty said, "What do you think?"

The paper towels were saturated. She switched to the cloth towel. Some had seeped under the couch and she lifted the flap. "About what?"

The purple Crocs shuffled away. "Who killed Eileen?"

Alexa looked up. Misty's back was turned. "I don't know. Who do you think killed her?"

"It had to be that man. Earl Hammer. Right?"

Alexa pressed the clean half of the towel into the ply. She spotted something under the couch. She fished it out and held it up. "A phone."

Misty turned. Her face paled. "Where did that come from?" She reached out a hand and took it. "It's Susie's. She couldn't find it this morning. Tore the house apart."

Alexa knew phones and teenagers were a unit. Where the hell was Constable Blume? "The police are doing everything they can to catch Hammer."

"Eileen being dead would have ruined our mum. Father too. I'm glad they're gone."

"I can understand that." She'd always heard parents losing a child was "the worst death." She remembered Misty's fingerprints had been on the Smart car door handle. It seemed inappropriate to bring up, but Alexa couldn't think of anything else to say. "Did Eileen ever lend you her car?" Misty stared at her. "Your fingerprints were on the door handle. We were wondering why."

Her eyes widened. "Don't know. It's probably a mistake."

Alexa wadded up the towel.

"Or maybe when Eileen gave Susie a ride home after driving lessons. Maybe I opened the door for her. I don't know."

"All good," came Constable Blume's voice from the kitchen. "Is this for me? Spot on." He came into the lounge holding a mug. "What's this then? Are you okay, Ms. Glock?"

Alexa got up. "We had a little spill."

"Vinegar will help, my mum says." He colored.

"Never heard of that." Alexa wondered if he still lived at home. Maybe that's why he blushed. "Mr. Tandy will be back soon. He gone to fetch their daughter."

"Why don't you sit, ma'am?" Constable Blume said.

Suddenly Misty was crying. Alexa raced down the hall for the box of tissues she'd seen in the bathroom. When she returned, Constable Blume was sitting with Misty on the couch, calmly talking about victim support counselors. "You can call, 24/7," he said.

The front door, which Alexa could see from where she stood, flung open. A girl, all legs, swirl of colors, ran in. "Mummy!"

冬天

WINTER

1903

Dear MaMa,

A flood swept away five miners camped along the Arrow River.
Forty souls were buried in an avalanche at Separation Creek. Do
not worry for First Son. This rock store I helped Cheong Tam build
withstands the howling winter. My bunk is built into the rock next
to the chimney, and the smooth river stone retains the heat of warm
summer days. Brother Tam tends to me even in death.

金石之交: Our friendship is as strong as gold.

I fulfill my duty for you to buy the house and with honor present
the funds with this cheque. I earned this money from running Tam's
store. Second Brother is past the age of school. Please use leftover for
his children's schooling.

Only seven of us are left on the banks of Bush Creek. Wun Long
and Hon Tie have despondency of heart and addiction in their bodies.
We are called 'Chinkie' by the townsfolk, but my fine vegetables and
teas bring them to my threshold. A hidden Pearl among the slag lifts
my lonesome heart. I sing like the robins who keep me company.

Like tea leaves added to the cup: first floating on the surface—my
birthplace—and then sinking to the bottom—Arrowtown, I will live
out my days here, finding happiness at last.

MaMa, you are a thousand pieces of gold.

Faithful First Son,
Wing Lun

Chapter Thirty-Two

As soon as the family liaison arrived, Alexa and the constable escaped the Tandy house. Constable Blume scowled at the various cars in the driveway. Mr. Tandy's sedan was behind his patrol car, and the liaison's car was next to them. "Gridlock," he said.

Alexa wanted to get the hell out of Dodge. Mr. Tandy had called them worthless and liable. Misty blubbered harder. Then the husband accused them of causing his wife's distress. He ripped the tissue box out of Alexa's hand and thrust it at Misty. The daughter Susie stood immobile, hugging herself, her hands buried in her sleeves. "Aunt Leeny," she cried over and over.

The family liaison's name was Bridget Kies. She would be the conduit between the Tandys and police, and work to build their trust and respect.

Good luck with that.

"Mr. Tandy is a jerk," Alexa said in the driveway. His accusations had smarted. Despite their failure to find Eileen alive, everyone—police, volunteers, SAR, tracker dogs—had worked hard on her behalf.

"People need someone to blame," Constable Blume said.

"How are we going to get out?" she asked.

"Miss? Can I talk to you?"

Alexa turned. The daughter had followed them outside. She prayed Susie hadn't heard what she'd said about her father.

Foot-in-mouth again. "Sure," Alexa said. "But can you get your dad to move his car? We're blocked in."

Susie sniffed and walked toward the sedan. "I can do it. I have my learner license."

"Bet you're a good driver," Constable Blume said, "but I'll move it. That way you can speak with Ms. Glock."

Susie relinquished the keys from the front kangaroo-pouch pocket of her tie-dyed hoodie. She had her mother's wide-set chestnut eyes and brown hair, but hers was styled in a bouncy way. A red splotch on her jawline looked inflamed, and she scratched at it while Constable Blume started the car. "Mum said you found Aunt Leeny."

"I didn't find her. A tracker dog did." *Was that too graphic?* "Let's get out of the constable's way." The driveway was gravel, with weeds sprouting here and there. Alexa walked toward the middle house and Susie followed. "I'm sorry about your aunt. Were you close?"

Susie buried her hands in her pocket. "Aunt Leeny is fun to hang with. She's way cool. I mean, she was way cool. I was, um, like a daughter to her."

Alexa hoped Benny and Noah would think she was way cool. *But why would they? I'm eight thousand miles away.* "Did your aunt give you driving lessons?"

Susie nodded. She was Alexa's height, but several inches came from her platform tennis shoes. "How did you know? Why are you asking me questions?"

Fair enough. Alexa leaned down and yanked out a weed. "I'm not sure how your aunt died. The forensic pathologist is with her body. He'll find out and let your family know."

"But that man did it, right? Earl Hammer?"

Alexa wondered what was happening at the Chinese settlement. Had they caught him? "We don't know."

The teen kicked into the gravel. "Well, did she like, suffer?"

"I don't know. I'm sorry. I can tell you really loved her, your aunt."

"I didn't think she was selfish. Mum did, but I didn't."

She pulled her right hand out and checked her nails. They were blue and chipped. Then she met Alexa's eyes. "What will happen to Aunt Leeny's car?"

Alexa kept her face neutral. *What was the expression? Barely cold in the grave?* "I don't know. Hopefully she has a will."

Susie kicked the gravel again. "On one of our driving lessons she said she'd give it to me when I graduated. It's almost new."

Before Alexa replied, Susie slouched away, her sweatshirt covering her short-shorts, her pale thighs and legs bare. *Was she a distraught niece or a gravedigger?*

In the patrol car, Constable Blume put a finger to his lips. "Repeat," he said into the radio.

A voice replied, "Suspect spotted on Arrow River Bridge Trail."

"They're closing in," he said.

Chapter Thirty-Three

The drive between Misty's house and the hospital was short. Alexa talked Constable Blume into a quick stop at the hospital canteen, where she bought a yogurt and a stale lemon scone. The constable watched her eat. Alexa felt defensive and checked her messages: Dr. Sally Weiner had CCed her on an email to Ana:

> DNA from S2's molar indicates a distant relative in Otago area. (This person completed a FamilyTree ancestry kit.) I contacted match through website to see if he/she wants to be involved.
>
> Strontium isotopic analysis results: geographical area of childhood residence is also Otago area.

Alexa got goose bumps; S2 had spent her childhood in New Zealand. She had most likely been born here. And died violently here.

"I'm ready," she said, throwing out her trash.

"Not sure I am," Constable Blume said.

Dr. McKenzie was in the anteroom. "We meet again," he said to Alexa, and then introduced himself to Constable Blume.

How strange it must be to go from examining skeletal remains in the morning to dissecting a fresh corpse in the afternoon, Alexa thought.

"Now that someone from the police department is here, we can get started," Dr. McKenzie said.

Constable Blume shot Alexa a look, which she interpreted as "You made this man wait while you fed yourself." *Oh, well.* She couldn't think straight on an empty stomach.

"Manhunt for Hammer, I heard on the news." Dr. McKenzie gestured to a computer screen. "The remains have undergone a full-body CT scan."

"Did you find anything?" Alexa asked.

"No foreign bodies, no other fractures except to the skull." He pointed to the screen.

There were jagged lines in the lower right side of the skull. Dr. McKenzie pointed to the largest line. "The fracture follows a linear pattern." He moved the pen lower. "The blow resulted in a depressed fracture."

It hurt Alexa's head to look. "A single blow?"

"Most likely."

"Can you tell what she was hit with?"

"No." He closed the CT scan and opened up a report. "These are my notes from my initial exam of the body."

His phone rang. He answered as Alexa and Constable Blume skimmed the report.

EXTERNAL EXAMINATION

The body is that of a well-developed, well-nourished, white female, 42 years of age, identified as Eileen Katherine Bowen. The body length is 165.1 cm and the estimated body weight is 62 kg. Body wrapped in vinyl bath curtain, clothed. Scalp hair is blond. Swelling on forehead. The right temporo-parietal area is fractured. No conjunctival petechiae. Soil in nose and mouth. Teeth are natural and in good condition. Ears single pierced, one earring present, right lobe. Left hole is torn, no earring. Two nails on right hand jagged. The breasts are symmetrical. The abdomen is slightly distended. The external genitalia are those of a female adult. No sign of vaginal tearing. The anus has no evidence of injury. The following scars are present: left knee, lower-right abdomen. No tattoos or birthmarks detected.

A life: snuffed out. A body: summed up.

Alexa traded her hiking boots for the gum boots, courtesy of the hospital, and advised Constable Blume to do the same. Unlike examining the skeleton a few hours ago, an autopsy on a fresh body could be messy, though most of the body fluids would be funneled to the side troughs of the exam table and into the sink. She started scrubbing her hands.

Dr. McKenzie aborted his call. "That was the FLO."

"The flow?"

"Family liaison officer. Ms. Bowen's family objects to a post-mortem and requests an external examination only."

Alexa scrubbed her nails with a brush. "We just met her—the FLO—and left the family. Why are they objecting?"

"The FLO didn't elaborate. She only told me as a formality. The body is part of a criminal investigation, so the coroner denied the request."

Alexa looked up at him. He smiled before pulling on protective goggles. "You don't have to scrub so hard. It's not like our patients can catch anything from you."

He had a point.

Alexa thought of suffocation by soil—a fate she hoped Eileen hadn't suffered. "Will you be able to tell if she was dead before she was buried? That would comfort the family."

"Lividity may us help determine that."

Alexa reviewed what she knew about lividity. When

circulations ceases, blood settles to the lowest parts of the body due to gravity and results in reddish-purple discoloration of the skin. After a certain time—she couldn't remember how many hours—the discoloration becomes fixed and won't disappear even if the body is moved from one location to another.

A woman rushed in. "Sorry I'm late. Snafu in the lab."

Dr. McKenzie introduced her as Ms. Bashar. "Best tech there is. Her Sam just turned ten. Did he like the karaoke machine? Our grandson picked it out."

Ms. Bashar wore a hijab and scrubs. "He's a crack-up with it. I appreciate that the amplifier is detachable."

She and the doctor laughed, then turned sober. They gloved up and entered the autopsy suite where Eileen's body was waiting. Alexa and Constable Blume followed.

Dr. McKenzie took his place by Eileen's head. "I'll summarize the known circumstances. The deceased was discovered by a cadaver dog buried twenty-two inches deep at…"

Alexa forced herself to look. Eileen was naked. Her shoulders balanced on a rest so that her neck was extended and her head tipped back. Her limbs were splayed, and her skin tone was slack. Her belly was slightly distended and greenish. *Was there a chance Eileen was pregnant, or was the distention the work of erupting gases under the skin? More work for blood tests to determine,* Alexa supposed.

Eileen had not been washed. Her hair was stiff with dried blood. A fruity smell emanated from her body. Ms. Bashar took photographs as the doctor spoke.

"…removed from ground at 14:40 hours. No weapon recovered with body." The doctor cleared his throat. "Does that sum things up, Constable Blume?"

He nodded earnestly.

Alexa studied him for signs of paleness or perspiration; the constable was bearing up well. He was a better cop than he gave himself credit for.

Alexa shared the temperature readings she had taken at the grave.

The doctor added them to his notes. "Ms. Bashar, will you open the medical examination kit now?"

Ms. Bashar set aside the camera and broke the seal on a brown box. She extracted containers for the hair, fingernail clippings, and hand swabs that Dr. McKenzie collected. Ms. Bashar would seal the box and turn it over to Constable Blume at the end of the autopsy.

Next Dr. McKenzie examined Eileen's eyes, nose, ears, and forehead. "There's slight swelling here. She may have fallen forward or been pushed."

Alexa hadn't noticed the bruise earlier. She had avoided staring at Eileen's face after her initial viewing. It distressed her knowing Eileen had been alive Thursday morning, going about her day, maybe dreading the school board meeting, and ended up dead.

She needed to disassociate, to be unclouded by emotion.

Dr. McKenzie probed through the hair, grunted, and asked Ms. Bashar for help in flipping the body. They did it proficiently, but one of Eileen's arms flung off the table, almost touching Alexa. She shuddered as she placed it along Eileen's side.

Eileen's shoulder blades, buttocks, thighs, and calves displayed mottled purple-red lividity.

"What was her body position in the grave?" Dr. McKenzie asked.

Alexa answered before Constable Blume could speak. "She was lying on her right side, legs straight, ankles crossed."

He raised an eyebrow. "Livor mortis suggests she spent the hours after death on her back. She was somewhere else before she was buried."

Killed, stored, and then buried.

"Shave around the wound, Ms. Bashar," he instructed.

Each scrape of the razor horrified Alexa. Eileen's hair—ruined. Her head—ruined.

When Ms. Bashar finished, Dr. McKenzie positioned a magnifying light over the wound and leaned in. After a moment's silence he said, "A full thickness laceration involving skin and subcutaneous tissue."

"Full thickness? What does that mean?" Alexa asked.

"Down to the bone," Dr. McKenzie said.

The gash was deep and ugly, and the skull looked concave. Alexa's stomach roiled.

"Any idea of what type weapon was used?" Constable Blume asked.

"It could be from a tool, a rock, even from a fall."

"A rock?" the constable asked. "Like Cindy Mulligan?"

Dr. McKenzie shrugged. "I can say her skull was fractured by the velocity of a blow or fall."

"But we need to know," Constable Blume blurted.

"The wounds are nonspecific." He measured the size of the wound and its location. "A blunt force injury to the head is the best I can do for cause of death."

"Can I look through the magnifier?" Alexa asked.

Dr. McKenzie stood back as Alexa leaned in. Up close, the gash lost its power to horrify her. In the margins she spotted grains of sand. She asked for forceps, extracted them, and dropped them in a vial Ms. Bashar held ready. "Might have come from the murder scene, eh?" Ms. Bashar said.

It more likely came from the grave, but it was worth examining in the lab. Ms. Bashar added the evidence to the exam kit.

Dr. McKenzie instructed Ms. Bashar to take fluid and blood samples. Then he told Alexa, "Your presence isn't required for the cutting part of the procedure."

Alexa fought to keep the relief from showing.

"Do you have a moment to look at my findings from this morning?" Dr. McKenzie asked.

Switching gears took a moment. "On the skeletal remains?"

"Our Jane Doe of European descent. I'll give you a quick recap in my office."

"I just received the strontium isotopic analysis results from her molar. She spent her childhood in Otago."

"Interesting," Dr. McKenzie said.

Alexa glanced at Constable Blume; he looked like a stricken child. "You'll be fine," she said. "Let me know when you deliver the examination kit to the station."

She and the doctor threw aprons, masks, and gloves in the bin. Dr. McKenzie moved to the sink. "This is when I scrub."

Alexa followed suit, changed back into her boots, grabbed her kit, and followed him to a cramped office one floor up. She was happy to see a window and blinked. The cars in the hospital parking lot were glazed with rain.

Dr. McKenzie handed her a skeletal diagram with two high-lighted areas: neck and lumbar. He sighed and sat down in his desk chair.

Alexa studied the diagram.

"The findings aren't official, and they aren't pretty." Dr. McKenzie picked up an identical diagram. "The injuries support my theory."

"Which is?" Alexa asked.

"Jane Doe was shoved to the ground. Then the attacker knelt on her spine, snapping it, and wrenched her neck backward."

"Jeez. Are you opening a case?"

"Everyone who knew her is dead. This will stay an unsolved mystery."

Alexa bristled. *Someone had gotten away with murder.*

Chapter Thirty-Four

SATURDAY EVENING

Alexa Ubered from the hospital to Touchdown Car Hire and rented a "compact special."

"Lucky, eh?" the attendant said. "We were just closing."

Finally, a car of her own. She stowed the shower curtain package in the back seat. It was the only evidence she left the hospital with, and it had been signed over to her. The rest would be delivered by Constable Blume. Then she opened the driver's side door.

"It doesn't come with a chauffeur," the attendant said.

Turned out not to be the driver's side door. She set the crime kit on the passenger seat as if she'd meant to do this and scurried through a light rain to the other side.

He wasn't fooled. "You know to drive on the left, eh?"

"I've lived here a year now, thanks." Driving on the left side of the road was getting easier, but she sometimes forgot which side the steering wheel was on.

She collected her thoughts before leaving the lot. Maybe the archivist at the Lakes District Museum would help her investigate missing women of the gold rush era. She vaguely remembered reading about a woman feared drowned.

Her phone buzzed. Her boss's name flashed on her screen. She swiped to accept the FaceTime call. Dan adjusted his round glasses and asked, "What's the latest?"

"I rented a car. Hope it's in the budget."

"A Ferrari?"

She laughed. "What are you doing in the lab on a Saturday night?"

"The monthly report."

"Sorry."

"No worries. Earlier I got to play with a drone. We're using it to digitally map crime scenes. I saw the press release about the principal."

The rain picked up and beat steadily on the roof. "The ex-husband identified her. I just left the autopsy." She glanced at her reflection in the rearview mirror. Her hair was a frizzy mess. "The forensic pathologist said COD is blunt force trauma."

"Ouch," Dan said. "Does he have any idea what weapon was used?"

"He was noncommittal."

"I hear they spotted Earl Hammer."

"He was last seen on the Arrow River Bridge Trail." She wished she was part of the team to hunt him down. She changed the subject. "Eileen Bowen was wrapped in a shower curtain. I'm heading to the lab to see if I can get anything from it." She reached over and patted the crime kit protectively. "There's a shovel, too, that might be involved."

"Shovel?"

"Lividity suggests Eileen was killed elsewhere, moved, and then buried in the Chinese miner's grave."

"Are you shitting me? On top of the bones?"

"We removed the bones. I sent you the report."

He modulated his voice back to Professional Dan. "What else do you have besides the curtain and shovel?"

She thought of the medical examination kit Constable Blume would deliver to the station. "The usual. Personal effects. Soil from the wound. Fingernail scrapings. I sent off DNA from a hat that probably belonged to Eileen, found in the creek." *But why was her hat in the creek and not her body?* This bothered Alexa.

"No other fingerprints?"

"Nothing of value. I'll run the ones from the shovel tonight."

"Continue assisting DI Katakana," he said. Alexa wondered if Dan wished he were out in the field instead of stuck at the lab, every day, all day. "Keep your reports updated."

They hung up. She turned on the blinkers instead of the windshield wipers. She hoped the car attendant hadn't seen.

The Queenstown Police Station was quiet. The desk clerk from this morning looked up as she strode in. His nameplate said Sergeant Dryer. He'd had a long day like everyone else. He hitched up his pants, tucking in his belly. Alexa put her package and kit on the counter and showed her ID in case he didn't remember her.

"Where's your shovel?" he asked.

"In the lab. What's the latest?"

"You're the CSI on the case, right?"

Alexa nodded.

He sniffed. His shiny nose was surrounded by broken capillaries. "Hammer. He's slippery as an eel. They're calling off the search as soon as it gets dark." He looked at his watch. "Which is ten, twenty minutes from now."

Alexa wondered if Ana's offer to join her at a Queenstown motel was still open. But her stuff was in Arrowtown, as was half the New Zealand police force. She'd be okay at the cottage. "Is Ms. Walker in the lab?" she asked.

The sergeant nodded.

Alexa stopped by the property room to log in the shower curtain. The room was the usual fare: computer check-in system, refrigerators, freezers, shelves, and storage lockers.

"Sign here," the clerk said. He accepted the shower curtain

package, logged it in, and then checked it out to her. Screwy, but necessary. A break in custody could let a guilty defendant walk free.

In the lab, Leigh looked up from a computer. "Hiya. I'm entering the shovel prints into AFIS."

"Good," Alexa said. "You can help with the shower curtain when you're finished."

Leigh discreetly checked her phone. "Um, forgot to mention DNA from the hat was a no go. Contaminated, the lab said."

"It was a long shot." Alexa surveyed the lab. The fuming chamber would be ideal to develop possible fingerprints, but the curtain was too big. Cutting it could destroy evidence. She wiped down a card table-sized workstation. Then she covered it with paper and spread the curtain, folded in half, so that the ring holes were visible. There were twelve across, and five were torn. Speckles of dirt and soil littered the paper.

She smelled the curtain. There was no strong chemical odor. She checked the hem. There was no mildew.

"Powders are in that cabinet," Leigh called.

Alexa chose black magnetic powder and a wand and returned to the curtain. She imagined obliterating the seahorses with the black powder; their smiling faces annoyed her. *Where would someone grab the curtain to yank it from the rings?* She decided two-thirds up the side. "Grip and rip," she murmured.

"What?" Leigh asked.

"Talking to myself. I'm glad you have mag powder." Her stomach growled. She tried to ignore it, but she was back to being starved again. She had passed a Fergburger restaurant on her way to the station, and the thought made her salivate. Her phone buzzed. She ignored it.

With mag powder there was no need for a brush. The wand had a magnet at the end. Alexa opened the powder jar and dipped the wand into it until a plume of powder hung below it like a black drip. It reminded her of the Wooly Willy magnetic toy she'd had as a kid, where she'd use a wand to give Willy a mustache and mohawk. Unlike poles attract.

Like her relationship with Bruce.

She ran the plume over the vinyl, forming big circles, leaving a faint blur of gray, waiting for the powder to adhere to the oils in a fingerprint. Nothing.

She tried another location, near the grommets. Nothing. For thirty minutes she plumed and hoovered. She had luck along the curtain ring holes, but the prints were partials and faint and degraded by humidity.

Nothing fresh.

"I'll help while we wait for results," Leigh said. They flipped the curtain and tried the other side. More seahorses taunted them. Nothing.

"To roll a body up and lug it around, the perp had to touch it," Leigh said.

"A fingerprint nailed Hammer for Cindy Mulligan's murder. This time he wore gloves," Alexa said. The thought chilled her. She replaced the curtain in the evidence bag as Leigh cleaned up.

The computer dinged, and like Pavlov's dogs, they raced to find out if the fingerprints on the shovel were compatible with any of their suspects. Alexa grabbed the chair, thought twice, and held it for Leigh.

"Ta." Leigh sat, opened the window, and scanned the results. Alexa turned her back, bit her lip, wondered where Hammer was.

"Three candidates for the first set," Leigh finally said. "Top one is Ana Luckenbaugh, your bone friend."

"I entered her fingerprints for elimination. It's her shovel."

"That's a hit then. Let me look at the lower prints."

Alexa sat at another computer and pulled up the photographs of Eileen in situ. Nothing stood out that she hadn't noticed before. Her photos prior to those were of the vandalized tent. "God is Watching You" and "The Wrath of God" in dripping red. *Was Hammer the tagger? If so, why?*

"I'm done," Leigh said. "Have a go."

Alexa marked the top candidate's print and then compared results: There were similarities. Both whorls. Both central pocket. But she also noted differences. So many that she excluded the print. It was the same for the others.

Leigh's results confirmed Alexa's.

Ana's fingerprints were on her own shovel. Made sense. Earl Hammer's were not. Some unknown person, whose prints were not in the system, left his or her ridges behind. Maybe Olivia had borrowed her boss's favorite shovel.

"Want to go get a burger?" she asked Leigh.

Leigh shook her head and took off her lab coat. "I can't. I have a thing."

Chapter Thirty-Five

She texted DI Katakana from the restaurant parking lot, the Fergburger Deluxe sitting heavy in her gut. No luck with shower curtain or shovel. Then she called Ana to let her know she'd be staying at the cottage.

"Probably a good idea," Ana said. "Shelby has a stomach bug."

"Tell her I hope she feels better," Alexa said.

The windows of the rental car were fogged. Where was the defroster? When she found it and the windows had cleared, she drove the slicked highway the twenty minutes back to Arrowtown, the wipers lulling and efficient. They hadn't saved Eileen Bowen; evil had triumphed.

Plum Tree Terrace hunkered in darkness. She pulled into the driveway of Prospector's Cottage, cursing herself for not leaving the porch light on. *Idiot.* At least her phone was charged. She used the flashlight app, inserted the key in the front door, the crime kit sliding off her shoulder. Her phone buzzed, scaring her.

Inside was dark as well. She scrabbled for the hall light, remembered it was out, and shined the flashlight toward the kitchen. Her heart leaped into her throat as she checked the back door. This time it was closed and locked. She turned on the light and set the kit on the table.

Her phone buzzed persistently. The screen said Unknown Caller. "Hello?"

"Ms. Glock?"

A man's voice, vaguely familiar. "Who is this?"

"DI Unger."

"What's up?"

She heard him take a breath. "I need you to come to my house."

"Why? Where do you live?"

"Not far from your place."

My place? How does he know where I'm staying?

"It's case-related," he added.

"Can't it wait until morning?"

"DI Katakana is on her way. She said for you to bring your crime kit. The address is 14 Norfolk Pine Street." Alexa kicked into gear. She turned lights on in the den and ran upstairs to turn the bedside lamp on. She made sure to turn the porch light on too and retraced her steps to the car. When she returned from whatever this urgent meeting was, the little house would beam its welcome.

Norfolk Pine was only four blocks away. She parked on the grass in front of Unger's green ranch. A porch light was on. A single car was in the driveway; she had beaten DI Katakana. She grabbed her kit and got out of the car. She sensed the mountains all around her—black hulks hunkering in the rain. She shivered and crossed the grass to the front door.

Unger opened it wide before she knocked. His face was gray and hollow, his eyes big. "Come in," he said.

Something wasn't right. She stepped back. A man shot out from a corner of the foyer and aimed a gun at Unger. "Get in here," he said to her.

Alexa gasped.

Earl Hammer. In DI Unger's house. Pointing a gun. Her hand inched toward her pocket where she'd stashed her phone.

"Don't," Hammer growled.

Alexa looked at Unger. He stepped back so she could enter. His face told her that Hammer would kill him if she refused. Maybe kill her.

She forced herself to step in. "Is DI Katakana on the way?"

Unger shook his head. "He made me lie."

Hammer motioned with the gun toward the den. Unger stumbled forward and Alexa followed. Her fear hadn't caught up with her tongue. "What's going on?" she asked.

Unger sank on a plaid couch. His voice was monotone. "He wants you to take his fingerprints. Wants you to compare them with the one used to convict him. He thinks I planted that print. As soon as you compare them, he swears he'll turn himself in."

Alexa eyed a stack of firewood next to a wood-burning stove. Could she grab a log? Hurl it at Hammer? Then she forced herself to look at him. He stood in the doorway. He had aged and shrunk compared to the image in her head. His dark hair was poorly cut. His eyes were menacing slits, like a rattlesnake's. He stepped toward her. "I been watching you," he said.

Her knees jellied. The crime kit slid to the floor. She eyed the gun. Was he going to shoot her?

Hammer slipped the gun into the waistband of his gray sweatpants. "Unger set me up, sent me to prison. Twenty-five years he stole from me." He watched her, gauging her reaction. She tried to hide her fear and disbelief. "Soon as I got out I came for this day of reckoning. Didn't expect the police to go hanging another murder on me. Sick as."

He crossed over and snagged her crime kit. She fought a mother-bear instinct to save it.

"I didn't set you up," Unger said. "Didn't do anything of the kind. The fingerprint expert said it was a one hundred percent match. He testified it was your print on the Discman."

"Weren't mine. Said it then and I'm saying it now." Earl Hammer slammed her kit on the kitchen table. He caught her eye and gestured to it.

Alexa straightened her shoulders. "Your fingerprints are already in the system."

"That weren't my fingerprint on the Discman." He held his large hands out and flexed. "I want the ink and paper kind. Then *you* see if they match. I never laid eyes on no Cindy Mulligan."

She looked at Unger. He was frightened. "Do it," he said.

"You'll turn yourself in if I do?"

"As soon as you tell me the results. World will know Unger planted that evidence."

Yeah, right. She looked toward Unger again. He looked old.

"I didn't plant any evidence," he said. "The fingerprint expert said it was a hundred percent match."

She walked to the table, thankful her legs worked. She pulled the kit, old friend, close to her and unzipped it. Words tumbled out of her dry mouth. "My boss made me get a mobile scanner. I have it here, but you want me to use ink and tenprint?" She didn't look at him and he didn't answer.

The crime kit had gotten a lot of use the past couple days. She rooted for the ink pad, willing her hands to stop shaking. She panicked that she didn't have it, but found it next to her magnifying glass. She pulled it out; it nestled in her palm. "This pad holds a two-year supply of ink. I got it in Raleigh. That's where I'm from."

She was blathering.

Hammer sidled closer. Her blood quit flowing. She glanced at the window behind him. The darkness was impenetrable.

"Raleigh is in North Carolina." She found the tenprint cards and tore one off. Across the top were boxes for First Name, Middle

Name, Last Name, and Aliases. *The Hammer.* She was going to leave them blank but Hammer noticed. "Fill it out," he said.

She found her Pilot G-2. "Earl, right?" Her fingers defied her command not to shake and *Earl* came out a wavy scrawl. "What's your middle name?"

"Tim. Timothy."

Her mind blanked on how to spell Timothy. She wrote Tim and then Hammer. She left Aliases blank. She forced herself to look at him. He stared back, his mouth slightly parted. Her throat constricted. She cleared it. "You should wash your hands. Dirt or other particles can obscure your unique characteristics."

He inspected his fingers, walked to the sink, and turned the faucet on. The gun handle was visible. She wondered if she could grab it and looked toward Unger. He shook his head.

Hammer rinsed and dried his hands. "Make em good."

Alexa took a calming breath and opened the ink pad. "You need to stand next to me."

His proximity was terrifying, and his body odor was ripe like garbage. Six feet or so, solid and muscular. No middle-aged tire ring. *Worked out in prison,* she guessed. She got a wet wipe ready.

He set his right hand, palm down, on the table beside the ink pad. She stared. Nails short, bitten. Two knuckles were scraped. Veins were visible, blueish purple and pulsing. She opened the pad and put her hand on top of his, trying not to shudder.

He flinched.

"Relax," she said. "I'll do the 4-4-2 method. Your four right-hand fingers first, followed by your four left-hand fingers, the thumbs last." Her voice came out calm and confident. She'd slipped into the comfort of science.

"I been threatened, scalded, beaten. Got death threats. My mum got the cancer and died. Do 'em right."

Like faint light through a crack, she let his possible innocence filter through. She helped him tuck all his fingers except the pointer. She rolled it so ink covered the pad from nail to nail, using just the right pressure. Too much ink would obliterate the ridges. She guided the finger to the tenprint box and rolled it in a continuous motion. She lifted his hand straight up to avoid a smear. She sighed with relief at the perfect dark gray print.

"Weren't no violence in my past. No record, either. Didn't matter to nobody."

She guided his next three fingers and then gave him a wet wipe. He tossed the wet wipe to the floor and narrowed his eyes at her. It took will not to cower. She repeated the process with his left hand. When he was ready, she did the thumbs. "All done."

Hammer stared at the tenprint as she waved it to dry and then slipped it into an evidence bag. As soon as she sealed it, fear lodged in her chest. Her task was complete. She was expendable now. She passed him a wet wipe for his black thumbs, but he slapped it away. He took out the gun—she saw now that it was a Glock—and aimed it at Unger. "I got his phone. Do your thing and call. No cops. I'll kill him if I hear from anyone but you."

Chapter Thirty-Six

Her fingers trembled as she punched DI Katakana's number from inside the locked rental car. "Glock? Got news?"

"Where are you?" Alexa asked. Damn rain. She turned the wipers and headlights on high and sped away from Unger's house.

"At the station, where else?"

There were no cars on the road. Alexa drove down the middle, one hand on the wheel, the other pressing the phone to her ear. "I need the fingerprint evidence from Cindy Mulligan's case."

"What for?"

"I'll explain when I get there. I know where Hammer is, but I need that evidence."

She hung up mid-DI-shout and didn't answer when her phone buzzed again. A possum scurried across a roundabout. She slammed on the brakes and the car hydroplaned. She took her foot off the pedal as the crime kit fell on the floor. When she felt traction, she accelerated again. "I'm alive!" she screamed into the night.

What if Hammer was telling the truth? Unger wouldn't be the first cop to tamper with evidence.

Her phone buzzed like an angry bee. She parked at a crazy angle at the station. She flashed her badge at Sergeant Dryer and ran past a huddle of cops toward the DI's office. She must have heard Alexa's footsteps because she met her in the hallway. "What the fuck is going on?"

Alexa pushed a hank of hair out of her eyes, suddenly exhausted. "Earl Hammer is at DI Unger's house. In Arrowtown. I just took his fingerprints. Did you get the evidence?"

The DI's face turned red. "I repeat. What the fuck is going on?"

Sergeant Dryer had followed her and was listening.

"Unger asked me to come to his house. He used you as bait, said you'd be there. I wouldn't have gone otherwise." TMI babble. "Hammer was there. With a gun. He told me to take his prints, with ink, which I did, and compare them to the one that was used to convict him. He says he's innocent."

"That's a laugh," DI Katakana said. "Fingerprint rate of error is zero."

"No, it's not," Alexa said. "That's a fallacy. And, well, Hammer said Unger planted the print. When I do the comparison and call with the results, Hammer said he'd walk out." She was proud of her coherency. "He said he never laid eyes on Cindy Mulligan."

"So he killed Eileen Bowen to prove it?" the DI asked.

"We don't know who killed Eileen," Alexa said.

"I'm calling AOS," DI Katakana. "We've got a hostage situation."

The Armed Officers Squad might end up shooting Hammer, maybe Unger. "Not a good idea. He said no cops." Alexa lifted the kit. "He'll turn himself in as soon as I call with the results."

"Call him now," DI Katakana said. "Tell him what he wants to hear."

She should have expected this, but it felt like a slap. "I'm not calling until I do the comparison."

The color in the DI's cheeks deepened.

"I'll track down that evidence," Sergeant Dryer said. DI Katakana stalked into her office. Alexa watched her pick up her phone, probably a direct line to AOS.

She hurried to the lab. Her hands shook as she scanned

Hammer's tenprint into the computer program, recording each fingerprint separately. She didn't know which finger left the print on the Discman. Right, index would be her guess.

She wished Sergeant Dryer would hurry. What if he couldn't find the twenty-five-year-old evidence? What if it had disappeared?

A theory formed in her head. If Unger hadn't planted the fingerprint like Hammer suspected, then maybe the analysis had been botched. She remembered such a case.

She opened a new browser and searched "Shirley McKie."

In 1997, a woman was stabbed to death in her home in Kilmarnock, Scotland. The police lifted several fingerprints at the scene, including one that matched a handyman who had worked for the victim. They later discovered a tin in the handyman's house that had the dead woman's fingerprints on it. The handyman was arrested and charged with murder.

Police solving crime. All good.

Alexa rubbed the bridge of her nose. The case took a disturbing turn. Four experts testified that a thumbprint lifted from a doorframe in the dead woman's bedroom belonged to Police Constable Shirley McKie. Shirley swore she had never been in the victim's bedroom.

No one believed her. McKie was suspended, fired, and later jailed for perjury. Her career was jerked out from under her.

The thought of losing her career was a nightmare to Alexa.

Two fingerprint experts from the United States examined the thumbprint and concluded it did *not* belong to McKie. She was exonerated, but her reputation was tattered. No apologies came from her department. No Welcome Back party. She ended up working in a gift shop. Alexa couldn't imagine selling stuffed kiwis and All Black caps.

Wait.

If McKie's fingerprint analysis was faulty, what about the handyman's? She read on: The handyman was released from prison because of "faulty fingerprint evidence."

Alexa thought of Earl Hammer. A fingerprint is only as good as the person who analyzes it. Could faulty forensics have sent him to prison? A weight settled on her shoulders, heavy as a sack of sand.

She pushed away from the computer and jumped up and down on her toes, did five jabs, five hooks, five squats, five kicks.

Sergeant Dryer rushed in, waving a manila envelope. "Signed, sealed, and delivered."

She willed her hands to steady as she signed the evidence transfer log and pulled on gloves. "What's DI Katakana up to?"

His eyes darted left and right. "A team is going in."

"Crap," Alexa said.

"They're surrounding the house, that's all. They'll be ready when, well, if he comes out."

That was to be expected, Alexa conceded.

The seal on the envelope was dated one year after Cindy Mulligan was murdered. No one had opened the envelope since then. She broke the seal as Sergeant Dryer watched. A single print on a white backing card waited inside a plastic sleeve. A singlet was unusual. The print was labeled Right Index.

Sergeant Dryer cleared his throat. "How is it?"

Alexa studied it with her magnifying glass. "It's suitable. Not smudged or partial."

"What's Hammer's game?" the sergeant asked.

Alexa didn't have an answer. She scanned the information at the top of the card:

Case Number: 0799970, Victim: Cindy Mulligan, Date: 24/ 02/93, Location: Arrow River Bridge Trail. Print

Lifted from: Sony D-T24 Discman. Print Lifted By: DI Mike Unger.

That worried Alexa. She showed the sergeant. "Detective inspectors usually delegate evidence collection to someone else."

"Might have been different back then," he said. "Are you going to look at them side by side?"

"It's better not to," Alexa said. "When things are right next to each other, people tend to note similarities. Like when you think someone looks like their dog because you see them walking together all the time?"

"I don't look like my dog."

Alexa's patience was kaput. "I'll need another analyst to compare them as well."

"I'll call Ms. Walker," the sergeant said.

"I'll send them to Auckland Forensic Service Center," Alexa said.

When the sergeant left, she called Dan. "What's up, Glock? It's my bedtime."

She explained breathlessly.

Wait," he said. "You know where Hammer is? You took his fingerprints?"

"He says he's innocent. He thinks the print was planted by Unger. He wants me to compare the new prints to the one that convicted him."

"What the hell, Glock? How do you get yourself in these situations?"

"Doing my job. I'm sending the prints to you. Get your best examiner to compare them. Well, that's me. Second best. Don't mention what it's about. We need a blind comparison."

"What if he doesn't like the results?"

Alexa thought of the gun. *Jeez.* "Just hurry."

She disconnected, punched the air, and emptied her brain of expectations. No preconceived ideas.

The fingerprint on the card was an ulna loop. Her fingers steadied. She made notes: ridges curve around core, exit from the same side that they entered. She located the delta. Jotted more details. More points for comparison. Then she scanned the fingerprint into the computer, enlarged the image, and marked several ridge endings. She counted bifurcations where the ridges forked: one, two, three. Another: four.

She closed the image, erased it from her mind, and pulled up the right index from the tenprint. Her heart hammered as she stared at the image. Ulna loop. Core similar. Spatial relationship between ridges similar. She counted bifurcations. One. Two.

Wait. She blinked, rubbed her eyes. Recounted. There were only two bifurcations. These prints were not compatible. If Unger had planted Hammer's print, it would have been compatible.

Some forensic analyst messed up all those years ago.

Alexa felt sucker punched. Earl Hammer had gone to prison based on the certainty that these prints were identical. "I never laid eyes on Cindy Mulligan," he said.

No one had believed him. People called him an animal. Remorseless. Evil.

She checked again. Some commonalities. More differences. *Holy shit.*

It took forever for Dan to call back. "No go," he said.

"That's the conclusion I reached."

Dan whistled. "There's going be major fallout from this. Audits. Accreditation review. Restructurings. Heads will roll. Maybe mine."

"It happened a long time ago," Alexa said.

"The public will want sacrificial lambs."

Hammer had been a sacrificial lamb, Alexa thought. *None of this was his fault.* "I need to tell the DI."

"Let me speak to her," Dan said.

Alexa kept him on the line, printed the reports, and ran to DI Katakana's office. She was yelling into her phone. "Helicopters? Hell, no. How is that undercover?" She hung up. "Give it to me," she said.

Alexa swallowed. "The print from the Discman is not compatible with the prints I just took from Hammer. Here's Dan Goddard, Director of Auckland Forensic Service. He had a verification done."

The DI snatched the phone. "Mr. Goddard?" She cocked her head. Sweat beads broke out one by one on her broad forehead. The lines around her mouth hardened. The argument Alexa expected didn't erupt. A single "bloody hell" flew out of her mouth, and then she handed Alexa the phone.

"I need to call him," Alexa said.

"The house is surrounded. Special ops is in place. I've got a direct line." The DI dialed, put her phone on speaker, and nodded when a man's voice said, "Agent Joe Leland, special ops."

"This is our forensic specialist, Ms. Glock," DI Katakana said. "She's got news."

"Hello?" Alexa said.

"Go ahead," Agent Leland said.

"The prints are not compatible."

"That can't be," he said.

"An independent examiner reached the same conclusion," Alexa said.

"A shitstorm is on the way," DI Katakana said.

"Are you still there, Ms. Glock?" Agent Leland asked. "Call Hammer and tell him what the results are. Tell him we're waiting out front and that no one will get hurt."

Her heart pounded as she dialed and set her phone on speaker.

"What took you so long?" Hammer said.

"Is DI Unger okay?" Alexa asked.

"He's not good, not my doing." Hammer's voice filled her ear canal. "What did you find out, fingerprint lady?"

Alexa met DI Katakana's eyes. "The prints I just took from you and the one from Cindy Mulligan's Discman are not compatible."

"They don't match? Is that what you're sayin'?"

"That's right."

"I knew it." He coughed, stuttered. "Unger set me up."

"The prints don't match, but it wasn't Unger." She could barely force the words out. "The fingerprint analyst messed up."

"Messed up is one way of putting it." After a moment Hammer said, "I don't have anything to do with this other lady's murder. Don't pin that on me."

Alexa swallowed. "Are you ready to come out?"

Hammer didn't answer. Alexa looked to DI Katakana for cues. The DI reached for her phone. "Mr. Hammer? This is DI Pattie Katakana." Her voice was steady, cool. "I have an officer at the house, ready to escort you. Walk out of the front door with your hands up. He'll bring you here. If what Ms. Glock says is true, there will be a full investigation into your unjust conviction."

Quiet.

"Do you want me to let Agent Leland know you're ready to come out?"

More silence.

Alexa grabbed her phone back. "I'm sorry for what happened," she said.

Chapter Thirty-Seven

Someone at the scene videotaped Hammer's surrender. Alexa watched with Sergeant Dryer in the break room. Earl Hammer came out first, hands up. Two police officers in riot gear cuffed him and led him to a patrol car.

Alexa saw tension drain from the spectators—most in black ops uniforms, a few in suits.

When an ambulance crew brought Unger out on a stretcher, the AOS squad watched solemnly. Had Hammer shot him?

The gravity of the situation was hard to process. DI Katakana popped in and announced a press briefing. "Scheduled for as soon as the deputy commissioner arrives."

"Do you want me there?" Alexa asked.

The DI paused. "Yes, but not to answer questions. No big reveal about the fingerprints. Just that Earl Hammer is in custody. The shit will hit the fan tomorrow."

"What happened to Unger?" Alexa asked.

"Heart attack. Mild. He's in hospital."

When it was time to meet the press, Alexa stood between DI Katakana and the deputy commissioner—a tall man named Garrett with a grave demeanor. The reporters gathered in front of the station, on the sidewalk. Alexa counted ten in all and blinked in their flashing lights.

DI Katakana said, "Thank you for gathering again and at such a late hour. After my sad announcement this afternoon about the discovery of Eileen Bowen's body, I have better news. Earl

Hammer, the escaped parolee, is in custody, thanks to members of the Queenstown Police Department, a team of special armed officers, and Ms. Glock, a forensics investigator. Hammer surrendered in Arrowtown."

The reporters cheered. One raised a hand. "*NZ Herald.* Has Hammer been charged with the death of Eileen Bowen?"

DI Katakana stiffened. "We aren't jumping to conclusions."

"John Blinkly, *News Stuff.* Was Hammer cornered? Is that why he surrendered?"

"No comment."

"Was he armed?" the same reporter asked.

"No comment," DI Katakana said.

"What role did Ms. Glock play?" another reporter asked.

"A crucial role, but we are withholding details at this time."

The deputy commissioner stepped forward. "We are in the critical incident debriefing process. It's been a stressful situation for our police and public, but we are thankful for a peaceful outcome. The public is safe. Earl Hammer faces numerous charges and is being held without bail. That's all we have time for now."

Afterwards, DI Katakana squeezed Alexa's wrist. "We have two murders to solve now. Team meeting, eight a.m, Arrowtown Policing Centre."

———

Her dreams that night came in relentless waves. Working in a gift shop that specialized in glass false teeth. Hammer's inky fingertips. Being buried alive. She woke in a sweat and gulped cold water in the bathroom. Her eyes in the mirror were wide and woebegone. "Happy birthday to me," she said.

The worst dream was an earthquake at dawn. The ground beneath her feet shifted, cracked, opened, and swallowed her.

Chapter Thirty-Eight

SUNDAY MORNING

She parked the rental car across from the miners' cottages on Buckingham Street at 7:50 a.m. The earth was soggy from yesterday's rain. The elms and oaks were mostly stripped bare, and what leaves hung on were bedraggled. She felt the same way.

Inside the center, the long-faced deputy commissioner and another man—dressed in black pants and black polo—conversed in urgent tones on one side of a table. Alexa sat opposite them, between two cops. She scanned their nameplates: Constable Kate Stafford sat on her left and Senior Sergeant Fielding sat on her right. She wondered if they'd been briefed. The guy with the deep cleft between his eyebrows said, "We've met."

He was right. She'd been a tad bossy to him at the cemetery. The man across the table caught her eye. He was bald, and his eyes were hard. He shot out a hand. "We spoke on the phone last night. I'm Agent Joe Leland. You're the fingerprint expert, eh? Hammer kept his promise to you."

Everyone stared at her. She flushed.

The volunteer Carrie hovered over a side table. "Coffee and tea are ready," she called.

DI Katakana and Constable Blume barreled in. "On time, thanks," DI Katakana said. She marched to the head of the table and took several binders out of her briefcase. "Good morning. First things first. I phoned DI Unger at hospital. It wasn't a heart attack. They're calling it tachycardia caused by stress. He's being monitored, but he was able to speak. Constable Blume, recap how Hammer abducted him."

Constable Blume stood and flipped his notepad open. "Retired DI Unger walked home from here at eight fifteen p.m. last night and entered his house. Didn't lock it. Hammer walked right in behind him. Stuck a gun in his back."

"Where the hell did he get a gun?" Senior Sergeant Fielding asked.

DI Katakana pulled at the cuffs of her navy blazer. "It was Unger's service gun. We're not sure how Hammer got it."

"Donuts, anyone?" Carrie asked.

"Not now," the DI snapped. She focused on Alexa. "Please inform the team what transpired with Hammer last night."

Alexa stood. "Unger called me. It was around nine p.m. He asked me to come over and to bring my kit. When I got there, I, um, met Hammer. He said he was innocent of Cindy Mulligan's murder and told me to fingerprint him. He said to compare them with the one used to convict him and that if I did, he'd let Unger go and turn himself in."

"Crazy bull," Senior Sergeant Fielding said.

Alexa swallowed. "DI Katakana tracked down the evidence from the case, and I compared the prints."

The cops stared, speechless.

Her heart rate climbed. "The prints are not compatible. My analysis was blindly verified by another examiner in Auckland."

"What do you mean?" Constable Blume asked.

Alexa was surprised the DI hadn't confided in him. Or anyone else, apparently. "Hammer's right index fingerprint isn't compatible with the right index fingerprint lifted from the Discman."

"So wait. What?" Constable Blume pushed back so that his chair screeched. "He's not the killer?"

"It wasn't Hammer's print on the Discman. From what I can tell, the fingerprint witness is at fault, not Unger or the police."

Senior Sergeant Fielding glared at Alexa. "Naff off. Who's to say you're right, and someone twenty-five years ago, who isn't here to defend his findings, is wrong? Fingerprint error is one in a million."

"An independent analyst confirmed it," Alexa repeated. She slid into her chair. The findings were a blow to forensic science, the foundation she counted on. Maybe that's why she'd had an earthquake dream.

The officers digested the bombshell. Shock and disbelief flickered across their faces.

"Then who killed Cindy Mulligan?" Constable Blume stuttered.

"And Eileen Bowen?" Constable Stafford asked.

"I've news on who *didn't* kill Ms. Bowen." DI Katakana's dark eyes roamed the room like a challenge. "I spent an hour with Mr. Hammer last night. He claimed he arrived in Arrowtown Friday afternoon. He had a petrol receipt in his wallet. Noon, Friday? He's filling up in Fairley, three hours from here. CCTV has confirmed it. According to the forensic pathologist's report, Ms. Bowen was dead by then."

"This is a total cock-up," Senior Sergeant Fielding said.

"Can't argue that," DI Katakana said. "We are not releasing this information to the public for the time being. Whoever killed Eileen Bowen needs to think *we* think Hammer did it. That will buy us time."

That wasn't fair to Hammer, Alexa thought.

DI Katakana shot daggers at the team. "Is that clear?"

Deputy Commissioner Garret stood. "What we have is an unfolding situation. No announcement about the finger-prints will be made for twenty-four hours. I've sent them to

independent analysts, some international," he said. "If their findings confirm Ms. Glock's discovery, we have a *national* cock-up.
False imprisonment is unconscionable. Shocking. We'll need to
investigate the extent of our forensic failures and whether other
people have been erroneously incarcerated."

"Public trust will tank," Constable Stafford said.

"The investigation will be handled by internal affairs,"
Deputy Commissioner Garrett continued. He took his jacket
from the chairback. "Work under the premise that Ms. Glock is
correct and the prints don't match."

"We don't use the word *match*," Alexa said.

He sighed. "The Crown will have to acknowledge a miscarriage of justice."

"I'll walk you out," DI Katakana said. "Five-minute break."

The cops huddled by the coffee, their backs to Alexa, even
Constable Blume. She got the message. She checked her phone
as she ate her sawdust donut. Bruce had called.

Finally.

She texted that she'd call him later. She couldn't wait to talk
with him, to fill him in, get his advice, hear his voice.

She had a text from Dr. Weiner: S2's descendant does not
wish to be contacted. 😟

Alexa thought of S2's violent death. Maybe it was for the best
that this descendant didn't learn the details. But who turns their
back on family?

She was sad for the skeleton. She was sad for the two murdered women. She was sad for forensics. She was sad she'd cast
her relationship with Bruce aside like it didn't matter.

Chapter Thirty-Nine

DI Katakana called them back. Alexa shook off her gloominess, grabbed a cup of coffee and returned to the table. For once she was glad she wasn't in charge. The DI started with: "I've made a big mistake."

That got everyone's attention.

"I've focused the investigation on Earl Hammer. What's that expression? Red herring?"

"Nah, yeah," Constable Blume said.

"According to the forensic pathologist, Eileen most likely died Thursday afternoon from blunt force trauma. Rock, shovel, crowbar, even a fall could have cracked her head.

"Or a push," Constable Blume added.

"Not much insect activity; she hadn't been buried for more than twelve hours. The murderer has had sixty hours to flee the area, or clean up, establish an alibi, make him or herself look innocent. Might even have helped with the search, eh?"

"I'll get the list of volunteers," Constable Blume said.

"To be fair, ma'am," Senior Sergeant Fielding said, "We've only known Ms. Bowen was murdered for twenty-four of those sixty hours. We were working our asses off to find her."

Good point, Alexa thought.

"Ta, Senior Sergeant. There's more news from the patholo-gist. Ms. Bowen was pregnant. Eight weeks."

Alexa's mouth dropped.

"Nah, yeah, a wee poppet," Constable Blume said. "Can't get it out of my head."

Eileen's bloated stomach hadn't just been signs of early decomposition.

The DI squared her shoulders. "I spoke with the boyfriend, Langston Johnston. Claimed he didn't know, but he reckons he's the father."

Pregnant at forty-two? Had Eileen wanted the baby?

"Think the pregnancy factors in her murder?" Constable Stafford asked.

"Maybe, maybe not. We'll consider a slim possibility that there is a single murderer," the DI said. "If we thought Earl Hammer was responsible for both Cindy Mulligan and Eileen Bowen's deaths, then someone else could be. This is our golden hour—when *he* doesn't know *we* know Hammer is innocent."

"If he is," Senior Sergeant Fielding said.

Alexa took a deep breath and focused on the stack of bind-ers in front of the DI. "Was anything used to convict Hammer besides the fingerprint? Any witnesses on the trail? Anything to link him to the scene?"

DI Katakana pushed the binders toward Agent Lee. "Find out. And find what other suspects there were."

"I'd like to review anything forensic-related," Alexa said.

Senior Sergeant Fielding narrowed his eyes. "Haven't you done enough?"

Alexa flinched.

"No shooting the messenger," DI Katakana said. "We're after the truth, no matter if it leaves us with our pants down."

Constable Blume laughed, and then flushed.

The DI pushed packets to everyone. "This is courtroom testimony of Earl Hammer versus Cynthia Mulligan trial. Read it, but not now. First we will concentrate on Eileen Bowen." She closed her eyes for a second. "She was killed somewhere, spent hours on her back, then was moved and buried. Where was she killed? Where was she stored?"

No one answered.

The DI riffled through the papers. "Personal information: divorced, no children—well,—one on the way—one sister, Misty Taylor. Career: Eight years as a classroom teacher, got a master's degree in administration, worked as assistant head at Livingston Primary, and has been principal at Arrowtown for four years. Well-liked, according to the secretary. All good, eh?"

"The students liked her too," Carrie said.

DI Katakana nodded. "We're waiting on mobile records. She's dead, and we're still song and dancing. The computer lads have turned over her emails. These are for you to wade through, Constable Stafford."

"Yes, Senior."

"Finances: Bank of Otago. Decent salary. Income from a rental property." She paused. "Someone find that property, get a search warrant. Maybe that's where she was killed."

"On it," Senior Sergeant Fielding said. "What about a will?"

"She didn't have one."

"With no spouse, children, or living parents, the estate is divided equally among siblings," he said. "The pregnancy—the baby—would have changed that."

"Could be a motive, eh? She paid cash for the Arrowtown house," DI Katakana added.

"Where did she get the money?" Constable Blume asked.

"Inheritance. The father passed away eighteen months ago.

Get the deets." She shoved a binder at Constable Blume and turned to Alexa. "Where are we with forensics?"

Alexa willed her voice strong. "The shower curtain the body was wrapped in was a dead end. I suspect the assailant wore gloves. Touch DNA from Eileen's hat was a no-go. Constable Blume took footwear impressions from around the grave. One is blurred, but the other is from a Wolverine brand boot, size eleven."

"Okay then," DI Katakana said. "That's something."

They're a mass-manufactured work boot, so it wasn't much, Alexa knew. "The fingerprints on her car door handle were compatible with the sister—Misty Tandy." She explained about the driving lessons.

"I'm towing the car so we can get inside. What else?" the DI asked.

"Ms. Walker compared the tool marks left in the grave soil with Dr. Luckenbaugh's shovel left in the tent and concluded they don't share a common origin." Ana's shovel did have some unidentified prints on it, though. Alexa made a note to ask Olivia if she had used it.

"Ms. Walker thinks a wheelbarrow was used to transport Eileen's body."

"That gives us something to look for," Constable Stafford said.

"The scrapings from under Eileen's fingernails have been sent off for processing," Alexa added.

"How long?" the DI asked.

"Usually ten days. I asked for a rush." *Maybe fingernail clippings had been taken from Cindy Mulligan,* Alexa thought, though DNA wasn't routinely collected in 1998. "Was biological evidence collected in Cindy Mulligan's case?" she asked.

"Unger will know. He wants to talk with you."

Great.

"While you're at it, collect prints from everyone on our Bowen suspect list. Except for Paul Bowen. He gave his the other night."

Alexa nodded.

DI Katakana stared at her. "What are you waiting for?"

Kicked out of class. Her cheeks reddened as she collected her belongings and left. She plodded toward the rental car. At least she didn't have to bum a ride.

"Ms. Glock?"

Alexa turned.

Leigh Walker caught up with her. She looked toward the center. "Are you leaving?"

Alexa nodded. "Did you hear about the fingerprint comparison I did last night?"

Leigh's face darkened. "The fingerprint evidence being faulty? How could it have happened?"

"Fingerprint comparisons are only as good as the analyst," Alexa said.

Leigh hooked her blond hair behind her ears. "Cops everywhere will be hacked off at us. Our cred is down the drain."

"We didn't cause this," Alexa said, but Leigh's fears were her fears. Part of her wanted to wither. But she needed to buck up. "DI Unger was the one who lifted the print. It's better when evidence is collected by trained forensics, right, like we do now? And we verify findings and don't use words like *match* or *one-hundred percent.*"

Leigh nodded. "It's still a cloud over our heads."

Chapter Forty

Facing Unger was the last thing she wanted to do. His world had cracked open. He would no longer be the hero of Arrowtown. She forced her foot to press the accelerator and maintain the speed limit.

Unger was sitting up in the hospital bed. He wore a gray gown and looked like hell. He was hooked up to a monitor. Respiration. Heart rate. Blood Pressure. Alarm. His eyes, though, were alert and followed her as she pulled up the chair. "How are you?" she said.

"Hanging in there."

The green lines on the monitor climbed and dove. *Were they supposed to be so steep?* His heart rate was ninety-nine. *He was nervous.* "DI Katakana said you wanted to speak to me."

"Me planting evidence?" His voice croaked. "Bullshit, right?"

His heart rate jumped to one-oh-three. "There's no sign of any tampering on your part, but the prints I took aren't compatible with the print from the Discman."

The green number jumped to one-fifteen. Unger's hand went to his chest. "How could that be? The fingerprint expert?" One-twenty. "He said it was a match. No chance of error."

"There's no such thing." She jumped up, ready to start CPR.

A nurse scurried in. "Give us some privacy, luv," she said.

Unger looked at her with despair as she backed out of the room. *God almighty.* She had felled forensic science and caused a cardiac arrest, all in a single morning.

She paced in the waiting room, avoiding eye contact with a woman knitting a baby sweater. A gender-neutral green and yellow. *Had Eileen wanted a baby?*

Hospitals reminded her of the accident. The scalding of her back when she'd just turned thirteen. Three skin grafts. Three hospital stays. The pain. The isolation. Missing school. She bent over and touched her toes, ignoring the knitter's funny look.

Upside-down in an upside-down hemisphere. Her scars protested; she'd neglected her stretches. Right-side-up she enjoyed the blood rush and checked at the nurse's station. Four women in scrubs looked up from various screens as she asked, "Is DI Unger okay?"

"Are you family?" one asked.

"I work with him. I was visiting."

"His heart rate has stabilized," the first Scrub said. "Since you're with the police you can go back in."

The bed was lowered this time. Unger stared listlessly at the ceiling.

"I'm back," she said.

He raised the bed. His silver ponytail snaked over his shoulder. She checked his heart rate: eighty-eight. "Let's get this over with," he said.

The ubiquitous cup with straw poking out waited on the table. "Do you need anything?" Alexa asked. "Water?"

"I need the truth."

"You have it." She pulled the chair up and sat. "The fingerprints were not compatible. This has been verified, blindly, by another examiner."

"So Hammer didn't kill Cindy Mulligan?"

Alexa stayed quiet.

His heart rate climbed to ninety-nine. "How could it have happened?"

"Breakdown along the crime-scene-to-lab-to-courtroom pipeline." Alexa kept her eyes on the numbers. "You lifted a good print. The fault is with the forensic examiner, the expert witness." She had read the courtroom testimony in the hospital parking lot; it had seared in her mind:

THE COURT FOUND THE FOLLOWING TESTIMONY SUF-
FICIENT TO CONFORM TO RULE:

[**State**]: *The latent-print card that was in State's Exhibit 3, did you compare those to the defendant's prints that were State's Exhibit 11?*

[**Expert Witness**]: *Yes, ma'am.*

[**State**]: *Did that latent print match the Defendant's prints?*

[**Expert Witness**]: *It was a 100 percent identification.*

"Who was the expert witness?" she asked.

"Tobias Drake." Unger rubbed his beard. "He testified in lots of cases. Retired by now."

"Was there other evidence linking Hammer to Ms. Mulligan's murder besides the fingerprint?"

Unger leaned for the cup. Alexa jumped up and handed it to him. "Outdoor crime scenes don't yield much." He sipped water. "The track, the rain, the fact she was dumped into the river. We had that Discman to show where she was killed. She still had the earplug in one ear. One witness, a woman, saw Hammer on the trail, in the vicinity at the right time, or thought it was him. Nothing else, even after divers searched the river and teams searched the bush."

"DI Katakana has assigned Agent Leland to the case. He'll want your help."

He placed the cup on the table and leaned back, sighing. The heart rate number dropped to ninety-five, then ninety-three. "I'm not going to press charges against Hammer. I've done enough damage."

"What other suspects did you have?" Alexa asked.

"Some man at her work. She refused his advances. A woman, also at her work. An accounting firm in Frankton. They argued about something. Might have been a few more. I can't remember."

She stood. "Do you remember if you took fingernail scrapings?"

He nodded. "It was a dead end."

Chapter Forty-One

Alexa pried her attention from Cindy Mulligan to Eileen Bowen. In the periphery of her mind, the hungry ghost flickered like a lightning bug. *Help me go home.*

What about S2? What would happen to her remains? Alexa was used to working more than one case at a time; in the lab, she processed ten to twenty per day. Police officers were always over-cased. Only TV investigators worked one case at a time. She looked down at her khaki pants and creased button-down shirt. *They dressed better too,* she thought.

DI Katakana has asked her to fingerprint all the Eileen Bowen suspects, except the ex-husband. Misty Tandy lived close to the hospital, but Alexa already had her prints. Susie and Martin Tandy made her uneasy. She decided to stop by the Tandy house and collect their prints. Sunday morning was a good time to find families at home.

Or not.

No car or van was in the driveway, and the garage door was closed. Alexa parked and got out. The house needed paint and the foundation had cracks. Misty wasn't spending her inheritance fixing it up.

There was no sound when Alexa rang the doorbell. She knocked, waited, and knocked harder, not expecting anyone.

Susie opened the door, scowling. She wore that tie-dye sweatshirt with flannel pajama pants. "What?"

"Hi, Susie. I'm Ms. Glock. We met yesterday."

Her eyes widened. She lifted her chin, and Alexa saw that patch of inflamed skin at her jawline. "I saw you on telly. You caught the man who killed Aunt Leeny. Is he in jail?"

"Yes, he's in custody. Are your parents home?"

"I don't know. I was sleeping." She yelled over her shoulder. "Mum? Dad?" There was no answer. Alexa wouldn't be able to fingerprint Susie without consent from her parents.

Susie turned back. "Did you find out about the car?"

This kid didn't waste a minute. "Your aunt's car?"

Susie nodded. She fluffed her bed-head hair with her fingers. A purple-cased phone was attached to her other hand like an appendage.

"Your parents will want to contact an attorney about Ms. Bowen's estate. Where do you think they are?"

"At a job or Papa's house, maybe. Aunt Leeny turned it into an Airbnb. I helped her decorate it. Mum cleans it between renters. Dad keeps up the yard."

"Who is Papa?"

"My grandfather. He died."

Alexa's heart skipped a beat. "Can I have the address?"

Susie frowned. "Why?"

"I have some information for your parents."

She opened the door wider and found the address on her phone. "It's eleven Bracken Street in Arrowtown."

"Thanks," Alexa said. "Are you okay? Home alone?"

Susie gave her a funny look. "Why wouldn't I be?"

Chapter Forty-Two

Kimiākau Jet, where Eileen's boyfriend worked, was on the way to the Airbnb. Alexa called the adventure tourism company and asked for him. "Lang is on the river," the friendly receptionist said. "He'll be back in twenty minutes. Can I book you a ride?"

"No," Alexa said quickly. "I'm with the police. I need to speak with him."

"Come along then."

She left a message with DI Katakana about the rental house. "It's in Arrowtown. It could be where Eileen went Thursday afternoon. Misty and Martin Tandy might be there. I'm headed there after I fingerprint the boyfriend."

A high, narrow bridge crossed the Shotover River. She had a few minutes to kill before Mr. Jet Boat returned. She got out at the overlook. A family did the same, and they stood together, staring down at the turquoise ribbon winding between canyon walls. Alexa was not immune to the beauty; it tugged at something poetic and beyond science and facts. She read a sign:

Gold was discovered in the Shotover River in 1862. The gold and the rush it brought helped build ports, roads, and railways to open up Central Otago.

Another sign was devoted to the bridge:

The original Shotover bridge was built in 1871, and then washed away by floods in 1878. After rebuilding and reopening in 1915, the Shotover Bridge is an impressive 172 metres long, and 16 metres above the Shotover River.

Her fear of heights triggered, she hustled back to the car. The GPS ordered her onto Gorge Road. She drove down and down and then crossed a narrow one-lane bridge which ended at Arthur's Point beach. She parked and watched tourists in life jackets board a bright red boat from a pier.

The river tumbled and tantalized. A pang of jealousy jabbed Alexa. *Oh, to be a tourist, with Bruce. His daughters Sammy and Denise would love a jet boat ride.* She shook it off and grabbed the portable fingerprint scanner. Inside, she told the perky ticket attendant that she was here to talk with Langston Johnston.

"He'll be back in six minutes. You can watch him come in."

Alexa walked to the bank and searched brownish sand for nuggets. She cupped her hands into the clear icy water and let it dribble out. Time was passing, dripping away, precious and ethereal. Today she was thirty-eight.

She clawed the wet sand for gold. Like clockwork a red boat shot into view and executed a 360. A veil of spray and screams surrounded it.

Showoff, Alexa thought. She rinsed her hands and approached the jetty.

An employee tied the boat to the dock. Langston helped people disembark, accepted tips, and laughed when a bedraggled woman said, "I'll do it again on my eightieth."

A drenched teenager said, "Crazy, man. I didn't know you could drive a boat like that."

When the last tourist left the pier, Alexa went to meet him. "Good ride?"

Langston untied the boat and smiled perfunctorily, his straight white teeth contrasting with his dark hair and beard. A headband held his longish hair away from his handsome face. "*Great* ride. How can I help you?"

"I'm Alexa Glock, a forensics investigator working the Eileen Bowen murder case."

His knuckles tightened on the rope. "I heard they caught Earl Hammer."

"That's right. He's in custody. DI Katakana has been in touch, right? She asked me to gather fingerprints of Eileen's family and friends."

"What for?"

She pegged him as in his mid-thirties, maybe older. Not a boy toy. "Process of elimination."

An eyebrow appeared over the sunglasses. "I don't have any reason not to. Let me fetch some rubbish off the river, and then I'll come up." He paused. "Unless you're interested in a quick ride?" He pointed to a life jacket next to the driver's seat.

Alexa considered the offer. There was a slim chance he had killed his girlfriend. Didn't want a baby. Didn't want to be tied down. It would be stupid to ride with him. While she debated, he contacted someone by radio. "Fanny? Two-liter plastic bottle snagged at Sprinter Point. I'm going for it. Back in ten."

He couldn't off her in ten minutes. She held up the mobile scanner. "Will this get wet?"

He pulled the boat closer and reached for a dry bag, which he tossed to her along with the life vest.

She secured the scanner, stuffed it in her coat pocket, and

adjusted the life jacket so it was snug. She took his hand to step on to the boat.

"Call me Lang. Hold on."

She sat and grabbed the bar in front of her.

The steep rock walls on either side of the canyon narrowed after the first bend. She looked up at a blur of red and yellow leaves and a sliver of sky. A gazillion horsepower engine vibrated throughout her body. The boat skimmed the water on its side, thrusting Alexa closer to Lang. Holy crap. He aimed at a rocky island and veered at the last second. She scream-laughed and squeezed her eyes tight.

A lessening of horsepower lured them open. Lang sidled around another bend, and eased toward a boulder that sliced the river like a razor clam. A stunted tree clung to the side of the rock, a soda jug wedged in its branches. "Hold the wheel," Lang said.

He hopped up before she could protest. She scooted over and held the wheel, the engine thrumming impatiently. Lang used a gaff to drag the trash toward the boat. The tool made Alexa's shoulder throb. She'd been gaffed a couple months ago during a case.

"I used to think rubbish was the worst thing," Lang said.

Alexa relinquished the wheel. "And now?"

He didn't answer.

In the shallows the water was gold-tinted, alluring. "The river is beautiful," she said.

Lang drove back slowly, without speaking. He tied them up and Alexa gave him her life jacket and the dry bag. On the way to the welcome center, he stomped the soda bottle with his boot: *Merrells*, she noted. "How long had you and Eileen been going out?"

Recycle bins lined the side of the building. He threw the

trash away and pointed toward an employees' entrance sign. "Almost six months. Do you know about the baby?"

Alexa nodded. She followed him inside and waited until he stepped out of an insulated jumpsuit.

"I just found out. Eileen didn't tell me."

When he removed his sunglasses, she saw that his eyes were the color of the river. She set the mobile fingerprint scanner on the break table and thought of how his photograph was on Eileen's bedside table.

He pulled out a chair and sat. "I'm gutted. I can't get over that she's gone, that I'll never see her again. I was moving in, gave up my lease."

"I'm sorry for your loss."

"Why didn't she tell me? About the baby?"

His eyes glistened. Alexa fished through her pockets for a tissue. All she could find was a pineapple lump.

"I wish we had the death penalty so they could fry him."

Alexa turned on the scanner and took his hand. "Start with your right thumb. Press here."

"Did she suffer?"

"I don't know. I'm sorry."

In the car she checked to see if he had a record. It came back clean, like he wanted to keep the river.

Chapter Forty-Three

Bracken Street sounded sinister. What was bracken, anyway? Brush? Undergrowth? Ferns? A spinney? A copse? The latter sounded like corpse. She found the address. The Tandy's tan sedan was not parked in the gravel driveway. She peered at the rental house. It was a cottage, painted brown, with a gabled roof, a wooden porch with ivy-twisted columns, and green shutters. Large trees loomed over it, shedding burnt-orange leaves, and like a lot of houses in Arrowtown, water ran behind it. Alexa wasn't sure whether it was the Arrow River or Bush Creek. She pulled into the narrow driveway and called DI Katakana. Voicemail. Again. "I'm at the rental house. There are no cars in the driveway."

A woman walked past the house, head held high, an unleashed dog waddling behind her. Alexa got out and waved. The woman looked at her curiously and turned down the next driveway. The dog—a short brown fireplug—did the same. Alexa scurried to catch up. "Hello?"

"Yes?" the woman said.

She did not look like her dog. She was tall, thin, Kate Hepburn-ish from *On Golden Pond*. Alexa related to that movie because of the strained relationship Jane Fonda's character had with her dad. "My name is Alexa Glock. I'm working forensics with the police."

Her faded blue eyes widened. "Forensics?"

"I have a few questions about your neighbors." She pointed to Eleven Bracken.

"That's the Topping place," the woman said.

"Topping?"

"Walter and Grace Topping. Well, they've passed on, and now poor Eileen has too. It's just too much."

The fireplug sniffed Alexa's Keds. She reached down to pet its fuzzy head. "It's a rental house now?"

"I don't know why Eileen bought the Plum Tree Terrace house instead of moving into this one. Size, maybe. This one is tiny. She turned it into one of those Airbnbs as soon as Walt died." The woman's voice even had the older Kate Hepburn's quaver. "Travelers coming in and out all the time now. I don't like it, but that's happening all over town. Tourists love Arrowtown. The colors in autumn, the gold rush charm."

This woman was a gold mine of information. "Is Eileen's sister a co-owner?"

"I wouldn't know. Misty and Walt didn't get along. Would you tell Misty to keep her lodgers out of my yard? Someone drove straight into the back. And tell her to finish cutting the Coprosma. Half of it is sprawling all over my garden."

What the heck was Coprosma? "When did you last see Eileen?"

"I mostly see Misty. She's in there now," the woman said. "Cleaning, I suppose."

Alexa eyed the house. Where was Misty's car? "Can you try to remember when you last saw Eileen? It's important. She has that little red Smart car."

The woman's chiseled chin quivered. "That's right. Looks like a ladybug. Poor girl. So young."

Alexa wanted more concise information, but she couldn't ask leading questions. "Any idea what day?"

"They all run together." She turned her back to Alexa and walked toward her house, which was yellow and cheerful.

The fireplug followed.

Alexa retrieved the mobile fingerprint gadget and headed up the path to number eleven. A basket of dirty linens was on the porch. Misty answered the door, scowling like her daughter. Or maybe it was the other way around. "Hi," Alexa said.

A screen separated them. "Thought you were the renters," Misty said. "They're always showing up early. Trying to slip in some free hours. The liaison said Hammer is in custody."

"That's right," Alexa said. "Can I come in? I have a few questions."

Misty stepped out instead. She wore rubber cleaning gloves and her purple Crocs. "Did he tell you why he did it? Why he killed Eileen?"

"No, sorry," Alexa said. "Is your husband here?"

"Marty?"

"DI Katakana asked me to fingerprint Eileen's family and friends, you know, for process of elimination." She tried to remember what Martin Tandy looked like, but couldn't. "I stopped by your house, and Susie said you might be here."

She flexed her gloved fingers. "You already took my fingerprints."

"That's right. Now I need Mr. Tandy's."

"Why? You've got Hammer."

"Loose ends," Alexa said.

"Marty isn't here. He'll be back soon." She pushed a hank of hair behind her ear. "I need to finish the cleaning."

"Who owns this house?" Alexa asked.

Misty stared at her feet. "I'm not sure."

"You don't know who owns it?"

"Well, Eileen does. Or did."

"And you clean it?"

Misty reddened. "We have—had—an arrangement. Eileen split the proceeds with me in exchange for cleaning it and keeping the garden tidy. Throw the dog a bone, Marty says—but we need the money."

"Why was Eileen the owner if it was your parents' house?"

The scowl returned. "Father left me high and dry. Or *Walter* left me high and dry. He never liked me calling him 'father.' Since Mum died first, he changed their will. Eileen got it all, and she *knew* that wasn't fair. After Airbnb takes their chunk, we split the rest."

Alexa's mind shifted gears. Her heart picked up speed. "Walter wasn't your biological father?"

"My daddy died. Car wreck when I was a baby. Mum married Walter when I was five. He never took to me, try as hard as I did to be good, you know, to please him. Eileen came a year or two later. So pretty, she was. Apple of his eye." She sniffed, wiped her nose with the glove. "Everyone loved Eileen."

Someone didn't. Alexa knew she was venturing beyond the realm of forensics, but soldiered on anyway. "The autopsy results showed Eileen was pregnant. Did you know?"

Misty's forehead bunched into unattractive knots.

"Did you?"

"Eileen told me a week or so ago. All excited and nervous. She did one of those home tests. She made me promise not to tell anyone. You know. She was at risk, being older, hadn't seen a doctor yet."

"Did you tell anyone?"

"'Course not."

Alexa looked toward the driveway. No Martin yet. No cops with a warrant either. She needed to buy some time. "Can I have a glass of water?"

"I just cleaned inside. I'll bring you one."

"I need to use the bathroom."

This time Misty frowned. "What game are you playing at?"

"Too much coffee?"

Misty huffed, but opened the door. There was a mirror above a table. A welcome sign, a guest book, and a stack of brochures were arranged on the table. Misty pointed to a hallway. "Down there."

The new vinyl shower curtain smell turned her blood cold. It was blue-and-white striped, half opened, and threaded directly through the shower rod instead of hanging from hooks. The bathtub was damp and smelled of disinfectant. A starfish hook hung on the back of the door. Alexa's mind went deep-sea fishing. *Is this where Eileen was killed?*

The sink and counter were spotless. Alexa lifted the blue floor mat—no drops of blood on the tile. She would come back, armed with Bluestar blood detector. A spritz here and there, turn off the lights, *voila.*

Misty stood in the hallway, holding a glass of water.

"Did Eileen meet you here Thursday afternoon?" Alexa blurted.

Her forehead bunched again. "Why did you ask that? I was working. Drove over to Eileen's house when Paul called."

"We don't know where she went after school. Maybe she came here. Was it rented out last Thursday?"

"Eileen kept the books. I don't know."

"You must know, if you clean between renters."

Misty set the glass of water on the welcome table and motioned toward the door. "You should go now."

"Can you ask Mr. Tandy to stop by the Policing Centre?"

Misty didn't answer. Alexa pushed the door open and stepped onto the porch.

Only she couldn't leave.

Martin Tandy's sedan fender touched the rental car's bumper, trapping her. He watched her from the driver's seat. She felt like a mouse trapped under a cat's paw. She whipped out her phone and pressed 111.

"Is this a fire, ambulance, or police emergency?" the operator asked.

"Police."

"Where are you?"

"I have a situation at Eleven Bramble Street, Arrowtown." She met Martin Tandy's eyes through the window. He sat there, expressionless.

"Someone is on their way," the operator said. "What's the emergency?"

Martin opened the car door and eased out.

"Hello, Mr. Tandy," Alexa called. "Can you move your car?"

"Who are you talking to?" he asked.

She put the phone on speaker. "The police."

"Ma'am?" the operator asked. "What is your emergency?"

"You're sending someone, right?" Alexa asked the operator.

"Yes, ma'am. Stay on the line."

"I've been speaking with Misty," Alexa told Martin. She checked his footwear: tennis shoes, not Wolverine work boots. "She said you wouldn't mind being fingerprinted."

"I can't hear you," the operator said.

Alexa stuffed the phone in her pocket and stepped onto the path. Martin Tandy's appearance hadn't imprinted on her, and now she understood why. He had beige-brown hair, and a bland broad face. His eyebrows were nonexistent, his eyes the color of weak tea.

"What do you want my fingerprints for? You caught Hammer."

"To clear things up, that's all."

He stepped toward her. "What about you leave us alone? Our family has been through enough."

Her knees weakened. She locked them in place and stepped back. "Where's your van?"

He didn't answer, just stood there, his eyes wary.

Misty called from the doorway. "Marty?"

"Go back inside," he called.

Alexa pivoted. Misty's face was gray and distorted behind the screen. "Can you ask your husband to move his car? Or the police will arrest him when they get here."

"Martin?" Misty pushed the door open. "What are you doing? Let her leave."

He chunked his keys to the ground and pushed past Alexa.

Chapter Forty-Four

SUNDAY AFTERNOON

Misty backed the sedan out without speaking, allowing Alexa to screech out of there. She didn't go far—just to the corner, where she pulled over to await the police. After five minutes, the Tandys drove by, Martin at the wheel. Alexa scrunched low but neither of them looked her way. They appeared to be arguing. At the sight of the taillights, Alexa let go the gallon of air she'd been holding.

What the hell just happened?

Constable Blume and someone riding shotgun finally sped by, siren blaring. Then DI Katakana and Senior Sergeant Fielding whizzed by.

Hail, hail, the gang's all here. Alexa turned the car around and followed them to number eleven. She beeped her horn to get the officers' attention before getting out of the car.

DI Katakana lunged toward her. "Why didn't you tell us the address?"

"What are you talking about?"

"None of your messages left the address, eh? Where are they?"

The gang had turned on her. "Martin and Misty left together—ten minutes ago."

Constable Blume came up beside her. "You confused the dispatcher."

"What do you mean?"

The officer riding with Constable Blume was the female

constable from this morning's meeting. "Bramble Street is in Cromwell," she chimed. "This is Bracken."

Bramble, bracken-frackin, Alexa thought. "I was nervous. Martin Tandy blocked me in."

"You're not blocked in now, are you?" The DI spread her blazer and put her hand on her hips. "Bloody hell. Where were the Tandys headed?"

"I don't know."

She pulled out her radio. "What are they driving?"

"A four-door tan sedan. Older model."

DI Katakana contacted the dispatcher. "Persons of interest left Bracken Street. Ten-One. Tan four-door."

The lady from next door stood at the foot of the driveway, the dog waddling behind her. "What's going on?" she called.

Constable Blume rushed to meet her. He spoke with the woman, looked toward her yard, nodded, and jogged back. "She's complaining the Airbnb lodgers trespass in her yard, mess it up."

The DI rolled her eyes. "Stay here for the search," DI Katakana told Alexa. She thrust the warrant at Constable Blume. Then she and the senior sergeant hustled to their car. "Wait," Alexa called. She wanted to share the information she'd sussed out.

DI Katakana ignored her and sped off. She turned to Constable Blume and Constable Stafford for an explanation.

"Eileen Bowen's phone pinged," Constable Blume said.

"From the grave?" It was a lame-ass thing to say.

"Like the battery was dead, and then someone charged it," he said. "Anyway, it pinged from Frankton."

Chill bumps broke out on her arms. "Remember when I was mopping the spilled tea in Misty's lounge? There was a phone under the couch. Misty said it was Susie's, but I saw Susie's phone a little while ago, and it has a different case. And guess what?" She pointed to the cottage. "There's a new shower curtain in the bathroom."

"And that's important how?" Constable Stafford asked.

"The new curtain might have replaced the one Eileen was wrapped in. I learned Misty is Eileen's half sister, and she was basically stiffed by the stepfather's will. And she knew about the pregnancy."

"That's a motive. Good on ya," Constable Blume said. "I'll text Senior." When he finished, he waggled the warrant. "DI Katakana said to look for evidence of a crime."

Alexa doubted they'd find anything obvious after Misty's cleaning. She grabbed the crime kit from the car, and the three of them pulled on booties, suits, and gloves.

Constable Blume rapped on the door. "Police. We have a warrant. Open up."

There was no answer, of course.

He tried the knob; it was locked. There was a lockbox next to it. Constable Blume opened it to reveal a keypad. He tried various combinations. "Take a squiz," he said. "The combo is 12345." He waved a key. "Beats forcing the lock."

The tiny house smelled lemony fresh and had a kitchen, living area, hall bath, and two bedrooms. The furniture was worn, but colorful pillows, throw blankets, and a few candles perked it up. The decorating touches that Susie had mentioned, Alexa decided. "I'll check the bathroom," she said.

The constables each took a bedroom.

She sprayed Bluestar in the tub, grout, and sink. Traces of blood, especially if they matched Eileen's, would be a huge help in reconstructing the primary crime scene. She turned off the light and held her breath. The reagent failed to oxidize and produce a blue glow. No trace of blood. Voices startled Alexa. She left the bathroom at the same time the two constables appeared from the bedrooms. "Who are you?" Constable Blume asked.

The woman let go of her suitcase handle. She and her companion stared open-mouthed at the three of them dressed in white hooded suits. "We're the Butlers. Here for holiday."

"You'll have to find another place to stay," Constable Blume said. "This is a crime scene."

"We have reservations," the man said. He flashed his phone.

"Like I said, the house is off limits."

"Will we get a refund?" the man asked.

"I'm sure that will be arranged," Constable Blume said. "If you'll step outside now."

"I'm giving the host a bad review," the woman said. Then her hand went to her mouth. "Oh, my God. Is the host the murdered woman? I thought the name was familiar."

Alexa kept her face passive. The Butlers left quickly.

The guest book caught her attention. The inside flap was dated last June. She opened it to a random page. Clara Rodriguez from California wrote: *April 22–26, Clean and comfortable, like living in a tiny nest, short walk to town.* Alexa flipped to the last entry: *Thank you for the lovely stay. Clean and cozy. Our son loved the rabbits in the garden and playing in the creek. Mud! A washing machine would be a nice addition. Stephen, James & Grayson, Sydney*

"This Sydney family left three days before Eileen was killed." She showed the constables. "I think the cottage was empty Thursday."

"I never sign those things," Constable Stafford said.

"There will be Airbnb records," Constable Blume said.

"No traces of blood in the bathroom. I'll check the backyard," Alexa said.

A hedge of rubbery red leaves separated it from Kate

Hepburn's yard. Branches and sprays shot from it willy-nilly like grabby hands. *Must be the Copso-what-so,* Alexa thought.

The tiny patio was slick with leaves. Alexa got on her hands and knees and inspected the flagstone closely. There was no sign of blood or struggle. Two wrought-iron chairs faced the creek. She opened the large wooden box between them. It held spades and big tin pans. "Strike gold in Bush Creek," a cheerful sign said.

Alexa crossed the wet grass, skirted a concrete firepit ring, and stood at the edge of the creek. It was swollen and angry. She followed its course; it flowed toward Prospector's Cottage. She thought of Eileen's hat. How did it get in the creek? She hopped back when the bank beneath her caved in, sending a trickle of pebbles into the creek.

A path followed alongside the creek. Alexa imagined Eileen taking the path from her house to here. Someone needed to check it for the primary scene of death.

Maybe she'd come back later.

The constables waited for her on the front porch. The basket of dirty linens was still there. The sight sent a spark to her brain. "If one of the Tandys killed Eileen, there was blood spatter, right?"

"Bound to be," Constable Stafford said.

Alexa nudged the laundry basket with her foot and looked at Constable Blume. "Remember when we visited Misty right after Eileen's body was discovered?"

He nodded, alert.

"She was coming out of the garage with a basket of wet laundry. It smelled like bleach. You hung it on the line. Can you get a warrant for the Tandys' garage?"

Chapter Forty-Five

After an hour, during which time Alexa ate fish and chips at the Fork and Tap, Constable Blume texted that he had obtained the warrant. Meet U there. She called Leigh Walker to request her assistance.

"Did you hear?" Leigh asked.

"No guessing game, please."

"There's an all-points out for the Tandys. Because of the phone pinging."

"Does the daughter know what's going on?"

"The liaison is with her."

Alexa brimmed with energy. She tried to explain the mission to Leigh. "If one of the Tandys killed Eileen, then Eileen's blood might be on that person's clothes. There could be traces of Eileen's blood on the washing machine in the Tandys' garage."

"And maybe a fingerprint to seal the deal," Leigh said. "I'm on my way."

She got it.

Constable Blume and Constable Stafford were waiting, warrant for house and property in hand, when Alexa arrived. They didn't wait for Leigh. She and Constable Blume knocked on the door.

Susie's eyes were fearful. The liaison stood behind her. "Where's Mum?" Susie asked.

Alexa refused to let her mind jump to "what ifs." "We're not sure. Has she called you?"

"About what?" Susie still wore pajama pants and the sweat-shirt. One hand was buried in the pocket and the other clutched her phone. "No one tells me anything."

"Everything is okay, miss," Constable Blume said. He handed the warrant to her. "This means we can come inside and look around, eh?"

They all turned at the crunch of gravel. Leigh had arrived.

Alexa turned back to Susie. "The warrant also means I can look in the garage."

"Why do you want to look in the garage? It's nothing but rubbish."

The roller door was down. "Is it locked?" Alexa asked.

"I don't think the lock works," Susie said. "You pull it up by the handle. I'll show you."

"That's okay," Alexa said quickly.

"Let's wait in the garden while the officers do their job," the liaison said.

Susie pouted. "I'm supposed to meet my friends."

Alexa couldn't meet her eyes. What if her dirty laundry hunch was right? The kid's world would implode. She set the crime kit on the gravel and suited up. After snapping on gloves, she bent down for the garage door handle. "Ready?" she asked Leigh.

The metal door shrieked across the ceiling on two tracks. Alexa gritted her teeth and surveyed the innards. The left half of the garage was a tumble of wheeled discards: a stroller, two bicycles, plastic toddler car, scooter, rusted mower, upside-down wagon, and a tricycle.

"They need a jumble sale," Leigh said.

Behind a few boxes marked "Mum's house," "girl's sz.2–6," "holidays" and "X-mas," Alexa spotted a wheelbarrow. She met Leigh's eyes. They both probably thought of it transporting

Eileen's body. "Let's work on this first," she said, her heart pounding.

"What-ifs" crowded in. *What if Susie's Dad killed her aunt?*

Leigh photographed the wheelbarrow, zooming in on the tires, handles, tray, and the legs as Alexa dusted the wooden handles for fingerprints. Nothing. "Wiped clean," she said.

"Or gloves," Leigh said. "By the way, Eileen's car had some unknown prints on the steering wheel. Not much else."

"They might be Susie's," Alexa said, thinking of driving lessons. "I'll take her prints when we're done here."

The washing machine was situated against the back wall. A light bulb dangled above it. A wooden shelf above it held the accoutrements of laundry: a jumbo box of detergent, stain remover, bleach, and scoops. There was no clothes dryer. Alexa thought of the clothesline in the backyard. Two days ago Constable Blume had hung the wash.

Filtered light seeped through a single dirty window. Alexa pulled the string attached to the light bulb above the washer and set up another light on a tripod. Her hands shook; she hoped Leigh didn't notice.

She took wide-angle photos and mid-range photos of the garage and then of the shelf. Then she took photos of the Maytag Dependable Care washer. It was off-white, and the control panel had three dials on the left and a larger one on the right. *Retro*, Alexa thought. There was an indentation for lifting the lid. Alexa zoomed in and clicked, willing latent prints to become visible. No go. "Lift the lid," she told Leigh.

The drum was empty, the agitator scummy.

What if Susie's mom was a killer?

Alexa imagined a garment draping down as Misty stuffed it in the washer. She switched from camera to Maglite and swept the beam along the surface, hoping for something visible. The light caught a smudge. It could be dirt. She switched back to the camera, zoomed in, and took several photos. She enlarged one in the viewfinder, added a filter, and showed Leigh. The smudge was a vague reddish-brown. She made out fingerprint ridges in the smudge. Her heart skipped a beat. The smudge continued in a smear.

As if a finger slid along the surface of the metal.

If the smudge turned out to be Eileen's blood, and *if* the fingerprint turned out to be Misty's or Martin's, then this was a goldmine.

"Should we test it for blood?" Leigh asked.

Alexa nodded. There were several presumptive tests on the market to determine if a sample was blood or some other fluid. She preferred phenolphthalein, although it didn't differentiate between human or animal blood. That would take another test in the lab.

She leaned back to plan. The trick would be to swab the outskirts of the smudge—not toward the center where the ridges were. That could ruin them. "I'll do it," she said. Her voice came out louder than she meant.

Leigh gave her a puzzled look.

"When I worked in Raleigh, I messed up a case by not swabbing for blood before I lifted the print." Her mistake had hurt the case.

"Where's Raleigh?"

"In North Carolina."

Alexa ripped open a test pouch, removed the sterile Q-tip swab, and moistened it with distilled water. Then she carefully swabbed the outer edge of the smudge. She could see the discoloration on the end of the swab. While Leigh watched, she added a few drops of her premixed phenolphthalein solution to the cotton tip, and held her breath. Expectations aside, holding her breath reduced chances of contamination.

In ten seconds the end of the swab was bright pink. Alexa smiled. "We've got the presence of blood." When she thought of the possible source of the blood, the smile evaporated.

"What next?" Leigh asked.

"Take two more swabs—one wet and one dry—from the same area. Don't get near the ridges. We'll send the samples off for DNA." That would be the possible link to Eileen.

What if the parents were in cahoots?

When Leigh finished, Alexa let out a whoosh of air. "Time to bust out the blood-enhancement reagent," she said. "Get the camera ready."

She used a spray bottle to apply the amido black. It looked like octopus ink. The dark color enhanced the visibility of ridge patterns. She watched the reagent adhere to the fingerprint, plumping the ridges up like magic and fixing them to the metal surface. She sprayed again, this time with distilled water, to wash away the excess.

The dark-blue fingerprint was easy for Leigh to photograph. "Let it dry, and then you can lift it," Alexa said generously.

A conversation Alexa had had with Ana's mom jumped into her head. Pam told her about a sixteen-year-old kid sentenced to life in prison for stabbing someone.

What if Susie had killed her aunt?

Chapter Forty-Six

Leigh zoomed off to the station with the evidence. The constables were still working in the house. Susie was alone, slumped on one of the backyard patio chairs. She waved her phone at Alexa like a distress signal. "I need my charger."

"Have you heard from your parents?"

"I got a text." She didn't meet Alexa's eye.

"What did it say?"

Susie hugged the phone to her sweatshirt and scowled. "I don't have to tell you."

The kid's evasiveness was irritating, suspicious. "That's true, but why wouldn't you? Everything you share helps us find who killed your aunt."

"Everyone knows who killed her. That man. The Hammer. That's what Dad said."

"Maybe. Where's Ms. Kies?" Susie looked toward the house. "She's gone to get us drinks."

"That's nice. I need her present so that I can take your fingerprints." Alexa paused. "Unless you're eighteen?"

Susie brightened. She looked younger when she wasn't scowling. "Almost. I'm fifteen."

Alexa sat. The bloody fingerprint in the garage pushed down on an imaginary pressure point. "Do you ever do the laundry?"

Susie made a face. "You're a crack-up. Mum does the laundry."

"Did you find your aunt's phone?"

Her face reddened. She picked at a nail. "I didn't. It was Daddy. He smacked me when I turned it on." Her bottom lip trembled.

"Where's the phone now?"

She shrugged.

Alexa watched the family liaison come out the back door, bearing a tray with a pitcher and glasses as if this were a summer picnic. She smiled brightly at Alexa. "Would you like some lemonade?"

"I need to take Susie's fingerprints and head to the lab." She turned on the mobile scanner and guided Susie's right hand. She blinked. Leaned closer. The kid had scratches on the top near the knuckles.

Raw and angry scratches.

Chapter Forty-Seven

SUNDAY EVENING

Martin Tandy pressed his pointer finger on the mobile scanner pad, just as his daughter had two hours ago. He and Misty had been detained at a roadblock between Arrowtown and Queenstown and escorted to the station for questioning.

"Where had they been?" Alexa had asked Constable Blume.

"At some house he was inspecting. That's what Mr. Tandy said. There's a team of cops checking it out and searching for the van. Now he refuses to speak."

Alexa studied the live image on the screen and pressed Capture. "Next finger," she told him.

His mouth stayed clamped, and his finger trembled. Misty was in a separate room, and DI Katakana was about to talk with her.

Martin barely pressed his little finger and the print was rejected. "Press harder," Alexa said.

In the hallway she checked the results.

Martin Tandy did not have a police record and neither did his daughter. She found Leigh in the lab. "Compare their prints with the one you lifted from the washing machine," Alexa said with gravity. "I want to hear what Misty has to say."

She watched through the two-way glass as DI Katakana and Senior Sergeant Fielding questioned Misty. The room was eight-by-ten, and the only furniture was a table and three chairs. Misty sat opposite the officers, squeezing the water bottle in her hand.

"Where's Susie?" she asked.

"She's okay," DI Katakana said. "Your husband's parents are coming to stay with her."

"Her Nana and Pop?" Misty dug her nails into the label and peeled the paper from the water bottle. "Why? What's going on? You have Hammer. He killed Eileen."

"We don't believe he did," Senior Sergeant Fielding said.

Misty's fingers stilled. Her mouth opened and closed like a fish, gasping for air.

"What do you know about the dig at the Arrowtown Cemetery?" he asked. "That's where your sister was found. Buried."

"I don't know anything about the cemetery."

Not true, Alexa thought. She had blabbed about the dig to Misty, trying to build rapport. That had been Friday afternoon; Eileen's body had been found Saturday morning.

DI Katakana consulted a sheet of paper. "Why did your sister's phone ping from your house?"

Misty shrunk into the chair. "Martin must have found it. I don't know."

"You told Ms. Glock it was Susie's phone. Why?"

She scratched the patchy spot on her neck, hard. "I didn't know whose phone it was. I thought it was one of Susie's friend's."

"How did Eileen's phone get there?" the DI asked.

"I don't know."

"What was it like, being Eileen's half sister?" she asked.

"Leeny wasn't a half to me. She was my sister through and through."

"But she didn't share her toys, right?" the DI said. "All you got was a job cleaning the house she inherited from *her* father."

"Mum would have wanted me to get half. Martin called her the princess. She always got what she wanted."

"I'd be jealous too. Want some of what she got."

Misty stared at her. "She said she'd give Susie Mum's diamond earrings, but she never did."

"Fancy that," DI Katakana said. "She was wearing them when someone ripped one off and brutally killed her."

Misty looked as if she'd been hit. Senior Sergeant Fielding leaned forward. The cleft between his dark eyebrows deepened. "Did you meet Eileen at the rental house Thursday afternoon? Is that where you killed her?"

Her mouth dropped. "My own sister?"

"Half sister," he said.

"I didn't kill Leeny. I was working Thursday afternoon. That's where I was when Paul called."

"Who can verify that?"

A fat tear slid down Misty's cheek. "I work from home." She clawed at her neck. "My eczema. You're making my eczema flare. Susie's is flaring too. All this stress."

Alexa cringed when she saw Misty's neck bleed. Maybe the raw patches on Susie's hand had been eczema.

"You knew Eileen was pregnant. Who did you tell?" the DI asked.

Misty bowed her head. "Eileen told me not to tell anyone. She was afraid something might happen. Her being so old."

"Something did happen," Senior Sergeant Fielding said.

Misty covered her mouth. "I want to go home," she whimpered.

"You told your husband about the baby, right?" DI Katakana asked. "Maybe Susie too?" Misty's shoulders jerked up and down and tears spilled from her eyes. DI Katakana shoved a box of tissues at her. "If Eileen had a child, you wouldn't inherit her estate, eh? The one you were cheated out of?"

Misty swiped at the tears. "I'm older than Eileen. I never would have inherited anything from her."

"Susie might have," DI Katakana said. "Were you planning for her future?"

Misty shook her head, back and forth.

The DI stood. "Let's bring Susie in. See what she has to say."

Misty stilled. "I don't know what he's done."

"Who?" Senior Sergeant Fielding asked.

"Marty. I don't know what he's done."

Chapter Forty-Eight

"Oh, my God," Leigh said when Alexa entered the lab. "The fingerprint in the blood is Martin Tandy's."

"I'll need to verify," Alexa said calmly.

"Right. Of course," Leigh said.

Alexa conjured a neutral mindset, and as if Earl Hammer was looking over her shoulder, painstakingly mapped the minutiae of each print. Twenty minutes later she concluded that they were similar. *Was there a name for men who killed their sisters-in-law*, Alexa wondered?

Bastards. Monsters. Devils.

"It's late. We won't get the blood test results until morning," Leigh said.

Alexa had lost track of time. "You've done good work. Go home. I'll update DI Katakana."

The DI, in her office, took a moment to digest the news that the fingerprint on the washing machine was Martin Tandy's.

"If the blood matches Eileen's, we'll have a slam dunk," Alexa finished.

"As it is, we have enough to hold them overnight. Now we need to figure out if Misty Tandy was in on it. You watched through the glass, right? Impressions?

"The phone, the laundry, the missing shower curtain. If she wasn't a partner-in-crime, she had to be suspicious of Martin."

"Accessory after the fact maybe. That's better than murder. A press conference is scheduled for nine a.m. Three independent analysts confirmed your Hammer print comparison." The DI snatched a bottle of Visine from her drawer, leaned her head back, and squeezed drops into her bloodshot eyes. "Deputy Commissioner Garret and a rep from the Innocence Project will announce Hammer was erroneously imprisoned and that the Cindy Mulligan case is reopened." She blinked and sighed. "It's a hell of a mess."

"How is DI Unger?" Alexa asked.

"Released from hospital. He won't press charges against Hammer, said that he deserves to go free. The press will eat Unger alive."

"It's the forensics they should turn on." Alexa felt like she had stabbed her bestie in the back, not that she had a bestie. "The expert witness misled the court. Is Hammer still in custody?"

"He was released to the company of a lawyer an hour ago."

Alexa would have liked to have watched him walk out.

The DI shook her head. "All these years a killer has walked the streets, free. Cat's out of the bag tomorrow, and if he's still alive, he's in for a shock."

"What's next?" Alexa asked.

"We're trying to find that van. I think it was used to transport the body."

Alexa went cold. "Misty gave me a ride to the station in the van. Friday afternoon."

They stared at each other. Alexa did the math. It was possible Eileen Bowen's body had been in the back.

"Don't suppose you saw a body and forgot to report it?"

"There's a partition. I..."

"Go home, Glock."

Chapter Forty-Nine

There was a country song about Earl in a car trunk. After stopping at a Countdown for frozen pizza and a birthday bottle of wine, Alexa found the song on her phone and listened to it as she drove to Arrowtown. The body was wrapped in a tarp, not a shower curtain.

In the cottage she kicked off her Keds and preheated the ancient oven for the pizza. She chose two hundred and fifty degrees Celsius. Her phone buzzed.

Dad—FaceTiming from Florida. He sat on a couch, his arm around her stepmother Rita, who wore a white spa-like robe. "Alexa. Look at that. What time is it in Australia?" he asked.

"New Zealand, Charles," Rita said. "Alexa lives in New Zealand."

The Beatles started crooning "The Long and Winding Road."

"No, Alexa. We don't want to play music," Dad yelled.

The song ceased. "Hi, Dad. Hi, Rita. It's eight p.m. What time is it there?"

"Four a.m."

"You don't have to shout," Rita said.

"You didn't have to get up in the middle of the night to call." Despite the witching hour, they looked good, Dad a little grayer, Rita's bob a tawny brown. Dad had retired from the civil engineering company he'd worked for and they'd moved to Naples, Florida, a few years ago.

"It's your birthday," Dad said. "Happy birthday."

"Thank you."

"I remember when you were born. Eight pounds, eight ounces. Your red hair stuck out all over. You got it from your mother."

"I had red hair?" Alexa conjured her mother, holding her newborn against her skin. *Oh, Mom.*

"It fell out and then you were bald."

Alexa snorted.

"How did you celebrate your birthday?" Rita asked.

Her stepmother's face made her back scars tighten. For the longest time she had held Rita responsible for the scalding, but she'd been wrong. "I'll celebrate later. I'm on a travel case, and it's been crazy busy."

"Taking a bite out of crime," Dad said. "When are you coming home?"

"I'm not sure."

"Charlie said you have a boyfriend, a nice police officer," Rita said.

"A detective inspector," Alexa clarified. Her heart did the foxtrot. Bruce had called. She had texted that she would call him back.

"We've booked a cruise to come see you," Rita said. "In November. Early in the season, but prices are better. Our ports are Akaroa—am I saying that right?—Bluff, and Bay of Islands."

"We'll tag on Auckland and visit you," Dad said. He covered a yawn and said he loved her. "How do we end this thing?" he asked Rita.

"Goodbye," Alexa said to a blank screen. She wondered if her dad had forgiven her for the decade she'd shunned Rita, her heart shellacked against all her stepmother's overtures. Dad had been caught in the middle.

Forgiving herself was another matter, for another day.

She'd picked up a package of Tim Tams too. She ate a cookie, put the pizza in the oven, and poured herself the wine. She didn't have to marry Bruce. She didn't have to move in with him. She didn't even have to trust him; that might build with time. Or not. She didn't have to commit to anything but seeing him.

Now or never.

Now or Scotland.

She dialed and he answered as if he'd been waiting. "Alexa."

Her greenstone pendant, warm against her skin, pulsated like a second heartbeat. *Say It Say It Say It.* "Bruce. I miss you."

He was silent. She'd botched it. Waited too long. His voice, when it came, was husky. "What took you so long to call?"

She laughed and said it again, joyful. "I miss you."

"What do you want to do about it?"

"See you."

"That can be arranged."

"It's my birthday," she said.

"It is? I'll cook you a steak when you get back in town."

He made her mouth water.

"I got the memo about Earl Hammer," Bruce said. "The big announcement is tomorrow morning, right?"

She sipped her wine and didn't mind veering into police biz.

"The scuttlebutt is that you did the fingerprint comparison," Bruce said.

"They've been verified. Twenty-five years locked away and Hammer's innocent." The weight of that pressed on her shoulders. "What if that so-called expert witness sent other people to jail too?"

"Every case he testified in will be dissected," Bruce said. "Any suspects for who killed the principal?"

She told him about the Tandys, about Martin blocking her

from leaving, about the pending blood test, about their daughter. "She's Denise's age." Denise was Bruce's older daughter. "I can't bear to think about what this will do to her."

"Kids are resilient," he said softly. "Where is the DI on who killed Cindy Mulligan?"

"She's busy with the Tandys. She assigned it to some guy from the Armed Officers Squad. DI Unger had been looking at a man at her workplace and some woman too." The aroma of melted mozzarella filled the little kitchen. Her stomach growled. "I'll track down her DNA profile in the morning. It might hold some clues."

"With the announcement tomorrow, the killer might panic," Bruce said. "Be careful."

Her eyes landed on the file of newspaper clippings and photos from the museum she'd left on the table. She told Bruce about the Chinese miner. "He's going home."

"That's a happy ending," Bruce said.

"I'm no longer a prime number."

"Got me there. What do you mean?"

"I'm thirty-eight. I'm divisible now."

The crust was burning. She reluctantly disconnected.

Washed down with another glass of wine, the pizza didn't taste so bad. She browsed through the gold rush articles from the museum: bone-cleaning, rice bowls, missing miners, floods and blizzards, the *Ventnor* sinking. It took her mind off her Susie worries. She looked for the photos. There had been two. One showed three Chinese men leaning against the fence. She found it and stared into their stalwart faces. Then she looked for the other photo, the one of a Chinese man holding an umbrella for a European woman. He'd been dressed in a suit with one of those chains leading from a buttonhole to his vest pocket. The woman had been identified on the back. She checked again and again.

The photo was missing. When the back door was wide open, the articles and photos had scattered across the kitchen floor. Her eyes darted around the room. She felt the presence of hungry ghosts, trying to tell her something.

Science. I believe in science, not ghosts.

Chapter Fifty

MONDAY MORNING

The press conference, which started thirty minutes late, was being held in front of Tāhuna District Court in Queenstown, a couple blocks from the police station. Alexa had guzzled her flat white coffee to arrive on time, and now wished she'd savored each sip.

"Mr. Earl Hammer was unjustly convicted of Cindy Mulligan's murder on the basis of a single fingerprint which was not his," the spokesperson from the New Zealand Innocence Project said.

The deputy commissioner, who stood next to her, blanched. A unified gasp came from the twenty or so gathered reporters and bystanders.

"We are seeking a full pardon on Mr. Hammer's behalf," she added.

Alexa stood to the right of the speakers, between DI Katakana and Senior Sergeant Fielding. She wore her last clean outfit: khakis and a floral button-down. She zipped her jacket. Snow covered the jagged peaks of the mountains this morning, a reminder that winter waited in the wings.

"We have ordered a full review of how and why it happened," Deputy Commissioner Garret said. "We know you have questions."

Hands shot up. The deputy commissioner pointed to a reporter in a TVNZ cap.

"If Hammer is innocent, then the real murderer has been roaming the streets free all this time. Is that right?"

DI Katakana stepped forward. "We have reopened the Cindy Mulligan case."

"Ya think," someone hurled.

"There will be a full internal investigation," Deputy Commissioner Garret said.

"Will whoever conducted this faulty science be held accountable?" a small woman with a Māori TV cap asked.

"No comment," Deputy Commissioner Garret said.

"Will the police be held accountable?" she asked.

"The investigation will be handled by internal affairs. We'll honor their recommendations."

"That's rank, man," a bystander yelled. He wore an Innocence Project New Zealand T-shirt. "You'll slap your damn wrists and go about ruining lives."

"Was the fingerprint evidence tampered with?" an *NZ Herald* reporter asked.

DI Katakana said, "Our forensic expert Alexa Glock can speak to what happened."

Alexa stepped forward. She had rehearsed her statement in the cottage kitchen. "The fingerprint comparison used to convict Mr. Hammer was erroneous."

"How can that happen?" the TVNZ reporter asked.

"It appears that the expert thought the prints were similar, when they weren't," Alexa explained. "There are specific differences between the two prints."

Three hands shot up. Deputy Commissioner Garret pointed to the reporter closest to him.

"I thought fingerprints were foolproof."

"Errors can happen," Alexa said. "There are better safeguards in place today than there were in 1998."

"So forensics is bogus?" someone shouted.

Alexa flushed and stepped back. She wanted to defend her profession, but in light of what happened to Earl Timothy Hammer, how could she?

"Every forensic lab in the country will be scrutinized, starting with the one right down the street at Queenstown Police Station," Deputy Commissioner Garret said. "Next question."

"What will Hammer's payout be?" the Māori TV reporter asked.

The Innocence Project spokesperson said, "There's a formal compensation scale for claimants who have been wrongfully convicted. We'll go for the fullest, but it will never make up for the loss Mr. Hammer endured. Our client never got to say goodbye to his mother, who died while he was in prison. How do you compensate for that?"

"What's your estimate of the extent of other wrongful convictions due to that expert?" the same reporter asked.

"An internal investigation has been opened, and we will look into that very question," Deputy Commissioner Garret said.

An *Otago Daily Times* reporter asked, "If Hammer didn't do it, who killed Eileen Bowen?"

"We have suspects in custody," DI Katakana said. She had told Alexa that the Tandys had lawyered up. The Tandy Home Inspections van was still MIA.

"Who?" he asked.

"No comment."

Her phone buzzed. Alexa waited until the conference ended before looking at her screen. It was a text from Leigh: Found DNA profile from Cindy Mulligan case.

Chapter Fifty-One

Alexa drove to the station while reflecting on the history of DNA. In 1995, New Zealand established a DNA data bank. It was the second country in the world to do so; the United Kingdom beat them to it. But it wasn't until 1999, a year after Cindy Mulligan's murder, that New Zealand police first used DNA to solve a homicide.

The DNA in that case came from a hair found at the scene. A suspect willingly gave the police a blood and hair sample. He had said, "I hope you catch the guy who did this."

The hubris. It was him.

Alexa parked in her usual spot at the station, straighter this time, curious to what the tissue and biofluids collected from under Cindy Mulligan's fingernail would reveal.

When DNA collected at a crime scene matched a DNA profile of a known individual, that individual was a possible suspect. Alexa mulled over the word *matched*, verboten now in the realm of fingerprints. DNA profiles don't provide matches, but probabilities. This person is one in a billion, maybe trillion, who has this profile.

Good enough.

DI Katakana wasn't back from the press conference yet, but Constable Blume waited for Alexa in the lobby and accompanied her to the lab. "Ms. Walker has big news," he said.

Leigh buttoned a lab coat over a bright yellow T-shirt. Before

Alexa let the lab tech share her news, she asked, "Any word on the blood test? Whether it matches Eileen Bowen?"

"Still waiting."

"No word on the Tandys' van," Alexa said. *How could you hide a van? Or a crime scene?* She set her kit on a desk. "When they find it, we'll scour it."

Leigh showed them the DNA profile. "There were no hits in 1998, eh? Everything was kind of new then. But loads of profiles have been added over the decades, so the analyst ran them again. Guess what?"

Alexa gritted her teeth.

"What?" asked Constable Blume.

"They don't match Earl Hammer."

Alexa got a solar plexus *oomph*. This was further confirmation that Hammer was a victim of injustice.

"Guess what?" Leigh asked again.

"No guessing games," Alexa snapped.

"The DNA profile has no Y chromosome."

It took a moment for Alexa's brain to work through this. Males and females share twenty-two similar pairs of chromosomes. A twenty-third chromosome is different in males and females. "So the DNA comes from a female?"

"Bob's your uncle."

"A lady killer," Constable Blume said.

Alexa got chills. "DI Unger mentioned a female suspect. A coworker."

Leigh's face shone with excitement. "The criminal investigations data bank links with familial searches like MyAncestry and FamilyTree. You know, genetic genealogy companies. I gave one of those kits to my dad for his birthday." The brightness drained from her face and she studied her tennis shoes.

Alexa wondered what worms had been in that apple. "Go on."

Leigh regained her footing. "The profile shows that whoever left DNA under Cindy Mulligan's fingernail has an ancestor in the Otago area."

"A relative of the murderer?" Alexa asked.

"An ancestor of the murderer."

"Does it give names?" she asked.

"It doesn't work that way. But this is where it goes over the top. I reckon you should sit down."

"No thanks," Alexa said.

"The profile linked to your skeleton."

Alexa grabbed a chair.

"You did the molar thing, right? And sent off the DNA?"

Disconnected wires in her brain connected. Alexa found her phone and scrolled. She located the text from Dr. Weiner and showed Leigh:

DNA from S2's molar indicates a distant relative in Otaga area. This person completed a FamilyTree ancestry test kit. I contacted the relative through the website to see if he/she wants to be involved.

"And the strontium isotopic results indicate she spent her childhood in Otago—was probably born here," Alexa said.

The constable's freckles popped out against his pale skin. "I don't get it."

Alexa kept her voice steady, but the news was electrifying. "S2 is the second skeleton. From the dig at the cemetery. It, well *she*, has a broken neck and back. Plus she was buried facedown."

Constable Blume rubbed his neck.

"So the skeleton that was in that vandalized tent, remember? It shares genes with whoever killed Cindy Mulligan." She couldn't believe it.

"Agent Leland needs to hear this," Constable Blume said.

While they waited for the constable to fetch him, Alexa scrolled forward. She showed Leigh the follow-up text from Dr. Weiner: S2's relative does not wish to be contacted. ☹

Leigh ducked her head. "My dad found out his dad, my granddaddy, isn't his biological father, and he didn't want to be contacted either. My gift shattered my dad. Those kits are dangerous. Do you know there are DNA NPE support groups?"

"What's NPE?"

"Nonpaternity event. It's devastating."

"I'm sorry," Alexa said.

Agent Leland rushed into the room. He wore black pants and shirt again. Alexa wondered why DI Katakana had assigned the cold case to a member of the Armed Forces Squad. "What do you have?" he asked.

She and Leigh explained the situation.

He asked a few questions and then said, "So what the hell next?"

Alexa thought of Dr. Weiner and the private lab, but this was police business. "We have a forensic genealogist at Auckland Forensic Service," Alexa said. It was a new position. "The genealogist might be able to produce leads or construct a family tree."

"Call," Agent Leland said.

"I'll have to go through my boss," Alexa said.

Once briefed, Dan connected her. Alexa hadn't met the genealogist. She put her on speakerphone and repeated the scenario. "Can you find out who did that ancestry kit?"

The woman laughed. "Privacy laws prohibit that. It's a dead end. Your best bet is the cold case DNA from Cindy Mulligan's fingernail, if the sample hasn't been contaminated or degraded."

Agent Leland rubbed his bald head. "How long will that take?"

"We don't have the specialized equipment," the woman said. "I'll outsource the biological material to a vendor laboratory to evaluate the genetic results. They may be able to construct a family tree and identify relatives."

Agent Leland's eyes hardened. "How long?"

"Depends on the backlog. A week, minimum."

It was a letdown after all the excitement. "Now we know the perpetrator is female," Alexa pointed out when they disconnected.

"Forget the DNA route," Special Agent Leland said. "DI Unger had a female suspect. Someone Cindy Mulligan worked with."

"Who?" Alexa asked.

"Stick to the lab," he said. He had a look in his eyes that scared Alexa: a predator hunting prey. "Let's go," he told Constable Blume.

"Wait," she called. "I have another idea. The skeleton had dental work done. A porcelain inlay. There was a dentist who came to Arrowtown. He advertised in the newspaper I saw at the museum. Maybe his records exist." She fiddled through her phone photos. "I took a picture of the ad."

Agent Leland looked at her like she was crazy. "That was what—a hundred and twenty-five years ago—something like that, and you don't even have a name."

"I know she was thirty to forty years old, raised around here, and could afford dental treatment. Not many people could at that time." She blinked. On her phone was a photo of the Chinese man holding an umbrella for a European woman. The photo that she had searched for last night. She'd forgotten she had a picture of it. Then she found the ad. She showed Special Agent Leland.

"Waste of time," he said.

Constable Blume gave her a thumbs-up as they left. Alexa was happy he was being treated as a team member, but that brush-off from the agent rankled. She showed Leigh the ad:

F. ARMSTRONG, Surgeon Dentist of Baker Street, Queenstown, Intends making a TOUR OF THE PROVINCE OF OTAGO. A Complete Outfit is carried. Continuous Gum Work, which is so like the natural gum. Bridge Work. Gold Stopings. Porcelain Jacket Crowns. The strongest system of Vulcanite work. Gas, Cocaine, or Chloroform administered.

Leigh looked dubious.

"I'm going to see if Armstrong's practice is still around," Alexa said.

"Okay by me," Leigh said.

Alexa searched her phone for Queenstown dentists. There were four in town. The number gave her pause. Raleigh, North Carolina, probably had five hundred dentists. It was a reminder that Queenstown and Arrowtown were small, remote communities surrounded by mountains and lots of ocean. *Insular* popped into her head.

She scanned the addresses: Beach Street. McBride Avenue. Autumn Terrace. Baker Street. Her heart rate accelerated. She clicked on the Baker Street website. "Longest Continuous Queenstown Dental Care," the banner claimed.

Score.

None of the dentists listed were named Armstrong, though. She told Leigh to call her if she was needed and left the lab.

DI Katakana flagged her down as she crossed to the main entrance. Her face was flushed. "I was on my way to the lab. That blood test? The pathologist called me directly. It's Eileen

Bowen's blood with Martin Tandy's fingerprint in it. You nailed it. Can't wait to hear what Mr. Tandy has to say."

Alexa arranged her face to look humble and mentally flip-flopped cases. "We need to corroborate it with more evidence. I thought of something. When we were at the Airbnb, the next-door neighbor complained that someone drove through her yard." Rain had probably washed evidence away, but it was still worth mentioning. "If Eileen was killed by the creek, maybe Martin drove the van back there to pick up the body."

"I'll send a crew to look."

The long-dead dentist could wait. Alexa lifted her crime kit. "I'll go."

The DI's flush deepened. "In light of the debacle in the Cindy Mulligan case, Deputy Commissioner Garrett has ordered a fresh forensic team to take over the investigations. I notified your boss. You can finish your reports in Auckland."

"What?"

"It's not my decision. Those were his orders."

Heat surged through Alexa's body. She'd worked her ass off every which way, followed the rules, bit her tongue when needed, helped solve Eileen Bowen's murder, and was hot on the trail of Cindy Mulligan's. "You're releasing me mid-case?"

"Deputy commissioner is releasing you. This is just the beginning. There's talk of closing our lab, of letting Ms. Walker go."

"But—"

Without another word, the DI walked away.

Alexa stood in the entrance, stunned. People stepped around her, casting curious glances. Sergeant Dryer, from behind his desk, averted his eyes. Senior Sergeant Fielding and another cop gave her a wide berth as they passed. She finally lifted her chin, determined not to abandon Cindy Mulligan, and left the police station behind.

Chapter Fifty-Two

The deputy commissioner couldn't prevent her from doing historical research on old dental records. While the team tracked down Cindy Mulligan's coworker and the others confronted Martin Tandy—she wished she could be there—Alexa would delve into the past.

And the twain shall meet. Or was it: *Never the twain shall meet?*

Alexa found a parking garage in the central business district. She locked the crime kit in the trunk and located Queenstown Dental wedged between a bank and a jewelry store. She entered through glass doors and approached the receptionist, who bared perfect white teeth. "Kia ora. How can I help you?"

She showed her forensic ID badge. "I need to ask questions about the history of Queenstown Dental."

"It has a long history," the receptionist said.

"Who started this practice? Was it F. Armstrong?"

"I don't know. I've only been here three years."

"Is there anyone who might know?"

"Mrs. Riggs works in accounting. She's been here forever."

Mrs. Riggs looked over her reader glasses as Alexa knocked on her open door. Her face was crisscrossed with lines, and her eyes were sympathetic. "Is it about a bill, dear?"

"No." Alexa stepped into the closet-sized office. "I'm a forensic odontologist. I'm tracking down old dental records for a case." She pulled out her phone and showed the woman the dental ad. "This is from 1901." Mrs. Riggs took her time reading it. "Vulcanite? What's that?"

"It's a hardened rubber that was used to make dentures. Since Queenstown Dental is on Baker Street, I'm wondering if this is the same practice?"

"It is, dear. Franklin Armstrong, Senior started the business and Franklin Armstrong, Junior took it over. Junior sold it to Queenstown Dental just after I started working here. They kept me on."

"Do you have dental records from back then?"

Mrs. Riggs glanced at her computer screen. "We are required to keep patient records for ten years from the day following the last date on which care was provided. After that, records are deleted."

Alexa didn't give up. "Records from back then wouldn't be computerized. I wonder if the first F. Armstrong kept handwritten logs or a ledger that was passed down in his family. Some doctors did."

She shrugged. "He's long gone, of course, and unfortunately Franklin, Junior has passed as well. Would you like his widow's number? I hope she's still with us."

"Yes, please."

The number, when Alexa tried it on the street, was no longer in service.

Just like herself.

Chapter Fifty-Three

Ana called. Reception was bad in the parking garage, so Alexa backed up and stood on the sidewalk.

"How's Shelby?" Alexa asked. "Does she still have the stomach bug?"

"She's better. Now I have it. Saw you on TV." Her voice was weak. "What a mess. Mum and I can't believe The Hammer is innocent."

"They're bringing in a fresh forensics team. I'm off both cases."

"Holy hell."

Alexa didn't want to wallow. She launched into the DNA revelations and the connection to the skeleton.

"Holy hell again. Our S2 shares genes with Cindy Mulligan's murderer?"

"The crazy part is that this person, or someone closely related, recently did a family genealogy kit that links back to S2. But privacy laws protect her."

"Her?"

"No Y chromosome."

"A woman? That's a shock. I always expect murderers to be male."

"Eighty percent are," Alexa said.

"My head is swimmy. Our female skeleton is related to whomever killed Cindy Mulligan. That must mean the murderer is from a family that has lived in the area since gold rush times."

"And maybe still does. I'll head to the museum and dig into the archives again."

"Aren't you off the case?"

Alexa sidestepped.

"Are you coming back to the cottage?"

"I don't want to get you sick. Can you meet Olivia at the cemetery this afternoon? She's removing the vandalized tent and our supplies. Mr. Sun and the benefactor are at the morgue, wrapping S1's bones in calico. Mrs. Wong is having a ceremony at the cemetery tomorrow afternoon. Then she's taking S1 home to China. You'll be there, won't you?"

Dan would want her back in Auckland. She was surprised he hadn't already called. She'd request some comp days since she'd worked straight through the weekend. "I'll be there."

"He'll finally rest in peace," Ana said. "Oh. Would you stop by the Gold Shoppe? They have that gold chain that was buried with S1. It belongs to the benefactor."

She agreed. "Remember how S1 was positioned in the grave? Pointing at something?"

"Probably pointing the way home," Ana said.

Alexa heard Shelby singing in the background as they said goodbye.

She drove the familiar road back to Arrowtown, letting the anger and shock of being dismissed slide through the cracked-open window. She was free to snoop, attend S1's farewell ceremony, and head home to Auckland.

To Bruce.

The sign above The Gold Shoppe door said "Specialists in Natural Gold Jewelry." Inside, Alexa was drawn to three gold nuggets in a glass case. The middle one was fifteen ounces and had been found in the Arrow River. The other two came from the West Coast. The man behind the counter—close-cropped brown hair and ruddy face—waited on two customers while simultaneously watching her move to a display of jewelry. She wasn't in the market for a locket of gold flakes for two thousand dollars. She waited until the man finished and then introduced herself. A gold signet ring gleamed from his ring finger. "Dr. Luckenbaugh said you'd be by. She asked me to examine this artifact from a miner's grave. I had a look. Let me show you."

He reached under a counter and retrieved a clear plastic bag with the chain in it. It had been cleaned and glistened enticingly. "A lovely piece, very pure, maybe ninety-five percent gold."

"Can you tell how old it is?"

"It was part of a single-strand Albert chain, and that style was popular in Victorian days."

"I've never heard of an Albert chain."

"They were named after Queen Victoria's husband Prince Albert. He was keen on them."

Wasn't there a joke about letting Prince Albert out of a can? She didn't mention it. "So it's gold rush-era?"

"Most likely. See the T-bar? That was used to affix the chain to a vest buttonhole."

"Chinese miners wore chains like that. I've seen them in photographs."

"European gold miners wore them too." He poured the chain onto a velvet-covered pad. "The other end would have had a swivel hook to attach to a pocket watch which would be tucked into the vest pocket. This one is severed. The link here is wrenched apart."

Like someone jerked it, Alexa thought.

"Albert chains had small chains added to display a decorative fob or gold sovereign. That's missing also." A man and woman entered the shop. He followed them with his eyes. "A single strand like this probably belonged to a working-class gent, could be a miner. Sometimes men wore them with the swivel chain attached to an empty pocket. To make it look as if he had a watch. I hope I've been of assistance."

He bagged the chain and handed it to her. It shimmied at the bottom of the bag, expectantly. "If this belonged to a Chinese miner, he had made the decision to stay in New Zealand instead of sending all his money home."

Chapter Fifty-Four

MONDAY NOON

Alexa recognized the woman at the museum desk. Her name tag said Stephanie Pincock. "I need to speak with the archivist."

"The archives are closed on Monday."

"It's urgent." Alexa showed Ms. Pincock her forensic ID badge.

She dialed the desk phone. "Maggie? The police are here."

Alexa almost corrected her, but Ms. O'Brien rounded the corner quickly. "You're back." Her fluorescent green pants shimmered as she walked. "Is it about Cindy Mulligan? They've reopened the case."

"Hammer was innocent all this time," Ms. Pincock said, "while a killer walks among us."

Alexa took that as her cue. "Cindy Mulligan volunteered at this museum, right?"

"It was before our time," Ms. O'Brien said. "Cindy was a docent and helped establish the archives."

"Is there anyone still here that knew her?"

Ms. O'Brien's earrings jingled. "Might be."

"Certainly Gayle Frost," Ms. Pincock said. "She's volunteered here for ages. No husband, no children—the museum is her life. She even has an office. Want me to call her?"

The name was familiar.

"No need," Ms. O'Brien said. "Gayle is due in any minute. She's still digitizing our photos. You can browse the art gallery while you wait," she said to Alexa. "Mrs. Frost's family foundation donated the funds for it."

"I'd rather read the old newspapers again. We're still trying to identify the remains we found in the cemetery. One skeleton was a Chinese miner. The second one grew up in this area. She's a mature female who could afford dental work. Her death was violent."

A young family gathered behind Alexa. She stepped to the side so Ms. Pincock could assist them. "There must be records to help us identify her," she said to Ms. O'Brien.

"Come upstairs again."

Ms. O'Brien plopped on a computer cubicle chair in the archive room and opened the Papers of the Past link. "Same parameters? Gold rush, Otago papers, Chinese miners, police records?"

"You have an amazing memory," Alexa said. "Add accidents and fatalities."

"After you left last time, I tracked down something that might help." She stood. Her eyelids were glittery blue. "The Arrowtown police chief kept logbooks during his twelve-year reign, 1894 until 1905. Mrs. Frost stored them in her office. Eventually, we'll digitize the lot."

A tingle crawled up the nape of Alexa's neck. "I'd love to see them."

"Any particular year?"

"Early 1900s."

Ms. O'Brien left the room and returned after five minutes bearing three leatherbound books. She set them on the table. "Let me know when you're ready for more." The tomes were dated 1902, 1903, and 1905. Alexa pulled 1902 close. The cover was black, the spine was red leather, and the edges of the pages were gilded in gold.

Naturally, Alexa thought.

She opened the book and sneezed. *How old were the dust*

particles? In a flourishing script, the inside cover was inscribed *Arrowtown Police Station, Chief Kevin Haywood, 1st June, 1902—1st June 1903.* This was followed by case totals: 132 exclusive of criminal offenses, 221 criminal.

Alexa flipped to May 12:

> *Mister William Bringezu: public drunkenness. Remarks: docile, remorseful, fine paid £2, released to Mrs. Estelle Bringezu*
>   *Loo Wan: unauthorized mining on Crown land. Remarks: vile, dirty, 3 days gaol, mining claim revoked*
>   *Teresa Callaghan: prostitution. Remarks: sinful strumpet, doped, latrine digging in lieu of fine*
>   *Yung Tie: breach of peace. Remarks: vile, diseased, fine paid £4, driven out of town*

Jeez, Alexa thought. She closed 1902 and opened 1903. It was set up the same way. She skimmed February 8th :

> *Charlotte Sloan: prostitution. Remarks: sinful cavorting with Chinaman, smoking opium, fine £4*
>   *Master W. G. Rees: hard swearing, throwing rocks at Chinamen. Remarks: released to mother*
>   *Lock Chong: theft of gold. Remarks: coolie insists innocence, whipped, fine paid £7*

Alexa's stomach cramped. Chief Haywood appeared to be a racist, sexist jerk. She skimmed 1903 for homicides.

On June 21, Mrs. Sarah Cobcroft was arrested for fatally stabbing her husband in the couple's Arrowtown home. She awaited transfer to Dunedin jail.

Alexa turned page after page. There were no accounts of a local woman disappearing or being murdered. The newspapers might be more efficient. She moved back to the computer cubicle and searched "fatalities" in Otago newspapers. People died gruesomely: kicked by a horse, drowned in flooded creeks, lockjaw, falling rock and trees, fire, even arsenic poisoning. None of the victims was a thirtysomething woman.

She searched "missing woman" and an article from the *Otago Daily Times* popped up. It was from 1904.

ARROWTOWN WOMAN MYSTERIOUSLY SPIRITED AWAY

Two months have passed and no trace of Pearl Haywood, spinster daughter of Calvin and Delphinium Haywood. To the sorrow of her older brother, our esteemed Chief Kevin Haywood, who spent the whole of his time in instituting inquiries in the hope of at last finding his sister, the Crown court declared Miss Haywood drowned in the Arrow River, with hopes her body will surface in the thaw.

That frisson crawled up her neck again. When she was here last time, she'd read another article about a missing woman, feared drowned. She searched the same newspaper and found it six weeks earlier.

PUBLIC NOTICE

Miss Pearl Ellen Haywood, spinster daughter of Calvin and Delphinium Haywood, failed to return Saturday last from paying a visit to friends. It is feared she drowned in the Arrow River or met with dark treachery.

Dark treachery?

"Hello."

Alexa jumped. When she twirled around, the woman from the cemetery—the one who sported a plastic rain bonnet and complained about the dig—stood in the doorway. She had a helmet of steel-wool-colored hair that matched her cardigan. Alexa had left the 1903 log book open, and the woman frowned down at it.

Alexa banged her knee as she stood. "Are you Gayle Frost?"

"I'm Mrs. Frost."

Alexa tried to figure out how old she was. Sixty, sixty-five? "My name is Alexa Glock. We met at the cemetery. I was part of the dig." She took a breath, expecting Mrs. Frost to launch into complaints about exhuming bones.

Mrs. Frost's thin lips parted. "Margaret said you wanted to speak with me."

"Yes. Thank you. We're making progress at the dig. We discovered one of the skeletons was born in China. The other, a mature female, grew up in this area."

It was as if someone had lit a fuse in her. She glowered. "Consecrated ground is God's domain."

Alexa stepped back, into the chair, and changed the subject. "Have you heard that the Cindy Mulligan murder investigation has been reopened?"

Mrs. Frost twisted a pearl button on her sweater. Her knuckles were slightly arthritic. "All this fingerprint poppycock when an eyewitness saw Hammer on the trail. It hurts the spine."

Alexa was confused until Mrs. Frost closed the logbook, set it on top of the other two, and pulled them to herself. Her faded denim blue eyes bore into Alexa's. "If you want to talk, you can come with me. I have work to do." She gathered the logbooks in her arms and left the room.

Alexa followed her down the narrow off-kilter hallway to an office opposite Ms. O'Brien's. A work table, covered with scissors, tape, rulers, markers, stacks of photos, and a scanner took up most of the room. There was a single chair with an almost full trash can next to it. Shelves of books and photo albums lined the wall. Mrs. Frost replaced the logbooks in a gap.

Eleven logbooks, Alexa counted. "Looks like the 1904 logbook is missing."

Mrs. Frost narrowed her eyes. "They belong to my family."

Alexa tried defrosting her with a smile. "Ms. O'Brien said you're going to digitize them. That will be a big job."

Mrs. Frost picked up a black-and-white photo, made a notation on a legal pad, lifted the lid of the scanner, and placed the photo in it. "What did you want to see me about?"

"Did you work with Cindy Mulligan?" Alexa asked.

The scanner whirred. "I didn't work *with* Miss Mulligan. Occasionally she assisted me."

Picky, from a fellow volunteer. "What were Cindy's duties?"

Mrs. Frost picked up a black-and-white photo of a dark horse pulling a buggy. She scanned it. "Miss Mulligan worked with school groups. She played the role of the schoolmarm."

Ms. O'Brien's comforting voice boomed from across the hall. Alexa continued, "Ms. O'Brien said Cindy helped in the archives too."

"Margaret said that?" Mrs. Frost's nose flared. "What archives? Back then it was boxes and boxes of discards with the occasional historic keepsake. Miss Mulligan helped consolidate materials and keep paperwork." She lifted her chin and stared at Alexa. "I had to keep an eye on her. She was unable to discern what was of value or keep her nose out of other people's business." She paused. "Like you."

Heat welled in Alexa's core. "What do you mean?"

"You disturbed the order of my photographs."

Alexa guessed she was referring to the two photos she'd

borrowed from the pile on her earlier visit. "I asked Ms. O'Brien to make copies for me." An alarm bell rang in Alexa's head: one of the copies had disappeared from the cottage. The photo of the Chinese miner holding an umbrella for a white woman. What was going on here? She parried. "It must have been a shock when Cindy Mulligan was murdered."

"It was disruptive. The police swarmed the museum."

Frost was an apt name; this woman was cold. "Was there anyone in the museum who didn't get along with her?"

"Miss Mulligan only came one afternoon a week and alternate Saturdays."

Not really an answer. Alexa switched subjects. "Ms. O'Brien said you've lived in the area all your life."

"My great-great-grandfather came from Ireland for the gold rush," she said proudly. Her stern demeanor relaxed a tad. "When the Chinese swarmed over the gold, he turned to sheep farming. He raised five children to adulthood. The oldest, Kevin Haywood, became the police chief."

"I was just reading his logs."

"My great-grandfather. He died before I was born, I'm sorry to say. The town was fueled by gold lust, alcohol, gambling in Chinatown, dope dens, prostitution, and thievery. He established law and order."

"Did he lose a sister named Pearl?"

Mrs. Frost picked up another photo, frowned, and lifted the scissors. She attacked the photo so that the pieces—snip, snip, snip—fell into the trash can. "Times were different back then. That's what no one understands."

Chapter Fifty-Five

It took a second flat white and a thick bacon butty at Wolf Cafe for Alexa to process the information she'd gleaned from Mrs. Frost, the log, and the newspapers. She opened her notebook on a tiny corner table, tuned out the happy chatter of diners, and jotted notes.

Arrowtown "spinster" Pearl Haywood disappeared in 1904.
Pearl was the police chief's sister.
Chief Haywood kept logbooks. The 1904 log is missing.
Cindy M volunteered with Mrs. Gayle Frost, the great-
*   granddaughter of Chief Haywood.*
Cindy M was bludgeoned along Arrow River Trail, not far
*   from the museum.*
The female suspect left a fingerprint on Cindy's Walkman and
*   DNA under Cindy's nails.*
The DNA indicates Cindy M's murderer shared genes with S2.
Mrs. Frost shares DNA with Kevin Haywood, ergo with Pearl.

Her heart skipped beats. Answers dangled just beyond her grasp. Her phone dinged, jarring her back to the Wolf Cafe.

Ana's email contained the Chinese miner's letters from Mrs. Wong. Alexa went to the counter and bought a thick slice of carrot cake, a belated birthday present. She savored the not-too-sweet moist cake as she read the first letter.

Wing Lun arrived in "New Gold Hill" in 1880 and shortly thereafter found a gold nugget in the Arrow River. Alexa smiled. In the next letter, dated 1884, he planted plum trees and sent money home.

The winter of 1886 was tough and cold. Wing Lun's gold was stolen. The birds ceased singing. He and the other miners were lonely. He wrote letters home for the other miners. He planned to go home in three years.

The year 1888 brought more hardships, and Wing Lun mentioned opium-smoking, rats, a cave where he escaped to carve a bellbird for a lady who bought his vegetables. Alexa stopped chewing, listening for the fairy-tinkle sound that bellbirds made.

Silly.

Was Wing Lun's cave the same one she'd entered with that retired gerontologist? A rusted shovel had been in the corner. She thought of that nice guy Julian and hoped he would find someone to share his busy life with.

She slipped back into the letters.

Wing Lun helped exhume some Chinese miners' graves in 1892 and mentioned the tomb ships. A lady shouted at them to burn in hell. Alexa thought of Mrs. Frost: history repeating.

The next year there were twenty Chinese miners left along Bush Creek. Boys from town taunted them. Wing Lun's heart hurt, and he had only love to send to his MaMa.

Alexa's heart hurt for him.

The year 1900, the year of the rat, was Wing Lun's twenty-first year in Arrowtown. Alexa couldn't believe her eyes. Wing Lun mentioned Sheriff Haywood, who spit in his face and told him to go home.

Alexa recoiled. Worlds were colliding.

In 1903, only seven Chinese people live along Bush Creek.

Wing Lun declared he won't be coming home, that he will live out his days in Arrowtown.

Alexa's eyes filled with tears. She blinked them away and reread the next lines:

> *A hidden pearl among the slag lifts my lonesome heart. I*
> *sing like the robins who keep me company.*

A hidden pearl? Pearl? Her greenstone pendant pulsed.

The final letter was dated 1904, Wing Lun's twenty-fourth year in Arrowtown. Cheong Tam was tormented by local boys and died of shame. *Was that possible?*

Birds continued to bring Wing Lun joy, and time would reveal his heart. Sometime after he wrote the last letter, his time ran out.

She wiped her eyes and pushed away the rest of her cake. *What to do and who to tell?* She had built a rapport with Constable Blume and called him.

"Eh? Ms. Glock?"

"How's it going?"

The constable lowered his voice. "Not right, what the DC did, kicking you off the case."

It gladdened her to hear him say it. She collected her belongings and left the cafe so she could hear better.

"That suspect? The woman Cindy Mulligan argued with at the accounting firm? She retired," he offered. "Her name is Mrs. Cass Racine. She said Miss Mulligan was outspoken and argued some such that the firm needed to be Y2K compliant, that was before I was born, eh. Miss Mulligan flat-out told Mrs. Racine her head was in the sand. She has grandbabies."

"Who?"

"Nah yeah. Three. Cindy Mulligan's death still haunts her.

Dreams about her. She gave a DNA sample and let me finger-print her. Ms. Walker will do the comparison with the print from the Sony Discman."

Alexa was jealous. "I have a lead."

"But you're off the case."

"A lead is a lead," Alexa said. "Gayle Frost at the Lakes District Museum. She volunteered with Cindy Mulligan. She may share genes with the female skeleton."

"Is she the one who did the FamilyTree thing?"

"It's possible. Her great-grandfather was chief of police during the gold rush. It factors in. You should send someone to the museum to question her and see if she'll give a DNA sample and fingerprints."

"You think *she* killed Cindy Mulligan?"

The woman was strange. Uptight. Scary even. "Maybe."

"What about motive?"

Alexa wrestled with the why. "Maybe Cindy pried into some-thing that Mrs. Frost wanted to keep buried. There are some log—"

"Gotta gap it," Constable Blume interrupted. "Agent Leland headed my way."

Chapter Fifty-Six

Alexa parked the rental car at the cottage and walked to the cemetery, unencumbered. No need for the crime kit. Its absence felt liberating. She had shared what she'd learned with the constable, and now—after she helped Olivia take down the tent and attended Mrs. Wong's ceremony—she was free to leave, to go home to Auckland. She'd said it. *Home.*

She'd call that secretary at Abertay University and say she wasn't interested in the position. *Didn't they eat weird foods like haggis and neeps in Scotland?*

The Preserving Heritage van wasn't in the cemetery parking lot. Olivia hadn't arrived yet. She crossed the withered grass and wove between tombstones, intent on visiting Chief Kevin Haywood. She'd seen his grave somewhere. Death; it was everywhere. Inevitable as the earth's rotation around the sun.

Chief Kevin Emanuel Haywood's gravestone was devoid of lichen and well-tended. Mrs. Frost, Alexa figured. He'd been born in 1870 and died in 1951. Alexa read the words etched in granite: PUT TO DEATH WHAT IS EARTHLY IN YOU.

What did that even mean?

She got that creepy feeling of being watched and scanned the cemetery in all directions. Nary a soul in sight. She sounded like a Victorian epitaph. She ignored other tombstones and statues as she hastened to the other side of the rock wall. Yellow caution tape still surrounded Wing Lun's grave.

It was his grave, but Eileen Bowen had been dumped there too.

Misty Taylor had given her a ride, and Alexa had blabbed about the dig and empty graves. *Had Eileen's body been in the cargo area of the van?* Misty had probably mentioned it to Martin, who seized the opportunity to dispose of Eileen's body in freshly turned dirt.

Lazy bastard.

She hoped the tape would be removed before Mrs. Wong and Mr. Sun's ceremony. She backed up and sat on the wall, the cold stone permeating her khakis. She pulled the sleeves of her jacket over her hands to warm them. Rotting apples littered the ground. She kicked one and cursed the racism the Chinese miners had experienced. She cursed the hardships that caused women to turn to prostitution and be belittled by Chief Haywood. She cursed Cindy Mulligan and Eileen Bowen's fates.

There but for the grace of God...

A robin hopped toward her, cocking its head, its eyes bright and beady. "Did you see Martin Tandy bury Eileen?" Alexa asked.

"Cheep cheep, twit, twit, twit," it answered.

Had Misty been in on Eileen's murder, or had she been unaware of her husband's evil? She must have recognized Eileen's phone. If she'd been innocent, that would have been the moment to speak up. Instead, she had lied. Said it was Susie's.

Alexa didn't want to think of Susie.

Her mind circled back to evil. Why would Martin Tandy kill Eileen? He had a decent job, a wife, a daughter. The inheritance from the father must have been a trigger. His wife being denied meant he and Susie had been denied too. But he had what was important. Didn't he know that?

Who was she to act all therapist and psychologist when she was a basket case with relationships?

I can change.

The robin hopped to her Keds and pecked. New Zealand robins had dark feathers and white breasts. Coop, a Māori cop Alexa had met during her first case in New Zealand, and who now worked in Auckland, had told her if you hear the cry of a robin from the right, good fortune is hurrying to meet you. From the left? Be wary.

The robin flew away.

The tent that had sheltered S2's remains was blighted by the spray-painted *God is Watching You* and *Wrath of God*.

What had Mrs. Frost spouted an hour ago? *Consecrated ground is God's domain.*

Alexa walked to the tent. The flaps were closed. The last time she'd been here, the inside had been a mess. She apprehensively opened them and blinked in the gloom.

The jerry-rigged light bulb was shattered, and the work table was still on its side. The tools had been tidied and were lined up in a row. The tarp was folded. The grave was half-filled. What would happen to S2? Would she be given a proper spot within the cemetery boundaries?

She tied the flaps back and got to work. She wrestled the table flat and attacked the hinges. The corroded metal resisted her efforts. She grunted and used force. The last leg was toughest. She pushed and pulled, said "hi ya!" and banged it. Motion caught her attention. The silhouette of a figure passed the side of the tent.

Olivia was here.

The leg gave. Alexa, triumphant, pulled that table on its side. She and Olivia could wrestle it to the van.

Mrs. Frost appeared in the tent's entranceway, not Olivia.

Alexa shook her head to clear it. Instead, alarm bells went off. "What are you doing here?"

"I came for a proper chat, to explain things."

Beyond the older woman, Alexa saw gray sky, the branch of the apple tree, the flank of a mountain. She took a deep breath and made her voice calm. "Explain what?"

"About Miss Mulligan snooping in the collection inventory." Her eyes landed on the grave. "*You* have no right to tamper with the past. You're just like Miss Mulligan. She blithely told me about what she discovered in the logbook. And the picture tucked in with it. She brought them to my attention." A tote hung from her shoulder. She reached in and pulled out a photograph.

Alexa's knees buckled. She locked them in place. It was the photograph of the Chinese man holding an umbrella for the white woman. She lifted the table an inch, tested its weight, considered hurling it at the woman.

But she wanted to hear more.

"This is the original. I destroyed the copy you made," Mrs. Frost said. Her face remained expressionless.

"You came into the cottage?"

"That photograph was not for your prying eyes. The logbooks and this photo are no one's business. Not yours. Not Miss Mulligan's."

"Cindy Mulligan is dead," Alexa said. Her confidence crept back. She could take this woman, barrel into her, run out of the tent.

Mrs. Frost didn't react. She fixated on the photograph. "My great-grandfather caught this chink raping his sister."

Rape?

"Dirty, dirty Chinaman."

Alexa thought of the letters. "His name is Wing Lun. He loved Pearl."

Mrs. Frost ripped the photo in pieces and let go. She ground the scattered parts with the heel of her gum boot. "Dirty dirty

dirty." She lifted her chin. "He rightfully killed him on the spot, with a pickax. He recorded the crime and punishment in the logbook. Miss Mulligan planned to show the director. She wanted to drag my family through the dirt."

Alexa tightened her grip on the table. "What happened to Pearl?"

Mrs. Frost stepped into the tent. Her voice never wavered. "She ran along the track toward town. 'Screaming like a banshee,' he wrote. He didn't have a choice."

No. No. No. Alexa pictured Kevin Haywood chasing his sister along the river, catching her, pushing Pearl down, kneeling on her spine, jerking her neck back. Alexa looked at the grave. Pearl's grave. Buried facedown by her own brother.

Mrs. Frost stepped closer. A hiss escaped her mouth. "She would have brought shame on the family. Shame. He had to do it. Times were different."

Alexa leaned the table against the side of the tent. Nothing was between them now. She could push past Mrs. Frost and tear out of the tent.

Mrs. Frost's nostrils quivered. "I burned the logbook. No one will know."

The woman was delusional. Unhinged. "You killed Cindy Mulligan?"

"She would have brought shame on the family. Like Pearl." Mrs. Frost lifted her chin righteously. "Like you're trying to do." She pulled a knife out of the tote quicker than a blink and lunged.

Alexa blocked the swipe with her arm. The blade sliced through her jacket sleeve. Searing pain shot through her system like a bullet train. Mrs. Frost raised the knife and plunged again.

Alexa sidestepped and kicked Mrs. Frost's knee.

The woman staggered but kept coming, knife raised.

Alexa jabbed her in the jaw. "Your fingerprint is on Cindy's Discman!" Burning pain. "The police know it's you."

Mrs. Frost froze. "Not so," she spouted. She held the knife in both hands and raised it. It hovered above her head indecisively.

Alexa made fists, ready to ward off the knife. "We have your DNA."

Mrs. Frost raised the knife higher, her stony face registering disbelief, then resignation. She closed her eyes and plunged the knife straight into her cardigan. Straight into her own stomach. She hissed, stumbled, fell face-first into Pearl's grave.

Alexa screamed.

Her scream was joined by another scream.

Olivia ran in. "What's happened? Who is that?"

Alexa clutched her arm and sank to Mrs. Frost's side. "Call an ambulance," she yelled. She seized the woman's shoulder and rolled her over. She grabbed the tarp to stanch the blood soaking Mrs. Frost's sweater, but she couldn't press it to the wound. The knife poked straight out. Mrs. Frost's fading denim eyes stared into hers. "It tore him up."

Alexa leaned closer. "What? Who?"

Her throat gurgled. She held Alexa's eyes for as long as she could, held on to secrets as long as she could, crazy murderous woman, held on until the electrical signals between her retina and brain shut down and her eyes ceased seeing the world in a narrow swath.

Chapter Fifty-Seven

MONDAY EVENING

Constable Blume stood over her like a father hen. "You lost some blood, see?"

Alexa sat on the side of a hospital bed, her legs dangling. A drop of blood blotched the shoelace of her right sneaker. "See what?"

"That's why they're keeping you in hospital overnight."

She looked down at the blue-and-white checked hospital gown she wore over her khaki pants. It was not her best look. Her blouse and jacket were ruined. Olivia had ushered her to the ambulance amid a swarm of arriving police cars, and then she had fainted.

She didn't have the energy to be embarrassed.

The knife slash on her left forearm was three inches long. "No muscular penetration; that's lucky," the doctor had said. "You'll have a less obvious scar if I stitch you up."

"Add it to the list," she laughed. He looked at her like she was loony or the meds had kicked in. He gave her a prescription for additional pain meds and assigned her to a room when he finished sewing.

DI Katakana burst in. Constable Blume jumped back from the bed. "Are you ready to talk?" she asked.

"No," Alexa said. The events in the tent were a horrifying jumble.

The DI adjusted her cap. "Gayle Frost is dead."

Alexa had watched the life leach from Mrs. Frost's eyes, but this proclamation made it official and all too real.

"We've got a new mess with the Tandys," she added.

The meds made it hard for Alexa to focus. "What's going on?"

"Susie. She called a teen suicide prevention line."

Bruce was wrong. Kids weren't so resilient.

The DI's shoulders sagged. "She threatened to kill herself if her dad went to jail. She said she killed Eileen, heard her head crack, what should she do? Told the whole frigging story to some volunteer who followed protocol and called us."

Alexa's head was fuzzy. "Susie confessed?"

"Mr. Tandy made her do yard work at the rental house. A father-daughter thing, but Susie hated it. Eileen shows up and tells her about the baby. 'What about the car? And those earrings?' Susie asks. Eileen says 'no-can-do.' The kid goes berserk, grabs Eileen's ear, rips it, shoves her. Eileen hits her head on the concrete firepit. Susie goes running to find Daddy, hands all bloody."

The firepit. Alexa had walked right by it.

"Daddy did everything he could to cover for her. Including burying the body. "

Alexa could not believe this turn of events. Did not *want* to believe it. "But it was Martin Tandy's fingerprint on the washing machine."

"Like I said, he did everything he could to cover it up, including throw their bloody clothes in the washer. Susie's being picked up as we speak."

"She could be lying," Constable Blume said. "To save her dad."

"Doubt it. Glad I never popped one out." She patted Alexa's knee. "I'm glad you're okay, well, not okay, but okay. Avoid the press if you can." She turned and left the room.

Alexa forgot about the pain, about her near-death experience. She scooched forward and stood up.

"Can you find me a top? T-shirt, sweater, anything?" she asked the constable.

He did so and reluctantly drove her to the Queenstown Police Station where Sergeant Dryer plied her with coffee and a left-over pastry. She brushed crumbs off Constable Blume's Super Rugby sweatshirt—he was sitting with her like a babysitter— and endured Agent Leland's questions.

"Now who was Mrs. Frost trying to protect?" he repeated.

"Her great-grandfather. The police chief. He murdered his sister and her lover, Wing Lun. Simple as that."

"Murder is never simple," he said.

Alexa agreed, but she wanted the questions to end so she could hear what Susie Tandy was saying. If she saw Susie with her own eyes, she'd be able to tell whether Susie was lying. "I didn't read the logbook entry, but Cindy Mulligan did. I imagine he recorded it as self-defense. There are a couple newspaper articles about the disappearance of his sister, Pearl Haywood. He let people believe she drowned. He buried them both outside the cemetery." *Like trash.*

"And you sleuthed all this out without involving us?"

Constable Blume thrust his shoulders back. "She contacted me, sir. As we were leaving Mrs. Racine's house. I told you."

"The DNA information made me suspicious of Mrs. Frost," Alexa said. "She was the link between Cindy Mulligan and the skeletons." Alexa had a question of her own. "Did someone take her fingerprints and compare it to the one on the Discman?"

"Fingerprint analysis? Bugger off," Agent Leland said.

Alexa glared at him. "One chop doesn't fell a giant tree. I'm sorry for what happened to Mr. Hammer, but fingerprints are still valuable if analyzed correctly and verified."

"Ms. Walker will do it," Constable Blume said.

A wave of jealousy flowed and ebbed. Leigh was perfectly

capable. Agent Leland was satisfied with the debriefing and let her go.

She found Sergeant Dryer in the hall. "Where's Susie Tandy?"

"She's at the youth detention center, not here. Senior is with Martin Tandy, though. Room one."

A stab of pain shot through her arm. She grimaced and slipped into the viewing room. Martin Tandy's head was on the table. His bald spot gleamed in the harsh light. The DI leaned toward him from the other side, hands splayed. "We found the van."

Martin lifted his head. His eyes were fearful.

"Eileen's tennis shoe was wedged in the tire well."

He made a sound, a moan.

"Your daughter called a suicide line and confessed that she pushed her aunt. Why didn't you just call for an ambulance?"

"She didn't have anything to do with this," he said.

Alexa rubbed her eyes.

"I think you panicked, wrapped the body in the shower curtain, and carried her to the creek path so you could pick her up in the van. That's what you did for Susie, right?"

"Earl Hammer killed Eileen."

"Earl Hammer never killed anyone, including Eileen Bowen." The DI pulled out a chair and sat. "But what a nice coincidence that you could try pinning Eileen's death on him."

"Susie didn't have anything to do with this," he repeated like a mantra.

Alexa thought of the DNA collected from under Eileen's fingernail. And the scratches on Susie's hand. She was glad she was off the case. Nailing a fifteen-year-old wasn't something she could stomach.

———

Constable Blume kept glancing at her as he drove her back to Arrowtown.

"I'm okay," she insisted. "I like the sweatshirt."

"It's yours now."

"Do you think Misty Tandy was in on it?" Alexa asked.

Constable Blume drummed the steering wheel. "Mr. Tandy swears Misty didn't know anything."

"She knew something," Alexa said. Her arm hurt. She felt woozy.

Pam and Shelby greeted her at the door of the cottage. The savory aroma of stew or casserole woke her stomach. "Ana sent us back so you wouldn't be alone," Pam said. Shelby wrapped her arms around Alexa's legs.

Constable Blume set her crime kit on the stairs. "Eh. Be careful," he told Shelby. "Ms. Glock has a boo boo."

While Shelby watched the TV, Alexa wilted into a kitchen chair and told Pam what happened, first about Eileen Bowen and then about Gayle Frost killing Cindy Mulligan. And trying to kill her.

"I wrote about him as if he were a monster," Pam said when she was through.

Alexa didn't follow.

"Earl Hammer. I covered his trial. Stepped right on the bandwagon. In my article I called him soulless. All along it was that woman. I'm ashamed."

"You believed an expert witness," Alexa said. "The jurors did too." It was all the ammo she had.

Pam sensed it. "Let me dish up tea, luv."

Alexa called Ana and told her the latest news too.

"You must be traumatized."

"I don't know what I feel," Alexa said.

Pam fed her and mothered her, which was exactly what Alexa needed.

Chapter Fifty-Eight

Bruce wanted to pick her up at the airport Tuesday afternoon, but she turned down the offer, and once her flight had landed, she drove her car to Auckland Forensic Service Center to debrief with Dan, update reports, and meet with the WorkSafe coordinator about her injury. Her pain meds were wearing off as she drove with one hand to Bruce's apartment.

She left her suitcase and crime kit in the car and ran up the steps. He lived on the third floor, and she always took the stairs.

Halfway up the third flight she slowed down.

What was she getting herself into?

Bruce whipped the door open and stared at her, waiting for her to decide.

It wasn't hard. When his arms went around her, she ignored the pain and relaxed against his chest, felt his fingers tangle in her hair, smelled his woodsy scent, felt his longing and vulnerability and acknowledged her own, she knew she had made the right decision.

He pulled back and looked at her, his blue eyes alight. "Medium rare?" he asked.

"Can the steaks wait?" she replied.

———

The joint reinterment ceremony was two weeks later, and Bruce flew with her back to Queenstown. "This reminds me of Kāhu's memorial," he said from the passenger seat of the rental car. "His bones had been hungry too."

Her pendant pulsed as she drove the familiar road to Arrowtown. She mentally thanked the greenstone carver for guiding her and keeping her safe. It had been at his service, at the end of another case, that Kāhu's mother had gifted her the pendant.

Did all her cases end with funerals? The thought made her cold. And then she thought of how Wing Lun and Pearl Haywood would finally rest side by side. Her mood lifted.

The cemetery stretched before them under a crisp blue sky and the parking area was bustling.

They got out of the car. Alexa pressed wrinkles out of her pleated wool dress. She hadn't wanted to wear black and settled on teal. The saleswoman had suggested something "younger, more stylish," but Alexa's mind was made up since the dress was on sale.

She avoided looking toward the other side of the rock wall, where the tent had been. Mrs. Gayle Frost would not be charged with Cindy Mulligan's murder and with Alexa's attempted murder. She was beyond the reach of the police and court. That left Alexa indignant on Cindy's part. If people could be pardoned after death, why couldn't they be prosecuted? Her arm ached daily, a reminder that evil wore many disguises.

The cemetery director, as if lying in wait, rushed over.

"You're back, you're back, Miss Clock."

"Ms. Glock," she said.

"Looking lovely." He stuck his hand out to Bruce. "Quentin Howard, Lakes District Cemetery director. Big crowd. Big turnout."

Townspeople, some dressed in colonial garb, milled about as if it were a party. Two men carried gold pans and cradles. A little boy skipped along the rock wall, his mother trailing. Two women of Asian descent handed out red envelopes to everyone they passed.

"I knew you'd find someone," Mr. Howard told her. "Just knew it."

Bruce raised an eyebrow at Alexa as Mr. Howard scurried off. She blushed. "He wanted to sell me a DIY coffin kit."

DI Katakana and Constable Blume greeted her as if she'd been a long-valued member of the team. "They released Misty Tandy on bail," Constable Blume told her. "Martin Tandy insists she didn't know what he'd done, didn't play a part. He's been charged with accessory after the fact."

"What about Susie?"

"Her DNA was under Eileen's fingernail," DI Katakana said. "She's in custody like her dad."

The revelation made her wobble in her one-inch heels. Susie—a kid—had killed her aunt. Bruce put his arm around her. She regrouped, thanked the officers for the update, and searched the crowd for Mr. Sun. She spotted him with two people by the freshly dug gravesites. Bruce stayed behind to talk shop with his fellow DI. Mr. Sun's eyes lit up as she joined him. "This is Mrs. Corrie Wong and this is Mr. Richard Lumb, our Otago Chinese Association representative."

Alexa remembered Mr. Lumb. His prediction about coming events casting shadows had been spot on. He bowed and she bowed back.

Mrs. Wong wore a satiny black dress and pearls. Her gray hair curled around her face, ending at her chin. Her lips were painted red. "I journeyed far to this port," she said in perfect English. "Always he called to me." She squeezed Alexa's hand. "Sorrowing hearts are unsettled. 'Bring me home,' he called. Sun Shing says that it is you that I need to thank."

"It was Dr. Luckenbaugh and her graduate assistant who found them because of you and the letters."

The clip and clop of horseshoes on pavement drew their eyes toward the entrance. A horse and buggy stopped there. The driver wore a black suit and top hat.

Mrs. Wong squeezed her hand harder. "But you discovered what was Wing Lun's heart and desire." She gestured to the cemetery, the mountains, the sky. "*This* is his home. He was only a hungry ghost because he was separated from his Pearl."

Alexa's mouth dried. She looked into Mrs. Wong's wise eyes, imagining the distance she had traveled to be here. "He was pointing in the grave." Her greenstone pendant pulsed, telling her that sometimes it was okay to ignore science and hear the hungry bones speak. "He was pointing to Pearl. To tell us he wanted to be with her."

Mrs. Wong slipped a hand into her pocket and pulled out the gold chain that had been buried with Wing Lun. It was now attached to a gold pocket watch. "They found the other end of the chain and the watch in that woman's house."

"Mrs. Frost's?"

"I will not speak her name. Or that of her great-grandfather. The links are rejoined. I am donating this and Wing Lun's boots to the museum. The archivist recorded me telling Wing Lun's story, and reading his letters."

"That's wonderful."

"The letters though, I will keep. They remind me of hardship and what's important."

Alexa heard a robin, off to her right.

Mr. Sun lit incense, and people gathered around them. Two sets of pallbearers unloaded simple wooden coffins from the buggy and started their slow procession toward the graves, now within the consecrated grounds of Arrowtown Cemetery.

"It must have been so hard for Pearl and Wing to be together," Alexa said. Bruce was suddenly by her side. He stared at her with eyes the color of the sky. Being with him was only hard if she made it hard.

Pearl Ellen Haywood and Wing Lun were laid to rest, side by side. Mrs. Wong and Mr. Sun left bowls of rice and cups of tea on the newly packed earth. The minister proclaimed, "Children of God, rest in peace."

Mr. Sun handed Alexa a red envelope in parting. "Read before you leave," he said.

Alexa opened the envelope. On thin paper was a quote from Confucius. She read it to Bruce. "Three things cannot long be hidden: the sun, the moon, and the truth."

"What's your truth?" Bruce asked.

She didn't censor her reply. "I've been wondering where my home is."

"And?"

"Home is here. In New Zealand." Her heart cartwheeled. She couldn't say the rest aloud. *Home is with you.*

Epilogue

NEW ZEALAND PRESS

Earl Hammer spent twenty-five years in prison for a murder he didn't commit. Our justice system failed him. So did I.
                           —Opinion by Pam Luckenbaugh
                    26 Sep, 2024 04:26 PM 4 mins to read

(**Editor's Note:** *Pam Luckenbaugh, a freelance reporter, covered Earl Hammer's trial in 1998 when she worked for New Zealand Press.*)

The outpouring of support that surrounded Earl Timothy Hammer when he was first exonerated for the murder of Cynthia Mulligan has faded. It took three months for him to find a landlord willing to rent him an apartment. He still hasn't found a job. "Don't matter if I'm innocent," he says when we meet. "No one will hire me."

He hasn't made a single friend.

The 49-year-old Hammer joins me at an Ashburton diner. His eyes are guarded, haunted. "I never hurt nobody, even in prison."

He stayed with his younger brother when he first got out. "Issac don't know what to think, plus his house is crowded. Only my mum knew I was innocent. The cancer *got her. Didn't ever get to see me pardoned. That's what makes me…"*

His words fade. He stares at his lap, I think, to hide tears. Or tamp his anger.

Hammer left school at age fourteen. "It was the reading. I never could do the reading. No one cared when I didn't show up."

Last Monday, Hammer's murder conviction was quashed by the Supreme Court in Wellington. Justice Allison Bartlett announced that a substantial miscarriage of justice had occurred. "Our judicial system robbed Mr. Hammer of the prime years of his life," she said. "A Criminal Cases Review Commission has been established to investigate forensic findings that have resulted in prison sentences."

The man sitting across from me, eating a steak-n-veg minced pie, knows I covered his murder trial in 1998 and that I believed the expert witness who claimed Hammer's fingerprint matched the one left on Cindy Mulligan's Sony Discman.

I failed Hammer by believing the witness, no questions asked.

I've learned expert witnesses must be vetted about their training, about how their findings are validated, and about the error rates of those findings. I urge you, if you are ever on a jury, to ask those questions.

Hammer will be compensated $150,000 for each year he served and he is eligible for up to an additional $100,000 per year in jail for loss of livelihood.

Perhaps when the money comes through, that is when he will make some friends.

"I blamed DI Unger," Hammer says. "Thought he planted my print on the music player. I planned a reckoning with him every day I was in my cell.'

That's 9,125 days, and DI Unger was the detective inspector who investigated Cindy Mulligan's murder.

"That forensic woman, Ms. Glock? She proved it weren't my fingerprint. My freedom is because of her."

Auckland Forensic Service Center investigator Alexa Glock compared Hammer's prints to the single print used to convict him. "There were more differences than similarities," she said. Glock also played a key role in finding the real murderer, Mrs. Gayle Frost, who killed Cindy Mulligan to keep dark family secrets from coming to light.

Earl Hammer meets my eyes. His look less haunted now. "There's other people in jail that don't have no schooling to prove they're innocent. You know, reading the laws, writing letters. No one helped me do that."

His final words before we part humble me.

"When that money comes in, that's what I'll do. Help them."

THE END

ACKNOWLEDGMENTS

With each Alexa Glock forensics mystery, my indebtedness to my Poisoned Pen Press/Sourcebooks editor Diane DiBiase grows. I think she understands Alexa Glock better than I do. Her support and suggestions always make my books better. Thank you, Diane.

Thanks to the Poisoned Pen Press/Sourcebooks cover design team—wow—and to Assistant Content Editor Beth Deveny. Her fact-checking and editing are extraordinaire.

Thanks to my agent, Laura Bradshaw of Bradshaw Literary Agency.

I am lucky to have Dr. Heidi Eldridge, director of Crime Scene Investigations at George Washington University, as my forensic consultant. She is over-the-top smart with a sense of humor. She saves me from errors big and small. In one fingerprinting scene Alexa used the word *pinkie*. Heidi said, "Little finger. No forensic scientist would say pinkie." :) (My face went pink.)

Dr. Leslie Anderson, Canterbury District Health Board forensic pathologist, read over my autopsy scenes and helped me understand more about blunt force trauma. (No—you can't tell from which way a blow came.) Dr. Anderson says it is a privilege to be the last doctor a person sees and to be able to speak on their behalf.

Dr. Charlotte King, professor of anatomy at the University of Otago, read my strontium isotopic analysis scenes. Dr. King's research focuses on the use of bone and tooth chemistry to solve forensic and archaeological problems. She read a scene where Alexa discovers notches on upper and lower teeth of an exhumed Chinese miner. Dr. King said, "It's really nice you've put the pipe facets on the incisors, as European pipe smokers tend to have pipe facets on their canines." (This was luck on my part.)

My writing group is my village. Thank you Nancy Peacock, Lisa Bobst, Denise Cline, Linda A. Janssen, Ann Parrent, and Karen Pullen.

Thank you to Brandon L. Garrett, Duke law professor and author of *Autopsy of a Crime Lab: Exposing the Flaws in Forensics*. His book and willingness to answer my questions helped me understand the devastating consequences of faulty science.

Thank you to the archivist and staff at the Lakes District Museum in Arrowtown, New Zealand.

Lastly, thank you to my husband, Forrest. He has my back throughout the writing-a-book process and doesn't mind when I ask (in a panic): What did Alexa's father do for a living? Not only that; he knows the answer.

ABOUT THE AUTHOR

© Morgan Henderson Photography

Sara E. Johnson lives in Durham, North Carolina. She worked as a middle-school reading specialist and local newspaper contributor before her husband lured her to New Zealand for a year. *The Hungry Bones* is the fifth Alexa Glock Forensics Mystery.